DIVINE
FATE

USA TODAY BESTSELLING AUTHOR
ALICIA RADES

Copyright © 2018 Alicia Rades

All rights reserved. No part of this book may be used or reproduced in any matter whatsoever without written permission from the author except in brief quotations used in articles and reviews.

This is a work of fiction. Names, characters, places, and incidents are either the product of the author's imagination or are used fictitiously, and any resemblance to actual persons, living or dead, business establishments, events or locales is entirely coincidental.

Published by Crystallite Publishing LLC.
Edited by Megan Linski.
Proofread by Emerald Barnes.
Cover design by Rebecca Frank.

aliciarades.com

DIVINE FATE

Chosen by Grace
Touched by Grace
Awakened by Grace

ALSO BY ALICIA RADES

DIVINE DESCENDANTS DUOLOGY

Concealing Magic

Exposing Magic

HIDDEN LEGENDS: ACADEMY OF MAGICAL CREATURES

The Fire Prophecy

The Water Legacy

The Earth Legend

The Air Omen

The Elemental War

The Soul Sacrifice

HIDDEN LEGENDS: COLLEGE OF WITCHCRAFT

The Coven's Secret

The Reaper's Shadow

The Cauldron's Curse

The Demon's Spell

The Warlock's Trial

The Witch's Fate

HIDDEN LEGENDS: PRISON FOR SUPERNATURAL OFFENDERS

The Villain Institute

The Criminal Lair

The Infernal Underground

The Assassin's Destiny

The Devil's City

The Elven Gate

The Phoenix Dawning

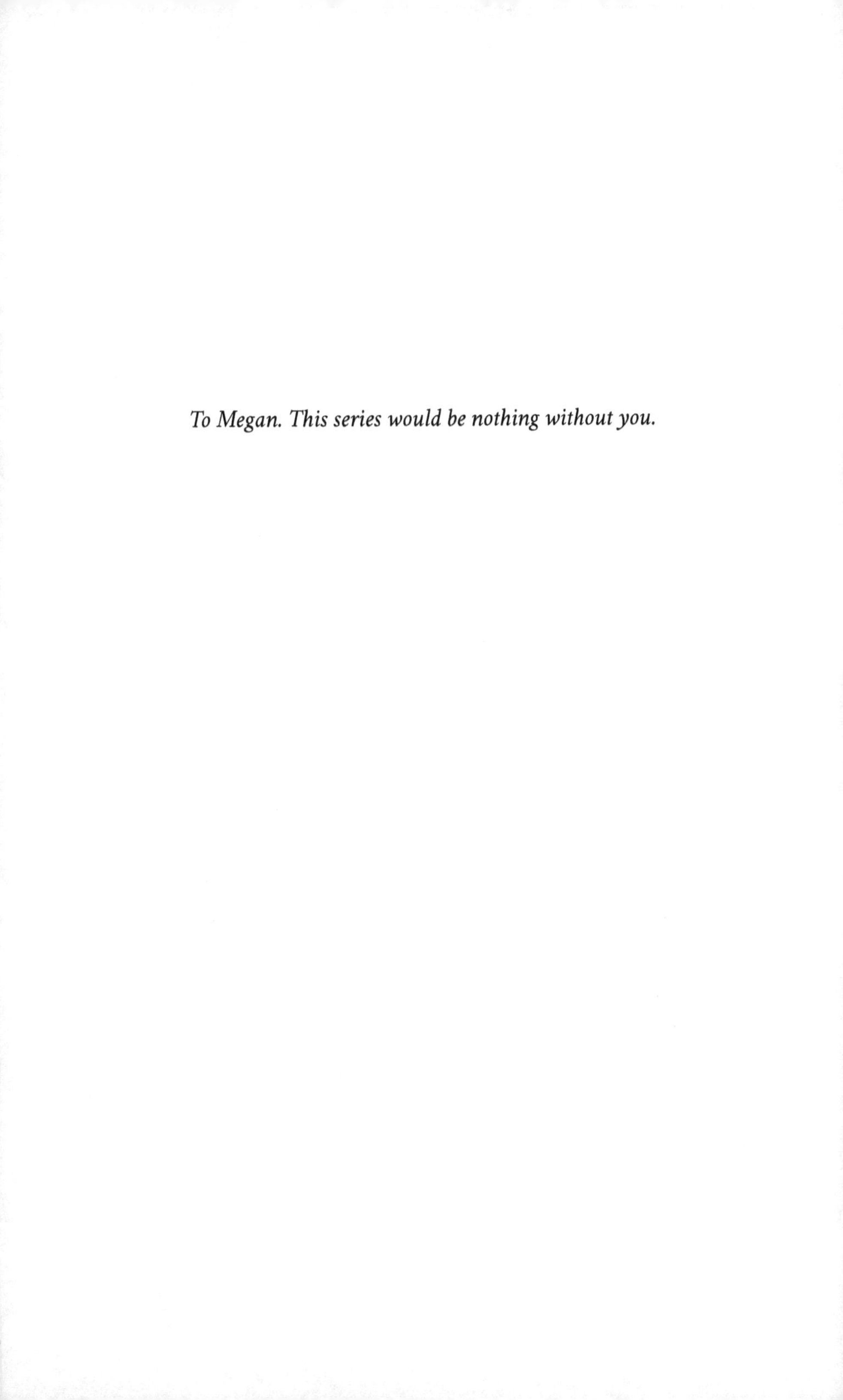

To Megan. This series would be nothing without you.

CHOSEN BY GRACE

DIVINE FATE BOOK ONE

1

$\mathcal{C}$onsidering I'd been seeing demons my whole life, I should've expected one of those sons of bitches to attack someday. And maybe I would've—if I'd known they were real. I'd become so accustomed to assuming the cloaked figures were figments of my imagination that I eventually stopped noticing them. The problem with closing your eyes? Sooner or later, you have to open them again.

I squinted across the lawn toward the old white farmhouse. Music pumped from somewhere inside and reached us where we were parked near the road. Silhouettes of dancing teens passed the front window. A short distance from the house, a large group stood around a fire pit and threw their heads back in laughter. My eyes landed on a hooded figure immersed in the crowd.

My fingers froze against my dangly earring I'd been fidgeting with.

Usually, I didn't notice the figures, but this was the first one I'd seen since moving to Eagle Valley. I thought I was starting to get over the nightmares of my childhood.

"Is something wrong?" Allie pulled her gaze from the rearview mirror to look at me.

I continued to stare at the crowd, but the hooded man I'd seen had vanished.

3

Just my imagination, I told myself. That phrase had become my mantra since I was eight.

"Ryn?" Allie prodded.

I turned to her. "Everything's fine. I'm just waiting for you. You know, your reflection will be there when we get back."

Allie laughed and tucked her lipstick into her makeup bag. "I would hope so!"

She stole one last look in the mirror. Allie had a natural beauty that came with her tan skin and sleek black hair, thanks to her Asian heritage. She'd expertly outlined her striking brown eyes with black liquid liner, and she'd even added false eyelashes for the occasion.

My version of going all out was borrowing a flowy purple top from Allie and letting her curl my hair. I hadn't even bothered to swap out my tennis shoes for something fancy.

She finally abandoned her reflection. "Ready?"

I'd only been ready for the last two hours. "Yep."

We stepped out of the car into the chilly Minnesota night air. Allie tugged down on her skirt and started down the long gravel driveway like she was walking down a runway. I followed beside her, but my hips didn't sway in the same confident manner. It definitely had something to do with the four-inch heels she was wearing.

As we neared the fire pit, I noticed what looked like a freshman chugging a beer.

"Are you sure we won't get in trouble?" I asked.

Allie shook her head. "Mike's parents are away for the weekend, and we're far enough out of town that no one will call in a complaint."

The smell of pizza and alcohol hit my nose at the front door, and the music was so loud I could feel it vibrating through the walls. Allie took my hand so we wouldn't lose each other. My eyes landed on several people on our way to the kitchen. A nervous sensation hit my gut as we waded through the crowd.

"Hey, you made it!" A tall guy with dark hair and a slightly crooked nose held an arm out to Allie.

She leaned into him with a smile.

"This is Kyle!" she shouted above the music.

She'd mentioned him before, how they weren't officially dating but had a thing for each other. By the way she talked about him, you'd think he was a god. Even with his crooked nose, he was attractive enough to be mistaken for one, at least.

"How about a shot for my girls?" Kyle didn't wait for an answer. He placed two plastic shot glasses on the kitchen island and poured each one full of a green liquid.

I eyed it skeptically. "I'm okay, thanks."

"It's sour apple. You'll love it." Kyle pushed the drink toward me.

"No, really," I insisted. "My mom would *kill* me."

Allie bumped hips with me. "Your mom's not here, is she? Live a little!"

A smile crept across my face. Allie was right. Mom *wasn't* here to tell me what I could and couldn't do. I might as well take advantage of the freedom while I had the chance. I snatched up my glass and downed the shot in one gulp. It burned as it flowed down my throat. I gagged.

"That a girl!" Allie tipped the shot into her mouth and asked for another immediately.

Kyle poured her drink and then turned to the fridge and handed me a hard lemonade. "Maybe you'd prefer something a little tamer."

I brought the bottle to my lips and welcomed the sweet flavor.

"Hey," Allie called to a group of three across the kitchen. "Come meet Ryn. She's starting at Eagle Valley High this year."

"Hi." I waved to two girls and a guy nervously. I'd already forgotten their names by the time introductions were over.

Allie had dragged me to this party so I could get to know people before school. I'd be attending Eagle Valley High my senior year while Allie was enrolled in the private school in town, Galen High.

Mom and I never stayed in one place for more than a year, so I never let myself get too attached to anyone. The only reason I spent time with Allie was because I'd moved in next door last month and she insisted we hang out.

Allie took a beer from the fridge. Her eyes instantly lit up when the song changed. "Oh my God. I love this song. We have to dance!"

She grabbed my wrist and dragged me toward the living room.

"Don't have too much fun," Kyle called after us.

"Don't worry," I laughed. "I'll bring her back in once piece."

Allie rolled her eyes.

"What?" I asked over the music.

She took a sip of beer. "Kyle. He's so protective."

"When are you going to make it official?" I swayed my body to the music.

Her brows shot up. "Ask *him*."

The room was so crowded that Allie and I nearly touched as we danced. Her eyes darted across the room.

She did a double take. "Creep alert, nine o'clock."

I glanced to my left. My eyes fell on a tall guy with ruffled brown hair standing alone in the corner. The music and chatter faded as our eyes connected. He had the strong jaw and perfectly symmetrical features of a movie star. Even from this distance, I could tell his electric blue eyes were worth getting lost in for hours.

Hot Stuff wore a leather jacket over his broad shoulders like he was some kind of badass biker dude. His lips curled into a slight smile the longer I held his gaze. He leaned against the wall as if amused and stuck a hand into the pocket of his tight jeans.

All I wanted him to do was turn around so I could see what those pants looked like from the back. He could get rid of the pants for all I cared.

My cheeks flamed at the thought. I turned back to Allie before I could completely undress him with my eyes.

"Cute guy? Leather jacket?" I asked.

"No, closer."

I checked my left again and found a muscular guy in a backwards baseball cap staring at us while he danced. As soon as he saw us look, he began making his way through the crowd.

"Do you know him?" I hissed in Allie's ear.

She shook her head. "I've seen him around. He goes to your school."

I quickly searched for an exit while Allie tried to work her way through the crowd casually, but we were squeezed too tight. The guy reached us far too soon.

"Hello, ladies." He dragged out the words and eyed us up and down.

"Um, hi," Allie said shyly.

Maybe I was too quick to judge, but based on what looked like a homemade tattoo on the guy's arm and the strong scent of alcohol on his breath, I could tell he wasn't the kind of guy either of us wanted to get involved with.

"Sorry, not interested," I said boldly.

Allie and I turned our attention back to each other and continued dancing like we never noticed his approach.

"Your friend here is *feisty*." He draped an arm around Allie's shoulder. The cup in his hand nearly spilled over the front of her blouse.

I cringed.

I grabbed Allie's arm and pulled her away from him, though there wasn't really anywhere for us to go. "Sorry, but she's taken."

"I don't see anyone claiming her," the guy challenged with a laugh.

Allie shot me a pleading expression, begging me to save her from this guy. I did the only thing I thought would make him get lost. I wrapped an arm around her waist and pulled her into me. She continued dancing like the guy didn't bother her.

I gave him an extremely fake, exaggerated expression of apology. "Like I said, she's taken."

He glanced between us like he was trying to figure out if we were for real. "A two for one deal? That's hot."

I wanted nothing more than to slap the ugly smile right off his face. "That's not how this works."

"How can you not want a piece of this?" He gestured to his body, which wasn't very impressive.

My jaw tensed, but my serious expression never faltered. "I'm not interested in dicks."

I wasn't talking about anatomy, either.

Douchebag huffed and walked away like he'd never been turned down before.

As my eyes followed him, I noticed Hot Stuff had made his way halfway through the crowd. He stared straight at me like he'd planned on stepping in to teach Douchebag a lesson. I shot him a small smile to let him know we were okay and didn't need his help.

"Thank you." Allie breathed a sigh of relief. "That was brilliant."

I couldn't suppress my laugh. "Did you see the look on his face?"

She nodded. At the time, we both thought that was the end of it.

It wasn't until we were leaving that we spotted Douchebag again. Allie had so much to drink that I finally cut her off and told her we were going home. I'd have to figure out how to sneak her past her dad's room later.

I supported her weight on the way back to the car. A cool breeze sent my hair dancing in the wind.

"Hey," someone called when we passed the fire pit.

I didn't realize they were talking to us until they called again. We turned.

Douchebag stepped forward with a beer in his hand.

"Well, would you look who it is?" He covered his mouth with his fist, and the word *bitches* slipped out between coughs.

A few guys around him laughed.

"That's not very nice," Allie slurred.

"It's not nice to turn down a nice guy like me, either." He shifted his weight rather unevenly between his feet.

"You," Allie pointed, "are *not* a nice guy."

"Me?" he feigned. "You never gave me the chance. You don't know what you're missing."

Allie opened her mouth to say more, but I pulled her away.

"Come on," I whispered in her ear. "Let's get you home."

I thought ignoring him might be enough, but his footsteps followed. I slowed, not wanting to lead him to the car. My fists clenched at my sides.

"Come on, Tad," one of the other guys said.

"Where are you going?" Tad insisted. "Take me with you. We could throw a party for three."

Allie whirled around and stumbled over her own feet before I caught her. "*That's* how I know you're not a nice guy."

Tad stepped toward Allie and lowered his voice. "So maybe I *am* a bad guy. If you take me for a test drive, you might find out you like the flavor." He reached out and placed a hand on her exposed thigh.

My heart lurched in surprise. Before he could get his hand up her skirt, I slapped it away. Noises erupted from the guys around us. I couldn't tell if they were on my side or Tad's. I had the overwhelming urge to barf and punch the guy at the same time. I was *not* going to let him touch my friend like that.

The anger I'd been suppressing bubbled to the surface. My skin heated and sizzled with rage, and the air around us suddenly seemed charged with energy. I let Allie go and raised my arm, but before I could throw the first punch, everyone went silent.

Fear entered Tad's eyes. He backed away but tripped over his own feet and fell to the ground.

Everyone gaped at me. Even Allie, who had fallen to the earth without anyone to support her, stared at me wide-eyed.

"What?" I snapped.

Before anyone could answer, I glanced down at myself and noticed for the first time what they were all staring at.

A white glow danced across my fist and lit up my arm like an electric charge. I opened my hand and tried to shake the substance off of it.

Bad idea.

A luminous white orb the size of a softball rose from my palm. My first thought was that I was hallucinating again, but I could tell by everyone's faces that I wasn't imagining it.

As soon as the shock overcame me, the orb disappeared, and my hand returned to normal. I scanned the crowd, hoping someone might be able to tell me what was going on. A dozen stunned faces stared back at me.

I noticed one guy in the back cloaked in a dark hood. A shiver ran down my spine, but I didn't have time to worry about whether I was imagining him or not. I had to get away from all those eyes and figure out what the hell was going on with my hand.

I turned to Allie and bent to help her up. Before I got her to her feet, a heavy weight crashed into me. The air left my chest, and I tumbled to the ground.

2

I rolled over to find Tad straddling me. Squeezing my eyes tightly shut, I expected the blow to come any second now.

Suddenly, his weight disappeared. My eyes opened, and I stared up at the dark, starless sky. The moon peeked out through the clouds.

I rose to a sitting position and immediately became alert when I saw two guys fighting in the grass to my left. The first thing I noticed about the second guy was his broad shoulders and leather jacket. My heart flipped in my chest.

Hot Stuff threw a punch. Before he could get in another one, Tad scrambled to his feet and ran off toward his friends.

My savior hurried over to where I sat and offered a hand to help me to my feet. In a silent mutual agreement, we both took one of Allie's arms and supported her weight as we distanced ourselves from the fire pit. Darkness enveloped us, leaving nothing but moonlight to guide us down the long driveway.

"Are you crazy?" he hissed. "In front of all those people? It's going to be fun explaining that one. You're lucky they're all drunk enough that we can convince them it was a trick of the light."

"What are you *talking* about?" I bit back through shallow breaths. "You think I did that on purpose?"

"You know you can't use essence to intimidate people. Have you not learned anything?"

I narrowed my eyes at him. "I don't know what you're talking about."

"*That*. Back there."

Oh, wow. That's helpful.

"I don't—ow! Allie, that was my foot," I complained.

She muttered an incomprehensible apology.

We reached the car, and I opened the back door. Allie climbed inside and melted into the seat.

I slammed the door and spun back toward him. "Who *are* you?"

"Who are *you*?" he demanded.

"I asked you first."

He hesitated. "James Marek. Most people call me Marek."

"Well, thanks for the help, but I think I can take it from here." All I wanted was to escape this place. Even the prospect of learning more about this guy couldn't make me stay.

I turned, but he caught me before I could get out of reach.

"Aren't you going to answer *my* question? I've never seen you around before," he said.

I jerked my arm away from him. "Of course not. I just moved here."

He stared at me like he expected me to say more. "What's your name?"

I wasn't sure I should answer, but I caved under the weight of his heavy stare. "I'm Ryn. And I'm leaving."

"Wait!"

The urgency in his tone made me stop.

"It's not like Davina drop out of the sky every day," he said. "I think I recognize essence when I see it."

I backed away from him. The cool metal of the car touched my skin.

"Are you insane?" My voice shook. *No, Ryn. You're the crazy one.*

"This is serious." Marek spoke through clenched teeth. "Do you know how much trouble you could get in for something like this?"

My pulse quickened, and my face grew hot. This had to be a dream or something. Maybe I drank more than I thought and had passed out.

"I think I can defend myself just fine," I said.

I started around the back of the vehicle toward the driver's side, but a second voice caught my attention.

"Maybe you should listen to your boyfriend."

I turned around, expecting Tad to be back. Instead, I found two cloaked figures approaching us. Their faces were hidden beneath the shadows of their hoods. My first instinct was to ignore them like I had my entire life. But when I glanced around and found no one else nearby, I realized the voice must've come from one of the dark figures.

That couldn't be right. They hadn't spoken to me in years.

Marek took a defensive stance.

"You can't see them, can you?" I asked him accusingly.

"Of course I can," he said, not taking his eyes off the men. Marek's tone shifted as he addressed them. "You don't want to try anything. Believe me."

The taller figure spoke first. "Little Angel looks fun to play with. How can we resist?"

The other man chuckled. "What do you think, Dorian? You take the guy, I'll take the girl?"

A muscle popped in Marek's jaw. "You shouldn't be here. You know you'll get yourself killed before you make it out of town."

"But it's so much fun when all you young angels gather together with no protection," the taller one said. "Your kind aren't the only ones who have fun killing. The fewer there are of you in the world, the better."

I inched away slowly, my hands shaking. Now would be a really good time to wake up.

"I wouldn't bet on that," Marek said.

Before I could process what was happening, a white light erupted from Marek's palm and hit the first man in the shoulder. He crumbled to the ground and lay on his back breathlessly.

"Oh my God! What did you do?" I tried to push past Marek to check Dorian's pulse, but he grabbed my wrist and pulled me behind him.

The second man crossed in front of Dorian.

Marek faced him and spoke in a strong voice. "I wouldn't try anything if I were you, unless you want to end up like your friend."

A second ball of energy formed in Marek's palm. It glowed intensely like some sort of magical fireball.

"You think you're better than me?" the man challenged. He extended a hand out from underneath his cloak. A similar object appeared to grow from out of nowhere. His fireball had a dark black center outlined in a reddish white glow that contrasted against the darkness of the night. "What do you say we do this hand-to-hand? No essence."

"Only if you don't want to survive," Marek said confidently.

An icy laugh erupted from the man's chest. "Have it your way." He swung his hand around, sending the dark fireball flying in our direction.

I couldn't think fast enough to duck out of the way. Luckily, Marek spun around and tackled me to the ground. The black ball disappeared behind us.

Marek shuffled to his feet and lunged toward the figure. His fist connected with the guy's jaw. Before the second punch could reach him, the man caught Marek's fist and twisted his arm around. A loud thud came when he shoved Marek onto the hood of the car.

"Stop!" I cried, but my throat closed up around my words. My knees shook as I rose to my feet.

Marek gasped for breath. The man stood over him and squeezed his fingers around Marek's throat.

"Stop!" I pleaded again. "You're going to kill him." Fear stalled me from making a move.

The man only laughed.

Anger instantly replaced my fear. Blood rose to the surface of my skin, and a warm sensation spread to my fingertips. Another white fireball settled in my palm. My mind instantly flickered back to what Marek had done just moments ago when he threw something similar at the last guy. I drew my arm back and heaved the object at the man choking Marek.

The next few moments passed by in slow motion. The man glanced up at me. Surprised, he loosened his grip on Marek's throat and shifted to fight back.

Somewhere on its course to him, the white ball of energy transformed into a dark purple. He made a move to dodge the object, but before he could get out of the way, the purple ball of energy hit him in the chest. His cloak crumbled to the ground in a heap as his body vanished in a puff of black smoke.

This is not happening to me again.

I'd been so preoccupied with saving Marek that I hadn't realized Dorian had sat up. He glanced between where his friend had vanished and me.

Marek coughed and sucked in several breaths.

Another white fireball formed in my hand.

Dorian stood, and a black ball of energy rose from his own fingers. Marek placed his feet firmly between us. Dorian hesitated for a moment and then closed his fist. The orb in his hand disappeared.

The light emanating from Marek's hand illuminated Dorian's face just enough that I could see his black irises. My gut twisted at the sight.

Dorian narrowed his inhuman eyes at me. "You shouldn't have done that, Little Angel. Now I know what you are, and—"

"You'll never get close to her," Marek said with conviction. "Not as long as I'm around."

Dorian scoffed. "You won't be around forever."

Marek's face twisted in anger. In one quick motion, he hurled his fireball at Dorian. Dorian spun out of the way, and the fireball exploded like a firecracker against the ground. Dorian snatched up his friend's cloak and rushed away from us, escaping into the darkness.

"Shit," Marek muttered under his breath. "He's going to be back. And it's going to be ugly."

3

𝒜xhaustion sent me tumbling to my knees. Marek rushed to steady me and slowly lowered me to the ground. I closed my eyes and pressed my head against the cool metal of the car door.

I'm hallucinating again.

Why, then, did it feel so real?

I opened my eyes. Marek sat beside me with his elbows rested on his knees, breathing in deeply.

He must be part of the hallucination, I thought. It's not like sexy hunks showed up every day to rescue me from figments of my imagination.

"Are you okay?" Marek asked.

Physically? Yeah.

Mentally? Maybe it was time to check in with a therapist again.

I wasn't worried about myself, though. My main priority was getting Allie home safely.

"I'm fine, but I have to get my friend home." I rose to my feet. "I'll see you around."

"Wait."

I didn't. I slipped into the driver's seat and grabbed Allie's keys from the floor where she'd left them. My hand shook as I stuck the key in the ignition.

It felt strange being in the driver's seat again. Mom wouldn't let me drive after what happened the last time I got behind the wheel.

Marek grabbed my door before I could shut it. "You can't just *leave.*"

"I can." I ripped the door from his grasp and narrowly missed squashing his fingers. Allie shifted slightly in the back seat at the sound of the slamming door.

"Seriously. This is a big deal." He knocked on the window.

I sighed and rolled it down. "Seriously, I have to get Allie home. Maybe we can talk about this later."

Marek gaped at me. "Let me come with you. You shouldn't be alone."

"I'm not. Allie's with me." Even if she wasn't exactly conscious.

"At least let me know how I can get in touch with you," he insisted.

I sighed. If I didn't give him something, he wasn't going to let me leave. I was too freaked out to stay.

"I'm staying at Allie's house."

"I can meet you there in the morning," he offered.

My brows shot up. "And you just happen to know where she lives?"

He nodded. "Yeah, we go to school together."

"Okay, I'll see you in the morning." I rolled up the window and shifted into drive. I had no intention of ever seeing Marek again.

I woke the following morning with a pounding headache and momentarily wondered where I was.

The first thing I noticed was the white vanity to my left, and then I spotted Allie's pink comforter hanging off the edge of her bed to my right. Allie's shoes were strewn at the floor near my feet. I'd taken them off for her last night and never bothered to put them away nicely. I still wore the same clothes I'd gone to the party in.

Allie stirred from the bed above me and cleared her throat. "How do you feel?"

"I'm fine," I lied. "You?"

"Like shit," she admitted. She attempted to sit up but immediately fell back onto her bed. "How'd we get home?"

"I drove you back and snuck you in."

"Thanks. I don't know what I would've done without you there. I'm so thirsty."

I climbed out of my sleeping bag and stood. "I'll get you some water."

"No," she insisted kindly. "I can do it."

"Relax," I told her. "You have a pretty bad hangover."

I walked out of the room before she could argue further. In the bathroom, I filled the glass next to the sink with water. My eyes landed on my hand as I twisted the faucet. I remembered the white orb forming in my palm so vividly. I'd never forget the deep purple it transformed into.

But things like this didn't happen in real life. There had to be another explanation. Had Kyle slipped something in my drink? It would explain my headache.

The cool water hit my skin as it spilled over the edges of the glass, pulling me from my thoughts. I immediately twisted the faucet off and returned to Allie's bedroom.

"Here you go." I handed her the glass.

She rolled over and thanked me.

"Hey, Allie. Kyle's cool, right?" I asked.

"What do you mean?" She sat up and sipped her water.

"I mean, he can be trusted, can't he? He wouldn't mess with someone's drink?"

"God, no. He'd never do that." Allie's eyes widened. "You think you were drugged? Because that douchebag—"

"No," I answered quickly.

Tad certainly seemed like a viable suspect, but he never got close enough to my drink to slip something in it.

"Do you know someone named Marek?" I asked.

She took another sip of water. "Yeah. We're in the same class at Galen. Why?"

"I met him last night."

Which meant everything had been real.

Holy shit. My knees shook so badly I had to sit in the chair next to her vanity to steady them. This changed everything I knew about my childhood.

"What'd you think of him?" Allie wiggled her eyebrows. "He's cute, right?"

"Huh?" My face flushed. "Yeah, he's cute. We didn't really talk much."

Allie wrinkled her nose. "Probably for the best."

I straightened. "What do you mean by that?"

Allie sighed and rested her drink in her lap. "He's just… a little too serious at times."

"Oh?"

"We're always in groups together in class," she explained. "I mean, we get along, but he can be kind of controlling. He thinks he's better than everyone else. Anyway, you don't want to get involved with anyone at Galen High. Dating someone from a different school is hard."

"I didn't say I wanted to date him!"

She giggled.

"I was just curious what his deal was and all."

Memories from last night flashed through my mind. Marek saw the cloaked figures. I wasn't alone.

Not to mention I can shoot freaking fireballs out of my hands.

I stood quickly. "I have to go."

"What? Why?" She asked in surprise.

I have to test out this fireball thing and confirm I'm not insane.

"I have chores." That wasn't exactly a lie.

"Okay." She relaxed. "See you later."

I grabbed my overnight bag from the floor. "Bye."

I left the house wondering how I was going to test what I'd experienced last night. Perhaps my anger at the time had something to do with it.

As soon as I stepped out of Allie's front door, my heart soared in my chest. At the end of her driveway stood the one thing that was sure to help me make sense of it all.

Marek leaned against a sleek black motorcycle looking even sexier than the first time I met him. He wore the same tight pants he had on last night, and his brown hair was tousled in the same manner. He'd draped his leather jacket over the handlebars of the motorcycle. Without it on, I had a great view of his thick biceps.

Heaven help me. I was undressing him with my eyes again.

Marek smiled at me, but it didn't quite reach his tired eyes. Had he slept at all? He stood there waiting for me like he'd camped out in Allie's yard last night.

"We need to talk," I stated as soon as I reached him.

He straightened. "Agreed."

"What the hell happened last night?" I demanded.

Marek gazed at me from under long lashes. "You really don't know?"

My brows shot up. "I really don't know. I mean… was it… real?"

A shocked expression crossed his face. "Of course it was real. What, you don't fight demons on a daily basis?"

My eyes widened. "You do that *all* the time?"

Marek chuckled. "No. We get idiots like that coming into town every now and then trying to show how tough they are."

"So, they're like… actually demons? From Hell?"

"No, that's just what we call them. Maybe we should go somewhere private to talk about it."

I glanced down the quiet residential street. It was completely deserted.

"It's private enough here. So, you can see them, too? I'm not the only one?"

He eyed me curiously for at least five seconds.

Say something already, dammit!

"You really have no idea?" he asked.

My mouth hung open, but nothing came out. *Uh, duh!*

Marek took my silence as an answer. "You're lucky I was there. I almost didn't come, but Kyle made me." He paused and pressed his lips together in thought. "I think I should introduce you to Fletcher."

My eyebrows pressed together. "Who's Fletcher?"

"He's the guy who can answer your questions. Should we get going?" Marek grabbed the helmet off his seat and shoved it into my hands.

"On *that* thing?" I squeaked.

"Why not?" he asked. "There's enough room for two."

"But there's only one helmet." I held it up to prove my point.

He slipped on his jacket and swung a leg over the bike. "That's why I gave it to you. Put it on."

I bit my lip nervously. I'd never ridden on a motorcycle before.

"Well?" Marek prodded. "Do you want answers or not?"

Mom didn't expect me home for hours, and I'd only ditched Allie so I could figure this all out. The answer was obvious.

But how did I know I could trust him?

Because he saved my life.

And there was nothing I wanted more than answers right now.

I shoved the helmet back into his hands. "Give me a second."

I hurried up my porch steps and dropped my overnight bag inside the front door. When I returned to the bike, Marek had his phone up to his ear.

"Okay," he said into it. "We'll see you soon."

He hung up and slid the phone into his back pocket.

"Here," he said, handing me the helmet.

"I don't need it." I pushed it back toward him.

"Yes, you do. I'd rather you wear it than me."

I was about to protest again, but then he reached for my hand. His touch was warm and electric.

Marek placed the helmet in my palm. "Put it on, Ryn."

If I knew hearing him say my name would melt my insides the way it did, I would've asked him to say it sooner.

I put the helmet on and swung my leg over the bike behind him. Not quite sure where to place my hands, I settled them on his shoulders. They shook in laughter.

"What?" I asked sharply. "Let's go."

"You've never ridden a bike before, have you?"

"No shit, Sherlock."

"Usually your arms go around my waist." He took my hands and pulled them around him.

My breath caught in my throat, and my entire body tensed. Shouldn't we at least go on a date before we got this close? I wouldn't know.

I could feel Marek's strong muscles under his shirt. My heart hammered so hard I was sure he could feel it against his back.

Lovely. I was going to die of a heart attack.

The engine roared to life, and before I knew it, we were speeding down the street.

There was no telling what kind of trouble I was getting myself into.

4

*I*t took a moment for reality to sink in. I'd just hopped on the back of a stranger's motorcycle so he could take me God knows where. *What was I thinking?*

Marek drove so fast through the streets of Eagle Valley that a scream erupted from my lungs. I squeezed my eyes shut and wrapped my arms around him so tightly I thought I might crush his ribs. Instead of slowing like I wanted him to, he took it as an invitation to increase his speed.

Relief flooded through me when I felt him apply the brakes. I finally opened my eyes. We were in front of Galen High.

Three stories of red brick complete with white stone accents towered above us. The third floor was mostly slanted roof, but three peaks with small balconies housed extra windows for the top story. The Jacobean-style building featured five chimneys and a beautiful ornate window above the front doors. The only thing standing between us and the brick beauty was a vast manicured lawn bordered by a deciduous forest.

This place looked more like Galen Mansion than Galen High School.

I steadied myself against the bike when I dismounted it.

"Are you okay?" Marek asked. He reached out toward me, but at the last second, he pulled away.

"I'm fine." I slipped off the helmet and shook my hair out like that proved something.

I followed Marek up the sidewalk to the front entrance. Each step closer to the school had me questioning my sanity. I tried to reassure myself I was safe. Aside from a middle-aged woman jogging across the road with earbuds in, the street was quiet. I had to remind myself I was doing this for answers.

Marek sat on the top step. "We'll have to wait for Fletcher to unlock the door."

I took a seat beside him. Just when I opened my mouth to ask more about this Fletcher person, Marek spoke again.

"So, tell me about yourself."

I felt a blush rise to my cheeks and tucked a strand of brown hair behind my ear. He couldn't actually be interested in getting to know me.

"What do you want to know?" I asked.

He shrugged. "How have you grown up your whole life not knowing what you are?"

Good question. "You mean, not knowing I could shoot fireballs out of my hands?"

"They're not fireballs," he said with a laugh, "but yeah. Are you adopted or something?"

The question caught me off guard. "No. Why would you say that?"

"I'm sorry. I just figured your parents would tell you—"

"Well, they didn't," I bit harshly. I took a deep breath to steady my tone. "My mom definitely doesn't know about any of this." If she did, she wouldn't have taken me to three different therapists by the time I was eight. "I guess it's possible my father knew…"

"But?" Marek prodded curiously.

I wasn't sure why I opened up to him. Part of me said it was because I wanted answers and figured the more I shared, the more he'd share. Another part of me suspected it was his inviting smile. Something about him held an air of trustworthiness.

"My dad has never been around," I told him vaguely. "He left before I was born."

"Oh," Marek said simply, dropping his gaze to his feet. I could tell he regretted asking the question. "So, what brought you to Eagle Valley?"

Silence settled once again as I considered the question. I remained quiet for so long that I was sure Marek was wondering if I'd actually answer.

"I did," I finally said.

He tilted his head in question.

"My mom and I move a lot," I explained. "She's always on the search for a new adventure. She can't stay in one place for too long. It's like no place is ever good enough for her."

I didn't mention why I thought that was. Mom would never admit it, but I suspected deep down, she hoped to someday run into my father again.

"Mom usually chooses where we'll go next," I said. "This time, she let me choose."

"Why Eagle Valley, though?" Marek asked.

"Fate, I guess." It was the only thing that made sense. Coincidence didn't just land you in the lap of a dreamy guy with all the answers, did it? "When Mom said I could choose, I knew I wanted to move to the Midwest. I've always loved it here. It's so green in the summer, and I love the snow in the winter. But I didn't really care what part of the Midwest we moved to, so I tacked a map to the wall and threw a dart at it. It landed on top of Eagle Valley."

Marek pressed his lips together and nodded, considering the information.

"Aren't I the one who's supposed to be asking the questions?" I teased.

He shot me a smile.

Dayum. He could smile at me any time he wanted.

"What do you want to know?" he asked.

"If those things were demons, what are we?"

Before he could reply, the sound of an approaching vehicle stole both of our attention. The gray crossover pulled into the school parking lot across the street and parked in the closest space.

Marek stood. "That's Fletcher. He'll be able to answer your questions."

A thin man with gray hair stepped out of the vehicle. He wore tan slacks and a blue button-down shirt. A messenger bag bounced against his hip as he rushed up the walkway. He stuck his hand out in my direction when he reached us. I shook it.

"Samuel Fletcher," he introduced himself. He sounded slightly winded like he was in a hurry. "Most students simply call me Fletcher. You must be Ryn. James told me about what happened last night."

I was about to ask who James was before remembering it was Marek's first name.

Fletcher stepped past us and stuck a key in the front door. He held the door open for us while he spoke. "He says it gave you quite a shock."

An uncontrollable laugh bubbled up from my chest. "You could say that."

I fell silent the moment I stepped through the doors. The architecture inside was even more spectacular than the exterior.

A large foyer opened to the second level, where a balcony overlooked the commons area. Plush sofas and chairs surrounded a massive antique fireplace to our right. To our left sat a large staircase with a dark walnut banister. The same wooden texture covered the floors and bordered the doorways. Even the white walls and ceiling featured carved wooden accents.

Hints of a lemon-scented cleaner filled the air, but it couldn't completely cover the smell that reminded me of an old museum. There was nothing modern about this building, but it contained a unique charm that made me feel at home.

"You're kidding me," I blurted as I took in the scene. "This place is a school?"

"It is now. It used to be a mansion," Fletcher explained. "It belonged to the brothers who founded Eagle Valley. My room is this way."

I followed behind him, but my attention remained on the architecture. Fletcher led us under the balcony and to a hall behind the grand staircase. I stole a glance inside a pair of open doors directly across from the front entrance. It was a small cafeteria dotted with dark wooden tables that matched the rest of the antique décor.

We entered a wide hallway and took the second door on the right. Three short rows of student desks faced a large desk at the front of the room. A modern whiteboard hung on the wall behind it.

"It's unfortunate you had to find out this way, but I'll explain the best I can." Fletcher dropped his bag on his desk and fell into the chair behind it so hard that it rolled across the floor a few inches. "Please, have a seat."

I followed Marek's lead and sat in one of the desks in the front row. My heart hammered quicker than I would have thought possible as I anxiously awaited answers.

"So... um..." I couldn't get the words out. Where did I even start? "Any idea what's happening to me?"

Fletcher straightened in his chair. "Well, it appears you're a Davina."

"What—what does that mean?" I tried to keep an open mind. "Am I, like, an alien?"

Both Marek and Fletcher laughed.

"Of course not," Fletcher said.

"So, what's a Davina?" If possible, my pulse grew even louder in my ears. "All I heard last night was something about angels and demons. I figured I was insane. But if Marek saw it all too..."

"We're not angels or demons," Fletcher said like he wasn't pleased with the terms. "We're similar, but the stories have it all wrong."

"So, you're not aliens or angels. Mutants?" This whole place definitely gave off an Xavier Institute vibe.

Fletcher smiled in amusement. "No, Ryn. We're where the stories of angels and demons came from, but we prefer not to use the terms as we have no religious affiliations. Not with any modern religion, anyway."

I glanced between the two of them. They stared back as if expecting me to take their word for it.

"Davina have been around much longer than humans have," Marek explained. "Unfortunately, so have the demons." He said the word *demons* with an air of disgust.

"I thought you said this wasn't an angels and demons sort of thing," I pointed out.

"Not like you're used to," Marek said.

"It's an insult," Fletcher clarified. "They're really called Aedes."

Uncertainty crossed my face. These guys must've been as crazy as I was.

"Who all knows about this?" I asked. "Everyone in Eagle Valley?"

"Oh, no," Fletcher said seriously. "We'd never reveal our secret. It's our duty as Davina to protect humans from the Aedes. We'd much rather they live in peace not knowing what was out there. We'd prefer not to cause a panic, and frankly, most of us aren't keen on the idea of becoming lab rats. Our secrets are kept within the walls of Galen High."

"Everyone at Galen knows?" I asked in shock.

"It's a Davina-only high school," Marek confirmed.

Holy shit. Allie went to Galen High. My best friend was an angel.

And here I thought I'd made normal friends this time.

"Here, and at other schools like ours, our students learn how to use their Davina skills," Fletcher explained. "Many of them go on to become Protectors and leave Eagle Valley to fight the Aedes. Eventually, most return to raise families, and we move on to training the next generation."

I remained quiet as I let the information sink in. How could *I* be a Davina? How could anything they were saying be true?

It can't be, I thought to myself. *It's all one big prank to psych out the new girl.*

"Show me that thing again," I demanded. I stuck my palm up in Marek's direction and wiggled my fingers.

He eyed me like he didn't know what I was talking about.

"The fireball thing," I said.

"I told you; they're not fireballs." Marek stretched out his palm, and a glowing white orb appeared.

I couldn't take my eyes off it. The longer I stared, the more I realized other colors swirled inside it. Though they were subtle, it was mesmerizing.

Fletcher stood and popped the cap off a marker. He began to write on the whiteboard like he was teaching a high school history lesson. "It's called essence. The Davina believe there are four energies that make up a person: their body, their life force, their consciousness, and their essence. The four are all interconnected and work together to create balance."

He drew lines on the board connecting each of the words. "The body is obvious. Life force is most closely tied to the body. It's the energy that keeps the body living. Consciousness refers to a person's thoughts. So, what's left?"

It took me a moment to realize he wanted me to answer. I stared up at the four words he'd written.

"Essence," I answered. *Whatever that means.*

"Right," Fletcher said. "But what *is* essence?"

How am I supposed to know?

I stared at him blankly.

"It's your *soul*," Fletcher said passionately. "It's your character, who you are as a person."

My eyes widened, and my words came out in a rush. "The fireballs are part of your *soul*? What happens when you throw one at someone? Are you throwing away part of your soul?"

What had I gotten myself into?

"No, no," Fletcher said quickly. "They're only a physical manifestation of your essence energy. It can be recharged."

Good to know.

"If a person's body is damaged and their life force severed, their essence returns to the earth to be used by later generations," Fletcher continued. "Essence is the only thing that survives after death."

I paused for a moment to think about it. "So, it's like reincarnation?"

Fletcher pressed his lips together in thought. "In a sense. Your energy gets recycled."

I took a moment to let this sink in. "Where do the demons fit in to this?"

"Good question." Fletcher returned to his chair.

I knotted my hands in my lap. How could this really be happening to me?

Fletcher began to recite the story like he'd told it a hundred times. "In the beginning, there were gods with unimaginable power. The gods yearned for children, but only the highest gods, called Divinities, were afforded the privilege. Their children didn't inherit all of their powers to begin with, and they didn't want the lesser gods diluting that power. Wanting the best for their children, the higher gods created a paradise they called Vehena. They gifted this realm to their children, the Davina.

"The lesser gods, known as Sanctities, saw what the Divinities had and began having their own children in secret. Their children were called the Aedes. When the secret got out, the Divinities called for the Aedes' execution. They believed their lack of power was an abomination, and they were furious that the Sanctities had broken the laws of their realm.

"The Sanctities begged for mercy and to spare the lives of their children. The Divinities agreed, but the arrangement didn't work out like the Sanctities hoped. Instead of sharing the god's realm or allowing the Aedes into Vehena, the Divinities stripped the Aedes of their immortality and marked them with darkness so they would never forget the sins of their fathers."

I glanced to Marek to see if he was buying all this. He stared up at Fletcher with a look in his eyes that told me he believed every word of it.

Fletcher continued. "The Divinities banished the Aedes to a dark, desolate realm called Malum. But even the gods couldn't stabilize the gateways between realms, and the Aedes returned.

"To remind everyone how powerful they were, the Divinities laid upon the Aedes a second curse. They could return to the god's realm, but they could do nothing but walk the realm and observe. Aside from the ground at their feet—and, of course, the Divinities and Davina—they could only interact with objects that originated outside the realm. Anything they brought from their realm wouldn't truly exist here. Their curse served as a constant reminder that this realm was not their home."

Fletcher took a breath. "The Sanctities were also cursed. They couldn't see, hear, or interact with their children or anything from their realm. This was to prevent alliances and keep the Sanctities from having more children. It was another way for the Divinities to exercise their power."

The Divinities sounded like a bunch of jackholes.

"This was the worst curse of all," Fletcher said. "It sparked a war, and the gods destroyed each other. The earth was what was left from the ashes of their realm."

"Shut up." I couldn't help it when the words flew from my mouth. "You're saying *gods* used to live on the earth?"

Fletcher nodded. "It was their realm before it was ours. After the dust settled, the earth acted as a bridge between Vehena and Malum."

And I was just supposed to believe in this religious nonsense?

Marek must've noticed the disbelief written on my face. "Let him finish the story," he whispered.

Fletcher cleared his throat. "The Davina had nothing to do with the Great War, and so they sought to form an alliance with the Aedes. The Davina didn't agree with the actions of their parents. They wanted to set things right again. To solidify their alliance, the Davina tried to bring back the Sanctities and reunite them with their children. They called upon the power in the sands of the earth, but instead of bringing the Sanctities back, a new race—the humans—were formed. The curse of the Sanctities remained."

"That's why humans can't see demons or their cloaks?" I interrupted. "Because of that curse?"

Fletcher nodded. "Precisely. In a sense, humans were created from what remained of the Sanctities, but they didn't possess any of their divine powers."

Goodbye, science.

"The Davina grew to love the humans," Fletcher said. "Several mated to create human-Davina hybrids that possessed the power of the Davina. That's where *we* come from."

"Except we're not as powerful as the original Davina," Marek clarified.

"Correct," Fletcher agreed. "Much of our Davina power has been bred out throughout the generations. We're a closer match for the Aedes now. They're getting tougher to defeat."

"You're at war?" I asked.

Fletcher nodded. "Since the dawn of civilization."

Seriously, what the heck was going on? I was being introduced to a whole new religion here. What if I didn't want to be a part of this?

I shot up out of the desk. "I—I'm sorry."

I took one look at Marek's shocked expression and knew I'd never find the words to explain myself. I did the only thing that made sense in that moment.

I bolted.

5

"Ryn, stop," Marek called down the hall.

My breath hitched as he caught my wrist and whirled me around to face him. I jerked my hand out of his grasp, but he only reached for me again.

"Stop it!" I struggled against him and accidentally elbowed him in the ribs. Hard.

I broke free and raced to the end of the hall and turned to the right. Before I could get my hand on the front door handle, Marek slipped in front of me and blocked my path. I ran straight into his chest and nearly tripped over his feet.

I stumbled back. "What's your problem? Are you planning to keep me prisoner here or something?"

His gaze dropped. "No, I just think you need to hear more before you run off. Believe me. I felt the same way when I first came here. There's so much more you need to know."

I crossed my arms and pursed my lips. "My whole world is being turned upside down, Marek. Everything I thought I knew… I just want the demons to go away."

He spoke softly. "I know. I can't make them go away, but I can promise you one thing."

I dropped my arms to my side. "What's that?"

"You'll never have to be alone in this again."

I didn't know how long we stood there staring at each other. It

32

could've been just moments or half an hour. The look in Marek's eyes begged me to accept my new reality. And I knew I would, because he'd been right. I wasn't alone anymore.

"Should we sit down?" Marek offered, gesturing to the plush chairs by the fireplace.

Before I could agree, Fletcher's voice came from behind me. "Maybe we should give her some time to think about things."

I turned to look at him. He stood next to the banister with his hands crossed in front of him.

He stepped forward with a sympathetic expression on his face. "It's a lot to take in. Perhaps you should take the day to come up with a list of questions. Maybe later next week we can go over some of the basics, get you introduced to things a little before school starts."

It took me a long moment to process the implication of his words. "You mean, you want me to attend Galen High?"

A smile twitched at Fletcher's lips. "How else do you expect to learn how to use your skills?"

"I—I…" I didn't know what to say.

"Perhaps it's best if someone escorts you home," Fletcher suggested.

"Shouldn't we tell her about—?" Marek started to say, but Fletcher cut him off.

"I think we should take this slowly. You know what can happen if we spring too much information on a person too fast." Fletcher turned his attention to me. "Are you going to be okay?"

I thought about it for a second and shrugged. "I don't know."

"I'll come by on Monday to see how you're doing," Fletcher offered. "We can discuss your enrollment then."

"Okay, thanks."

When no one said anything else, I turned to the doors beside me and slipped out into fresh air. It had become warmer in the short time I'd been inside, and the air was dense with humidity, causing my shirt to cling to my skin. Though it was muggy and unpleasant, my head began to clear once I stepped outside. I was already to the end of the walkway when I heard Marek calling my name.

"Wait up, Ryn."

I stopped and turned to him. My hair danced in the light breeze.

"Do you want a ride home?" he asked.

"Oh, I—um…" I glanced to his bike. "No, it's okay. I'll walk."

Marek's brows shot up. "You sure you can find your way back?"

"Yes," I lied.

It was only when he pointed it out that I realized I wasn't sure how to get home. When Allie had shown me around town, we spent the whole day walking. All the landmarks blended in my mind. Plus, I hadn't been watching this morning when Marek drove me here.

I could tell by the smirk on Marek's face that he knew I wasn't telling the truth.

"Well, maybe not exactly," I admitted, "but I know the general direction, and Eagle Valley isn't very big. I can't exactly get lost."

"Get on the bike. I'll drive you home."

The tone in his voice told me I didn't have a choice. At least he'd save me time wandering around aimlessly.

"Yeah, okay," I caved.

He drove slower this time but still made me wear the helmet. Relief washed over me as soon as we made it to my street.

Marek didn't part with me at the curb like I thought he would. Instead, he followed me up the creaky wooden steps to the front door. He stared down at me with a hint of a smile. His eyes danced around my face like he expected an invitation inside.

My cheeks heated under his gaze. "What?"

"I just want to make sure you're all right."

My heart fluttered. It was nice for someone to actually care.

"It's all so scary, Marek," I admitted.

"I know." He truly sounded like he meant it. "I can help you if you let me. Let me give you my number. Then you can call me when you're ready."

I pulled my phone from my back pocket and handed it to him. He programmed his number in and gave it back.

"Do you have more questions?" he asked.

"I do." The problem was there were questions I was afraid to ask. "Later, though."

I pushed past him and into the house.

In the following silence, I glanced around the house, letting the light filtering in through the stained-glass window by the stairs distract me. That was one thing I liked about this house. It had character, from the big brass door handles to the ancient hardwood flooring. I was always finding something new in this house that gave it a bit of character.

After a deep breath, I dragged myself into the living room and fell onto the couch. I closed my eyes. If I could just fall asleep, maybe this would all be over.

This is really happening. It will never be over.

Several minutes later, a knock sounded at the front door. I sighed heavily and rose, wondering what Marek could possibly want from me.

But it wasn't Marek. It was Allie.

"Hey," Allie said softly. "How are you doing?"

I caught a glimpse of Marek retreating down the street on his bike. "He told you?"

Her face fell. "Yeah. You don't mind if I come in, do you?"

"No." I opened the door wider. "Are you feeling any better?"

"A little," she told me. Even with a hangover, she'd found enough energy to flawlessly reapply her makeup.

I led Allie up the stairs to my room. I knew she'd want to talk about what happened, but I didn't know how to approach the topic.

Allie entered the room behind me and glanced around. "You haven't finished unpacking yet?"

I followed her eyes. The white walls were bare, but I hadn't left any packing boxes lying out. "I did finish unpacking."

"Oh," she said. "I don't see any pictures or anything."

"I have pictures!" I defended. I sat on the bed and pointed to the framed photo on my dresser.

Allie walked over to it to get a better look.

"It's from when I was in seventh grade," I told her. "Just after Mom and I ran our first half marathon. That was when she was going through her fitness phase. It was right before her photography phase. Here, I'll show you."

I hopped up from the bed and crossed over to my closet. I

pulled a thick scrapbook from the top shelf and handed it to Allie. She gazed down at it curiously and sat on my bed to flip through it.

"Oh, wow," she said in amazement. "These pictures are really nice."

"Yeah, but they're all from junior high. Like I said, my mom was going through her photography stage and photographed *everything*. And that led right into her scrapbooking phase."

Allie never took her eyes off the book. "Your mom's a really interesting person. She's talented at a lot of stuff."

I wouldn't exactly say *talented*.

I took a seat beside Allie. "She never sticks with one thing."

"What other kinds of things has she done?" she asked as she flipped through the pages.

"Mm…" I thought. "We had a martial arts phase and a cooking phase. Then obviously we had the running one and the photography and scrapbooking. She tried sewing once, but that didn't last long. For a year, all she did was read books. She read something like three hundred books that year."

Allie's eyebrows shot up. "Wow."

I'd never been impressed. It was like nothing could ever please my mom.

"What about you?" Allie asked.

"What do you mean?"

"What are you into? Are you like your mom, always changing your hobbies?"

I sighed heavily. "You know we move around a lot. I never get to be a part of anything for long. I was in martial arts classes for a few years in elementary school, and I played softball in junior high."

I shrugged. The truth was, Mom changed hobbies so often that I never had much of a chance to pursue my own interests. We didn't have the money for it. Her job as a virtual assistant didn't exactly pay a whole lot.

"I like cooking," I said. "That was my favorite phase she went through. Oh, and earrings! I *love* earrings."

I jumped up from the bed and pulled open the drawer at my desk. Allie closed the scrapbook and stood. When she saw my collection, she drew in an audible breath.

"I noticed you wore different earrings almost every day," she said, "but I never thought you'd have *this* many."

I smiled and opened the next two drawers, each displaying another set of my collection. Allie's eyes grew even wider.

"It looks like a lot because I keep the packaging for all of them so they don't get mixed up," I told her.

"It's still pretty cool," she said. "Have you checked out Celeste's yet?"

I shook my head. "What's that?"

"It's a jewelry store in town. I think you'd like it. It's on Main Street right next to Angela's Café. We should go sometime."

"Sounds like fun," I agreed.

I noticed I was still wearing the same dangly cubic zirconia earrings from the night before. I slipped them off and stuck them back where they belonged. I swapped them out for a pair of dark purple studs.

Allie sat on my bed. "Ryn, we need to talk. Marek told me about what happened last night. I wish I could've seen it."

I turned to her from where I sat in front of my mirror. "You saw part of it."

Allie sheepishly dropped her gaze. "I don't remember much of last night. I am *so* sorry I wasn't there for you. I didn't know about you. I never thought you'd be in danger. I never thought *any* of us would be in danger, not here."

"So I guess it's true, then. You're a Davina?" The word felt strange on my tongue.

Allie nodded. "Yeah. I can't believe you're one, too. Marek said you never knew."

"It's... definitely a surprise. I'm still trying to process it all."

Allie looked at me with a sympathetic expression. "I can't imagine not knowing."

I thought back to my childhood, wondering how things would be different if I knew. Would I have faced the demons sooner? What if I hadn't grown up thinking I was crazy?

"What was it like for you, growing up?" I asked curiously.

Allie twisted her lips in thought. "I don't know. It's always been normal for me."

"Could you always do that fireball thing?"

"You mean, conjure essence?" Allie stuck out her palm. A white fireball formed in it and floated just millimeters from her palm.

I stared at it, mesmerized.

She closed her hand into a fist, and the ball of energy disappeared inside it. "No, not always."

"How'd you learn how to do it?" I held out my hand and concentrated, but it remained empty. "You make it look so easy."

Allie shrugged. "I don't know. You just… do it."

"Is that how you learned? You just… did it?"

"Kind of," she admitted. "It should come naturally by now. The ability to manipulate essence comes later in our teens, after puberty. That's why we don't start our training until high school. Your essence is always there; you just can't access it until later."

"But if you don't develop your powers until your teens, how come…" My voice trailed off. I'd conjured essence once before when I was little, although I didn't know what had happened at the time. I wasn't sure if I should tell Allie about it.

"What is it?" Allie prodded. "It's okay, Ryn. I'll answer any questions you have. That's what friends are for." She gave an encouraging smile.

"If you don't develop your powers until later, how have I been able to see the demons my whole life?"

Allie suppressed a giggle. "All Davina can see demons. They probably left you alone until now because they never knew you were a Davina. They can't tell the difference between us and humans. Unless you show your essence or make eye contact, they wouldn't know."

I pressed my lips together. I didn't dare mention to her that they hadn't *always* left me alone.

"What?" Allie asked, sensing I had more to say.

I paused for a beat. "There don't seem to be many demons here in Eagle Valley."

It was one of the first things I noticed when we came here. I thought it meant I was finally growing out of my insanity.

"Of course not. There are far too many Davina here. They'd get themselves killed."

"Then what about the two last night?"

Allie dropped her head. "They were idiots. Sometimes the brave ones will stumble into town for fun. They don't usually make it very far."

I nodded. "Marek mentioned that."

"You're lucky he was there," she said seriously. "I wouldn't want to face a demon on my own."

I opened my mouth to ask more questions, but I cut off when my door opened.

"Kathryn, I'm headed to the store—" Mom stopped as soon as she saw Allie. "Oh. I saw your bag downstairs. I knew you were home, but I didn't realize… Are you coming to the store with me? I want to find some more yarn for that afghan I'm making."

Mom's latest thing was crocheting. If you asked me, it was a waste of time and money. She'd never stick with it.

"No, that's okay," I said.

"Why not? I thought you had fun the last time we went."

Where'd she get that idea? I hated yarn shopping. It was so dull, and the craft stores were always filled with that sickening scent like someone had lit too many candles.

"Mom," I complained. "I have a friend over."

She huffed like she couldn't believe I'd rather spend time with Allie than with her. "If you're going to stay home, I expect your chores to be done by the time I get back."

"Fine," I reluctantly agreed.

"Bye, Mrs. Tyler!" Allie called after my mom.

"Ugh. Don't call her that. It sounds weird."

"Sorry. Should I just call her Gloria?"

"Yeah, I guess that works." I stood from the bed. "I'm sorry, but I have a ton of cleaning to do before my mom gets home."

"I'll help you," she offered.

"You really don't have to do that." I didn't want to take advantage of her.

"Yes, I do," she insisted. "The sooner you get your chores done, the sooner I can teach you to manipulate your essence. You'll need to learn how to defend yourself. Should we get started?"

7

*A*llie thought it best if we practiced somewhere with more space than my bedroom. After we finished cleaning, I took a shower and grabbed some lunch. I sent Mom a text letting her know I was hanging out with Allie the rest of the day.

I stared out the passenger side window of Allie's car. The bright sun from earlier had disappeared behind a layer of clouds. I wasn't sure where we were going until I noticed the red brick of Galen High at the end of the street.

"How are we going to get into the school?" I asked.

I wondered if maybe there was a back door that was easy to jimmy open with the right tool. That's how the seniors at my last school got in for their senior prank. They'd covered the entire gym floor in balloons.

"We're not going inside," Allie said simply.

"Where are we going, then?"

"It's behind the school."

I hesitated. "I don't think that's a good idea, Allie. I don't want anyone to see us."

"Don't worry. They won't," she said with a knowing smile.

Allie parked the car and led me around the side of the building into a forest of dense trees.

I followed behind her and kept my eyes on the dirt path. "Are you sure no one will see us?"

41

"Relax," she insisted. "This is at the edge of town, and the land belongs to the school. No one comes here who isn't supposed to. We use this place to train all the time."

"Fletcher said you train to become Protectors?"

"Yeah."

"What's a Protector, exactly?" I asked.

"They're like soldiers," she explained, "but Protectors usually work alone or in small groups so they don't draw attention. They kill demons."

"Kill them?" I asked warily.

Allie glanced back at me but didn't slow her pace. "Well, yeah. Demons feed off human essence. We protect them from that. Didn't Fletcher tell you?"

I stared down at my feet. "We didn't get that far. But it makes sense."

That didn't mean I wanted to have a hand in killing them, though.

"What if you don't want to become a Protector?" I asked.

"The Davina Council will assign you another job."

I relaxed slightly. "The Davina have their own government?"

"Mm-hmm."

"What kind of jobs do they assign?" I'd always thought it'd be cool to be a chef. I wondered if there were any options for that in the Davina world.

Allie shrugged. "Teaching, keeping track of records, protecting ancient Davina artifacts, things like that."

"And you?" I asked curiously. "You're planning to become a Protector?"

"Yeah," Allie said like it was obvious. "Most Davina start out as Protectors and then go on to teaching or whatever once they get older. It's kind of frowned upon to never become a Protector."

Lovely. I never thought I'd be able to list *soldier* on my résumé.

"Allie, are you sure this is the right way?" I complained.

The forest was so thick and dark that I was sure no one would see us out here. The only problem was there didn't seem to be any room off the path to practice much of anything except dodging overgrown roots.

"It's not much farther," she promised.

Just as she said it, I noticed a break in the trees ahead.

"Is that it?" I pointed.

She glanced back at me with a smile. "Yep. You're going to love it."

We stepped out of the trees and into the vast clearing. My eyes widened at what I saw.

We stood at the top of a large hill taller than any building in town. The base of the valley extended the length of several football fields, and the grass below us had been well manicured. The entire valley was surrounded by vibrant green trees at its highest points. It looked like something straight out of a Costa Rica travel magazine, only on a much smaller scale.

All it needed was a little log cabin at the base of the hill. Then, when I made my millions as a celebrity chef, I'd retire here.

My jaw dropped. "I can see why you train here."

"Right?" Allie agreed enthusiastically. "No one will ever see us."

To our right sat a stretch of wooden steps. I headed for the stairs, but Allie quickly stopped me.

"Don't be lame!" She lowered herself to the ground. Before I could ask her what she was doing, she began rolling down the hill on her side, tumbling over and over again.

"Allie!" I called.

Her laughter echoed throughout the valley.

"Be careful," I yelled.

Her voice rang back. "As… you… wish…"

I couldn't help but laugh at her *Princess Bride* reference. I took a deep breath and sat on the grass below me.

"Here goes nothing…"

I lay down on my side, spreading my arms above my head. Then I let my body tip until gravity took over and I could no longer control my momentum. Hysterical laughter erupted from my lungs as the world tumbled around me faster than I thought possible. My laughter turned into screams as my speed increased. What seemed like far too soon, I slowed and came to a halt at the base of the hill. My head spun as I pushed myself up.

"Crazy fun, right?" Allie asked from several yards away where she was still recovering.

A wide smile spread across my face. "So much fun. Can we do it again?"

And we did. We raced up the stairs. My legs burned, and my face flushed. Allie insisted we lie head-to-head and hold hands. We could've only been holding on for a few seconds before the momentum was too strong and our fingers slipped from each other's grips.

At the bottom of the hill, our laughter filled the valley. I stared up at the spinning sky, taking in the strange sensation. I felt unstable, almost like I was flying. I had this urge to do it again, only instead of rolling down the hill, I wanted to jump off it and spread my arms, hoping they would hold me up.

Obviously, that wasn't going to happen.

Allie hopped to her feet and ran her fingers through her hair. Bits of grass fell out of it and back to the earth. "You ready?"

I stood and dusted the dirt off my jeans. I couldn't help but feel slightly disappointed that she'd put a stop to our fun, but I needed to focus. If I could get the hang of this, maybe I could make sense of all the madness.

"How does this work?" I asked.

Allie extended her hand to demonstrate. "Think of it like flexing a muscle. It's something you just tell yourself to do, and you do it."

"Okay," I said.

This is never going to work.

I held out my arm, imagining the orb growing out of it like Allie was doing. I flexed my fingers, working my muscles all the way up through my bicep and to my shoulder. My hand remained empty.

"It's okay. You've got this," Allie encouraged.

I narrowed my eyes as if my fingers might combust by sheer will. Eventually, I found myself tensing every muscle in my body. Not so much as a flicker entered my outstretched palm. A headache began to form.

"Relax," Allie instructed. "Don't think about it so hard."

I resisted the urge to roll my eyes and ask how I was supposed to do that. Instead, I gave in and released the tension in my muscles. Still, nothing happened.

I dropped my hand. "It's not working."

"I'm sorry. Maybe I'm just a bad teacher." Allie frowned.

My heart sank.

"No, it's not that," I assured her. "I'm probably a bad student."

Allie shot me a half-hearted smile. "I have an idea."

She held out her hand, and a white fireball formed in it without a single sign of struggle.

"Hold out your hand," she instructed.

I did, but I immediately recoiled when she reached out toward me.

"Don't worry," she said. "It's not going to hurt. I promise."

Warily, I let her take my hand. I *did* trust her, but that didn't keep my arm from shaking. Slowly, Allie raised her right hand above mine and tipped it until the fireball inside fell into my outstretched palm.

My fingers warmed for a mere second, and hope surged throughout my chest, but the sensation immediately dissipated. The orb vanished as if it was made of mist.

"Dang it," Allie said. "I thought that might give you an idea of what it feels like. I thought it'd be easier to sustain it than to conjure it."

"But it's *your* essence," I pointed out. "Does it work to transfer it to someone else?"

Allie shrugged. "Never tried. Should we test it again?"

"I guess so." There wasn't an ounce of confidence in my voice.

Allie and I spent the better part of the afternoon in the valley trying to get *something* to appear in my hand. But nothing did.

My frustrations grew. How could Allie act like this was so easy? She wouldn't know what struggle was if it slapped her in the face.

Maybe she needs a slap in the face. The girl's too perfect for her own good.

After several hours, I thought I felt something out of the ordinary sizzle in my palm, but it only lasted a second. The next moment, voices coming from the top of the valley distracted me.

"Crap," Allie muttered.

I glanced toward the top of the staircase to see three figures headed our way. "What is it?"

Allie crossed her arms and pursed her lips. "It's trouble."

8

A thin girl with long blond hair led the way down the stairs. Two muscular guys followed behind her. She laughed at something one of them said.

"I thought no one came here," I said to Allie.

Her expression contained a hint of disgust. "Only people from Galen High."

I could tell when the group spotted us because their laughter died down instantly.

"Uh, maybe we should go," I suggested. "We've been here long enough. They can have the valley to themselves."

I didn't need an audience.

"No way," Allie argued. "We were here first."

My eyes followed the group of three. The blonde held her head high and her back straight as if she owned the place. The two guys were good looking, even from this distance, but they almost looked *too* old to be in high school. It was like I'd stepped into some super-natural TV drama where all the actors were in their thirties even though they were supposed to be seventeen.

"Allie," I pleaded. "I haven't made any progress since we've been here. I don't think I'll start any time soon. Let's go."

Allie's shoulders dropped. "Yeah, okay. It's really not fun training around these guys anyway."

"You don't get along?"

That much was obvious.

She sighed. "They think they rule the school, but really the Saints are better than the Beasts."

"Saints? Beasts?"

"We train in groups," Allie explained. "Every group gets to choose their own team name. Marek, Kyle, and I train together with a couple others. Fletcher says the rivalry helps make us better."

I wanted to ask more questions about the inner workings of Galen High, but before I could, Blondie and her two bodyguards reached us.

"What's going on?" Blondie asked curiously. I half expected her to cross her arms and demand an answer.

"Uh, this is Ryn." Allie gestured to me. "She just moved here. She's starting at Galen this year."

Blondie tilted her head slightly. "I didn't know we were getting any new kids."

"It was a last minute thing," I told her vaguely.

"Welcome to Eagle Valley," she said with a smile. "I'm Casey. This is Troy and Trenton."

To my surprise, Casey held her hand out in my direction. I shook it, knowing I couldn't refuse.

"What school did you used to go to?" Casey asked casually.

"I've been to a couple—ow!"

A pain shot through my toe. I glanced over at Allie, wondering why she'd stomped on me. By the look on her face, she didn't want me to answer the question. When I glanced back at Casey, I realized she was asking which *Davina* school I'd been to. It was too late. Casey had already caught on.

"You mean you've never been to a Davina school before?" Her blond brows shot up.

"Well, uh... no, not exactly." I began to feel vulnerable. I certainly wasn't making a good first impression.

Except that Casey didn't make fun of me or throw a snide remark my way like I thought she might.

Instead, she simply smiled. "Don't feel bad. Trenton didn't show up until sophomore year, and he's going to be one of the best Protectors once we graduate. It's loads of fun. You just want to make sure you end up on a good team. Some can be *better* than others."

Her eyes darted toward Allie for a moment, who was desperately trying not to make eye contact.

I smiled back at her. "Thanks. I think I have a great team of people in mind already. Allie and I were just leaving. Have fun training."

I grabbed Allie's elbow and dragged her toward the stairs.

"She's really good, you know," Allie called back to Casey.

Casey crossed her arms and rolled her eyes. "If you mean by *your standards*, I feel sorry for her."

"Bite me," Allie called, but my grip dug deeper into her arm as we distanced ourselves from the group of three Davina. "Ryn has powers you wouldn't believe."

"Okay." Casey didn't sound convinced. "I'll believe that when I see it. Though, maybe your team could use the extra help."

Allie finally drew her attention away from Casey when we hit the stairs.

"What a *bitch*," she said under her breath. "She thinks they're so much better, but we get ratings based on how good we are. We totally crushed them last year."

"Allie," I tried, but she didn't respond between her complaints about Casey.

"Her team wouldn't be half as good without Troy and Trenton on it. I could totally take her one-on-one."

"Allie," I hissed again halfway up the stairs.

"What?"

"Why would you say that?"

She blinked several times. "Well, she *is* a bitch."

"No, not that. Why would you tell her I had amazing powers? I can't even conjure a basic fireball. Do you *want* her to have something else to ridicule you with?"

Allie and I reached the top of the steps and entered the trees before she spoke again.

"First of all, they're not fireballs. And besides, it's not like it's not true. Marek told me what happened the other night. I *wish* I was sober enough to have seen it. He said you were amazing."

"I didn't know what I was doing! I wasn't any better than he was. He knocked one of them out."

"Yeah, but you—" Allie's voice stopped dead.

"What?" I demanded.

"Oh, I'm sorry." Her tone grew soft. "They didn't tell you, did they?"

"Tell me what?"

Our pace slowed, but Allie moved ahead of me. A waterfall of black hair concealed her face. "I'm not sure I should be the one to tell you. I think Fletcher should."

"What's going on?" My voice rose.

I knew there was a lot left to learn, but I didn't like the idea of anyone omitting information. I thought being one of them meant I could trust them.

Allie brushed her fingers through her hair like she was uncomfortable. "I'm sure they didn't mean to keep it from you. Honestly, it's easy to forget how much you don't know. The rest of us grew up with this stuff. It's kind of common sense to us."

My skin heated. "Are you saying I'm stupid?"

"What?" Allie looked genuinely shocked. "No. Of course not. I just—I don't think I can explain it well enough."

We stepped out of the trees at the back of Galen High. Allie stopped and turned to me.

She spoke in a small voice. "I don't think it's something you should hear from me. Please trust me."

I sighed, feeling bad for how uncomfortable I made her. "We don't know each other that well yet, Allie, but I *do* trust you."

That doesn't mean I can't be mad at you.

We drove home in silence.

Allie turned to me when we pulled into her driveway. "You should stay the night."

"I can't." Not if she was going to keep secrets from me. "Mom's going to throw a big enough fit as it is about how we never spend time together."

"Maybe I should stay at your house, then," she suggested.

Sure. Just invite yourself over. How nice of you.

"I'd have to ask my mom," I said.

"You really shouldn't be alone, Ryn. Not with the demons out there."

I made a point to glance up and down our street. "I don't see any demons. I'll be fine, Allie. I'll see you tomorrow."

I opened the door and hurried across her lawn to my house. I started up the stairs to my room, but the sound of my name stopped me.

I peeked into the living room. "What?"

Mom sat on the couch crocheting her afghan. "Why didn't you finish your chores?"

Excuse me? I'd done the dishes and cleaned the bathroom and the living room. I'd even gone so far as to scrub the toilet and vacuum the carpets. Did she somehow know Allie had helped me?

"What do you mean?" I asked innocently. I *was* innocent.

"You have a pile of dirty laundry in the basement."

Oh, right. *That.*

"I'll get to it. I promise."

Just not now.

"Okay..." She didn't quite sound convinced, but she didn't push it.

I took it as an invitation to ignore her.

In my room, I plopped down on the bed and pulled out my phone. If Allie wasn't going to tell me the truth, I'd talk to someone who would.

❧

Can we talk?

I stared down at my text on the screen. I'd texted Marek thirteen minutes ago, and he still hadn't responded. What kind of freak goes longer than ten minutes without texting someone back?

Maybe he was out riding his bike.

The phone shook in my hand. I contemplated sending him another text in case he hadn't seen the first notification, but I didn't want to seem desperate.

Except I was desperate.

Thirteen minutes turned into twenty. Twenty-three minutes after sending the first text, I began typing out a second message.

Before I could finish and hit send, my phone chimed. Butterflies fluttered in my stomach.

Sorry, I'm busy.

My excitement quickly died. What could he possibly be doing? Modeling underwear?

I need to talk to you, I texted back.

His response came six minutes later. *No time.*

I stared at the screen and read his text at least five times. Allie wasn't willing to talk to me, and Marek was busy. Did I have any other options?

Do you have Fletcher's number? I texted.

At least *he'd* tell me the truth.

Marek's next text came almost instantly. *Are you in trouble?*

No. Why would he think that? *I just have more questions.*

Sorry. He's busy, too.

My fingers pressed hard against the screen as I typed. *Doing what?*

He's with me.

Obviously, they couldn't both be modeling underwear. What were they up to?

We'll talk tomorrow, his text said. *Gotta go.*

Tomorrow seemed too far away.

9

$\mathcal{B}$y the way I screamed, you would've guessed I was being murdered. Over the roar of the wind, I didn't think even Marek could hear my screeching. We sped quickly down a secluded road near the edge of town the following afternoon. I wrapped my arms tightly around his torso.

"Slow down!" I cried, but I didn't think he heard me. I tried to peek over his shoulder to view the speedometer on his bike, but I didn't want to loosen my grip on his body. We had to be doing at least twenty miles per hour over the speed limit, and our speed was only increasing.

My screams turned into laughter. "Seriously, slow down," I called, but I sounded anything but serious.

Marek had said he wanted to show me something fun. I didn't think he meant *this*. I squeezed my eyes shut. For a moment, I could imagine myself flying.

Marek slowed the bike. I was surprised to find a wave of disappointment wash over me. He pulled over to the side of the road and twisted toward me. I forced myself to release him. Cool air rushed between us.

"Having fun yet?" he asked.

No matter how much I tried to suppress the smile on my face, it only grew wider. "I'm having more fun than I thought I would."

"Good."

"I thought you said earlier you were going to show me magic."

"No," Marek corrected. "I said I was going to show you something *like* magic."

I laughed. "That's not fair."

Marek smirked. "Oh, you thought the bike ride was it? No, this is just a warmup. What I'm going to show you is much, *much* more amazing."

Excitement sizzled in my bones. What could he possibly have in store?

"Ready for another go?" He winked before facing forward and revving the engine.

Before I knew it, we were back on the road again. I could've sworn Marek went even faster this time. Too soon, he slowed as we neared Galen High.

My knees shook when we stopped and dismounted the bike. I removed the helmet and shook my hair out.

"Are we going to the valley?" I asked in enthusiasm. "It was *so* pretty there when Allie took me."

Marek's smile widened, and that weakness returned to my knees. "We sure are. You ready?"

I nodded and eagerly followed behind him. "What are you going to show me?"

Marek threw back a knowing smile.

"You mean it's a surprise?"

His smile didn't fade. "You're going to love it."

"What is it?"

Marek ignored my question. "There's a lot to learn about Davina, and unfortunately, you freaked out before we could tell you much."

"I'm sorry. I must seem like a total foreigner."

Marek shrugged. "Don't feel bad. You're not the only Davina to grow up not knowing what they are."

I wanted to ask who he was talking about. Before I got a word out, we broke through the trees and into the clearing that opened to the valley.

The cloud cover had grown thicker since yesterday afternoon, casting a dull gray hue across the landscape. It looked like a storm was rolling in, but it didn't smell like rain.

Marek began stripping off his jacket without saying a word. Caught off guard, I remained silent.

"There are a few things you should know about Davina," he said as he tossed his jacket aside. "And this is one of them."

An involuntary intake of breath passed my lips as he pulled his t-shirt over his head. I knew it was rude to stare, but I couldn't tear my gaze from his torso. Marek flexed his upper body, accenting his six pack and his tan, toned arms. I was so mesmerized by him that I didn't take a moment to ask what he was doing. Surely he didn't mean to show me that all Davina were drop-dead gorgeous.

A moment later, I realized Marek wasn't showing me his muscles at all. As he flexed, two white shapes rose behind him. They grew increasingly larger until I could finally make them out.

I gasped.

What looked like massive eagle wings had sprouted from his back. They were covered in silky white feathers and stretched wider than his arms. They were so beautiful; I wanted to reach out and touch them.

Without saying a word, Marek turned from me and took off sprinting toward the steep decline in front of us. His wings pulled into him for a moment. In a single leap, he hurled his body forward and spread his wings wide once again.

I stared in disbelief. Marek flapped his wings several times and then held them straight out parallel to the ground. He looked like the most majestic bird in the sky.

As soon as he began losing altitude, his wings pumped again to push himself higher. His body tilted to the left and circled around the empty field below us.

He began his flight back toward me. My body remained frozen at the top of the hill, completely mesmerized. Marek came so close to me that I thought he might land, but instead, he shifted course at the last second. Wind rushed by my face, and I beamed.

Marek locked his wings out, and they carried him on a graceful descent. Just when I thought he might touch the ground, he flapped his wings in one powerful, agile motion and shot straight into the air again.

I cheered and clapped in exhilaration.

Marek landed beside me. His massive wings flapped to slow his momentum, blowing my hair away from my face.

"Oh my God!" I managed to say. "No wonder people call you angels. I had no idea. Marek, they're beautiful."

Involuntarily, I reached a hand toward his outstretched wings. I thought better of it at the last second and jerked my fingers away.

"It's okay," he said kindly. "You can touch them."

My breath wavered as I inched closer to him. Carefully, I reached my hand out. My fingers connected with the soft, velvety feathers, and my breath hitched. Forget the fact that I'd just seen *wings* sprout out of Marek's back; what really got me was how soft and perfect his wings were. I couldn't wrap my head around the fact that they were real.

"But… how?" I asked, barely able to get the words out. "How do you do it?"

Marek shrugged, and his wings moved with him. "We just do. Think of it like shape shifting."

I ran my fingers down the feathers. "Are you saying Davina are like… shape shifting eagles?"

I caught Marek smile from out of the corner of my eye. It was the first time I managed to pull my gaze off his wings.

"Why do you think this place is called Eagle Valley?" he asked. Before I had a chance to answer, he spoke again. "No, we're not eagles. And before you say it again, we're not angels, either."

"I wasn't going to say that."

Marek rolled his eyes and pulled his wings into his back. I retreated a step to give him space. The wings shrunk behind him until they vanished. A wave of disappointment washed over me; I wanted to stare at them longer.

"I wasn't thinking," he said. "I should've had you change before we came."

"What do you mean?"

"You want to fly, don't you?"

I drew in a breath of excitement. "You don't really think I can do that, do you?"

Marek furrowed his brow. "Of course I do. You're a Davina."

"Well, I didn't have much luck when Allie was trying to show me—"

"That's because Allie's never had to teach anyone before. Besides, the wings are easier. Let's start with that. But you'll have to change first. Most of the girls wear racerback tank tops. They won't get in the way of your wings. You have one, right?"

I nodded.

Marek turned to grab his t-shirt from the ground. For the first time, I got a look at his back. My gut instantly twisted.

Two raised scars ran along the length of his shoulder blades. It was as if his wings had sliced right through his skin… Except, the raised, discolored lines looked like they'd been trying to heal for years, not mere seconds.

He didn't notice me staring. "We'll go get it and then come back—"

"Marek." I spoke softly, but the shock in my tone got him to look at me. "Are you hurt?" I stepped forward and ran my fingers across his back.

Marek shrugged me off and slipped his shirt on quickly. "No, it doesn't hurt."

"Does everyone get those scars?" My back heated as I imagined wings tearing through my flesh.

Marek bent again to scoop up his jacket. He stepped toward me and spoke quietly, like his words were meant only for me. "Everyone has scars, Ryn."

He was so close that his breath danced across my face.

"Am I going to get scars like that once I… you know?" My voice dropped to a whisper.

Marek started for the trees. For a moment, I thought maybe he didn't hear me.

"Not like this," he finally said.

I followed behind him. "Well, if everyone has them—"

"Not everyone has the same type of scars, Ryn. These are mine."

For every step he took, I had to take two. "What are they from, then?"

Marek whirled around so fast that I nearly rammed into him.

"Do you want me to show you how to fly or not?" he snapped.

I blinked in surprise. "I—I just wanted to prepare myself in case…"

"In case of what?" he asked sharply. "Nothing bad is going to happen to you." He sounded more irritated than reassuring.

I crossed my arms. "How can I be sure of that if I don't know what gave you those scars? I don't know anything about this Davina stuff. What if I mess up?"

I thought I caught a hint of an eye-roll in Marek's expression.

"You're not going to mess up. Again, do you want to learn how to fly or not? Because we're just wasting time."

I stood my ground. "I'm not in a rush."

Marek sighed in annoyance and turned from me. Instead of heading down the path, he veered off into the trees in a straight shot toward his bike. "Whatever. If you're going to push it, maybe I don't *want* to teach you."

He muttered something else about respecting privacy, but I didn't hear the rest of it because this time I didn't follow him.

Watching him walk away caused a guilty sensation to settle in my gut. As soon as he disappeared through the thick brush, I felt like I might hurl.

"Marek, wait!" I called after him.

At that point, I wasn't sure he could hear me.

I hurried into the trees, intent on apologizing, but I had no way of knowing where exactly he went. I followed my best guess and continued toward where his motorcycle was parked. I still didn't catch a glance of him.

I increased my pace to try to catch up. Almost immediately, my foot caught a root, and my body lurched forward. On the descent, I caught a flash of a black object flying by my head.

It took a moment for me to realize what had happened. I snapped my head in the direction the essence came from.

My heart jumped at the sight of a cloaked figure stalking my way.

10

"Marek!" I cried as I scrambled to my feet. I told myself I should run, but I stood grounded by fear.

The demon let out the kind of laugh that sent a shiver down my spine.

"You're all alone now, Little Angel," he said.

I recognized his voice from the party on Friday night. *Dorian.*

My hands shook. "I thought your kind didn't come into Eagle Valley."

His face was shadowed under his hood, but I could sense the smirk in his voice. "Not usually, but I've made an exception for you."

A dark fireball formed in his hand. This time, I was prepared. As he hurled it my way, I dodged his attack and fell to the earth. I raised my dirt-covered palms and tried to conjure a fireball myself, but my hands remained empty.

The demon lunged for me. His body crashed into mine and knocked me on my back. Almost immediately, he was on top of me, straddling me.

I managed to get my knees under him and forced him off of me. I rushed to my feet, but I was back on the ground a moment later. His cold fingers gripped my ankle. My foot connected with his face, but he only tightened his hold on me.

Before I knew it, he was on top of me again. He squeezed my

wrists together tightly and held them above my head with one hand.

"Marek!" I tried to scream, but Dorian slapped his free hand over my mouth.

I lifted my hips to shove him off me, but it was no use. He was bigger and stronger, and I didn't know how to use my essence yet to defend myself. My legs thrashed against the ground, sending dry leaves flying.

"You're a fighter." Dorian sounded amused. "Should we get started now, then?" His ice cold hand slithered up my abdomen.

Nausea slammed into my gut.

"Marek!" I shrieked. Tears rose to my eyes, and my vision blurred.

Dorian's hand reached my breast, and he squeezed. I writhed beneath him, but there was nothing I could do to free myself.

"Please stop!" I sobbed.

He lowered his face to mine. I squeezed my eyes shut and twisted my face away from him.

His cool breath rushed across my ear. "You don't have to fight this. With you on my side, we could do anything." His fingers moved to my waistline.

Oh, hells to the no.

"Screw you!" I did the only thing I could think of. I spit in his face.

Dorian recoiled like he couldn't believe what I'd done. His hand left my skin, and he reached beneath his hood to wipe the spit away.

"Bitch!" he roared.

His palm cracked across the side of my face, and I cried out in pain. The moment I expected another blow to come, Dorian's weight vanished.

When I opened my eyes, Marek was scrambling on the ground beside me. He rose to his knees above the demon and brought his fist down onto his face. I heard a crunch as the two connected.

Dorian's hood fell. His face was so pale and thin that he could easily be mistaken for a skeleton, and his black irises hinted at a darkness beyond human capacity.

I shuddered.

The blood streaming from Dorian's nose contained hints of red, but it was darker than I expected. It looked like someone had mixed black paint with the crimson liquid.

Marek shifted to wrap his arm around the demon's neck. Dorian flailed, struggling to breathe. His face darkened the more Marek squeezed.

"Stop it, Marek." My hands shook against the ground as I pushed myself to my feet. The left side of my face still stung.

Marek only squeezed Dorian harder.

"You're going to kill him!" I shouted.

"*He* was going to kill *you!*" Marek roared without loosening his grip.

"I don't care," I cried. "It's not right!"

"This is what we do, Ryn. This is a war. Don't you realize that?"

It didn't matter. I couldn't watch him do this.

"You can't fight evil with evil," I protested. "There has to be another way."

Marek hesitated for only a second, but it was enough for Dorian to gain the upper hand and slip out of his grasp.

Dorian balled his hand into a fist and smashed it into the side of Marek's face. Marek stumbled to the side. I let out a screech in surprise. Before either of us could fight back, Dorian raced away into the forest.

I rushed to Marek's side and dropped to my knees beside him. "Are you okay?"

Marek glared at me and wiped the blood from his lip. "You're going to regret that, Ryn. He's going to come after you again."

Tears welled in my eyes, but I remained silent.

Marek stood and reached out a hand to me. "Let's get out of here."

11

My heart hammered, and it didn't stop all the way home.

As soon as Marek parked in front of my house, I pulled the helmet off and shoved it his way. I couldn't bring myself to go inside. Instead, I paced back and forth on the sidewalk next to him. He opened his mouth to say something but closed it again. The silence was agonizing.

"What?" I snapped.

Marek recoiled.

"Clearly you have something to say," I accused.

"I…" He trailed off.

"Are you hiding something from me? Just say it."

Marek sighed. "I'm not trying to *hide* anything from you. We just didn't think he'd attack, not when…"

My brows shot up. "Not when, what? What aren't you telling me?"

Marek wouldn't look at me. "I shouldn't have left you alone. Not even for a second."

"I'm alone all the time," I pointed out.

"Not recently." Marek finally lifted his gaze to meet mine. "I was going to say… we didn't think he'd attack when one of us was nearby… protecting you."

I froze. "What are you saying? You've been stalking me?"

Marek's eyebrow twitched. "Well, that just makes it sound creepy. We've been keeping an eye on you."

"Who's *we?*" I demanded.

"Me, Allie, Fletcher. Kyle took a shift last night watching your house."

I gritted my teeth. "You didn't have to do that."

Marek climbed off his bike. "We did. Clearly you can't defend yourself."

He had me there.

"What did you expect to happen?" he asked rhetorically. "I said he'd be back, or don't you remember?"

"I—" I went silent.

I remembered his words from Friday night. For some reason, I hadn't processed them at the time.

"I don't know what I thought," I admitted. "Frankly, I was sure I was going crazy."

Marek stepped toward me slowly, as if testing to make sure I wasn't going to run away from him. "We *were* going to tell you everything, but then even the basics overwhelmed you. We thought it was best to show you a little at a time rather than dumping everything on you all at once. Honestly, I thought you might run away and get yourself killed."

"I have no plans of getting myself killed."

Marek raised an eyebrow and took another cautious step forward. "And running away?"

I sighed and threw my hands in the air. "Well, sure, it might be something worth considering. I don't know if I can actually trust you people. I don't know if any of this is even *real.* I don't know if—"

Marek grabbed my wrists, but I jerked away immediately.

"Don't touch me," I bit harshly.

"Calm down, Ryn," he said in a soothing voice.

Marek reached out for me again. I wedged my arms between our chests and pushed away. I had no desire to be touched right now, not after what happened.

"Stop trying to comfort me," I said with an edge to my tone. "I barely even know you."

"But you trust me, don't you?" he asked softly.

It took me several moments to ponder the question. He *had* saved me from the demons twice now. That had to count for something. And I had no reason to believe he was lying about anything he'd told me so far.

I searched his eyes for signs of dishonesty. I couldn't find any.

"I don't know," I finally said in a whisper. "I don't think I have a choice."

"Please let me help you," he said softly.

This time, I came to him. I allowed him to wrap me in his arms. Marek was nothing like Dorian. His embrace was warm and comforting, a sanctuary in stark contrast to Dorian's icy cold touch. I let myself melt into Marek's chest, and I inhaled the scent of his leather jacket.

"You can trust me," he whispered.

I swallowed the lump in my throat. "Am I going to be safe, Marek?"

He paused for a beat. "Demons won't come this far into town. And during the school year, there are a lot more Davina coming and going from the valley. That place is usually pretty safe, too."

"Usually?" I asked warily.

"Well, it's not every day you offend a demon and become a target. They don't usually try to mess with us like that."

"You're using that word a lot."

"What word?"

"*Usually.* Why would he be after me? Why not you? You were the one who hurt him the other day."

"Oh, um…"

"You're doing it again," I accused, pulling away from him. "You're hiding something from me. What is it you don't want to tell me?"

Marek dropped his gaze. "I thought you understood."

"Understood what? Marek, just tell me."

He finally looked at me. "Ryn… you killed his friend. He's out for revenge. And he won't stop until he kills you."

12

I drew in a sharp breath.

"No," I insisted. "No way. I would *never*."

It didn't matter that Marek had just pointed out that my life was in danger. All I could focus on was the fact that I'd killed someone.

"You didn't know what you were doing. It was an accident." He said it like that justified what I'd done.

Suddenly, I felt like I couldn't breathe. I grabbed onto his shoulders to steady myself. My fingers dug into his leather jacket.

After deciding I wasn't going to puke, I relaxed my grip and drew away from him.

"You really had no idea?" Marek asked curiously.

"That I killed someone? Yeah, because that happens every day." My face grew hot.

"He vanished in a puff of smoke," Marek pointed out. "What did you think happened to him?"

"I don't know! I've spent my entire life thinking the demons were in my head. I thought I was hallucinating."

That's what everyone told me the last time something like this happened.

"He could've teleported or something," I said. "It'd make just as much sense as the rest of this. Besides, you used the same thing on the other guy, and he got right back up and is apparently doing fine."

"It's not—Ryn, calm down."

I covered my face with my hands, still unable to believe it. "Why'd he disappear like that?"

What kind of fantasy world had I fallen into?

"It has something to do with the demon's curse," Marek explained. "They live on a different plane of existence. Without their life force tethering them here, their bodies fall into a plane we don't have access to."

I shuddered at the thought of demon bodies piled up throughout the world, rotting away on another plane of existence we couldn't see. It quite literally sounded like Hell.

"It's not a bad thing," Marek assured me. "He was just a demon."

"Just a demon?" I balled my hands into fists and paced away from him several steps. "That doesn't change the fact that I *killed* him."

"That's what Davina *do*, Ryn. We help protect the world from demons."

"Then why are there so many of them still running around?" I couldn't help the accusation from slipping out.

"Believe it or not, they're actually not that easy to kill. We can't just shoot them." He paused momentarily. "It's complicated."

"I have all day," I challenged.

Marek sighed. "What do you want, Ryn?"

I closed my eyes and attempted to steady my breath. There were so many answers to that question. I wanted to erase the last hour of my life. I wanted to escape all of this, to live in a world where I never saw the demons and never learned I was a Davina. At the same time, I wanted to learn what I was capable of. I wanted to be able to defend myself.

"I want to see Fletcher," I said in a small voice.

Marek nodded. "Okay, we'll go see Fletcher. I'll give him a call." He pulled his phone from his pocket.

Just as he placed it to his ear and the other line began ringing, a familiar voice called from behind me.

"Hey." Allie crossed her lawn toward us.

Kyle followed behind her.

"What's going on?" Allie stopped beside me and glanced between us. "Is something wrong?"

How did I even begin to answer that question?

"Hey," Kyle said cheerfully. He lightly elbowed me in the side. "Don't look so glum. Cheer up."

I glared at him.

I noticed Marek subtly shake his head at Kyle out of the corner of my eye. Kyle's expression instantly fell.

"Hey, Fletcher," Marek said into the phone.

"What happened?" Allie asked me, her tone full of concern.

I looked up to the overcast sky then down at the sidewalk. Anything not to meet her gaze.

"We're meeting up with Fletcher," I told her like it explained everything. I didn't think I'd ever be able to truly explain it.

"The school?" Marek's voice came into focus again.

My head instantly snapped in his direction. "No!"

He furrowed his brow at me as he listened to Fletcher on the other end of the line.

"I don't want to go back there," I whispered.

Marek nodded in understanding. "Forget the school," he interrupted Fletcher. "We'll meet at your house."

"What's going on?" Allie demanded as soon as Marek hung up.

A muscle popped in Marek's jaw. "The demon found her. We're going to see Fletcher."

"We're coming with," Kyle insisted.

"Yeah," Allie agreed. "You two go together. Kyle and I will take my car."

"I'll come with you, too," I suggested.

"No," Allie insisted, pushing me toward Marek's motorcycle.

He was already sitting on it and holding the helmet out toward me.

I huffed. Now was not the time for Allie to play matchmaker. But I didn't want to waste the time arguing. I grabbed the helmet and put it on. I wrapped myself around Marek again, and we sped down the street.

We pulled up in front of a small ranch-style home at the end of a cul-de-sac. It was a simple one-story house with gray siding and stone accents. Two well-kept flowerbeds lined the edge of the house, and a carved wooden bear stood next to the front door with a welcome sign in his hands.

Marek placed a hand on my back as we approached the house.

Fletcher opened the front door for us before we even had a chance to knock. He wore tan slacks and a white button down shirt.

It wasn't until we were inside that I realized I was still wearing Marek's motorcycle helmet. I pulled it off and breathed in a deep breath. The house smelled like dryer sheets and freshly baked bread. It's what I thought my grandparents' house might smell like —if I'd ever met them.

"Sit down," Fletcher said, gesturing to the couch.

I set the helmet on the coffee table and sank into the couch cushions. Fletcher's living room was small, housing only a couch, recliner, and TV. Several photographs hung on the walls, but they were just to add a pop of color to the space; I didn't see any pictures of his family. The room was bathed in earthy tones. That, coupled with the smells I detected earlier, gave it a welcoming, homey ambiance.

I felt safe here.

Allie and Kyle entered a moment later. Allie sat beside me, and Kyle leaned against the arm of the couch next to her. Marek took my other side, and Fletcher sat in the recliner.

Fletcher fixed a serious expression on his face. "Tell me what happened."

My gut twisted. I didn't know if I could. I exchanged a wary glance with Marek. He took charge and began to recount the details from earlier. My hands shook against my knees when he told them how he'd returned to find Dorian attacking me. I was grateful he didn't go into detail. I could still feel Dorian's hand cupping my breast. The last thing I wanted to do was relive that moment.

The more Marek talked, the angrier he became. He rose from the couch and began pacing back and forth across the living room.

"I made a mistake," he said. "I had the chance to kill him, and I didn't."

"Calm down, James," Fletcher insisted.

Marek glared at him. "We should go back out there and hunt him down."

Kyle scoffed. "Yeah, because that worked so well the last time."

I instantly became alert. "What do you mean?"

Marek stopped pacing and raked his fingers through his hair. "He's talking about last night. Fletcher, Kyle, and I were out there trying to hunt this guy down."

So that's what he'd been busy doing when I texted him.

"He knew we were on his tail, though," Marek said. "We never got close enough to him. I was hoping we'd scared him off, but…"

Tension formed in my head. "You still don't have to kill him."

"Would you rather he kill you first?" Marek's voice rose.

"Calm down," Fletcher repeated. "Sit, James."

Marek's chest rose and fell rapidly, and his lips pressed into a thin line. After several moments, he finally gave in and sat next to me.

Nobody spoke for several seconds.

I was the first to break the silence. "I don't think he was trying to kill me, Marek. He was trying to…" I couldn't finish the sentence.

"He was having fun with you," Marek said with disgust. "He would've killed you as soon as he was done."

Nausea returned, and a lump rose in my throat. "That doesn't make killing him okay."

I had to believe Marek was better than that.

"What do you suggest?" Marek snapped. "It's not like there's a prison we can lock him up in."

"He has a point," Kyle said.

"Everybody needs to calm down," Fletcher said in a commanding voice.

The four of us stared back at him.

"Ryn," Fletcher said softly, "are you okay?"

My shoulders relaxed. I appreciated that he cared.

"I'm scared," I admitted. "But I'm okay for now."

Fletcher's gaze dropped. "There's something you should know."

Oh, crap. I had no idea what to expect. I couldn't even manage to come up with insane possibilities in my head.

"I'm not going anywhere," I stated. I just hoped I meant it after I heard what he had to say.

"Good," he said. "Because if you did, the entire human race would be put in jeopardy."

I forced my shock down so it couldn't overwhelm me. I could hear it in Fletcher's voice. There was something bigger going on here, bigger than the age-old war he'd mentioned before.

And somehow, I had something to do with it.

13

"What—what do you mean?" My voice wavered.

Fletcher leaned forward. "We believe you have the Power of Grace."

I glanced around the room, hoping someone would elaborate without me having to ask.

Thankfully, Fletcher continued. "Marek knew when he met you. It's evidenced in the color of your essence—purple. Most Davina can only conjure white essence. Yours, Ryn, is special."

This must be what Allie wouldn't tell me about before.

"What does it mean?" My hands shook slightly as I thought about what I'd done with it. "It's more powerful?"

"Yes. Most Davina can't kill with their essence—only stun," Fletcher explained. "We have to turn to other means or use weapons to kill the Aedes, the same way they do with us."

"Other weapons?" I asked cautiously.

"I told you the Aedes' curse doesn't apply to materials that originate from another realm," Fletcher said. "When the Davina first returned here, they brought certain things from their realm back with them. We have a small collection of what we call Davina Blades. They're daggers that came from Vehena. We can use those against the Aedes. You, Ryn, are another type of weapon."

My body gave an involuntary shudder at the word *weapon*.

"Your essence is unique," Fletcher said.

I crossed my arms. I tried to remain as calm as I could, but my words came out flat and accusatory. "Because I can kill. What if I don't want to?"

Allie placed a comforting hand on my shoulder. Her eyes pleaded with me to hear Fletcher out before jumping to conclusions.

I uncrossed my arms.

"There's more you should know about our history," Fletcher said. "When the Davina created humans, the Aedes believed it to be a form of trickery. They thought the Davina created humans in an attempt to build an army faster and to force the Aedes back to Malum. They felt betrayed; they'd once again been cast aside by those who were more powerful than they were. The Aedes soon realized, however, that humans were powerless, and they became power-hungry. They were finally stronger than someone else, and they exploited that."

I considered this for a moment. "Allie said they feed off human essence."

"Yes," Fletcher confirmed.

"But humans don't have essence," I stated.

Fletcher's forehead creased. "Of course they do. Remember what I told you. Essence is the energy that makes up who you are as a person. Humans simply can't access their essence physically like we can. The Aedes, however, found a way to tap in to it. It's essentially an unlimited power source. But that doesn't mean it can be stolen without consequences. When an Aedes feeds off a human's essence, it throws the balance of their four energies off. Humans can easily be manipulated then. Many will go into deep depressions as long as their essence is being fed upon. Others will be overcome with greed or jealousy, all the things that make the Aedes themselves evil. The Aedes do it for amusement."

I trembled. Fletcher's story brought back too many horrible memories. And now those memories were starting to make sense.

"How do I fit in to that?" I asked.

"Because of the way the Aedes treated the humans, the Davina became protective," Fletcher continued. "That's what started the second war, the one we're still fighting today. The Davina believed the earth belonged to the humans. They forced the Aedes back to

Malum and sealed off the portals to that realm. They decided to seal off their own portals to Vehena as well to prevent any of their own kind from exploiting the humans.

"Sixteen original Davina stayed behind to seal the portals. Afterward, they found their power so drained they'd nearly given up their immortality. Remember that the Divinities tried sealing off Malum before only for the gateways to reopen?"

I nodded.

"The Davina knew it could happen again. The realms touch and can't be broken apart. They made a difficult decision. At the time, their work was finished, but they feared what might happen if another war broke out and they weren't around to help. They decided to freeze their bodies in time by sending their consciousness and essence into the earth, where it would be safe until they made their return. As legend tells it, their essence would return if we had to call upon the Originals once again for protection."

I couldn't believe what I was hearing. It all sounded like make-believe, but Fletcher told it like it was fact, history.

"What does that have to do with me?" I asked.

Fletcher took a deep breath. "Your power is a sign that we're in danger. If the Power of Grace has returned, it means the line between the realms is thinning. The problem is that we don't know where to find the portal that poses the threat. Even if we could find it, we'd need an Original's power to close it. This is why the Power of Grace is important."

The room went silent for a beat.

"Grace was among one of the Originals," Fletcher explained, "and she's our last hope."

Was Fletcher out of his mind? He didn't actually think I played a role in this, did he?

"So," I said, "I have some other Davina's power inside of me?"

Allie and Fletcher nodded in unison.

"What am I supposed to do with it?" I wasn't sure I wanted the answer.

"It's your job to wake Grace." Fletcher said it like it was so simple.

"Excuse me?" My eyes must've widened to twice their size.

Fletcher frowned. "I apologize if I'm not explaining it well enough."

"I get it," I said. "It's just a lot to take in."

Fletcher nodded in agreement and then continued. "A group of Aedes managed to stay behind when the portals were sealed. When they heard about what the Originals had done, they turned to hunting them down so they could never awaken and use their powers again."

I drew in a sharp breath. "Why would they do that?"

Fletcher shook his head like he'd never quite understand. "Same reason they want to kill the rest of us. Power. If we're not around to stop them, they can play their games with the humans and manipulate them like puppets. They've never been in a position of power before; this would put them there."

Marek cut in. "Not to mention that if we don't have the power of the Originals, we'd never be able to seal off the portals to Malum again."

I stared at him in confusion. "Why is that a bad thing, though?"

"Have you seen the world today?" Marek asked rhetorically. "The demons have bred and grown their numbers so much that things are bad enough as it is. They're the ones corrupting the world. If the portal opens, the rest of the Aedes get through. Their numbers skyrocket; they kill us off; and they manipulate the humans to extinction. It's how they get revenge for their ancestors."

I looked between Fletcher and Marek, still trying to absorb all this information. "Do you really believe all this?"

Everyone nodded in unison.

"So, if the demons hunted the Originals, where are they today?" I asked.

Fletcher sighed. "When it started, the Davina formed a secret society called Praesid dedicated to the protection of the Originals. They thought it was best to split the Originals up, and so members of Praesid moved the Originals across the globe. Every few centuries or so, they'd move again to keep anyone from tracking them down. Unfortunately, the Aedes managed to hunt down fifteen of the sixteen Originals and destroy their bodies with the help of humans through manipulation if needed."

"I thought you said the Originals were immortal," I pointed out.

Fletcher nodded. "In a sense. They didn't age, and they had incredible healing abilities, so they didn't die natural deaths. But that didn't mean they couldn't be destroyed. When the Originals sent their essence into their earth, their life force remained intact, which meant all four energies survived. They were only temporarily separated. When the Aedes destroyed their bodies, it severed their life force. Their consciousness ceased to exist, and their essence mixed with that of their ancestors to be recycled by later generations."

I dropped my head and pressed my fingers to my eyes. This was all too much to take in. How could *I* possibly have anything to do with this?

I took a deep breath. "So they killed fifteen of the sixteen, which means Grace is the only one left."

"Yes," Fletcher confirmed.

"And she needs me to bring her back to life?"

"She's still alive," Fletcher said. "Her body is essentially frozen. By awakening her, you can restore her essence, and she can close the portal."

I glanced around the room in disbelief. Four pairs of eyes stared back at me, but nobody said a thing.

"Even if I was capable of something like this, I'd never know where to find her," I said. "Anyone else have any clues?"

I didn't expect an answer.

"Grace was lost over a century ago," Fletcher said. "Some believe her body was destroyed along with the others. Your power is evidence that she's still out there somewhere."

My mouth grew dry. "How—what—?" *Why me?* "You really think so?"

A smile crept across Fletcher's face. "Yes. I believe that Grace is somewhere in Eagle Valley."

I inhaled an audible breath. Even Allie made a noise beside me like this was news to her, too.

"Our town was settled over a hundred and fifty years ago by a group of Davina," Fletcher said. "It's very possible that they were part of Praesid. They would've brought her here and hidden her during settlement. And since there are so many of us here, she would've always been protected by default."

"But you're not the only town of Davina, are you?" I asked.

"Of course not," Allie said.

"No, no," Fletcher answered at the same time. "It's not the Davina population that made me think that Grace might be here. It's the fact that you showed up, Ryn. I think you might've been brought here for a reason."

My jaw dropped. "You're talking about fate?"

Fletcher shrugged. "In a sense, yes. I think you're here because Grace led you here."

I had to sit silent for a moment to let all of this sink in.

"Why didn't you mention this before?" I asked calmly, though my heart hammered. I guess I never gave him a chance.

"I was afraid it would all be too overwhelming for you," Fletcher admitted. "I've seen how some students react when we throw too much information on them at once."

He and Marek exchanged a glance, like they both knew exactly which student he was talking about. Neither of them cared to elaborate.

"How do you expect me to find her?" I asked.

Fletcher shifted in his chair. "I'm not sure I have an exact answer. You were chosen by Grace. Her magic will lead you to her."

Suddenly, Eagle Valley didn't seem so small anymore. I couldn't believe what he was asking me to do. Someone like Allie who had been exposed to this her whole life should have the Power of Grace, not me.

"What if I can't?" I challenged. "I have no idea what I'm doing."

"We'll figure it out," Fletcher assured me. "You'll be training with Marek, Allie, and Kyle. They're the best in their class. I'm sure you'll catch on quickly."

"And Fletcher is the best mentor in school," Allie said.

Fletcher shot her a smile. "Ryn, you're not alone. We'll teach you how to use your essence. We'll be here to help in any capacity we can. In the meantime, however, I would like you to train in private. I think it's best if no one knows you have the Power of Grace. If word gets out, it may not be long before the Aedes find out and realize, as I have, that Grace might be here in town. Then Eagle Valley would really have a war on their hands. Let's keep this between us five."

"But what about the demon that's after me?" I asked. "Doesn't he realize I'm different? Won't he tell?"

Fletcher took a long moment to breathe. "The recent incident is personal to him. He'll want to finish you off himself."

I didn't like how casually he said the words *finish you off.*

"I've been in touch with other Davina in town," Fletcher said. "We have a group of people looking for him. Obviously, we haven't caught him yet, which is why I want you with one of us at all times. If you stick by us, you won't have to worry. We'll take care of him."

The tension in my head intensified. I pressed my fingers to my temples.

"I can see we've overwhelmed you with information once again," Fletcher said in a regrettable tone.

"No, it's fine," I lied, still rubbing my head. "I had to know all of this anyway."

"Why don't you return home and think about it?" he suggested.

I nodded, not really looking at him even though my eyes were on his.

"Once you're ready, we'll get started on your training." He smiled. "The first step, after all, is teaching you how to use your powers. I believe as you become more in tune with them, you'll have a better sense of your connection with Grace. We'll discuss the next steps once you have a firm grasp on your essence."

I nodded when all I really wanted to do was shake my head and refuse. I wasn't equipped to handle all of this.

And I definitely wasn't interested in being the *chosen one* Fletcher thought I was.

$\mathcal{M}$arek stood. "Come on, Ryn. I'll drive you home."

I grabbed the motorcycle helmet from the coffee table and followed behind him. I walked slowly, still trying to make sense of everything Fletcher had told me.

Outside, Allie and Kyle waved goodbye to us and climbed into her car.

Marek swung his leg over the seat of his bike, but I didn't make a move to climb on. I stared down at the helmet in my hands.

"What's wrong?" Marek sounded genuinely concerned.

Everything.

"Life is never going to be the same again, is it?" I whispered.

Marek's shoulders dropped. "No, it's not."

"I guess that means I'll never be normal." Not that I ever was.

Marek laughed lightly. "Where's the fun in being normal?"

I shrugged.

Marek quickly became serious. "Is there anything I can do to help? If you get on, I'll take you home."

Home. I wondered what that was like. Mom and I moved so much that nowhere ever really felt like home.

"I don't want to go home," I heard myself say.

"What do you want?" he asked kindly.

I finally looked at him, but I didn't answer. The truth was, I didn't know what I wanted.

A long silence stretched between us.

Finally, a small smile crept across his face. "Get on."

"Where are we going?" I asked.

"You want to be normal. Let's forget about all this stuff. Let's do something normal." His smile widened.

I couldn't help but smile back, even though that smile was filled with uncertainty. I placed the helmet on my head and climbed on the bike behind him.

"Do I even dare ask where we're going?" I shouted as the engine roared to life.

"You mean you don't like surprises?"

The bike lurched forward before I had a chance to answer.

Lately, surprises had been nothing but bad news, but I could tell by how excited he seemed that this one would be good.

Marek pulled into a driveway next to a two-story house. It looked a lot like our rental with the same big front porch, but there were clear differences. The brown vinyl siding made this house look a lot newer than ours, and the two-car garage had a basketball hoop attached to the front.

Marek cut the engine, and we both climbed off the bike.

"Do you play?" I asked, gesturing to the basketball hoop.

"Yeah, whenever Kyle comes over."

I handed Marek the helmet, and he tucked it under his arm.

Marek headed to the back door and led me inside a mud room. He placed the helmet on a small bench and hung his jacket up on a hook above it.

"James?" a high-pitched voice called from the next room.

I stepped into the kitchen behind Marek. A young girl who looked around eight stood on a chair at the counter and dug through one of the cabinets. She wore a red apron that was far too big on her.

"What is it, Piglet?" Marek playfully tugged at one of the ringlets in her pigtail.

She slapped his fingers away but smiled. "Me and Mom are making cookies."

"Mom and *I*," Marek corrected her.

She stuck her tongue out at him. "Mom and *I*. Want to help?"

"Not right now." Marek exchanged a glance with me.

The girl noticed me in the doorway for the first time.

"Ooh," she teased. "Is she your girlfriend?"

I had to refrain from bursting into laughter.

"No, Bailey," Marek answered. "She's just a friend."

Bailey set a bag of flour on the counter and hopped down from her chair. She eyed me curiously. "What's your name?"

I smiled at her. She was adorable.

"My name's Ryn."

She tilted her head. "That's an interesting name."

"It's short for Kathryn," I explained.

"I thought Kathy was short for Kathryn."

"Kathy makes me sound old," I told her. "I like Ryn better."

I'd been around Bailey's age when I chose the nickname for myself. It was the first time Mom and I moved. Mom called it our fresh start, and I took those words to heart. I told everyone at my new school to call me Ryn, and the name had stuck with me ever since.

Bailey looked up at me with bright eyes. "Do *you* want to make cookies with us?"

Cookies sounded delicious.

"No, Piglet," Marek answered for me.

"Actually, I love baking," I said. "Or did you have something else in mind?"

Marek's gaze shifted between mine and Bailey's. "Okay, Piglet. What kind are we making?"

Bailey jumped up and down in excitement. "Sugar cookies. You get the cookie cutters out." Her voice rose to call down the hall. "Mom! James brought his girlfriend over. They're going to help me make cookies."

A middle-aged woman entered the kitchen a moment later. She looked exactly like Bailey minus the pigtails. Her eyes brightened curiously when she saw me.

"You didn't tell me you had a girlfriend," she said with a smile.

"She's not my girlfriend," Marek objected.

At least he didn't sound offended by it.

The woman crossed the kitchen and stuck her hand out toward me. "Hi, I'm Faith."

"Ryn," I introduced, shaking her hand.

"Well, Ryn," Faith said. "Welcome to our home."

All I heard her say was *welcome home.*

Marek and I spent the next several hours in the kitchen with Bailey baking and decorating cookies.

Marek swiped his finger across the inside of the bowl before I added the flour. He stuck his finger in his mouth and sucked the cookie dough from it.

"Get out of here." I swatted at him with my dirty spatula.

Marek's eyes widened innocently. "It's *my* kitchen."

I added the flour and started up the mixer. "You're throwing off the recipe."

"You're just going to eat the dough anyway," he pointed out.

I turned to Bailey, who was putting the flour away for me. "Help a girl out, would ya, Bailey?"

She hopped down from her chair and pushed at Marek. "If you're not gunna help, get out of the kitchen."

Marek laughed as she tried to push him out of the room. "I'm helping eat the cookies."

"You're ruining them," she complained.

I turned off the mixer.

Marek skirted around Bailey. "Look, they're done! I can eat them now."

Marek was closing in on me fast. I didn't know what came over me. I made the split second decision to scoop my finger into the bowl and fling a bit of dough at him. It hit him square between the eyes and bounced off his forehead.

He caught it with one hand and stopped a step away from me. His eyebrows rose in my direction.

"Nice shot," he said before popping the dough in his mouth.

Eventually, Bailey ate so many cookies that she began to complain about a stomach ache.

Marek encouraged her to relax on the couch, and he put a movie in for her.

I noticed it was starting to get dark outside, but I wasn't prepared to leave yet.

"Your sister's cute," I said when he returned to the kitchen. I nibbled on a heart-shaped cookie.

He leaned against the counter. "She's not my sister. She's my cousin."

"Oh," I said in surprise. "So, Faith isn't your mom?"

He shook his head and then swallowed a bite of cookie. "My aunt."

Marek didn't bother elaborating, and I didn't want to push him to tell me about his family situation. I had a feeling it wasn't a fun story.

"What do you do when you aren't making cookies?" I asked.

Marek shrugged.

"All you do is play basketball and ride your bike?"

"No," he said defensively. "The bike's just for transportation, anyway."

"So you're *not* a badass biker dude?" I teased.

He laughed. "I never said I wasn't badass. As for a biker dude? I only bought the bike because my uncle's friend was selling it. It was cheaper than buying a car. I'd already been saving up from three summers of bailing hay and even more winters shoveling snow. I was sick of waiting for my own ride."

Marek motioned for me to follow him. He led me down a flight of stairs, and we entered an unfinished basement with cinderblock walls and a concrete floor. Exercise equipment lined one wall, and a TV stood against the other.

"This is basically what I do outside of school." He motioned to the exercise equipment.

Weightlifting definitely explained his abs.

I eyed a dumbbell on the floor. Maybe I needed to pick up weightlifting. I'd never understood the appeal before, but if I were stronger, I could defend myself better.

"Is it fun?" I asked.

Marek shrugged. "I don't do it because it's fun."

I sat at the bench press. "Why do you do it, then?"

"Training," he said simply.

"To become a Protector?" I already knew the answer.

Marek sat beside me on the bench. "Yeah."

Was I the only Davina who wasn't interested in fighting?

"Allie told me most Davina become Protectors," I said.

Marek nodded. "Yeah, but I'd do it even if it weren't so highly encouraged."

I looked at him curiously. "Why?"

Marek took a deep breath. "Because there's enough evil in the world already. If I can help get rid of some of it, then it'll be worth it."

He sounded so noble.

I tucked a strand of hair behind my ear. "You'll be good at it. The way you protected me earlier... I never said thank you."

He leaned in closer and spoke softly. "You didn't have to."

My breath hitched. He was so close to me. Close enough to kiss.

"Yes, I do," I whispered. "Thank you for everything."

He leaned even closer. My pulse quickened.

"Everything?" he asked like he didn't know what I meant.

"For earlier today..." I couldn't bring myself to talk about it. My skin crawled at the memory. "And for bringing me to meet your family. It made me feel normal. For a few hours, at least."

He gave a half-hearted smile. "I figured you could use a break."

And now I had to face reality again.

I dropped my gaze.

"What?" He pulled away slightly.

I shrugged. "There's just so much information, and there's still so much I don't know."

Marek shifted to straddle the bench facing me. "What do you want to know?"

I didn't have to think about it. "What are demons capable of? How much can they hurt us?"

"Their essence can stun you, but in case you didn't notice before, they have other means of hurting us."

"You mean strangling us to death?"

The image of the demon strangling Marek the night I met him flashed across my vision. My throat began to close up.

"Yeah," he said quietly. "They're pure evil."

I shook my head in disbelief. "That's horrible."

"They grow up in a different world than we do, quite literally."

I went silent for a beat. "Grow up? Like, there are baby demons?"

Marek laughed. "Well, are there baby Davina?"

"Um, yeah…" I said like it was obvious.

"The demons aren't immortal. The Divinities stole that from them. They have to reproduce the same way we do."

I'd never thought of that.

"Are they more powerful than we are?" I asked.

Marek shook his head. "The original Davina were a lot more powerful than the demons. But now our powers have been diluted by our human blood. The more time passes, the more magic we lose while theirs stays the same it's always been through every generation. Now we're closer to equals."

"That's what makes this war so dangerous?"

Marek nodded. "They used to be easier to defeat. The only way we've been able to grow our numbers is breeding with humans, but the power gets diluted every generation. Now the demons outnumber us. You see, not everyone with Davina blood develops full Davina powers."

I bit my bottom lip.

"I didn't mean you, Ryn. I saw what you can do. You're a Davina through and through."

"Then why is it so hard for me to conjure essence? You do it so effortlessly."

"Believe me, it wasn't always so easy." Marek reached out and forced my chin toward him.

I didn't resist.

He held my gaze intensely, never dropping his fingers from the side of my face. "You're doing amazing so far. I mean it."

I stared into his mesmerizing blue eyes, trying to convince myself he was telling the truth.

Marek shifted forward on the bench until we were just inches apart. It would be so easy to lean over and kiss him.

My phone buzzed in my back pocket, and we instantly jumped apart. I sighed and stood. It was my mother.

Where are you?

Hanging out with friends, I texted back. Just like I'd told her earlier.

It's getting late. Which was code for *I want you home right now.* Probably so I could cook her dinner.

I'll be home soon.

I turned back to Marek, who looked at me curiously. "Sorry. My mom wants me home. I should go."

Marek stood abruptly. "Let me drive you."

"No—" I started to say, but I cut off. I didn't want to walk home alone in the dark. "Okay, but on one condition."

"What's that?" he asked.

I smirked playfully. "Drive slow this time."

15

We pulled up in front of my house too soon. I wanted to hold onto him longer.

I was surprised when Marek walked me to the door. I turned to him with my hand on the doorknob. The porch light illuminated his features. His eyes danced across my face, and his lips curled into a hint of a smile.

I hardly knew Marek, and already I had this urge to give him a hug goodbye. After everything he'd done for me, I felt like he at least deserved that much.

"What?" he asked curiously.

I wasn't bold enough to hug him first.

"I still have so many questions." It was only an excuse to keep him here longer.

"Like what?" he asked.

He reached out a hand to tuck a strand of stray hair behind my ear. My skin heated where he'd touched me. It didn't even seem like he noticed what he'd done.

I dropped my hand from the doorknob. I'd much rather stay out here talking to Marek than go inside. I didn't want him to leave.

"I don't know. Is there more I *should* know? Besides the fireballs and flying, what else can we do?"

"We can heal," he said. "Ever been sick, Ryn?"

85

"No," I answered automatically. The reality of it hit me so hard it nearly took my breath away. I sank into the porch swing.

Marek sat beside me. "What is it?"

I knotted my hands in my lap. It wasn't exactly a deep, dark secret, but I hadn't really talked about it before. It was the reason Mom wouldn't let me drive anymore.

"I was in a bad car accident last spring," I said. "The doctors couldn't believe how fast I healed."

Marek gazed at me with a look of concern. "What happened?"

I was surprised at how easy it was to open up to him. "We didn't have anything worth cooking in the house, so Mom sent me to the grocery store to pick up a few things. On the way home, a group of people from my high school ran a red light and hit me. I fractured my leg and broke a couple of ribs."

Marek gasped. "Ryn, I'm so sorry."

"I'm okay now," I assured him. "The funny thing about it is that the accident is one of the reasons I came here."

He tilted his head. "What do you mean?"

"I told you Mom always chooses where we move next."

Marek nodded.

"Well, when I was in the hospital, Mom asked if there was anything she could do to make things better. My only request was that I got to choose where we moved next. She agreed."

Not that she cared about any of that anymore. It was like she didn't even remember the accident happened.

"Instinct told me to take another route, but I ignored it," I said. "After that, I swore I would listen to my instincts more often. I guess my instinct led me here."

"*Grace* led you here," Marek emphasized.

His words struck me, and we both fell silent as we rocked back and forth on the porch swing. My mind flew through everything I'd learned over the past few days.

A thought suddenly occurred to me. If we had the power to heal, what had given Marek those scars on his back?

"How good is this healing power?" I asked.

"Pretty good." He shrugged. "I mean, it still hurt when you broke your leg, didn't it? You'd heal about three times faster, though."

"What about you? Do you heal the same as other Davina?" I

thought about how Marek said some Davina didn't have full powers and wondered if he was one of them.

His features hardened. "It's not the perfect power. It doesn't heal everything. When things are bad enough…" He didn't finish.

My hand inched closer to his. "You can tell me."

He immediately swatted me away. "I told you before I didn't want to talk about it."

I stared at him in confusion. "Why did you show me if you didn't expect me to ask about it?"

"I didn't mean to." He grew irritated with each passing second.

"You told me everything else."

Marek stood abruptly. "Don't make me out to be the jerk, Ryn. Some of it you don't need to know. Maybe some of it I can't talk about."

I gaped at him. How could he go so quickly from being playful, fun-loving Marek to the irritated, closed-off guy standing in front of me?

"Go inside, Ryn," Marek said. It wasn't a suggestion. "Stay safe."

My heart sank. I hadn't meant to offend him. I was only trying to offer him comfort while trying to make sense of everything I'd learned so far.

I pressed my lips together and stood. I wasn't interested in picking a fight with him, so I did as he ordered.

But inside didn't offer me sanctuary.

I'd stepped away from one fight just to walk into another.

"Where have you been all afternoon?" Mom stood in the hall with her hands on her hips.

"I told you, I was hanging out with friends."

Mom pressed her lips into a thin line. "When you said friends, I thought you meant Allie. Who's the guy on the bike?"

Crap. She'd seen that.

"A friend," I insisted vaguely.

Is that what we were? Friends?

"He's a friend of Allie's," I clarified. "He offered to drive me home."

"Home from where?" she demanded.

"His house," I told her truthfully.

She crossed her arms over her chest. "That's completely irresponsible. I haven't met his parents."

"So?" I snapped. "I'm almost eighteen."

Mom's eyebrows raised so far they nearly touched her hairline. It was like she couldn't believe I had the audacity to point it out.

"You're not eighteen *yet*." She said it like it was a threat. "And until you are, I want to know where you're at."

Yeah, I doubted that was going to end once I turned eighteen.

"I don't want to have to worry about you," she said.

I wasn't buying that line. The truth was she wanted to control me as long as possible.

"I'm fine." I heard the lie in my own voice. Maybe she had a reason to worry, but it wasn't like I could tell her about what happened earlier.

By the way, Mom. I'm a Davina. Ever heard of them? I wasn't sure that was a conversation I wanted to have.

Best not, I told myself. *Mom's better off not knowing. She said goodbye to my insanity a long time ago. I don't need to drag her back into it.*

"And I don't want you riding a motorcycle," she demanded. "With a guy I don't even know, no less."

"There's nothing wrong with him. And he's a good driver." No point in mentioning how fast he liked to drive. She'd never let me see him again.

"That doesn't matter," she argued. "Motorcycles are dangerous."

She was just jealous she didn't have a hot biker dude to run away with. She hadn't dated my whole life.

"How am I supposed to get around town, then?" I asked. "You won't let me drive."

She didn't seem to care that the accident wasn't my fault. I still couldn't get behind the wheel.

"You have two feet," she pointed out. "And there's a bicycle in the garden shed."

So my only options were to walk or bike anywhere I wanted to go? I was seventeen, not twelve.

I rolled my eyes. After everything that happened to me today, I didn't deserve this. "Whatever, I'm going to bed."

I stared up the stairs, but Mom apparently wasn't done chewing me out.

"Don't you use that tone with me," she scolded.

She huffed when I ignored her. She mumbled something about *teenagers*, but I didn't hear her as I hurried down the hall and into my room.

As soon as I fell down onto my bed, exhaustion consumed me. As I was falling asleep, something Fletcher had said resurfaced in my mind. He said he'd stop by on Monday to talk about my enrollment at Galen High.

I had a feeling after the way I just spoke to my mother, she wasn't going to be easy to convince.

16

Fletcher's visit couldn't come soon enough the next day.

I waited eagerly in the living room that morning untangling balls of yarn Mom had bought from a garage sale. I didn't put up a fight when she'd asked me to do it because I wanted to stay on her good side.

By the time lunch hit, the doorbell still hadn't rung. I was starting to wonder if Fletcher would actually show.

Finally, the sound of footsteps on the porch caught my attention. I hopped up from the couch when the doorbell rang. The floorboards in Mom's home office creaked above my head.

I swung the door open a bit too quickly.

Fletcher greeted me with a smile.

I was surprised to see a woman standing beside him. She was a head shorter than him, with short dark hair and an air of professionalism in the way she held herself.

Fletcher wore his usual button-down collared shirt, and the woman had on a navy pantsuit. They both looked strangely formal standing on my front porch.

"Miss Tyler," Fletcher greeted. "This is Mrs. Presley. We've come to discuss your enrollment."

"Yes, come in." I opened the door wider. "Just so you know, Mom doesn't know about the Davina." And I didn't intend to tell her.

Fletcher nodded in understanding.

The soft pad of footsteps on the stairs caught my attention. Mom descended the stairs slowly, and a confused expression settled on her face. I hadn't known how to tell her about Fletcher earlier. I thought he might have a better idea how to introduce the topic.

"Ah," Fletcher said, looking up at her. "You must be Mrs. Tyler. I'm Mr. Fletcher, an advisor at Galen High School. This is Mrs. Presley, our principal."

Mom reached the bottom of the stairs and stretched out a hand. "Hello. For what do I owe the pleasure?" She didn't sound anything like herself.

Mrs. Presley spoke for the first time. Her voice was at least a pitch higher than I expected. "We're partnered with Eagle Valley High to review incoming students' transcripts, and we believe that Kathryn would be a great fit at our school. We'd love to discuss the opportunity with you."

"Sure," my mother agreed, confusion still layered in her tone. "Why don't we have a seat in the living room? Can I get you anything?"

"No." Mrs. Presley sat on the couch and adjusted the coat on her pantsuit. "I'm fine, thank you."

"No, thank you," Fletcher told her.

Mom and I sat on the loveseat across from them.

Mrs. Presley opened a folder on her lap and glanced up at my mom with a smile. "I apologize that this is on short notice, but seeing as you just moved to the area, it's to be expected. As I said, we've reviewed Kathryn's transcript and think she would make a great fit at Galen High."

She glanced back down at her papers. "Her grades are good, all A's and B's, and she's been involved in extracurriculars all throughout high school."

I didn't know what record she was looking at, but it couldn't have been that accurate, unless she counted the prom committee at my last school.

"I'm sorry," my mom stopped her. "Public school has served Kathryn well her whole life. What is it that Galen thinks they can offer her?"

My jaw nearly dropped to the floor at her words. Did she not want me to go? I had to go. I needed all the help I could get if I wanted to learn what I was capable of.

"But Mom," I started.

Fletcher was already speaking. "We have a very intense curriculum that would suit a student of Kathryn's talent."

"I apologize," Mom said. "I know my daughter is talented, but—"

"Mom," I interjected. "I want to go."

She stared at me. "Is it because Allie goes there? You'll make new friends at Eagle Valley High just as well."

"It's a smaller school," I tried. It sounded unconvincing, even to me. "I'll have an easier time getting to know people and connecting with my teachers. I've always liked smaller schools anyway."

Mom pressed her lips together. "Maybe we should discuss this a little more."

Mrs. Presley shifted uncomfortably in her seat. "I'm sorry, but is there something wrong with our school?"

Mom looked shocked. "No, I just—we just..." She glanced at me like I might be able to help her find the right words. Her confession came out in a near whisper. "We don't have money for a private school."

The two Davina across from me relaxed.

"Not to worry," Mrs. Presley assured her. "Kathryn is eligible for a full scholarship. It won't cost you a penny more than putting her in public school."

I hadn't thought of the costs, but it's not like there was any other option. I was a Davina. I belonged at Galen High.

The thought sent a nervous shiver down my spine—in a surprisingly good way. Mom and I moved around so much that I never felt like I belonged anywhere. For the first time in my life, I did.

I wasn't alone. The demons weren't just in my head. Sure, I'd been able to ignore them for the better part of a decade, but they were always there, lurking in my peripheral vision, their voices filling an otherwise quiet room. The other Davina knew what that was like.

More than that, the demons didn't come into Eagle Valley. I could stay here and forget about them.

"Can I go, Mom?" I pleaded.

She didn't answer for a moment. "We should really talk about this more, in private."

"But there's only two weeks left before school starts!" I argued.

I knew my mom. She was going to put off talking about it for so long that I'd miss enrolling by the first day of school. She never let me have anything I wanted.

"If you need the time to think about it, we can leave the paperwork here," Mrs. Presley offered. "You can take your time reading through it. I'll write my cell number down so you can call with any questions."

I gave her a reluctant smile. I felt anything but cheerful. "Thanks."

"Yes, thank you," Mom said. "We'll consider it."

Sure we will, I thought sarcastically.

Mrs. Presley stood and shook both of our hands. She held onto mine a little longer. "We hope to see you soon."

I smiled back. "Thank you."

Fletcher shook my mom's hand and then mine. What felt like far too soon, they left.

Mom turned to me after leading them out the door. She crossed her arms over her chest and looked at me with a hard expression.

Here we go again.

I bit my lower lip. "So, can I go to Galen?"

I expected Mom to sit on the couch across from me so we could talk about it, but she remained standing.

"Why are you so interested in going?" she asked with an edge to her tone.

Because I'm a Davina like the rest of them.

"Have you seen Galen High?" I asked rhetorically. "It's beautiful. It'd be cool to go there my senior year."

She pressed her lips into such a thin line that they practically disappeared. "Does that boy go there?"

"What boy?" I asked innocently.

"The one with the motorcycle."

Oh. *That* boy.

"Yeah, but that's not why—"

Her brows shot up. "Oh, *that's not why*. I was a teenager once, too, you know."

Oh, hells no. She wasn't keeping me from Galen High just to keep me away from a boy.

I shot up out of my seat. "You don't want me to go because you think I'm *whoring around?*"

Her nostrils flared. So much for staying on her good side.

"I never said that!" she defended.

My eyebrow twitched challengingly. "You didn't have to."

Mom dropped her arms to her sides and huffed. "Kathryn, you're being ridiculous."

I rolled my eyes. "So I guess that's a no. I'm not going to Galen High."

"I'm still considering it, but if you keep up this attitude, the answer *will* be no."

"There's no reason not to let me go," I insisted. "They're giving me a scholarship."

"And I said we'd think about it."

I huffed. "You never let me do anything I want to do."

"Oh, really? Who chose to move us to Eagle Valley?"

"*You* chose to move us," I emphasized. "You *always* choose to move us. We move so often I never get a chance to make any real friends. Allie's the best friend I've had in over a decade, and now you're taking my last chance at making real friends away."

I stormed past her into the hall. Eager for a door to slam, I turned to the first one and slammed it behind me as hard as I could.

17

I pounded down the steps into the basement. Next to the washer stood two full laundry baskets. Mom definitely wasn't going to let me go to Galen if she saw my laundry still wasn't finished.

Gritting my teeth, I dumped the entire contents of the first basket in the washer, not caring about mixing the whites with the colors. I tossed in some soap without measuring it and slammed the lid shut.

My skin grew hot in anger. I barely knew what I was doing when I swung my foot angrily at the shelf in the corner. A gallon of paint teetered on the edge. I just barely caught it before it smashed into the concrete floor. My foot throbbed, and my heart raced.

I sank to the dusty floor and set the paint can beside me. I wanted nothing more than to cry—to scream—but even as I buried my face in my hands, nothing came.

I curled myself into a ball on the floor.

Why was Mom so selfish? She always got to do what *she* wanted to do but never seemed to care about my feelings. Forget the fact that I was destined to save the world and Galen High could actually help me do it. She had too much pride to allow me the chance.

Maybe I'd sneak off and go there anyway.

A banging in the corner of the room pulled my attention from my self-pity. I glanced up to find the washer violently shaking, indicating an uneven load. I reluctantly rose from the floor and walked over to it. I threw open the lid and rearranged the clothes inside.

Turning back to the shelf behind me, I sighed heavily. It didn't matter how long I sat there in the cold, damp basement. Sooner or later, I had to face her again.

I picked up the can of paint I'd knocked over and went to place it back on the shelf, but something caught my eye. I lowered myself to peek past the shelf to the wall behind it. I had to tilt my head to each side several times to make out what I'd found.

What looked like a carving of an eagle had been etched into the stone of the house's old foundation.

Another thing to add to the list of traits that give this house character, I thought.

Only after a moment of staring at it did I realize something was off. The figure had the wings of an eagle but the body of a woman. For a moment, I could almost imagine it was me.

The thought settled in my mind.

Forget Mom. Forget Galen High. I was a freaking Davina. I could fly. I didn't have to take this crap.

I shoved the paint can back in its place and pounded up the steps, not stopping until I made it to my bedroom. I stripped off my shirt and tossed it in the corner then flung my dresser drawer open to find a sports bra and a racerback tank.

I can do this, I told myself. My breaths grew shallow, and my hands shook as I tensed my muscles.

Come on, Ryn.

I squeezed my eyes closed and concentrated on my back as if wings would sprout from it simply by wishing for it. After about a minute, I opened them, more frustrated than before.

I gripped onto the back of the chair in front of my desk so hard that my knuckles turned white. I didn't quite like what I saw in the mirror. Despite my quickened heart rate, my face looked drained of color, and my eyes drooped.

"What are you doing, Ryn?" I asked my reflection. *I'm not cut out for this.*

The longer I stared at my reflection, the more I got the feeling that something was missing. I could picture myself with the wings

Marek had shown me earlier. A strong desire to fly—like I'd felt when Allie and I rolled down the hill—overcame me.

My mom could move me all across the states. She could refuse to send me to Galen High. But she couldn't control *this*.

This one was all me.

Something in the mirror caught my eye. The studs in my ears were all wrong for this.

I quickly slipped them out of my ears and threw open my drawer to find my pair of angel wing studs. A sense of comfort washed over me when I put them on. They reminded me of the carving in the basement.

I've got this.

I closed my eyes again and took a deep breath. My mind focused on the angel wing earrings like I actually thought they might hold some power that could bring me the strength to overcome this.

I flexed my shoulders again. This time, my hands didn't quiver. Tension built within my muscles, and a tingling sensation radiated across my back.

Slowly, I opened my eyes. What I saw in the mirror took my breath away.

Two glorious white wings rose behind me. Each one was as tall as I was. Fluffy white feathers lined the top of the wings and grew steadily larger until they reached the size of my hand at the bottom.

I twisted to get a better look and noticed immediately how the white feathers seemed to shimmer purple in the light. I couldn't take my eyes off them.

A knock came at my bedroom door.

Shit.

18

I whirled around so fast that my right wing caught the chair and knocked it to the floor.

"Don't come in, Mom!"

How do I make these things disappear?

"It's me," a different voice called back. "Allie."

I relaxed.

"Your mom let me in," she said. "Are you okay?"

"Yeah. You can come in."

Allie pushed the door open. Her eyes instantly grew to twice their size. "Oh my gosh! You did it!"

I couldn't help but beam.

"This is great!" she exclaimed. "You're making progress."

I shot back a shy smile. "Thanks, but how do I… you know… make them go away?"

The corners of Allie's lips twitched like she was trying not to laugh.

"Not that I want to," I said quickly. "I just thought you were my mom, and I realized I didn't know how to."

"You just relax," she said simply.

"Great," I mumbled, stealing another glance in the mirror. "These things will never go away."

Allie laughed. She took a deep inhale and spoke softly on the exhale. "Just… relax."

98

I mimicked her patterned breathing. Slowly, the wings began to shrink behind my back. I turned my back to the mirror to inspect my skin. Wrapping my arm around my body, I felt the area where the wings had grown out of. It was completely smooth.

I turned back to Allie. "I don't get it."

She sat on the bed and tossed her dark hair over her shoulder. "What don't you get?"

"It didn't hurt or anything." I took a seat beside her on my white comforter.

She furrowed her brow. "No. Why would it?"

"Well, I—" I paused. "I saw Marek's scars."

"Oh, yeah," Allie said like it was no big deal. "Those are totally different."

"How'd he get them?" I burned to know.

She bit her lip. "Sorry, but it's not my place to tell. I don't really know the full story."

I got the sense that no matter how much I begged her for information, Allie wasn't going to spill.

Allie eyed me curiously after a brief silence. "Are you okay?"

I thought about it for a moment. "Yeah. Mom and I just had a huge fight. She doesn't want me to go to Galen."

Allie let out a breath in disbelief. I half expected her to call my mom out for being a bitch.

"Did you tell her about the demon?" Allie asked.

"No. I haven't told her any of it. She would never believe me."

"Why not?"

I sighed and resituated myself on the bed. "When I was little, I told my mom I could see the demons. I didn't call them that, though. I didn't know what they were then."

Allie nodded along in understanding.

"She told me I was imagining things," I continued. "She sent me to three different therapists before I lied and told her I'd stopped seeing them."

Some of the tension I constantly held in my body eased. It felt good to open up to her.

Allie's eyes widened. "I'm so sorry, Ryn. Your mom might be more willing to let you go to Galen if she knew the truth. I could help back you up."

I shook my head. Allie's gesture was nice, but I wasn't ready to talk to my mom about any of this.

"If she knew a demon attacked you and that you were in danger —" Allie started, but I cut her off.

"I don't want to talk about that." My voice came off harsher than I intended.

Allie looked at me in confusion, and then realization dawned. "Ryn, what did he do to you?"

"He attacked me," I said simply. "Like Marek told you."

"Marek was pretty vague about it," Allie said.

I twisted my hands in my lap. "It could've been worse."

"That doesn't mean you're not allowed to feel something," Allie said gently. "Someone will always have it worse than you. That doesn't invalidate your feelings."

I sat silent, letting her words sink in. If I was going to tell anyone, Allie would be my first choice.

"His hands were all over me," I admitted. "If Marek hadn't come to my rescue…"

Allie drew in an audible breath and leaned over to pull me in to an embrace.

I inhaled the comforting scent of her cherry blossom perfume. It was like hugging the sister I never had.

"The demons are evil," Allie said as she pulled away. "They killed my mom."

My heart broke. I knew her mom wasn't around, but I never knew why.

"Kyle's dad, too," Allie said. "I guess that's why we work well together. We both lost something to the demons."

"Allie, I'm so sorry." I pulled her back into a hug.

"Don't worry about it," she said. "It happened a long time ago."

"Is that why you want to be a Protector?" I asked.

Allie nodded shyly. "The demons hurt enough people as it is."

Her words hung uncomfortably in the air.

Finally, I broke the silence. "What'd you come over for?"

A smile twitched at the corner of her lips. "Well, it looks like you already figured out your wings. Do you want to try flying?"

My heart flipped at the thought of flying for the first time.

"Yes!" I answered eagerly.

If Mom lets me out of the house.

Allie rose from the bed. "Let's go. We'll meet the guys at the valley."

I paused momentarily. "The valley?"

"Yeah, that's where we fly."

Which meant I had to walk through those woods again.

"Isn't there another place in town we can go?" I asked.

Allie shook her head. "Not anywhere we won't be spotted."

I bit my lower lip.

"Hey," Allie said gently. "You're going to be all right. We'll be there with you."

Her words were incredibly reassuring.

I gave her a timid smile. "Thanks, Allie."

She stood from the bed. "Ready for your first flight lesson?"

19

Given everything that happened recently, I should've been screaming while someone dragged me away to a mental institution. Instead, I was excited about my first flying lesson. Flying was sure to make everything better.

By some miracle, Mom agreed to let me go—and even said I could stay the night at Allie's house. Something I'd said to her earlier must've stuck.

Allie and I took her car and parked across from Galen High.

My fingers quivered against the door handle. I stared past the edge of the school to the trailhead that led to the valley. My mouth went dry when I thought about what had happened the last time I was here.

A knock came at my window, startling me.

"You ready?" Marek asked. I hadn't noticed his arrival.

I forced my heart rate to slow and opened the door. "Yeah."

Allie glanced at her phone. "Kyle's already waiting for us."

"You okay?" Marek asked when we began walking.

"Yeah, I'm fine," I told him, but I could feel my face had drained of color.

"Don't worry," Marek said in a low whisper so Allie couldn't hear. "I'm not going to let you out of my sight this time, okay?"

As if to prove I could trust him, Marek grabbed my hand and squeezed it. I stared into his blue eyes.

102

Marek lifted one side of his mouth into a twisted smile. "Let's go have some fun."

"Are you two coming?" Allie called from several paces away.

I snapped my attention back to her. Marek dropped my hand, and it suddenly felt cold. I didn't realize I'd slowed at the entrance to the trail until Marek placed a hand on my back.

"It's okay," he whispered in my ear.

I needed to believe him, so I pushed forward.

I couldn't stand the silence. "Hey, Marek?"

"Yeah?"

"I'm curious. What all can Davina do? We have wings, and this sort of… magic."

"Well," Marek said, "it's not as cool as it sounds, I'll tell you that. Mostly, it's a weapon. We can stun demons with it, just like they can do the same to us."

"How else are they similar to us?" I asked curiously. My eyes remained on the path.

Marek shrugged. "They have wings."

My brows shot up. I shouldn't have been surprised, but I'd never seen them. "Really?"

"Well, yeah. Theirs are black, ours are white." He shrugged like it wasn't a big deal.

"What about the cloaks?" I asked. "Why do they wear them?"

"It's about tradition," he explained. "Originally, it was to set themselves apart. We used to wear white robes for the same reason. We eventually dropped the robe practice, but at least we had other clothes to wear. The demon's cloaks come from material brought from their realm long ago, when the portals were still open. They don't have any other choice."

"Kyle!" Allie shouted in excitement ahead of us.

I didn't have a chance to ask more questions as Marek and I broke through the trees into the clearing.

I noticed movement at the far end of the valley. What looked like the largest bird I'd ever seen soared near the tree line. It was unlike any other bird in the sky, though, with the body of a man and the wings of an eagle.

Kyle spread his wings wide and glided toward us gracefully. Air rushed by his wings when he landed, and the grass rustled beneath us. Kyle brushed his dark hair out of his eyes. His wings were bigger than Marek's, but he wasn't quite as toned.

"Anyone want to race?" Kyle asked.

"You're on!" Allie quickly stripped off her cardigan.

I watched in awe as white feathers sprouted from her back and grew into beautiful wings. Though my wings shimmered a slight purple, Allie's had a bluish tint to them. It matched the subtle blue shine in her black hair.

She lit up with a smile. She truly looked like an angel.

Without another word, Allie and Kyle raced to the edge of the hill and took off in unison. Their wings nearly touched as they spread out beyond their arm span.

I kept my eyes on Allie in wonder. She pumped her wings and shot forward above the landscape. She flew so effortlessly that it was as if magic kept her afloat. Even with the sun hidden behind an overcast sky, I could still make out the blue shimmer in her wings from a distance.

My heart felt as if it was soaring alongside her. The more I watched, the more excitement filled my chest.

Allie's wings were smaller than Kyle's, but that seemed to work to her advantage. She was much quicker than him. She was also several inches shorter and fifty pounds lighter, so she didn't have to work as hard to keep herself airborne.

As soon as they reached the other end of the valley, they both turned around and headed back toward Marek and me. Allie sped up until her ankle was in line with Kyle's head.

"Should we move?" I glanced at Marek to find him smiling at the couple.

"No, they'll be fine."

"Are you sure? They're coming right for us."

Marek laughed. "They know what they're doing."

I contemplated diving out of the way as Allie made her landing, but Marek placed an arm around me, forcing me to stay. My first instinct was to be annoyed with him, but then his arm relaxed against my shoulder. I relaxed, too.

Allie hit the ground and immediately tumbled into a summersault to slow her momentum. She landed on her feet and shot her fists into the air in victory. Her wings had vanished.

"You suck!" she gloated when Kyle landed.

He laughed. "You know I let you win."

Allie rolled her eyes. "Whatever."

"You ready for a go?" Kyle asked. It took me a second to realize he was talking to me.

My eyebrows rose. "Me? I'm not racing."

Kyle smiled. "Why not? I need to beat a girl one of these days."

Marek jumped to my defense. "Give her a break, Kyle. She's never flown before."

"That's why I'll finally be able to beat someone." He stood so confidently that I wasn't convinced he was as bad as he was suggesting.

"Relax," Allie told him. "You beat Casey all the time."

"Yeah, well, Casey's not as good as she thinks she is," Kyle said.

Even I could've guessed that based on my first impression of her, and I hadn't even seen her fly yet.

"I'm not going to race, but I'd like to try flying." I spoke to no one in particular. "How do we do this?"

A smile twitched at the corner of Marek's lips. "You know how birds learn to fly by being pushed out of the nest?"

"Yeah…"

Marek raised his brows.

"What? You're not going to push me off a cliff, are you?"

Everyone laughed beside me.

"No," Marek assured me. "But it really doesn't get much simpler than that. Allie says you've figured out your wings?"

I nodded.

"Well, let's see them," Kyle insisted.

I bit my lip and glanced between my friends. I didn't want to make a fool out of myself.

"We'll all do it together," Allie suggested. She flexed her shoulders, and her wings returned.

"Okay," I agreed.

Beside me, Marek stripped down to expose his toned torso.

Note to self: Keep your eyes off Hot Stuff while airborne—unless you plan to crash and burn. He's too damn distracting.

"Ready?" Marek asked.

I noticed his fingers twitch in my direction like he was about to take my hand. At the last second, he pulled away.

I nodded and then took a deep breath, flexing my back. I felt the afternoon air brush across my feathers. This time, it was easier to let them out now that I knew what it felt like. I stretched them as wide as I could.

I'd never felt more refreshed than I did in that moment... like something had been missing my whole life, and for the first time, I'd embraced it.

I turned my attention back to my friends. Allie stared, Kyle rose his eyebrows, and Marek smiled.

"What?" I pulled my wings closer to me.

Allie blinked several times. "There's just something... magical about seeing you discover your wings. You look so happy."

I realized I was smiling. "I never knew what I was missing."

"Ready to give it a try?" Kyle asked.

I nodded.

"Start by trying to flap your wings," Marek suggested. "Don't try to take off. Just move them to get a feel for it."

I did as I was instructed. It felt like I'd grown another set of arms, but strangely, the movement came naturally.

"How does it feel?" Allie asked enthusiastically.

I glanced behind my shoulder to watch my wings move up and down. If it wasn't for the tightening and relaxing of my muscles with every motion, I'd never believe they were my own.

"It feels great," I told her.

"You ready to try flying?" Marek asked.

I took a deep breath. "I'm ready."

"We'll fly alongside you," Marek explained. "One on either side and one in the back. That way, if you feel you might fall, we can catch you."

I nodded.

"It helps to get a running start," he continued. "Once you do, take a big leap and spread your wings out to glide. Flap to gain height, and tilt your body to change direction. It's not too hard to get once you're in the air. The trouble is finding the courage to get off the ground." He smiled at his last comment. "Remember, this is the easy part of being a Davina."

"Ugh. Don't remind me," I complained. "That means I have a lot more to learn."

Marek laughed. "Yeah, but you'll catch on quickly. Let's do this together."

Marek stood to my right while Allie situated herself on my left. Kyle took the spot behind me.

"Run, jump, and spread your wings," Marek reminded me. "Don't forget to flap them once you start losing height."

I rolled my eyes. "I'm not a child. I've got this."

Though my voice came out strong and commanding, I wasn't sure. Frankly, I was afraid I might break a leg, but I couldn't sit back without at least giving it a shot.

"Okay," Marek agreed. "On the count of three?"

I took off toward the hill before he finished the countdown. I saw Marek and Allie racing alongside me in my peripheral vision. Just as the hill dropped to a sharp decline, I dug my feet into the dirt and launched my body forward, spreading my wings out at the peak of my jump.

The ground dropped away from me. And so did my stomach.

My tummy tickled in the same way it felt to drive too fast over a hill. It was like someone flipped off the switch to gravity and my insides remained suspended high within my abdomen.

"Flap your wings!" Marek reminded me.

I immediately followed his instruction after realizing how quickly I was losing height. Wind rushed through my hair, tangling it into a wild mess. But I didn't care. I welcomed the air beneath my wings as it pressed against me and kept me afloat.

I dared to steal a glance below me. The base of the valley seemed miles away.

My heart slammed against my rib cage in exhilaration, and a satisfying tingle spread across my skin. It was the kind of rush that came with riding a rollercoaster. Only better.

I flapped my wings harder, daring to press the limits.

"Don't go above the tree line!" Allie warned. She had to shout for me to hear her.

I did as I was told. Instead of focusing on gaining height, I turned my attention to pressing forward.

I didn't fly as gracefully as the rest of them. Each flap of my wings seemed to shoot me into the air. The next moment, I'd fall several feet before counteracting gravity with another flap of my wings. At the very least, I managed to stay airborne, and my fear of breaking a bone slowly eased.

Once we reached the opposite end of the valley, Marek called to me. "We're going to circle around and try landing. Follow my lead. We'll glide and land at the bottom of the valley."

"Okay," I called back.

Marek leaned his body to the left.

I followed him. Where he made turning look effortless, I had to flap my wings double time to maintain my height.

As soon as he was headed in the right direction, he spread his wings wide and began to glide through the air.

I copied him and found myself descending toward the ground slowly. I actually felt for a moment like I might look graceful while doing it.

"Bend your knees when you land," Marek shouted my way. "It'll help absorb the impact."

As the ground grew closer, I feared we may be coming in too fast.

Allie charged ahead to demonstrate the landing. At the last second, she pulled her body back and swooped her wings up, landing perfectly on two feet.

I braced myself for impact. Though I did my best to mimic her motions, I stumbled and fell face-first into the grass. The inside of my right arm skidded along the ground. I pulled my wings back in and flipped over to examine my arm. Dirt had embedded itself into my raw skin.

"You okay?" Marek asked, landing beside me.

"Yeah, I'm fine." I bit back a cry as I tried to dust off the dirt. It stung.

"It was a good first flight," he said. "A few months at it and you could be the best flyer at Galen High."

I rolled my eyes, knowing he was just saying that to encourage me. "Don't use up all your compliments at once."

Marek smirked. "I'm sure I can come up with a few more."

Allie knelt beside me to take a look at my arm. "Doesn't look too bad. By tomorrow, there won't be any evidence of your landing."

"Ha ha," I said dryly.

"Uh," Kyle said to get our attention. "I wouldn't be so sure of that. We have witnesses."

We followed his gaze to find Blonde Bitch and her two body guards staring down at us from the top of the hill.

20

asey wasted no time making her way down to us. Her wings spread out behind her as she glided our way. She landed gracefully at my feet. She plastered a fake smile on her face and clapped her hands in a condescending manner.

Troy and Trenton landed behind her.

"Impressive." Casey dragged out the word, clearly not meaning it. She turned her attention to Allie. "So this is the talent you were talking about. You guys *really* have a shot at beating us this year."

Marek helped me to my feet.

"Bite me, Barbie." The words came out before I could think to stop them.

Casey blinked rapidly. "Excuse me?"

I glanced at Allie. Her eyebrows were raised in surprise.

I dusted the dirt off my jeans while I spoke. "I'm sure you weren't that great the first time you flew, either."

She narrowed her eyes at me. "I was, like, five."

"And?" I challenged, finally standing upright.

Casey opened her mouth once then closed it without saying anything. She rolled her eyes so heavily I thought they might fall out of her skull. "Whatever. Clearly they've already turned you against me." She shot both Allie and Kyle a disgusted look.

I crossed my arms. "Believe it or not, we don't sit around talking about you. We have more important things to do."

"Right. I heard there was a demon hanging around town. Word is he wants you. What'd you do to upset a demon?" Casey looked positively pleased with herself.

How did she know?

"That's none of your business," Allie snarled. She took a step forward, but Kyle placed a hand on her shoulder to hold her back.

Casey eyed her with loathing. "It's *my* dad out there hunting this thing. To protect *you.*"

"To protect *everyone,*" Allie pointed out.

"He's not the only one out there," Kyle said.

I realized Casey's dad must've been one of the Davina Fletcher had said he'd recruited to help.

"I still don't think he should be risking himself," Casey said.

Marek stepped forward. "Everyone relax."

I crossed my arms over my chest. "If your dad's out there, why hasn't he found him yet?"

Casey pursed her lips but didn't answer.

"Calm down, Casey," Marek insisted. "We're all Davina. We're on the same side."

Casey raised her blond eyebrows like she couldn't believe he'd suggest such a thing. "Competition is a good thing. It makes us stronger."

"But it doesn't make us enemies," Marek stated.

A muscle in Casey's jaw popped. "No, James, it doesn't. That one's on you."

An uncomfortable silence filled the air.

I glanced to Allie like she might have an answer.

"This is a waste of time," Casey finally said. "Enjoy your training session, but don't expect to have the place to yourself forever. We'll be back later. Come on, guys. Let's go."

She pushed past Troy and Trenton, knocking one of them in the shoulder—I couldn't remember which was which. Then she spread her wings to fly back to the top of the valley. The group disappeared through the trees.

It seemed to take a lifetime as we watched them go. The uncomfortable silence still hung in the air where we stood. I wasn't about to be the first to speak.

"What a bitch," Allie muttered under her breath.

"Don't call her that," Marek countered.

Kyle scoffed. "Why not? It's true."

Marek shook his head and ran his fingers through his brown hair. "It's rude."

"You don't have to be so bossy all the time," Allie said, raising her voice. "You don't still have feelings for her, do you?"

My jaw dropped.

"Of course not! I never had feelings for her," Marek argued.

"Sure you didn't," Allie said like she didn't believe him.

I looked to Kyle, hoping he might be able to explain. He shook his head, suggesting I shouldn't even ask.

"It's true." Irritation entered Marek's tone. "Can we just forget about it?"

Marek turned to me. "Ryn, I think we should move on to something else. You did really well with the flying, but it's not going to help you much in combat. Remember that demons can fly, too. We've got to get you comfortable using your magic, and you should know some hand-to-hand stuff in case you need it."

I started to agree with him, but Allie grabbed my arm and cut me off.

"Excuse us a moment." She dragged me several paces away.

"What?" I hissed.

"Would you rather Kyle and I leave?" she whispered.

I looked at her in confusion. "Why would I want that?"

"If Marek's really forgotten about Casey, you have a chance with him. It'll give you two a chance to get to know each other better." Allie wiggled her eyebrows. She was playing matchmaker again.

A blush rose to my cheeks. "You think I have a chance with him?"

Allie scoffed. "Girl, I've never seen him look at someone the way he looks at you."

I glanced over at Marek. He spoke to Kyle but kept his gaze on me. My heart flipped inside my chest like I was flying again.

I let my hair hide my face from him as I turned back to Allie. "He looks at me in a special way?"

Allie nodded like she couldn't believe I hadn't noticed. "If you want to spend some time alone with him, we'll give you space."

"I—uh—" I didn't know what to say. Of course I wanted to get to know him more, but was now the right time?

"You can do whatever you want," I told her.

She smiled wide. "Great. I'll see you later tonight. We can paint our nails and read through gossip magazines while you dish the juicy details."

I wasn't actually sure if she was kidding or not.

Allie turned back to Marek and Kyle. "Kyle, we have to go."

He looked at her in confusion. "Why?"

"I just realized…" She didn't finish her lie. She simply took his hand and led him away toward the stairs.

As soon as they were out of earshot, I turned back to Marek. "So, about Casey… I feel like I'm totally missing something."

He sighed heavily and shoved his hands in his pockets. "It's kind of a long story."

"I have time."

He gazed down at his feet, avoiding my gaze. "Okay… When I was new at Galen, Casey and I trained together. Long story short, I thought we were friends. She thought we were more."

The idea of Marek and Casey together made me want to puke.

Marek raked his fingers through his hair. "After I turned her down, she became pretty difficult to work with. She's been trying to prove how much better she is since then."

"So, you two weren't a thing?" Hope entered my tone.

Marek shrugged. "I guess I can see where I might've led her on, but I didn't mean anything by it."

"Does she still like you?"

Say no.

"God, no. I don't think she even realizes why she hates me so much. She's not good at letting things go, but half the time, she doesn't know what she's holding onto. I just—" Marek shifted his weight between his feet.

"What is it?"

He didn't look at me. "I don't have an easy time opening up to people. I think Casey took that personally."

I stared into his face sympathetically and spoke softly. "I'm sorry."

Marek continued to avoid my gaze. "For what? You didn't do anything."

"I did. I was a jerk to you."

I shouldn't have tried to push him into telling me about his scars. Involuntarily, I reached out to him, hoping it would get him to look at me.

He didn't pull away like I was afraid he might. Instead, he let me run my hand down his arm until our fingers entwined. He took a breath and gazed down at me. Our bodies inched closer together.

"Believe me," he said, "you're anything but a jerk. I was impossible to work with when I first came here."

I quieted, hoping he would elaborate. Instead, silence settled over the valley once again as he stared down into my eyes. His gaze flickered to my lips for a moment, and I swallowed hard. I was sure he could feel my fingers quivering in his.

This was it. He was going to kiss me.

Marek closed the distance between us in what felt like slow motion. Our eyes connected, and my breathing grew shallow. The sound of my own heartbeat echoed in my ears.

The kiss I'd been expecting never came. Marek let out a breath of shock, and then he crumbled to the ground, unconscious.

$\mathcal{I}$nstinct overcame me, and I dropped to my knees next to Marek. A moment later, I was on full alert, glancing around the valley frantically in search of an explanation.

The answer stood at the top of the hill with his feet spread apart in a confident stance. Another dark fireball was already forming in his fist.

Dorian.

Anger flared through my body, and my skin heated. What felt like an electric current ran down my right arm. The white essence I'd conjured last Friday night had returned. My anger subsided for only a moment, replaced instead by a wave of pride and victory.

The sound of flapping wings snapped my attention back to Dorian. I'd let myself be distracted for too long.

Two feathery midnight-black wings rose out from somewhere in the tangle of robes he wore. He landed just yards away from me.

I didn't know what to do next. With Marek on the ground, I felt so alone.

I knew exactly what Marek would tell me to do, though. *Kill him.*

I can't, I told myself.

The electricity in my palm fizzled away.

Shit. Dorian wouldn't care if I was unarmed and defenseless. He'd probably have more fun this way.

I gave one last glance down at my hand, but no matter how badly I wanted it, my essence didn't return.

"Why don't you lower your hood?" I challenged. I knew words were the only weapon I had at the moment. "Face me like a man."

Dorian took a step toward me, sending my heart racing.

"I'm not a man." He laughed. "You know that."

Keep him talking. Keep him talking. I didn't know what to say, but I had to come up with something. And fast.

"And you know what *I* am," I stated.

I could tell I piqued his interest by the way his hand twitched.

"So what if I do?" he asked.

"You saw what I did to your friend. Are you *really* sure you want your revenge like this? You know what I'm capable of."

I tried to sound confident, but I wasn't. Dorian sustained a fireball in his hand. It would take only a second for him to knock me out and strangle me to death.

He let out a bone-chilling laugh. "You think I'm doing this for revenge?"

I accidentally let my voice falter. "If not revenge, then what?"

"I know you have the power of an Original. No other angel I've seen has magic like yours." Dorian relaxed his hand, and the magic in it disappeared. "I'm not here to hurt you."

I forced down the lump in my throat so I could speak past it. His words didn't help reassure me. "Then why *are* you here?"

He held his head high. "I've come to convince you to join me."

Well, damn. That's definitely not what I expected to hear.

"Join you?" I asked curiously.

"With your magic, the Aedes could grow strong. We could build an army together, one that could win this war and stop the bloodshed."

I narrowed my eyes suspiciously. "How does my magic help you?"

"An Aedes child with your kind of power could lead an army. With enough of them, we'd be unstoppable. And with me as their father, I'd become a god to my people."

My breath froze in my chest. This was way worse than I could have ever imagined. Dorian wasn't planning to kill me. He was planning to turn me into a baby cannon.

Out of the corner of my eye, I noticed Marek's arm twitch beneath me. He was starting to wake. I had to keep Dorian talking.

I inched back a step. "What makes you think I'd go along with this?"

"Because one way or another, I *will* have you." He sounded so sure of himself. "You don't have a choice. You can either come with me nicely… or I'll make you."

I scoffed. "You think you'll be a hero to your people, yet you don't fight like it. Attacking me when no one else is around? Knocking my friend out to make sure he can't save me this time? You're not a hero. You're a *coward*."

Dorian laughed again. "We'll see about that." He stretched his hand out to conjure another fireball.

"You just made one mistake," I said with a raise of my eyebrow.

The orb in his hand instantly stopped growing.

"And what's that?" he growled.

Marek's voice came as I knew it would. "You kept talking."

Marek leapt to his feet and shot a white fireball at Dorian. A smile spread across my face before Marek's magic even made it to Dorian, but that smile quickly faded when Dorian dodged out of the way. Marek was quick and had already sent another ball of magic toward him.

Dorian ducked out of the way again. He launched himself forward and knocked Marek to the ground. His wings disappeared beneath his cloak. He pulled a fist back and smashed it into Marek's nose. Blood spirted across the grass.

Before I knew what I was doing, my foot connected with Dorian's ribs. Hard. He grunted and rolled off of Marek.

My nostrils flared, and my breath came in shallow heaves. "Do *not* touch him!"

Dorian pushed himself up, and his hood fell. Those dark, callous eyes glared at me like he was trying to burn a hole through my soul.

An electric tingle spread through my fingers. I was surprised to see a purple fireball form in my hand. I glanced to Marek uncertainly.

He held a hand over his bleeding nose. His eyes widened in urgency, but I hesitated.

If Marek had my powers, Dorian would be dead already.

Despite how much Dorian terrified and angered me, I couldn't bring myself to do it.

"Go!" I shouted at Dorian.

I held a weapon in my hand that could end him in a heartbeat. What was he still doing hanging around?

Dorian smiled sardonically. "You don't have the guts to kill me."

"Do you really want to stick around and find out?" I threatened. "Get out of here before I change my mind!"

Dorian sighed in a way that sounded like he was mocking me. "I'd hoped you'd come willingly. It would've made this a lot easier." He rose to his feet. Dark feathery wings grew out of his back again. "Remember, Little Angel, I'm not giving you a choice."

He launched himself into the air. His wings flapped vigorously, carrying him away from us.

Marek wiped the blood from his face and rose to his feet.

"Don't say it," I warned before he had a chance to speak.

I could already tell by the hard expression on his face what he wanted to say.

I shouldn't have let Dorian go.

But I wasn't going to make myself—or Marek—into a killer.

Dorian had to realize his plan would never work. My magic was stronger than his. I could only hope that would keep him away.

Marek tore his gaze from the horizon as soon as Dorian disappeared. He took my hand.

"Come on," he said in a commanding tone. "Let's go."

We raced up the stairs and down the trail without saying a word. My legs burned in protest. I sucked in large gulps of air without really feeling like I was breathing. Marek slowed and pulled out his phone near the end of the trail.

"We need to meet up," he barked into the phone. "Now." He paused for a moment. "At the school." He punched the screen so hard I thought he might crack it.

"Who—" I inhaled a deep breath. "Who are we going to meet?"

Marek was already scrolling through his phone for another number. He ignored me and pulled the phone to his ear. "Hey, Allie. Something happened again. We're meeting up with Fletcher. You and Kyle should come, too." It didn't sound like a suggestion.

He hung up and slipped his phone back in his pocket.

"I'm sorry," he said through labored breaths.

"For what?"

"I promised you nothing would happen. I just didn't think that… He must've been watching us, waiting until we were… vulnerable." Marek's eyes fell on the school building in the distance. "Come on. We need to tell the others."

2 2

llie and Kyle hadn't made it far. They were engaged in what looked like a heated conversation next to her vehicle. Allie stopped mid-sentence when she noticed our approach.

"What the hell?" She rushed to us. "We were *just* with you guys! What could've happened in the last five minutes?"

"Dorian." The name barely came out past the lump in my throat.

"Dorian?" she asked.

"The demon," Marek clarified with a scowl.

Kyle's eyes grew wide. "He attacked again? I thought he was being taken care of."

I crossed my arms. "I thought so, too."

"We need to talk to Fletcher," Marek said.

Just then, Fletcher's car pulled up and parked unevenly next to the curb.

He jumped out of the vehicle with a worried expression on his face. "What's wrong? What's happened?"

Marek glanced around. He seemed to decide it wasn't safe to talk out in the open. "Let's get inside."

Fletcher nodded and hurried toward the school, fumbling with his keys as he went. "Everyone's okay?"

Marek looked at me. "Ryn?"

My heart began to slow. "I'm fine. For now."

Fletcher led the way to his classroom. The remaining four of us filed into seats in the front row. He sat behind his desk and crossed his hands.

"Dorian attacked again," Marek stated flatly.

Fletcher pressed his fingers to his eyes, looking positively distressed. "Tell me exactly what happened."

Allie and Kyle leaned in closer.

"Ryn and I were down in the valley. She'd just taken her first flight, and everyone else left. We were going to get started on conjuring essence, but then the demon attacked me from behind."

Fletcher dropped his hands. "Then what happened?"

Marek looked to me for explanation.

"Dorian was standing at the top of the hill," I said. "He flew down to me, and I conjured essence. I thought I might be able to use it on him. But it was just a little bit. I couldn't sustain it. I knew I didn't stand a chance, so I tried to keep him talking to stall. He said…"

Everyone looked at me expectantly.

I took a deep breath. "He said he wants me to join him."

Fletcher furrowed his brow. "Join him?"

My gut twisted when I thought of Dorian's plan.

"He wants me to help him build an army of demons who have my power," I admitted.

"*What?*" Allie asked in shock. "How would that even work?"

"He wants to—" How could I put this into words? "He wants to *breed* with me. He wants our kids to lead a demon army. He says they'd be unstoppable."

Fletcher shook his head like he couldn't believe what he was hearing. "He clearly doesn't understand your powers."

"What do you mean?" I asked.

"The Power of Grace isn't genetic," Fletcher answered.

Relief washed over me. If what Fletcher said was true, Dorian would *have* to give up on me.

"It takes a physical body to manipulate essence," Fletcher explained. "That's why Grace needs someone else to wake her. Originals couldn't just hand their essence over to a mortal, though. It would destroy the mortal. She, however, can send it *through* you. You, Ryn, are a conduit."

My brows shot up. "A con-du-what?"

"A conduit," Fletcher said. "You've been chosen by Grace to reconnect her essence and consciousness with her body and life energy. Once that connection is restored, she'll be able to access the full potential of her essence once again."

I thought about it for a moment.

"So, what you're saying is—" I stared.

"Grace's power isn't yours to keep," Fletcher finished. "Once you restore the connection between Grace's essence and her body, your powers will return to normal—like the rest of ours."

I was stunned by Fletcher's words. I didn't know what to think.

"How'd you get away from him?" Fletcher asked.

"Away from Dorian? I threatened him," I said. "Marek woke up, and he was trying to help. Then Dorian hit him, and I conjured a purple fireball—"

"They're not fireballs," Marek muttered under his breath.

I shot him the evil eye for interrupting. "I told Dorian to go before I changed my mind."

"You shouldn't have let him," Marek said through gritted teeth.

"You think the alternative is better?" My voice rose. "I'm not going to kill someone!"

Reality slammed into me as soon as I said it. *I've already killed before.*

"Not on purpose, anyway," I clarified in a small voice.

Marek turned to Fletcher. "If Ryn's not going to kill him, someone else has to. He's not going to give up."

"We could reason with him," I argued. "We could tell him what Fletcher just said, about how his plan couldn't ever work."

"You think he'd give up?" Marek asked harshly. "If he's not using you to build an army, he'll use you for something else. The demons would rather kill you than let you wake Grace."

Allie cut in. "What about the team of people you have looking for him, Fletcher?"

"Yeah," Marek agreed. "I thought the Davina in Eagle Valley were supposed to have practical experience."

Fletcher sighed. "Unfortunately, some Davina haven't been as cooperative as I would like. I've essentially been looking for him myself. While I've asked the rest of you to keep an eye on Ryn, I've been canvassing the outskirts of town hoping to run into him. But he's on high alert. I haven't been able to get close enough for combat."

"What's everyone else doing?" Marek snarled. "Casey said her dad was out there looking for him."

"Casey's father, along with the others, don't know about Ryn's… talents," Fletcher said. "They know the demon won't come all the way into town, and though they know Ryn is his target, they're confident she's safe. They aren't trying very hard to find him. They don't see him as a threat."

"That's bull!" Kyle yelled.

"Then we have to tell them about her powers," Marek insisted at the same time.

Fletcher held up a hand to get them both to calm down. "We're not telling them. The more people we tell, the more danger we put Ryn in. Yes, we can trust the Davina, but it's not a matter of trust. Rumors will fly. It just takes *one* person to overhear what Ryn is capable of to put her in more danger."

"Tell them he attacked me, too," Marek suggested. "If they know he's not just out for Ryn, then maybe they'll think twice about how dangerous he is."

Allie shifted in her chair and raised her hand apprehensively, waiting for her turn to speak.

Fletcher raised his eyebrows in interest. "Yes, Allie?"

She cleared her throat. "Well, it's just… I agree with you. Maybe we shouldn't tell the others. But you already have a group of people who *do* understand the situation and can help out. You have us."

Fletcher shook his head with conviction. "No. I don't want to put any of you in more danger. I want all of you to stay in town until I can get this sorted out. No more going to the valley until next week. Without enough people coming and going during school hours, it leaves you too exposed. Ryn, I want you to continue trying to conjure essence but at home instead of the valley. Once we eliminate this threat, we'll have much more time for lessons."

I nodded.

"I know a way we could end this sooner," Kyle said.

We all looked to him in question.

"We use Ryn as bait."

"*What?*" I practically choked.

"No," Marek protested.

"Kyle," Allie said in disbelief.

"Just hear me out," Kyle insisted. "This demon's attacked her twice now at the valley. We go back out there and set up a similar scenario but have people surrounding the valley to attack *him* as soon as he shows."

I couldn't believe what I was hearing. "You can't really think he's that stupid, can you?"

Kyle shrugged. "It's worth a shot. He either shows up and we get him, or he doesn't and no one gets hurt."

"Kyle—" I started, but Fletcher cut me off.

"No. We're not using Ryn as bait. Ryn, I want you to go home and stay there. I'm getting a better feel for this Aedes' movements. I should have him taken care of before school starts."

"Can't we at least do something to *help*?" Marek asked.

Fletcher raised his brows. "Yes. You can keep Ryn company."

"Fine." Marek sounded slightly irritated, like he'd rather be out there with Fletcher than babysitting me. He stood.

"Wait," Kyle insisted. "Can't we talk about this more? The sooner we get rid of this demon, the better."

Marek turned to Kyle with a hard look on his face. "You think I don't know that? I want to get rid of him, too, but Fletcher's right. We have to protect Ryn." He turned to me and softened his voice. "Let's get you somewhere safe for the night."

My heart melted. How'd I manage to find this guy who wanted to protect me at any cost?

Allie, Kyle, and I stood to follow him.

I paused at the door. "Fletcher?"

I could see the apology written all over his face. He obviously felt bad that he hadn't caught Dorian yet.

"I'm really grateful for all your help," I told him. "Thanks for watching out for me."

A smile crept across his face, melting away the disappointment on it. "That's what I'm here for. Please do me a favor, Ryn."

"Yeah?"
"Stay safe, okay?"
I nodded. "I will."
I wasn't sure I'd be able to keep that promise.

23

We stepped outside into heavy air. The clouds had thickened, darkening the sky.

"What are we supposed to do now?" Kyle asked. "Just sit around and do nothing?"

"I don't know." Marek ran his fingers through his hair.

"I have an idea," I offered. "We could go back to Allie's and you could show me how to conjure fireballs."

Marek frowned at my use of the term *fireballs*.

"If I can learn to conjure white fireballs by will, I'll be able to defend myself without hurting anyone." I stared at Marek pleadingly. He had to know how much I didn't want anyone to get hurt.

We stopped beside Allie's vehicle.

"I'd personally love to see Ryn use the Power of Grace," Kyle said.

"Me, too," Allie agreed. "And Fletcher said he wanted her to keep trying with it."

Marek pursed his lips.

"What?" I asked. "You think it's a bad idea? I won't hurt anyone in a controlled environment."

Marek sighed. "It's not that."

"Then what?" I demanded.

Marek gritted his teeth like he didn't want to say. We all stared back at him expectantly.

He finally caved. "Forget what Fletcher said. I want to go after this demon."

"No!" I objected. The last thing I wanted was for him to get hurt.

"You can't," Allie agreed.

"Calm down, Marek," Kyle said. "You're not going anywhere."

Marek glared at Kyle like he couldn't believe he was giving orders. He ran his fingers through his hair again.

"I know." Marek crossed his arms. "That's why I need someone to talk me out of it."

"Fletcher's taking care of it," Allie said.

Somehow, I didn't think that would convince Marek.

I stepped forward until Marek and I were just inches apart. I stared intensely into his eyes.

"You can't," I said in a near whisper. "Who would protect me if you weren't around?"

Marek's expression softened. He held my gaze for several seconds but didn't say anything.

"Um, hello?" Kyle said. "Allie and I aren't completely useless."

Thanks, Kyle. You just invalidated my entire argument.

Allie elbowed him softly in the ribs.

"Ow!" Kyle elbowed her back.

Marek laughed lightly and relaxed his shoulders. "Ryn's right. I can't leave her alone with you two idiots. Let's go conjure some essence."

We spent the next hour in Allie's basement while I tried to conjure what essence I could. No matter how hard I tried, I couldn't manage more than a spark.

Kyle sprawled himself in the bean bag chair in the corner, making comments every now and then about how I was doing it wrong or how I wasn't trying hard enough. Allie told me at least six times to ignore him.

Eventually, my annoyance turned to anger. I tried to let that fuel my power, but it didn't work as I'd hoped. It was only when Kyle turned to criticizing Marek for his teaching methods and no one was paying attention that I felt a surge of electricity pass between my fingertips. As soon as I got their attention, it was gone.

"Stop being a jerk, Kyle," Allie snapped at him.

He spread his arms wide as if to ask what he'd done wrong. "I'm only trying to help motivate."

Allie rolled her eyes. "Yeah, well, you're doing it wrong."

Kyle let out a puff of air and turned his attention to his phone.

"It's okay, Allie," I told her. "I think Kyle may have actually helped a little. So far, it seems to only work for me when I'm angry."

"See?" Kyle said without looking up. "I *was* helping."

"I'm sorry I'm being so slow," I told them.

"It just takes practice," Marek assured me.

"Let me try again." I raised my palm and took a deep breath in concentration.

As the seconds ticked by, the tension in my head intensified. I glared into my hand like I could make it combust by sheer will.

Nothing happened.

I sighed. "Forget it. Maybe I'll do better another time."

"It's fine," Allie assured me sympathetically. "We'll try again tomorrow."

I forced a smile. "Thanks."

"Maybe we should take a break," Marek suggested.

I nodded. "Is it okay if I step outside for some fresh air?" I needed a chance to clear my head after the long day I'd endured.

"Yeah," Marek agreed. "Let's go out back."

I hadn't intended it as an invitation, but after everything that happened, I didn't think any of them would be letting me out of their sight anytime soon.

Allie and Kyle stayed behind as Marek and I climbed the stairs and stepped out into the back yard.

A slight breeze had picked up, chilling my exposed skin. I wrapped my arms around myself and sank into one of the swings on the playset next to the house. The whole thing was rusted and looked like it hadn't been played on in years. Marek sat in the swing beside me and swayed slightly.

I stared down at my feet in the dirt, but I could still feel Marek's gaze on me.

"I'm sorry," I whispered.

"For what?"

I closed my eyes and focused on the wind rustling through my hair. I thought for a moment that turning my attention to something so mundane might help take my mind of things, but the emotions I'd been feeling lately bubbled even closer to the surface. I didn't even know at this point *what* I was feeling, but I knew that most of it wasn't good.

"I don't know." I shrugged. "For being such a wimp. For having to turn to you every time I need my ass saved."

"Hey," he said with a hint of a smile. "Don't be sorry about that. It's what I'm here for."

I shot back a half-smile of my own, but it didn't last long. "I feel so useless. According to Fletcher, I'm some prophesied last hope, but I'm the furthest thing anyone would want to bet on. I might literally cause the end of the world because I won't be able to live up to my calling."

Marek frowned. "You shouldn't feel that way."

I couldn't bring myself to believe him.

"I don't get why *I* have this special power," I said. "It should be you, or Allie, or someone else who actually knows what they're doing."

Marek dug his feet into the dirt, stopping his swaying. "I didn't always know what I was doing."

I glanced his way for a second and then returned to staring at my feet. "You know what you're doing now."

Marek breathed a heavy sigh. "It took me almost a year after moving here before I could use my powers properly. You've already conjured essence a handful of times. It's not going to be long before you learn to control it."

It took him a whole year?

"How'd you learn?" I asked.

He shrugged. "I figured out what was holding me back."

"What was it?" I wondered if it could it be the same thing holding me back.

Marek let out a light laugh. "Me."

I looked at him curiously. "What do you mean by that?"

"*I* was holding me back. I didn't want to be a part of this world.

My mom was born into a Davina family, but she didn't have Davina powers."

I remembered Marek said not all Davina developed powers. I hadn't expected him to know one of those Davina.

"When we found out I was a Davina, she wasn't exactly happy about it," he admitted. "When I moved in with my aunt, she tried to explain some of it to me, but Fletcher laid on all the details. It was too much. That's when I ran away."

Shock riveted through me. I definitely wasn't expecting to hear that. But I didn't dare interrupt his story.

"The thing was, I had no money and had nowhere to go," he continued. "I just wanted to get away, to erase my past and start over fresh."

I wanted to ask him about his past; I wondered if it had anything to do with his scars. But I didn't want to intrude on his privacy.

"I didn't realize at the time Eagle Valley *was* my fresh start," Marek said. "I was gone two weeks before they found me. Between walking partway and stowing away the other part, I'd only made it about a hundred miles from here. I was so hungry and tired that I didn't really have any choice but to come back."

My heart broke at his story.

"It took another year before I finally embraced what I was and conjured essence for the first time." He shot me a half-hearted smile that didn't reach his eyes. "So, like I said, you're not doing bad for having just discovered what you are."

We both went silent. I had no idea what to say to him. I wanted to offer him my comfort, but Marek was already so tough. I wasn't sure it would help.

"Why are you telling me all this?" I asked.

Marek looked at me intensely. "Because I want you to know that you're stronger than you think you are."

A blush rose to my cheeks. Could he really mean it?

"Besides," Marek continued, "everyone else at Galen already knows. I'd rather you heard about it from me first."

It was evident in his voice that telling me about his past had been difficult for him.

I twisted my swing toward him. "Thank you for telling me."

Hopefully he knew how much I truly meant it.

"Trust me," he said, "you'll learn eventually. You've only just discovered your powers."

Or so you think.

I bit my lip and avoided his gaze.

"What?" he asked. He clearly knew I was hiding something.

Should I tell him?

"The thing is," I said shyly, "I've conjured essence before."

Okay, I guess I'm telling him.

I twisted my hands in my lap. "I didn't know what had happened at the time, but..."

I went silent.

"But what?" Marek asked.

What if he thinks I'm crazy?

I slowly lifted my gaze until our eyes connected. Marek stared back at me with a look of trustworthiness in his eyes. I couldn't explain the sudden desire to tell him everything.

The words tumbled out of me before I could stop myself.

"Friday night wasn't the first time my essence killed someone."

24

I didn't know what possessed me to tell Marek. I hadn't told anyone before in my life.

"I'm sorry," I said in a breathless whisper.

Is Marek the right person to tell about this?

He leaned closer to me in his swing. His face was so close that I could see the small flecks of brown spotted in his blue irises. "It's okay. You can tell me."

Can I?

"I'm afraid you'll tell me I'm crazy," I admitted.

Marek reached up a hand to tuck a strand of brown hair out of my face. My breath caught in my chest.

"I won't," he promised.

I knew he was telling the truth. And maybe that's why my subconscious decided to toss the confession out there. I'd never told anyone before because I knew they wouldn't believe me. Marek was different.

I took a deep breath. "Growing up and not knowing what I was, I didn't know the demons were dangerous. Pretty much as soon as I could talk, I started talking to them."

"And?" Marek encouraged me to continue.

"There was one demon in particular who always hung around. Clinton. He'd talk to me and play games with me. My mom would play along, but I could always tell she didn't quite believe that he was real. She'd sometimes say something about my *'imaginary friend.'* I knew she was talking about him because he could talk directly at her and she wouldn't respond. Is that normal for demons? To befriend kids?"

Marek pressed his lips together. "It seems strange. Demons would normally feed off your essence rather than befriend you. You never felt influenced by him?"

I shook my head. "I don't think so."

Then again, who knew what it felt like?

"Maybe it was different because you're a Davina," Marek suggested.

I shrugged. "Knowing what I know now, I wonder if he was more interested in my mom than me. She wasn't in a good place during my childhood."

How much should I tell him?

"Once I was a little older," I said, "I thought it was because she lost my dad. Now I wonder if all that bad stuff was because of Clinton."

"It's pretty normal for humans to have a demon—sometimes even more than one—attached to them," Marek said.

I frowned. "You haven't heard the half of it. Like I said, my mom was in a bad place. She—"

No, I can't tell him.

This wasn't exactly something you tell a guy you just met. At the same time, I wanted the weight lifted off my shoulders. I'd been holding onto this secret for too long.

"She what?" he prodded. "It's safe to tell me. I'm not going to judge."

I took another long breath. "My mom drank a lot."

I was surprised at how good it felt to finally open up to someone.

"The thing was," I continued, "Clinton would always egg her on. I was so young, I didn't realize what was happening. Most of the time, I thought he was joking around. And it seemed harmless, you know? All he was doing was *talking*. Things like *'one more drink'* and *'Kathryn would be better off without you.'*"

Marek's eyes filled with sympathy, but he didn't say anything.

"I guess when I was seven or so, I started to realize how awful he was being," I said. "I'd tell him to stop. I'd tell him he was lying to her. By that time, my mom had already sent me to therapy. She said it was because I should be past my stage of imaginary friends."

My chest knotted. The next part of the story was the hardest.

"Then what happened?" Marek asked softly.

I forced the knot to ease. "One night when I was eight, my mom drank so much she passed out on the couch. I yelled at Clinton and asked him why he encouraged her to drink so much. All he did was laugh at me. That was when I decided I hated him."

The memory of Clinton left a bad taste in my mouth.

"I told him to leave," I continued. "I said I was going to call the cops on him. I mean, I was eight. What else was I supposed to threaten him with? And obviously I wasn't going to do it because at this point, I knew no one else could see him."

Marek nodded like he understood.

"I locked myself in my bedroom," I told him, "but he didn't leave. I couldn't bring myself to fall asleep because I was so mad. Eventually, I heard my mom creep down the hall to her room across from mine. I waited a couple of minutes and decided I wanted to sleep by her that night. Only, when I opened the door—"

An involuntary sob caught in my throat. Marek touched my shoulder lightly.

"It's okay," he said.

I shook my head, unable to choke out the words. It really *wasn't* okay.

Maybe I should stop, I told myself. *I've told him enough.*

Except I wanted to tell him more. Getting it off my chest was a relief. I couldn't stop now.

My breathing wavered. "When I opened the door, he was standing over her... telling her to kill herself."

I couldn't help it as the tears fell down my cheeks and my body shook in sobs. I covered my face with my hands and barely noticed when Marek wrapped an arm around me. I wanted his warm embrace to soothe me, but nothing could help erase the images burned into my memory.

"I just remember so much blood," I cried into his chest.

Marek didn't say a word. He only pulled me closer as we lightly swayed back and forth in the swings.

I didn't know how long we stayed there. When my tears finally dried, I pulled away and wiped at my face.

I swallowed down the lump in my throat. "I saw the cuts on her wrists, and I yelled at Clinton. I told him it was his fault. He told me he knew, that it's what he *wanted*."

Bile rose to my throat at the memory.

"The night my mom tried to kill herself, I used essence on Clinton," I admitted. "I don't really remember it. I just remember this bright purple light shoot across the room, and then he was gone… vanished into thin air."

I paused. "All that was left was his cloak. I never touched it when we moved. Since she's human, my mom never knew it was there in the first place."

Marek took a deep breath beside me like he was going to say something, but he remained silent.

"As soon as Clinton was gone, I called 911 then wrapped my mom's wrists with the blanket on her bed. I saved her life." My voice cracked. "Sometimes, I wonder what would've happened if I hadn't walked in on her, if I had fallen asleep or something."

I couldn't bear to think of that. "I'd spent so long trying to forget that night. All these years, I felt like I was somehow to blame, like Clinton was some sort of omen telling me it was coming…"

I sniffled and wiped at my eyes again. "Mom got better after that. I told her I'd stopped seeing Clinton because, well, it was true. And I pretended like I couldn't see the rest of them. If I acted like I could, I was afraid something bad might happen again. So I ignored them, never made eye contact, never once spoke back to them."

Marek nodded in understanding.

"It was hard at first," I said. "I wanted to be homeschooled to avoid them altogether. But that was right when Mom started working from home so we could move around—and 'see the world,' she said—so she didn't have the time to homeschool me."

She never made the time for me at all, and then she'd act like it was my fault.

I sighed heavily. "I've spent most of my life believing I was imagining it all. That's why I thought I was hallucinating—or drugged—the night we met. I never knew what really happened to Clinton until you told me I'd killed that other demon."

My gaze finally locked on his again. After sharing so much about myself with Marek, all I wanted to do was stare into his eyes. They remained soft, like he really cared about what I was saying.

I wiped at my nose. "I'm sorry about crying."

"Don't be sorry," he said gently, pulling me once again back to his chest. "*I'm* sorry all that happened to you. You have every right to feel upset over it."

I forced a smile, even though he couldn't see it. "Thanks."

Marek loosened his hold on me, and I drew away. He stared down at me.

"What?" I asked shyly.

His eyes danced across my face. "I just want to protect you."

My heart flipped in my chest. "From what?"

"From Clinton. From Dorian. From everything."

"You can't protect me from everything," I told him.

Marek frowned and pulled me back to his chest. His breath was warm against the top of my head.

His words came in a low whisper. "I can try."

25

"Marek! Marek!" I cried.

I glanced around frantically, searching for an indication of where I was and what I was doing there. In front of me spanned a large patch of grass, but beyond that, nothing. A thick layer of gray fog obscured my view.

"Marek!" I called again.

"Ryn?" An unfamiliar voice cut through the fog.

"Who's there?" I demanded.

"It's me," the voice said.

A figure stepped forward. It was a young man who looked to be about thirteen. He stood shirtless and shaking in front of me. White wings rose behind him, giving him away as Davina. His blue eyes looked familiar, but I couldn't place him.

"Are you okay?" I asked, quickly rushing to the boy.

His bottom lip quivered, and his eyes filled with terror. "Ryn, I need your help."

"It's okay," I told him, but I couldn't be sure without knowing what was actually wrong.

A woman's voice echoed from somewhere past the fog. "I will NOT raise a Davina. You are a disgrace!"

I surveyed the area in a heartbeat, searching for the woman the voice belonged to, but I saw nothing. When I glanced back to where the boy

137

stood, he was gone. Instead, Marek stood in his place, complete with his leather jacket and a hard look on his face.

"We shouldn't be here, Ryn," he said, stepping forward to take me by the elbow.

I dug my feet into the grass and pulled away. "We have to save the boy!"

He reached for me again. "We can't, Ryn."

Marek's grip was so tight that I couldn't pull away this time. He dragged me alongside him.

"Why not?" I insisted.

"Because, Ryn, he's already gone."

"But Marek!" I jerked away again.

"Come on, Ryn," he insisted. "We have to go. He'll be here soon!"

"The boy? He was just here."

"No, not him."

"Then who?"

Laughter echoed around me, but I couldn't tell where it was coming from. As the eerie sound intensified, the fog began to clear. A hill rose in the distance, and I noticed for the first time I was standing at the base of the valley. I could just barely make out a dark figure with massive black wings at the top of the hill.

"Dorian?" I turned back to Marek for confirmation, but he was gone.

Panic entered my chest. How could he just abandon me?

I heard the flapping of wings and turned my full attention back to Dorian. By now, the fog had completely lifted, but the atmosphere remained a grayish tint that sent a chill down my spine.

With every increasingly rapid breath, Dorian got closer to me. I should've run, but I stood my ground.

"You can't win this fight, Dorian!" I shouted.

A dark fireball had already settled in his palm when he landed.

"That's where you're wrong." He didn't waste another second as he hurled the fireball toward me.

Instinct overcame me, and I jumped to dodge it. I expected my feet to hit the ground a moment later, but I was surprised to find myself airborne. A strong wind passed by my face. I flapped my wings harder, rising above Dorian.

He threw another fireball.

I dodged that one as well as the next.

I landed gracefully beside him. "This is a war you can't win, Dorian."

"Of course I can," he said, that cold laugh returning. "You may be the chosen one, but there's just one problem."

I swallowed, not sure if I wanted him to elaborate. My curiosity got the better of me. "What's that?"

Dorian's laughter stopped dead. "They chose wrong."

Then he hurled the essence in his hand at my chest, and everything went dark.

I awoke suddenly. My heart raced, and my body was covered in a sheen of sweat. The side of my face stuck to the arm of a leather couch, and a TV played quietly in the background. It took me a moment to remember where I was.

After Marek and I came inside, Allie had put on a movie in the living room. I'd fallen asleep next to Marek. Now I lay alone on the couch with a blanket draped over me that hadn't been there earlier.

I tried to hold onto the memory of my dream, but it was slipping away quickly. Who was that boy I'd dreamt about? He reminded me so much of someone… of Marek.

I realized it as soon as I asked myself the question. He'd been a younger version of Marek, the version who'd run away from Eagle Valley. The woman's voice had been his mother's.

I continued to play the dream back through my mind until I recalled how it ended. Could Nightmare Dorian have been right? Did Grace choose the wrong person?

I looked to Allie and Kyle in the loveseat beside me. Allie lay against Kyle's chest with his arm around her shoulder.

I sat up. "How long was I out?"

Allie shrugged. "Half an hour or so."

"That's it?" I asked in shock. "Where's Marek?"

"He went home a few minutes ago," Allie said.

My heart dropped. It was already dark out, but he could've stayed longer.

"Are you hungry?" Allie asked. "My dad left some chili on the stove. We didn't want to wake you."

"Thanks." I stood.

Allie hopped up from the loveseat to join me in the kitchen. "Do you remember where the bowls and spoons are?"

"Yeah." I helped myself to the silverware.

Allie pulled a bowl down from the cupboard and handed it to me. I ladled chili into my bowl and leaned my hip against the counter to eat.

"So, you and Marek were outside for a while." Allie wiggled her eyebrows. "Anything fun happen?"

I rolled my eyes at her. "Could you at least give us a month to get to know each other?"

"A whole *month?*" she teased, sticking her bottom lip out. "You never let me have any fun."

I swallowed my chili and laughed.

Allie pulled a clean glass from the drying rack and began filling it at the sink. "No, but seriously. I saw you two hugging."

I rose my eyebrows at her. "And what were you doing spying on us?"

Allie's eyes widened innocently. "I wasn't! You can see the swing set from the window." She gestured to the window above the sink.

I glanced outside. I could just barely make out the silhouette of the swing set through the darkness. Lightning lit up the clouds in the distance.

Allie sipped on her water. "What'd you two talk about?"

I shrugged. I knew I could tell Allie about Clinton because she was a Davina, but telling the story once today was enough.

I stared out the window. "Marek was just telling me I wasn't doing so bad. He told me he ran away when he came here."

Allie frowned. "Yeah, he did."

Another bolt of lightning lit up the sky. The thick cloud cover diffused the light.

"Who did what?" Kyle stepped into the room.

"Marek ran away," Allie said simply, taking another gulp of water.

Kyle crossed his arms in amusement and leaned against the counter. "Oh, that story."

I barely processed what they were saying. My attention remained locked on the lightning in the distance. Something was *off* about it.

And then I saw it.

A light shot up into the sky, illuminating the clouds. As fast as the flash came, it was gone.

"What are you looking at?" Allie followed my gaze toward the horizon.

I set my bowl on the counter, never taking my eyes off the night sky. "Is it just me, or is there something strange about that lightning?"

Kyle joined us at the window to get a good look. The light shot into the sky again and flashed through the clouds. Kyle let out a breath in disbelief. Allie and I looked at him for explanation. He twisted his lips and shook his head.

"That son of a bitch," he said in amusement.

"What do you mean?" I asked.

Kyle laughed lightly. "That's not lightning."

Allie drew in a breath of surprise. Clearly she understood something I didn't.

"If it's not lightning—" I stopped dead.

We were in Eagle Valley. What else could it be?

"Essence?" I asked.

Kyle nodded.

"I thought that was supposed to be kept secret," I said.

Allie frowned. "It is."

"Then why's someone out there doing that?" I asked.

Kyle scoffed. "Isn't it obvious?"

No, you dimwit. I'm not exactly familiar with this Davina stuff.

I shook my head.

Kyle smiled in amusement. "I'd bet you anything it's your boyfriend out there. He's going after the demon himself."

26

"He can't!" I cried. My eyes widened in shock.

Kyle shrugged. "He did."

"How do you know it's him?" I demanded.

"Because it's something he would do," Allie answered with an eye roll.

Kyle gestured out the window. "And check out where it's coming from."

I considered it for a moment. "The valley."

Kyle nodded.

"We have to go!" I was already on my way to the back door. Marek wasn't going to get hurt because of me.

"Hold on," Allie called. "Ryn!"

I raced through Allie's back yard and across the neighbor's.

"Marek's such an idiot," Allie mumbled from several paces back.

That, or my hero. We have yet to find out.

Kyle and Allie caught up to me when I reached the sidewalk, but I didn't slow my pace. I sprinted as fast as I could in the direction of Galen High.

My legs burned as we neared the school. It felt like a weight had settled on my chest as I sucked in shallow breaths. But it never felt like I was getting enough oxygen.

I definitely needed to pick up running. And maybe cut back on the cookies.

The three of us ran around the side of the school. We increased our speed as soon as we hit the trail. Through the trees, I saw Marek's essence shoot upward and illuminate the sky again. What was he thinking?

As we raced closer, I heard his voice cut through the sound of the wind.

"Come on!" he shouted. There was a raw passion in his voice I'd never heard before. "I know you're out there."

I broke through the trees and came to a sudden halt next to Marek's bike. Allie stumbled into me but caught herself on my shoulder. Kyle stopped beside her.

Below us, Marek stood in the center of the valley. Another fireball was ready in his hand, illuminating him. He paced back and forth aggressively with his head tilted toward the sky.

"Where are you, you jackass?" he roared. "Come fight me. Let's see who really deserves her!"

Marek closed his fist, and the fireball inside it disappeared. Darkness enveloped the valley. The next moment, a white fireball erupted from his palm and shot straight into the sky like a firework. It reached the low-hanging clouds. They lit for less than a second before the valley became dark again.

"Marek, stop!" I called from the top of the hill.

I hardly thought about it when I flexed my shoulders and wings grew out of my back. I threw my body forward and spread my wings out.

Marek conjured another fireball to illuminate his face. He looked in my direction as I descended toward him. I could hear Allie's and Kyle's wings flapping behind me.

I aimed for landing next to him, but I hadn't perfected my landing yet. I stumbled into him and caught myself on the sleeve of his jacket.

The fireball in his hand disappeared. He grabbed my arms to steady me, but the valley didn't go dark. I glanced behind me to see that Allie and Kyle were holding fireballs of their own.

Marek gripped my biceps hard and forced me to look at him. "You shouldn't be here."

"*You* shouldn't be here," I accused. "What were you thinking?"

His eyes searched mine, but his voice remained strong. "I was thinking I wanted to protect you."

"But Fletcher said—" I started.

"Forget what Fletcher said," Marek growled. "You need to get out of here. All of you."

"We're not going anywhere without you," I stated confidently.

"Please," Marek pleaded. "You weren't supposed to follow me. If he got my message, he's almost here."

Kyle stepped forward. "Marek, you're being an idiot."

Thank God someone agreed with me.

"You're not going to talk me out of it," Marek declared.

"I know," Kyle said. "You're too stubborn for that. The least you can do is let us fight alongside you."

Apparently Kyle wasn't taking my side after all.

Jerk.

"No." Marek's voice was strong and commanding. "Not Ryn. I left her with you so you could protect her."

Kyle frowned. "Then you should've told me your plan."

Allie stepped between them. "You're both being ridiculous. Fletcher is taking care of this demon. We need to get out of here before—"

An explosion like a firecracker at our feet cut her off. Every muscle in my body contracted.

It took me only a moment of confusion to realize what it'd been.

Essence.

A warning.

I whirled around quickly. What I saw sent my heart tumbling out of my chest.

A dark winged figure I recognized all too well swooped out of the sky and landed just yards away from us.

If at any moment I'd felt hopeless in all my encounters with Dorian, it was nothing compared to how I felt when six other cloaked figures soared out of the shadows behind him.

27

$\mathcal{S}$even demons surrounded us.

A dark fireball with its red and white outline glowed in Dorian's palm and illuminated the bottom half of his thin face. Fear instinctively hit, but it was quickly overshadowed by anger when I noticed his smirk.

He's not going to win.

Marek grabbed my wrist and pulled me behind him.

Allie and Kyle stood facing the circle of demons with their backs toward me. I was enclosed in a protective triangle between the three of them. Allie's and Kyle's wings helped hide me.

I stared past Marek to Dorian. "I thought you wanted all the glory for yourself."

Marek pushed me further behind him.

Dorian grinned. "I told you I wasn't going to give you a choice."

"Didn't think you could take me on alone, did you?" I taunted.

"Don't worry," Dorian said with a laugh. "You're still mine. I only recruited a few people to take care of your friends."

Dorian reached up with one hand to lower his hood. He looked mostly human, but there was something evil about him that made my stomach twist. His eyes held that same darkness in them I'd noticed before. This time, it was even more apparent and terrifying.

"Sorry to disappoint," I said, "but you've recruited for nothing. There's nothing you can do to make me go with you."

"Quiet," Marek hissed. He scanned the circle of demons like he was calculating how to take them all out.

"I wouldn't be so sure about that," Dorian mocked. "I'm giving you one last chance to join me. If you refuse, you can say goodbye to your friends."

Someone might as well have dropped a cinderblock on my stomach. We were outnumbered. If I didn't go with him, my friends were going to die.

There has to be a way out of this.

"Your plan will never work," Marek snarled. "The demons will never have the Power of Grace."

"Shut up, Lover Boy," Dorian barked.

"It's true!" Allie cried. She never took her eyes off the other demons. "Her power isn't genetic."

"You're lying!" Dorian accused.

"She's not," Kyle defended.

Marek stepped further in front of me for protection. I couldn't see Dorian's reaction.

After a few moments, Dorian spoke again. "Doesn't matter either way. Her power is too unique."

And he wants every bit of it for himself.

My chest tightened. Marek's words echoed in my head.

If he's not using you to build an army, he'll use you for something else.

Marek squeezed my hand. "If you want her, you'll have to come through us to get her."

Dorian scoffed. "If that's how you want to do this…"

Everyone moved in a blur. The six other demons closed in on us, and my friends immediately sprang into action. Marek's hold on me vanished as he aimed a punch at the closest demon.

Before I could make a move, Dorian had closed the distance between us and had me in his grasp. He spun me around and held me to his chest, pinning my wings at an awkward angle between us.

I watched in horror as a demon sank a foot into Marek's abdomen. Marek conjured a fireball. Nearby, Allie threw a kick into a demon's gut and elbowed another in the face. Kyle tackled one to the ground and smashed his fist into its face over and over again.

Dorian's cold breath across my cheek sent a chill down my spine. "Are you ready to come with me now?"

I squirmed. "I'll never go with you."

Dorian clicked his tongue. "Not the answer I wanted to hear, Little Angel. Though, your resistance is a bit of a turn-on." Dorian pressed his hips into my backside and trailed a hand down my stomach to my waistline.

I gritted my teeth.

"Stop!" I demanded.

"Stop what?" he taunted. "Stop my friends from killing yours? Or stop this?" His fingers slid across my hip.

"Please," I cried.

How had this happened? How had I let him get me in this position again?

Dorian squeezed me tighter. "That's it, my Little Angel. Beg for it."

My breath grew hot on my upper lip. "I. Am. Not. Your. Little. Angel."

A strength I didn't know I had overcame me. I lifted my foot and slammed it down hard on his toes. His grip on me loosened, and I took the opportunity to swing my elbow up into his nose. He stumbled back and released me.

I raced away from him as fast as my legs could carry me and launched myself into the air. A ball of black magic flew by my head, narrowly missing my shoulder. I didn't look back, but I knew Dorian was flying close behind me.

I'm going to die. Just like in my dream.

I somehow missed another one of Dorian's attacks. I was quickly reaching the end of the valley and didn't know how much longer I could hold him off. Any moment, he could knock me out of the air.

Don't let him get to you, I told myself.

Instantly, I knew the only thing I could do was hide. I didn't worry about landing gracefully. My only mission was to get into the trees—and *fast.* At least in there, I had some cover.

I landed hard at the top of the valley opposite the trail we normally came in on. I stumbled to my knees but quickly got to my feet and took off running. I pulled my wings into me so they wouldn't slow me down.

Rather than dodging Dorian's attacks, I found myself dodging around trees and jumping over thick roots. There was no path here, and the forest was denser than I thought it would be.

My hand scraped along the bark of the trees as I passed each one. I used their sturdy trunks to help me stay upright. Just as my hand found another tree, a dark fireball passed through it and fizzled out just feet ahead of me. I didn't let my shock slow me down. I was immediately on to the next tree, still jumping over roots and fallen sticks as fast as I could.

As another fireball rushed by my head, I knew Dorian couldn't be far behind. I gave up using the trees as support and let my legs carry me through the thick forest. I concentrated as much as I could to get that white fireball to appear in my fist.

Nothing came, not even a tingle.

How had this worked every other time fear overcame me, but it wasn't working now when I needed it the most?

Not fear, I reminded myself. *Anger.*

I dodged around another tree and shifted course to the left, hoping to confuse Dorian even if it only put him another second behind me.

My body continued to move forward, but my mind focused on all the things I could possibly think to be angry about.

I was angry at my mom for making us move every year, even though I pretended like I was fine with it. I was angry at Allie for acting like being a Davina was so easy. I was angry at Marek for trying to face Dorian on his own instead of letting Fletcher take care of it.

I was angry at Grace for choosing *me* and expecting me to do something with her powers when I had no clue, at my father for abandoning me and never coming back to explain any of it, at Clinton for all he did to my mom and our family, and at Fletcher for expecting so much from me.

My skin heated, and not just from running. All these thoughts bubbled to the surface. I thought for a moment that I might have to stop running to let myself puke.

You can't stop. Dorian isn't far behind.

I focused my anger on Dorian. If I had anything to be angry about, it was the sadistic pig on my tail. All the anger I felt sent me sprinting forward even faster.

I glanced behind me to see Dorian's body pass through the nearest tree like he was a ghost. With the curse keeping him from interacting with this realm, the trees weren't an obstacle for him.

He lunged for me. His solid body slammed into me, knocking me into a thick tree. Dorian fell to the ground. My shoulder ached from the impact, but I quickly recovered and continued running.

A distant scream reached my ears.

Dammit. My friends were still in danger, and I'd abandoned them.

I switched course again. My lungs grew heavy from the sprint. Ahead, a dull glow from the town's light pollution broke through the dense canopy. I'd circled around and was almost back to the valley. I sprinted out of the trees, tensed my shoulders, and hurled my body into the air.

Over my own labored breathing and the rush of air around my ears, I just barely caught the sound of battle below me. Grunts, screams, and the occasional firecracker pop of exploding essence echoed throughout the valley.

"No one's going to save you," Dorian shouted.

He was close. Too close.

He was also wrong.

A white-winged Davina flew high above the valley, surveying the area. Marek immediately dove for us with a white fireball ready in his palm. He hurled it at Dorian, but it only caught him in the ankle. Dorian faltered for a moment, but it wasn't enough to knock him out of the sky.

Below us, five demons remained, looking like nothing more than shadows in the night.

I noticed an extra pair of white wings. Another Davina had come to join the fight. He smashed a fist into the closest demon, sending him stumbling to the ground.

Beside them, Kyle raised his arm toward a nearby demon. A dagger glistened in his hand, reflecting the light from his essence in his other palm. He slashed downward, and the dagger sank into the demon's chest. Death was immediate, and the demon vanished from the valley.

The wind picked up, throwing off my balance in the sky. My wings began to tire as I wove a random path to keep from becoming an easy target.

Come on, Marek, I begged silently. *Knock him out of the sky already.*

The sound of Dorian's flapping wings grew closer.

Allie let out a scream.

My heart stopped in my chest when I saw a demon had knocked her to the ground and kicked her hard in the abdomen. He rose his foot above her face.

"No!" I cried. I immediately dove toward the demon.

I closed in on him fast, but before I made it, something struck my right wing. My wing seized up, paralyzed. I spiraled the remaining fifteen feet out of the sky and collided with the demon. The wind left my chest, and we skidded across the dirt.

I instinctively pulled my wings into me and quickly got to my feet before air returned to my lungs.

The first thing I noticed was the new Davina fighting a demon beside me. He was older, with graying white hair. His bare torso was toned, and he wore his regular tan slacks.

Fletcher.

I didn't have more than a split second to consider his presence. Dorian swooped down out of the sky with another ball of essence ready. I realized immediately that's what had struck my wing, though it hadn't been enough to knock me out. I threw myself to the grass, ducking out of the way of his next attack. Dorian continued flying with Marek still close on his tail.

Out of the corner of my eye, I caught the moment when Kyle raised his dagger to another demon. The demon lunged for him and seized his wrist. Kyle stumbled back but resisted against the demon's hold. The demon's elbow connected with Kyle's face. He snatched the dagger from his grasp and slashed it in Kyle's direction. Kyle dodged out of the way.

I scurried to my feet and rushed toward Kyle to offer my aid.

Allie made it to him first. Her weight crashed into the demon, but she wasn't strong enough to knock him off his feet. The demon grabbed ahold of her and pinned her to his chest. The blade he held pressed into her throat.

I stopped dead in my tracks as time slowed down. It felt as though someone had swung a baseball bat at my gut. Blood pulsed loudly in my ears, drowning out all other sounds.

I couldn't hear Marek above me shouting obscenities at Dorian. I never heard the *pop* of the fireball that exploded against Fletcher's shoulder and knocked him out. I never heard Kyle's body hit the ground as a demon tackled him and pinned his throat beneath his hands.

All I knew was that my best friend was about to die and there was nothing I could do to save her in the split second it would take the demon to slit her throat.

A panicked shriek ripped out of my lungs. "STOP!"

The valley went dead silent.

28

$\mathcal{E}$lectricity sizzled in my palm. A vibrant purple glow illuminated everything nearby—the grass, the demons, Allie.

A moment of clarity struck. I suddenly realized what had been holding me back all this time, why the Power of Grace only appeared intermittently.

Now was the time to use it to my advantage.

I raised my right palm threateningly at the demon holding the blade to Allie's neck. "Let. Her. Go."

Dorian's laughter reached my ears. I turned to find him standing just yards away with his head held high in confidence. His hand tangled in Marek's hair.

Marek's head tilted back, and he grimaced in pain.

Each remaining demon had ahold of one of my friends. I was the last one standing.

My knees shook. There was no way I could take them all on at once.

Dorian smiled in amusement. "Finally. You've been holding out on us, Little Angel."

That son of a bitch needed to stop calling me that.

My jaw tensed. "Let my friends go."

Dorian clicked his tongue and shook his head. "I'm afraid I can't do that. I told you this would happen."

It couldn't. I wouldn't let my friends die.

"How do you expect this to work out?" I demanded. "You have no power in this realm."

An evil grin spread across Dorian's face. "That's not true. Look around you. Who's in the position of power here? *I* call the shots now."

I swallowed the lump in my throat. I couldn't see a way out of this without my friends getting hurt.

"Isaac," Dorian called in a commanding voice. He gestured to the demon pinning Allie to his chest. "Over here."

Dorian forced Marek to his knees beside an unconscious Fletcher.

"Hands on your head," he commanded. "Or Isaac will slit the girl's throat."

Marek did as he was told.

Dorian snatched up a cloak left behind by one of his fallen comrades and tore off a piece of fabric. He forced Marek's hands behind his back and began tying them together with it.

Fletcher stirred on the ground.

One of the demons grabbed him by the neck and forced him to kneel beside Marek. He followed Dorian's example and tied him up.

Fletcher raised his eyes to mine. He had apology written all over his face.

The remaining two demons brought their hostages over and restrained them.

My hand with the fireball inside of it shook. "Please don't do this."

Dorian held his hand out to Isaac, who placed the blade inside it.

Dorian turned toward me with a hard look on his face. "I want you to watch as the life drains from each one of your friends' eyes. It's important that you know *this* is what happens to people who don't follow my orders."

He began pacing in front of the line of Davina kneeling at his feet. "Let's see… which one should we start with? The mentor, the boyfriend, the best friend, or…" His lips curled into a smile, and he pointed the dagger toward Kyle. "What's this one to you?"

"He's my friend!" I cried. "And I swear to God, if you touch one hair on his head—"

"What?" Dorian asked in amusement. "You'll use your powers to kill me? Honey, you've had every chance to knock me down, and so far you've failed to do so. Why is that?"

I hesitated. The purple fireball continued to glow in my palm, and I still couldn't bring myself to use it.

Because I won't stoop to your level.

"It's because you're *weak*," he barked.

"Then what do you want with me?" I snapped.

Dorian smirked. "You may be weak now, but you have potential. You just need a little direction, a little… motivation."

Dorian made a quick decision on his target and grabbed Allie.

"Stop! I'll go with you." The words shot out of my mouth before I consciously made the decision.

"NO!" Allie and Marek cried together.

"You can't do this, Ryn," Fletcher warned.

Dorian paused with the blade to Allie's throat. "You mean it?"

I didn't have any other choice. Even if I wanted to kill Dorian, my friends would immediately die at the hands of his recruits.

Allie stared at me intensely and shook her head the smallest bit.

The purple essence in my palm fizzled away. "Yes. I'll do whatever you want. Just don't hurt her."

"Good girl." Dorian released his grip on Allie and took a step toward me.

"Don't go with him, Ryn," Marek objected. "We're not worth it."

My eyes fell upon each one of them. In the past few days, they'd shown me a world that didn't just accept my insanity; they shared it with me. Marek had saved my life more than once. He was definitely worth it. All of them were.

"I'm sorry, Marek," I whispered. "You were right. There's no reasoning with him."

I stepped forward to accept my fate.

"Ryn, stop!" Marek insisted.

A demon kicked him in the head from behind. His face smashed into the dirt.

I drew in an involuntary breath. I made a move toward him but stopped myself when the demon raised his foot again. If I tried to save him, they'd only hurt him more.

"You can't go with him," Fletcher said. "Don't worry about us."

Marek lifted his head. "He's right, Ryn. The Davina need you!"

The demon kicked him in the gut, and he cried out in pain.

Kyle cringed beside him, and Allie let out a sob.

I glared at Dorian in horror. "Make him stop! I'm going with you. Let my friends go!"

Dorian grabbed my wrist tightly and pulled me toward him possessively. "I said I wouldn't kill them if you came with me. I never said I wouldn't hurt them."

Marek swung his leg around and knocked the closest demon off his feet. He tried to stand, but a second demon was on top of him a moment later, forcing his face into the dirt.

"Here, Isaac." Dorian held the handle of the blade out toward his friend. "Have fun."

Isaac took the blade. He bent beside Marek and pulled his head back by his hair. He laughed as he ran the blade across the side of Marek's face without breaking skin.

They're going to torture him. All of them.

"NO!" I screamed. "You can't do this!"

Dorian wrapped an arm around my waist and began dragging me away.

"Stop!" I kicked my feet out, but Dorian only squeezed tighter.

Suddenly, every muscle in my body contracted. An electric tingle began in my toes. With each inch it traveled up my body, the sensation intensified. Purple energy danced across the surface of my skin, lighting up my entire body like I was made of mystical lightning.

The demons beside Marek shot to their feet in alarm.

The energy grew in my chest, building exponentially each second until the feeling was so strong I couldn't breathe.

Dorian must've released me, but I never noticed. Every inch of my body was being crushed by an unseen force. I urged to cry out in pain, but I couldn't find my voice. In that moment, I thought for sure the energy would break me.

The next, the Power of Grace burst from my chest. A crack like thunder reverberated around me, and a purple energy wave rapidly swept across the valley in all directions. It blasted the standing demons backward in a single heartbeat.

The pain instantly subsided, and a numbness took over. I could no longer feel my limbs. Without warning, my body crumbled to the ground.

Real thunder roared above me. The first of the heavy raindrops hit my face a moment before the world completely faded away.

a bright light shone above me when I opened my eyes. I blinked the world into focus and saw I was lying in an unfamiliar bed. A door stood beyond a half-closed curtain to my right. Sunlight filtered through the window, casting a yellow ray across the tile floor.

My eyes continued to scan the hospital room until they fell upon my mother seated at my bedside. She stared down at the yarn she was twisting into knots. The afghan she was working on nearly touched the floor.

I cleared my throat.

Her eyes instantly met mine. "Kathryn."

She sounded surprised to see me awake. She quickly set her crocheting supplies aside and leaned forward to take my hand.

"How are you feeling?" she asked.

I carefully considered the question. I wasn't in pain, but I felt exhausted and hungry.

"I'm okay," I said in a scratchy voice. "What happened?"

I ran the events of the past few days back through my head. Had it all been a vivid dream I'd made up while in a coma?

Mom handed me a water bottle from the small table beside my bed. "Your friends said you passed out."

My friends? So it *had* been real.

"The doctors ran some tests," she told me. "They were worried about your heart when we brought you in, but your vitals have normalized since then. They wanted to keep you overnight for observation. They have no idea what happened."

And they never will.

I took a greedy gulp of water.

"Where are my friends?" I demanded.

Had they all gotten away from the demons safely?

"They went home last night. I said I'd let them know when you woke up."

"I want to see them." I didn't even give it a second thought.

"Let's wait a bit," she suggested. "We'll have the nurses check you again now that you're awake."

I would've much rather jumped out the window and flown back to Eagle Valley to check on my friends.

Mom pressed the nurse's call button.

I glanced around the room in search of my phone, but it wasn't on the table beside me or anywhere else within view. I didn't see my clothes anywhere, either. I wore nothing but a hospital gown.

"Where's all my stuff?" I sat up in bed, panicked.

Mom stood over me. "Calm down. It's all in a bag right there."

My eyes followed hers to see a plastic bag next to her chair with my clothes in it.

"Give me my phone," I insisted. "I need to call Allie."

"After the nurses take a look at you," Mom insisted.

I huffed and fell onto my back in the bed.

A nurse walked into the room. While she was checking my vitals, I turned back to my mom.

"You saw Allie last night?" I asked. "She's all right?"

My mom sat back in her chair. "Of course she is. Is there any reason she shouldn't be?"

I ignored the question. "Who else was with her?"

"Her boyfriend and that guy with the bike," she answered.

I didn't bother correcting her that Kyle wasn't Allie's boyfriend.

Mom frowned. "I really wished you would've told me where you were going. I said you could stay the night at Allie's, not wander around town at all hours of the night."

Of course. I was lying in a hospital bed and she still found something to chew me out about. I thought back to my car accident not even a year ago. This reminded me so much of that. Mom acted like she cared in the moment, but by the time I'd left the hospital, nothing had changed.

The nurse removed the blood pressure cuff from my arm. "Everything looks good for now. We'll get your doctor in here shortly." She smiled and left the room.

"You're lucky Mr. Fletcher was working late," Mom said.

"What do you mean?"

"You don't remember where you passed out? It was right in front of the school. One of your friends rushed to find help. Another called 911. Your advisor helped keep everything under control. I'm just glad there was an adult around."

"*My* advisor?" I couldn't help but notice her strange choice of words.

Mom tried to hide a smile. "Yes, I signed the paperwork. You're going to Galen High this year."

"Are you serious?" I squeaked, shooting upright in bed.

Mom surrendered to the smile. "Yes."

I sprang out of bed and threw my arms around her neck. "Thank you!"

Maybe something *had* changed between us this time.

My friends arrived an hour later. The doctor hadn't come to check on me yet. I guess when you're not dying, you don't get the expedited hospital discharge procedure.

I convinced Mom she should visit the craft store while we were nearby and that I'd be fine without her. I needed the privacy.

Allie rushed into the room and pulled me into a hug. "How are you?"

I shrugged. "A little weak, but I'll survive."

My eyes traveled past Kyle and Fletcher to land on Marek. His face was covered in bruises, but they already looked a few days old thanks to his fast healing abilities.

Marek stared at me like I was the only person in the room. He stood still for several long seconds, holding my gaze. Then, like he couldn't hold back any longer, he closed the distance between us in two long strides and bent to place a kiss on my forehead.

My heart danced in my chest.

Marek pressed his forehead to mine. "I'm so glad you're okay," he whispered. "Don't ever do something like that again."

It took me a moment to recover from his sudden display of affection.

I pulled away from him. "What do you mean?"

"Sacrificing yourself for the rest of us," he said. "Dorian was bluffing, Ryn. He didn't have the power to get you on his side; you're so much stronger than him. He was playing off your loyalty. Every move he made was meant to scare you."

I let out a breath in disbelief. "And you couldn't have pointed that out to me sooner?" I swatted at him.

He caught my wrist and laughed lightly.

I glanced toward everyone else. "You're all okay, then?"

Allie sat in the chair beside my bed. "We're all fine. It's *you* we're worried about."

"Don't be," I insisted. "Just tell me what happened. Did Dorian get away?"

Fletcher stuck his hands in his pockets and stepped forward. He gazed down at his feet like he was about to deliver bad news.

"What?" I asked in alarm. "What happened?"

"I know you dislike the idea of killing the Aedes," Fletcher said, "even if it's what Davina do, but it had to be done."

"You killed them?" I asked. "How? They had you all tied up."

Fletcher shook his head. "No, Ryn. *You* killed them."

Confusion struck. Had I heard him properly?

I furrowed my brow. "No, I didn't."

At least, I didn't remember.

Marek took my hand and nodded. "You used the Power of Grace."

My eyes widened. "That explosion that came from me… it killed them?"

"Yes," Fletcher confirmed. "It almost killed you, too."

I was struck silent, trying to make sense of it all.

Finally, I spoke. "How'd it kill the demons and not the rest of you?"

"We were lucky," Kyle said.

"It was a matter of circumstance," Fletcher explained. "The power came from your heart. It expanded at chest-level and missed those of us on the ground."

I suddenly realized how close I'd come to killing my friends. If the demons hadn't forced them to their knees, they'd be dead, too.

I dropped my gaze to my hands. "I didn't mean to kill anyone."

Marek squeezed my hand tighter. "No one's judging you, Ryn. You did what had to be done. Any other Davina would've done the same."

I looked up at him. "But I didn't know what I was doing."

"Perhaps that's what allowed you to summon so much power," Fletcher suggested. "It was never your intention to kill. It was your intention to save."

I considered Fletcher's words. I'd done what I had to in order to save them.

"Maybe the power came because I discovered the secret to unlocking it," I suggested.

Fletcher raised his eyebrows. The other three leaned in closer.

"I thought I conjured essence when I was angry," I told them. "But I was *really* angry when I was running through the woods, and I still couldn't manage to defend myself. It was only when that demon attacked Allie that anything actually happened. This whole time, that's been the key. I've only conjured essence when I was trying to *protect* someone."

I thought about the first time I'd conjured essence when I was eight. It was because Clinton was a danger to my mother.

"The first time at the party, I was defending Allie from that douche bag Tad," I pointed out. "That same night, I was defending Marek from the demon I killed. When we were practicing, I only felt a spark when Kyle was going off at Marek about stuff. See? I've only been making it work when I thought one of my friends was in danger."

"Hey," Kyle said defensively. "I wasn't putting Marek in danger."

"You were still being a dick," Marek accused.

Kyle shrugged like he couldn't argue with that.

"It's an interesting theory," Fletcher mused.

I stretched my hand out in front of me. "I think now that I know what was holding me back, I may be able to break through this."

I concentrated hard on my palm, flexing my muscles and picturing a white fireball.

Allie drew in a breath beside me.

A white orb rose from my palm. It wasn't the powerful purple it had been when we were fighting, but it was *progress*. I smiled involuntarily and then closed my palm. It disappeared in my fist.

I looked back at Fletcher. "I still have so many questions. How'd you end up fighting with us?"

Allie laughed and shot a glance at Marek. "Same way we did. Marek's fireworks display."

Marek scowled at her.

Fletcher nodded. "I was out in search of signs of the Aedes when I saw James's light show. I thought it was lightning at first."

"Yeah, so did we," I said. "I'm also curious about the knife. How'd it work on the demons?"

"It's a Davina Blade," Fletcher answered.

I remembered he had mentioned them before, about how they came from the Davina realm and were one of their only weapons.

"You had one this whole time?" I asked.

Kyle smirked beside him. "It was my dad's. He was a Protector. And a damn good one."

Fletcher nodded. "I knew him. Your family should've returned that blade after your father's death. Someone's surely wondering why the Protectors are a blade short."

"It was my *dad's*," Kyle bit harshly. "Besides, it came in quite handy. You're not going to make me return it to the Protectors, are you?"

Fletcher fell silent for a moment while considering the question. "No. I think we may want to keep it for now."

"Good. Because I'm not giving it back," Kyle said.

I took a deep breath. "What happened to me afterward?"

"I told you before that the power of an Original is too much for a mortal body to handle," Fletcher explained. "You accessed too much at once. You went into cardiac arrest."

I gasped. "Oh my God. How did I—?"

"Marek," Kyle answered. "Marek saved you."

I looked up at Marek.

He nodded slightly. "I used the blade to cut the fabric off my wrists. I gave you CPR until the medics showed up."

Tears of gratitude rose to my eyes.

"Thank you," I whispered.

He shook his head lightly. "You don't have to thank me."

I didn't care what Marek said. To me, he was truly an angel.

30

"Why are you stopping?" I asked.

Marek slowed his bike outside of town the next day. He parked along the shoulder of the road. "I told you I wanted to show you something."

"In the middle of nowhere?" I glanced around us.

A large hill covered in trees rose above us on the left side of the road, and a lush green meadow spanned the landscape to our right. A calm breeze rustled through the grass.

"Yeah," he answered, climbing off the bike.

I wasn't ready to let him go. All I wanted was to hang onto him tighter, but I reluctantly released him. I stepped onto the pavement and removed the helmet.

"Leave it on the bike," Marek said. "No one will bother it. Come on, it's this way."

Butterflies danced in my stomach when he grabbed my hand.

He didn't seem to notice. He looked both ways before leading me across the road.

I scanned the sunny landscape as we walked down the shoulder of the road. "Where are you taking me?"

A wide grin spread across his face. "It's right there."

Several paces later, I noticed a break in the trees ahead of us. Slowly, the wonder he'd pointed out began to reveal itself. Piles of

164

rock climbed the hill between the trees, forming a natural staircase. I imagined a waterfall once trickled through the area.

"Let's go." Marek released my hand and began climbing the dry falls.

I followed behind him.

Heaven help me. His ass looked perfect from this angle.

I tried to focus less on that and more on maintaining my footing. I used my hands to pull myself over tall rocks.

I tried to keep up with Marek, but he rushed like he'd done this a million times. He seemed to know exactly where to place his hands and feet to propel him up the hill.

Soon, the rocks became smaller and easier to climb over. I stood upright. I dusted my hands off on my jeans just as we broke through the trees onto a rocky hilltop.

"Where are we—?"

I was stunned into silence when we reached the top of the hill. In front of us spanned the entirety of Eagle Valley. More trees than I ever realized filled the town, and houses of all colors and sizes graced the landscape.

The vibrant green landscape stretched for miles past our small town. I longed to fly above it and explore the gorgeous scenery from new angles.

Up here, the world felt full of possibilities.

Marek lowered himself to the ground and rested his elbows on his knees. I sat beside him.

We gazed out onto Eagle Valley in silence. I noticed the roof of Galen High peeking up through a thick layer of trees at the other end of town. I concentrated close on where I thought the valley was. I spotted a thinning of trees, but it was nearly impossible to see unless you were looking for it.

Marek broke the silence. "Did I mention yet that I'm sorry?"

I turned to him. "Sorry for what?"

Marek raked his fingers through his hair. "I feel terrible about what happened. I never meant to put you in danger. I was supposed to protect you."

My heart sank. I hated to see him so upset.

"It all worked out in the end," I reminded him.

He stared straight ahead, not looking at me. "*This* time. What about the next time you're in danger?"

I shuddered at the thought. "Dorian's gone. I'm not *in* any danger."

Sadness fell across his face when he looked at me. "You can't know that. You have the Power of Grace, Ryn. There are a lot of people who would like to see you dead before you can find Grace and wake her. The demons would love to see the gateways to their realm open again. Right now, you're the only thing standing in their way."

"But they don't even know I *have* the Power of Grace. They don't know a war is coming," I argued.

"You don't know Dorian didn't tell anyone."

I hated to think Marek was right, but as far as I knew, I'd killed everyone Dorian told.

"If Grace is somewhere in Eagle Valley like Fletcher thinks she is, it won't take that long to find her," I pointed out.

Marek raised an eyebrow. "Do you have any clues on where to start?"

I bit my lip. "Well, no. But Eagle Valley isn't very big." I gestured to the town to prove its size.

"Ryn," he said softly. He glanced down at my hand resting on the ground then back up to my eyes.

My cheeks heated under his gaze. "Yeah?"

Marek reached out to slip his fingers into mine. "I want to be there to help you."

The air between us suddenly seemed charged with energy.

"Help me what?" I asked breathlessly.

"Search for Grace. Prevent a bigger war."

I nodded gratefully. "And I trust you'll be there."

It struck me how much I meant it. It'd been a long time since I felt I could count on someone the way I could with Marek.

His eyes danced across my face. "Just promise me something in return."

I fell so deep into his eyes that I practically forgot where I was. My mouth grew dry. "Yeah?"

"Promise me you'll be careful." He spoke so softly that I barely heard him.

"I—I'm not sure I want to be," I heard myself say.

"What do you mean?"

I could feel our bodies inching closer. "Sometimes, Marek, you have to take chances, even when they scare you. Even when the outcome could be as equally amazing as it could be devastating. You never know until you take that chance, until you—"

Marek's lips connected with mine, silencing my words.

In that moment, I forgot what I was going to say. I forgot all about the danger we'd just been discussing. All that seemed to matter were his lips against mine, his fingers tangling themselves in my hair, and my hands running down his back.

My fingers grazed against the scars beneath his shirt. For a moment, I was shocked. Then I only wanted to drag him closer to me, for him to let me kiss him all over and heal whatever emotional pain he'd been through. I knew trying to erase his past would be futile, but in that moment, I thought maybe I had the power to help the boy I'd seen in my dream.

Marek pulled me even closer. His tongue grazed across my bottom lip.

Good lord. This was even better than flying.

Far too soon, we parted.

For a moment, all seemed well in the world, but I couldn't help but hear Marek's words echo in my mind.

This time.

This time, things *had* turned out okay, but I couldn't shake the feeling that Marek was right. There was going to be a *next time*. And I had the strangest feeling that next time would be even worse. We'd only just won the first fight.

I knew what lay ahead was going to be a very long battle.

END OF BOOK ONE

TOUCHED BY GRACE

DIVINE FATE BOOK TWO

1

Flying through the sky in the midst of a raging thunderstorm was *not* how I pictured my first day at Galen High. Mrs. Anders called this a training exercise; I called it insanity.

Rain pounded down hard on my wings. I had to work ten times harder than normal to lift them and stay airborne. My soaked clothes weighed me down, and wet hair stuck to the side of my face. The frequent wind gusts weren't any help, either. My shoulders ached. I wasn't sure how much longer I could keep this up, but I'd be damned if I admitted defeat on my first day.

A hill rose ahead of me.

Only a lap and a half left.

The task was simple. Fly from one end of the valley to the other and back. Repeat five times. It reminded me of the grueling pacer tests I took at my old schools. Only this time, there was lightning.

Thunder cracked above me when I reached the far end of the valley and turned. Just when I thought it couldn't get any worse, the skies opened wider. I could hardly see through the thick downpour. My classmates had disappeared from view.

I pushed forward faster, flapping my wings as hard as I could. I hadn't been flying my whole life like everyone else in class had, but I *wasn't* going to be the last one back.

A wind gust rushed by me, throwing me off balance. My body lurched several feet to the left. In a moment of panic, my heart felt like it was falling out of my chest. I quickly steadied myself, but I couldn't tell if I was still on the right flight path.

I blinked away the rain and squinted ahead of me. Water continued to rush across my face, obscuring my view.

Lovely. Mrs. Anders was trying to kill me. Too bad she didn't realize my death would cause the end of the world.

Without warning, a blonde figure burst through the rain and slammed straight into me. Casey's screech filled my ears as we spiraled out of the sky. My legs twisted under me when we landed, and pain shot through my ankle. Casey fell on top of me. I gasped for breath as rain continued to beat down on us.

Blonde Bitch groaned and pushed herself to her feet. "Are you crazy, Ryn? If we were flying any higher, you'd have gotten us both killed!"

Air finally returned to my lungs. I rolled onto my stomach to keep from inhaling the rain.

"I couldn't see anything," I defended. "This whole exercise is suicide!"

Mrs. Anders swooped out of the sky and landed beside us. Her tall, muscular frame towered above me. Apparently *she* wasn't having any problem seeing through the rain. She'd been standing at the top of the valley with a damn umbrella watching us try to kill ourselves.

"What was *that*?" Mrs. Anders demanded. Her voice rose to be heard over the wind. "Didn't I emphasize at the beginning of class how important it was to stay in your own lane?"

Maybe she should've had us flying laps instead of sprinting in imaginary *lanes.*

Several students who'd already finished landed behind her to see what was going on. I didn't know most of them, but I recognized one of the guys who always hung out with Casey. I still wasn't sure if his name was Troy or Trenton.

I pushed myself to my feet. I tried not to put too much pressure on my right foot. "I'm fine, thanks for asking."

It wasn't exactly true. I was pretty sure I'd sprained my ankle from the fall.

"I'm glad to hear that," Mrs. Anders said. She didn't sound like she meant it. "But maybe we should have you sit out until you've had a little more practice."

I could hear it in her voice. She was *so* not pleased with having a total noob in her class.

I crossed my arms. "Or maybe *you* shouldn't run drills like this in the middle of a freaking storm!"

I realized what I'd said a moment too late. I'd never talked back to a teacher like that before. But who could blame me when rain was pounding down on us like this?

Mrs. Anders's brows shot up. "Are you trying to tell me how to run my class?"

Detention, here I come.

"No, I just—" I started, but Mrs. Anders cut me off.

"If you want to become a Protector, you're going to have to learn how to fight in even the most difficult circumstances."

The thing was, I wasn't sure I *did* want to become a Protector. Celebrity chef still sounded like a good job title, but that wasn't exactly Davina-specific.

"You never know when you'll have to fight a demon," she continued. "It could happen in the middle of a storm like this. I suggest you pay attention in your strategy class."

Didn't she realize this was literally my first day?

"Thanks, I'll be sure to do that," I said flatly.

Mrs. Anders stared down at my foot and frowned. She must've noticed I wasn't putting any weight on it.

She turned to Casey. "Miss Harris, would you please escort Miss Tyler back to school? Have Mrs. Banks check on her ankle."

Casey huffed. "Fine."

I limped along beside her as we headed toward the wooden stairs built into the tall hill. Casey reluctantly wrapped an arm under my shoulder to help steady me. I suspected she was only helping to get out of the rain.

We entered the forest along the trail that led back to school. The thick tree cover helped shelter us from the bulk of the rain, but the wind continued to rush through the trees.

"Is Mrs. Anders always like that?" I asked.

"Yeah, she's kind of a hardass," Casey answered.

"I take it she doesn't like new students."

"She doesn't like *incompetent* students," Casey emphasized.

Clearly she had some harsh feelings about being knocked out of the sky. That, or there was another reason she hated me. Namely, the hottest guy on two wheels in our class.

I had half a mind to tell Casey just how wrong she was about my incompetence, about how I'd killed five demons at once. But Fletcher didn't want anyone to know I had the Power of Grace. He didn't seem to trust all the Davina in town, and he certainly didn't want the demons hearing about it. Otherwise, I'd have more than just the *one* who wanted my head. Instead of telling everyone what really went down a week ago, Fletcher told them he'd taken care of Dorian himself.

Dorian. The thought of him twisted my stomach.

Casey and I hobbled across the school grounds. Galen High—or Galen Mansion, as I thought of it—towered three stories above us. We entered through the back door. Water squished through my tennis shoes and trailed behind us as Casey led me to the cafeteria.

I pulled a heavy mahogany chair out from the closest table and sank into it. Without a word, Casey turned from me and disappeared behind a swinging door that led to the kitchen. I took a deep breath and began wringing my hair out onto the hardwood floor. I shivered.

My eyes scanned the cafeteria. Four long rows of dark antique-looking tables spanned the length of the room. Each was lined with ten chairs on both sides. A large serving window was cut out between the kitchen and the cafeteria in the corner of the room. This place looked more like a reception hall than a high school cafeteria.

Casey returned shortly with a red-headed lady wearing a hair net.

"Hi, I'm Mrs. Banks," she introduced herself.

I returned her smile. "I'm Ryn."

"And I need to go change." Casey turned on her heel and left the room.

Mrs. Banks pulled out a chair and gestured for me to lift my ankle. She peeled back my wet jeans and inspected it while she spoke. "I'm sorry we don't keep a nurse on staff, so you're stuck with me. But don't worry; I have a background in medicine."

"Why doesn't Galen have a school nurse?" I asked.

"There aren't enough students for it to make sense," Mrs. Banks answered. "Out of the eighty kids who attend, we maybe have two or three a year who require medical attention."

She pressed on my ankle in search of tender spots. Luckily, there didn't seem to be too much damage.

"I think I'll be fine," I said. "Can I get some ice?"

"Sure." Mrs. Banks gently set my ankle down and stood.

Just as she disappeared into the kitchen, Fletcher walked by the cafeteria doors. He stopped when he noticed me. Fletcher wore his usual tan slacks and button-down shirt. He'd rolled up the sleeves, which looked strangely casual on him. It wasn't exactly the type of look I expected to see on a sixty-something-year-old guy.

He stepped into the room. "Are you okay, Ryn?"

I pushed my wet hair out of my face and smile reassuringly. "Everything's fine. I've just been introduced to Mrs. Anders's flying class. She's a lovely woman."

Fletcher smirked. "I take it things didn't go well?"

"Nah. I only fell a mile out of the sky and twisted my ankle."

Fletcher raised his eyebrows. "A whole mile, huh?"

I held back a laugh and nodded.

Mrs. Banks returned with an ice pack and a towel to mop up the wet floor beneath me.

"Can I borrow that?" I asked as soon as she was done.

She handed me the towel.

I used it to dry my hair out. Too bad I didn't bring extra clothes. I wasn't looking forward to walking around in wet underwear all day.

Allie should've warned me.

I handed the towel back and looked at Fletcher. "Why aren't you in class?"

"It's my prep period," he stated. "I was working on copying some papers. Since you have some free time, why don't you stop by my classroom once you get cleaned up? There's something I'd like to discuss with you."

It sounded like bad news. This had to be the worst first day of school ever, and I wasn't even a full hour into it.

I thanked Mrs. Banks and then hurried to the bathroom. I pushed through the door just as Casey was making her way out. She'd changed into dry clothes and brushed out her hair. She breezed past me without saying a word.

I sighed and turned to the hand dryer on the wall. I did the best I could drying out my hair and shoes, but my jeans still stuck to my legs like packaging tape.

I turned to the wide mirror above the sink. My eye makeup had been smeared from the rain, and the cute curls I'd put my hair in this morning were now flat. I ran my fingers through my hair to help with the tangles, but it didn't help. Even the pretty purple dangly earrings I'd put in this morning couldn't help improve my disheveled appearance.

I eventually gave up and headed down the hall to Fletcher's classroom.

"Miss Tyler," he greeted. He stood from his desk and grabbed a large roll of paper the size of a baseball bat.

I sank into one of the desks at the front of the room and pressed the icepack to my ankle. "What am I in trouble for?"

Fletcher furrowed his brow. "You're not in trouble. I just wanted to give you this." He unrolled the paper across my desk.

I scanned it for several seconds before realizing it was a map of Eagle Valley.

I looked up at him. "What do I need this for?"

"I thought if you had a visual, you might have an easier time pinpointing Grace's location," he said.

I sighed heavily. *Grace,* the ancient Davina who remained our only hope for defeating the Aedes. For reasons that still baffled me —and probably everyone else—it was up to *me* to awaken her. I just had to find her first.

I could hear Fletcher's voice in my mind. *You were chosen by Grace. Her magic will lead you to her.*

He'd said that to me two weeks ago. According to him, some sort of divine fate had brought me here. Apparently that was proof Grace was nearby.

I wasn't sure I believed him. But maybe this map would inspire me.

I could only hope, because if something didn't happen soon, the Davina would be facing the end of the world alone. And I wasn't sure we'd win.

2

I took the time I had before second period to drop the map off in my locker outside Fletcher's classroom. The modern lockers looked strange in contrast with the older architecture of the mansion.

The bell rang while I stood at my locker double checking my schedule for the day. The hall filled with students. Several people stared at me as they passed, no doubt wondering about the new girl.

I noticed Allie immediately. She seemed well within her comfort zone, shooting smiles and waving at people as she passed. She hadn't held back on the makeup today. Her eyes were outlined in black, and she'd twisted her dark hair into a cute updo with loose tendrils framing her face.

Allie's face fell when she saw me. I probably looked like a drowned rat.

"A little warning would've been nice," I said lightheartedly.

Allie leaned against her locker beside mine. "I'm so sorry. You must've had Mrs. Anders first period."

I ran my fingers through my damp hair. "That obvious?"

She nodded. "Don't feel bad. I totally forgot a change of clothes. I have her later today."

I kept my schedule in my hand and shut my locker. "What'd you have first period?"

"Magical defense."

I scanned the schedule I'd received this morning. "I don't see that class on here."

Allie's brows drew together. She stood beside me to inspect my schedule. "Maybe Fletcher got you out of it. You know, because…"

Because I still wasn't great at controlling whether or not my magic would stun or kill. And we didn't want to accidentally reveal I had the Power of Grace. That's why Fletcher and Marek had been training me in private.

"You have Fletcher next period with me," Allie said. "That's our mentor group. That class is a little different. They like to mix up the grades for training so we can mentor the younger ones."

I barely heard the last half of what she said as my gaze locked on Marek. His brown hair stood up in the front like he'd put effort into styling it that way. He strolled down the hall with his hands tucked casually in the pockets of those tight jeans I liked. He'd ditched his leather jacket and wore a light blue t-shirt that matched his eyes. A confident smile touched his lips like he was happy to be back at Galen High after a long summer.

I had the strongest desire to kiss those lips.

It'd been nearly two weeks since our first kiss. Since then, I hadn't gotten so much as a peck from him. The guy hadn't even *held my hand* in days. Sure, he had a thing for saving my life, but apparently kissing me more than once would be too much to show he cared.

It wasn't like we didn't spend time together. In fact, we'd spent every day training together since the kiss. I'd been practicing how to fly and learning how to conjure fireballs. Though, in Marek's words, *they're not fireballs.*

He smiled at me as he entered Fletcher's classroom.

That's it?

I had half a mind to call Marek out on his behavior right then and there. I scowled and followed behind Allie into the room.

Fletcher gestured to the desks in front of us. "We don't have assigned seats. You can sit anywhere you'd like."

I returned to the seat at the front of the room where I'd left my icepack. Marek sat on my right while Allie took the desk to my left.

Two terrified freshman boys had claimed the desks farthest from the door.

"Hey," Marek said with a sympathetic smile.

I ran my fingers through my hair nervously. "Hi."

Marek glanced down at the icepack. "Are you okay?"

"Just a mishap in flying class," I answered.

Kyle found his way into the room a minute later, followed closely by two girls I didn't know. He sat next to Allie. An uncomfortable silence hung in the air. It was cut only by the sound of the bell.

A young boy rushed into the room and shyly took a seat next to the other freshmen. "Sorry I'm late," he breathed.

"Not to worry." Fletcher stood from his desk. "To some of you, welcome back. To the others, welcome to Galen High."

The freshman boys sank in their seats with wide eyes, looking positively terrified.

"I'm your mentor, Fletcher. This class gives you the chance to hone your skills and improve in any areas you might be struggling in. We all work together to help each other reach their full potential. You may come to me at any time with questions. Now, take a look around you."

My eyes scanned the room and met several other gazes.

"This is your team," Fletcher explained. "We're here to lift each other up and learn how to fight together. This is the team you'll be with for battles. At times, we will be divided based on skill level."

Wonderful, I thought. *He's going to place me with the freshmen.*

"For example," he continued. "The upperclassmen have their first battle next week during the last period of the day. Obviously, we don't want the freshmen going up against other upperclassmen so soon, so your first battle will be in about a month."

One of the freshman boy's eyes widened.

"Don't worry," Fletcher assured him. "You'll start out up against people of your own skill level. We don't have any juniors in our group this year, so the sophomores—" he gestured to the two girls I didn't know "—will have a chance to battle with the seniors."

Fletcher turned to the whiteboard behind his desk and popped the cap off a black marker. "First things first. Let's hear some suggestions for this year's team name."

"We're sticking with the Saints," Kyle said, like he'd made the decision for the whole group.

Fletcher wrote *Saints* across the board. "Any other suggestions?"

"I like Saints," the red-headed sophomore said.

"We've always been the Saints," Marek pointed out. "I say we keep it."

Fletcher turned from the board. "This is an entirely new team this year, but if everyone is in agreement, we can recycle the name from last year's team."

The freshman boys seemed too afraid to say anything. The rest of us agreed to call our team the Saints.

Silence fell over the room. I took the opportunity to raise my hand nervously.

"Yes, Ryn?" Fletcher called on me.

"Yeah, I have a few questions. First, what are the battles?"

Fletcher leaned against his desk. "Good question. They're mock battles. Your team will go up against another team of students to practice your skills in a real-life setting. You'll be able to use your wings, your magic, or your hand-to-hand skills. There are a few variations. Sometimes you're allowed to stun, and the last team standing wins. Other times, stunning is off limits, and you'll have to rely on your combat skills to beat the other team."

My jaw dropped. "Don't people get hurt?"

"It wouldn't be fun if nobody got hurt," Kyle said with a smile.

A boy gasped from behind me.

"Where do you think this came from?" Kyle gestured to his slightly crooked nose. "Started healing before we could set it."

"The battles are supervised, and there are rules," Fletcher clarified. "You have nothing to worry about. The accident Kyle's referring to took place during an unscheduled and unsupervised training session, and he didn't seek medical attention as he should have."

Kyle smirked and shot Marek a glance like they shared some sort of inside joke.

"The battles are like football," Kyle said. "Sure, someone's bound to get hurt once in a while. But instead of playing other schools, we play against other Davina."

"So, it's like a sport? A game?" I asked.

"Yes," Fletcher answered. "Each win earns you points."

One of the freshman boys shot his hand into the air.

"Logan?" Fletcher called on him.

Logan spoke softly. "Do we have to participate?"

A sympathetic expression fell over Fletcher's face. "I will not *force* anyone to do anything they don't want to do, but I will point out that the purpose of Galen High is to prepare you to become a Protector. You're going to have to know how to fight. Unless you'd rather be working in Galen High School's kitchens as soon as you graduate."

Yes, please! Where do I sign up?

He raised his brows like that would be the worst thing in the world. "One day, perhaps sooner than you think, you'll be up against the Aedes. As Davina, it's our duty to protect the earth. We do that one Aedes at a time."

Another boy raised his hand.

"Yes, Ethan?" Fletcher said.

"My mom says that fighting the demons is pointless. That there are so many of them that the Protectors will never be able to keep up."

Fletcher raised his brows. "Yes, there are a lot of Aedes, but—"

The final boy cut in. "My parents say being a Protector is super dangerous, that you're just as likely to kill a demon as they are to kill you."

A shiver ran down my spine at the thought.

The room broke into whispers. The three freshman boys leaned together to discuss all the rumors they'd heard. Kyle hissed something in Allie's ear about how dumb the freshmen were.

Marek leaned over to me. "Don't worry. That's what your training's for."

"Calm down," Fletcher commanded.

The room went silent.

"Yes, there are a lot of Aedes out there," Fletcher said. "But how many do you think there would be if there *weren't* Protectors minimizing the threat? As for fighting them, there's a chance they'll kill you first, just like in any war."

Chatter began its way around the room again.

"Why are we even fighting them?" Ethan asked, sounding genuinely curious.

Fletcher tilted his head like he couldn't understand why anyone would ask such a question. "Because, Ethan, they feed off human essence. We fight them because this is our world, too. If we don't strike first, the Aedes will wipe us out. Then they'll get the humans to destroy each other. We may not have the numbers to eliminate every threat, but we will certainly do what we can."

Ethan raised his hand again and began speaking before Fletcher could call on him. "Doesn't legend say the portals to the demon realm could open back up one day?"

My breath stopped.

Fletcher answered calmly, but I sensed a hint of fear in his expression. "It's always a possibility, Ethan, but so is the chance that the Davina realm will open again as well. If such a thing *did* happen, you'd want to be prepared, wouldn't you?"

Fletcher's eyes connected with mine for only a split second. I still managed to catch his silent message.

Time was running out, and I wasn't prepared yet.

"Did you see the look Fletcher gave you?" Allie asked after second period.

Even after all the questions that filled the last half hour of class, I still couldn't get that look out of my head.

"You noticed?" I asked.

Marek stopped beside us. "How's that coming, by the way?"

"What do you mean?" I opened my locker and placed the warm icepack inside.

Kyle leaned against the locker next to mine. "We all saw the look. Fletcher's obviously curious how things are coming along."

"They're not really coming along at all," I admitted. "I need more training. Maybe there's more to my powers than I've discovered so far." I paused. "Or *maybe* he could be a little more helpful than handing me a map and hoping I'll be able to point at a spot and solve all our problems."

"I'm sure he doesn't expect that of you," Allie said kindly.

I resisted the urge to roll my eyes and tell her just how much it felt like it.

"We'll figure it out," Marek said with certainty.

He was so close in the crowded hall that I could feel the warmth radiating off him. I wished he would pull me into his arms.

"What's your next class?" he asked.

"Physical combat," I told him.

"Me, too. Let's walk together." That was all it took to make me feel ten times better.

"Kyle and I are in that class, too," Allie said.

The four of us walked upstairs together. We entered a small classroom that mirrored Fletcher's and sat in the back corner.

My stomach dropped when Blonde Bitch entered the room and took the seat in front of me. She didn't even look like she'd been flying through a rain storm earlier today. I noticed a couple of other students from first period had also cleaned up.

A dark-skinned man who looked to be in his fifties stood at the front of the room. His blue polo shirt must've had slits in the back for his wings since they rose out of his back.

My class schedule told me his name was Mr. Collins.

"Calm down, everyone." Mr. Collins rose his voice over the thick chatter.

The room quieted.

"Unfortunately with the rain," he said, "we're going to be having class inside today."

"Upstairs?" one of the guys across the room asked.

Mr. Collins shook his head. "No. Today, we'll cover this year's curriculum."

I shot Allie a questioning look. "Upstairs?"

She leaned over and whispered to me. "We sometimes train on the third floor when it's too cold outside."

"Quiet please," Mr. Collins said sternly.

I looked to the front of the room to see he was staring straight at me.

"You must be Kathryn Tyler, our new student."

"Uh, yeah. Call me Ryn."

"Why don't you come up and introduce yourself?"

Ugh. I was hoping I wouldn't have to do this.

I tried not to limp on my sore ankle as I stood from my desk and walked to the front of the room. The class was small—with maybe only a dozen people—but it didn't make me any more eager to introduce myself.

I faced the class. "Hi. I'm Ryn. I just moved here."

There. That should satisfy him. It's not like there's much else to say.

"Which school are you transferring from?" Mr. Collins asked.

I opened my mouth to answer, but then I realized he wasn't talking about just any school.

"This is my first time at a Davina school," I said.

He frowned. "And they put you in my combat class? Do you have any experience?"

Were all the teachers at this school asshats?

"I took martial arts as a kid." Not that I remembered a whole lot from it, but I knew how to block a punch.

Mr. Collins pressed his lips together like he wasn't impressed. When he didn't say more, I returned to my seat. It looked like I was going to have to work extra hard to get my teachers to like me.

Casey's eyes followed me all the way back to my desk. She scoffed and tossed her hair over her shoulder as she returned her attention back to the front of the room. She didn't seem to notice her hair spilling onto the top of my desk.

I gritted my teeth in annoyance. *She's probably trying to mark her scent all over me as a way to get to Marek.* I narrowed my eyes at the back of her head. It was because she realized she had competition, and not just in the romance department. I certainly had a shot at beating her in a battle. *Maybe.*

"If looks could kill…" Allie mused on our way to the cafeteria after our fourth period battle strategy class.

"What?" I honestly had no idea what she was talking about.

Allie smirked. "I saw you throwing daggers at the back of Casey's head in physical combat."

"I'm obligated to hate her," I pointed out. "I'm your friend, and you despise her."

I didn't mention there were other reasons I wasn't fond of Casey. I worried she still liked Marek. But that whole thing apparently happened way back in freshman year. Casey should've moved on by now.

Besides, Marek would never go for her anyway, I told myself.

My second inner voice quickly countered. *Then why doesn't he seem interested in you lately?*

I ignored the voices battling it out in my head. Instead, I focused on the smell of burgers and tatertots wafting from the cafeteria. In the lunch line, Mrs. Banks winked and slipped me a few extra tots. So far, that was the highlight of my day.

Allie led me to a table in the far corner of the lunchroom, where Marek and Kyle joined us shortly after.

"Hey, Ryn," Marek kept his voice low. "I was thinking about what you were saying earlier."

I swallowed my food quickly. "About what?"

"About Fletcher expecting you to point to a spot on the map he gave you."

"And?" I raised my eyebrows.

"I think you might be on to something. Maybe try the dart thing," he suggested. "It worked for you before."

Allie tilted her head in question.

"It's what brought me here," I explained to her. "Mom let me choose where we were moving this time. I left it up to fate by tacking a map to the wall and throwing a dart at it. Landed right on top of Eagle Valley."

Maybe Marek was right and fate would lead me to Grace again.

Allie's eyes widened. "You really think that'll work?"

I shrugged. "Doesn't hurt to try. Want to come over after school? We'll see if we can find Grace."

4

"**W**as it terrible?" Allie asked on our way home from school.

"Was what terrible?" I tore my gaze from the gray sky and looked at her from where I sat in the passenger seat. My backpack and the map sat in my lap.

"Your first day," she said. "Was it as bad as you thought it'd be?"

"Not too bad," I lied. My jeans were still damp from this morning. "I'm used to being the new kid. Except, I think people seemed a little more interested in me than normal."

I swear every person I walked past had to stare at me.

"It's because it's a tiny school," Allie said with a shrug. "What else are people going to be interested in? Besides, you're pretty. It makes you more interesting."

I batted my eyes at her. "You think so?"

She laughed.

I quickly composed myself. "In reality, they were only staring because I look like I just crawled from the depths of Malum."

Allie shot me a shocked expression.

"Sorry," I said regrettably. "Was that offensive? I just meant—"

"No," Allie interrupted. "I just didn't expect you to make a Davina joke."

I relaxed.

"And you were worried you wouldn't fit in," she teased.

"I wasn't worried." *Okay, maybe a little bit.*

I quickly changed the subject. "Is it just me, or did it seem like Fletcher was ignoring me during history?"

Allie pulled into her driveway. "He wasn't ignoring you. He was teaching. He has, like, two totally different personalities. One minute, he's in mentor mode; the next, he's in teacher mode. It's like somewhere between second and sixth period he turns into a completely different person. Don't take it personally."

"I'll try not to," I said, stepping out of the car.

Allie and I crossed her lawn onto mine and headed up my porch steps.

"How was school?" Mom called when we entered the house.

I poked my head into the living room. "It was good. Lots of homework. Allie and I are going upstairs to work on it."

Mom looked up from the scarf she was crocheting. "Okay. Don't forget about your chores."

I turned so she wouldn't see me roll my eyes.

Upstairs, I dropped my bag at the foot of my bed and unrolled the map across the mattress.

"Feel anything?" Allie asked hopefully.

I shook my head. I couldn't believe Fletcher actually thought this might work.

"Maybe we should start in our history book," I suggested. "There might be a clue about Grace in there."

Allie looked uncertain. "Wouldn't someone have found her already if there was?"

My shoulders dropped. "I guess so."

"I like Marek's idea," Allie said with a shrug. "You made it to Eagle Valley. You've come this far already."

And there was still no guarantee Grace was here. It was only a theory.

I sighed. "Okay."

I turned to my dresser and opened the top drawer. I rummaged around through the junk and found two stray pushpins. I used them to tack the poster-sized map to the wall.

I turned to my closet and felt around in the darkness for my pile of shoeboxes.

"Here," I said, handing Allie a shoebox. "Check to see if there are any darts in there."

Allie sat on my bed and pulled the top off the box. "I thought you said you'd unpacked everything."

My voice became muffled as I stuck my head deeper into my closet. "I did. I just keep a few boxes of junk that never get unpacked. There's no point in it."

"Then why do you keep this stuff?"

"I figure it might come in handy at some point. Like this." I drew away from the closet and held up a dart in triumph. "You ready?"

Allie set her shoebox aside. "You betcha."

I stood across the room and angled myself toward the map. Nerves fluttered in my gut when I drew my arm back, closed my eyes, and hurled the dart toward the wall. I heard it land softly—not a noise I was expecting.

I slowly peeled my eyes open. Confusion hit when I saw the map remained dart-free. The dart never made it that far. Instead, it stuck straight into my carpet.

Allie burst into laughter and rolled herself onto the bed like she couldn't control herself.

"Maybe... you should keep... your eyes open," she suggested between laughs.

Maybe you should bite me.

I snatched the dart up from the ground. "I wasn't trying to *aim*."

She composed herself enough to sit back up. "Well, at least aim for the *map*."

I sighed and turned back to face the wall. Keeping my eyes open this time, I locked my gaze on the map, not focusing on any area in particular. This time, when the dart flew from my fingers, it hit the wall with a satisfying *thud*.

"Yes!" I cried in victory.

Allie and I hurried over to the map to see where it hit. It landed near the center atop a small, clear section of grass.

I let out a breath in annoyance. "Great. According to this, we'll find Grace in the middle of nowhere."

Allie leaned closer to the map. "No, that's the park. We should check it out."

I plopped down on my bed. "I'm not sure I feel fate guiding me on this one."

"It's worth a shot," she said. "Would you rather sit here reading our history book or be out there taking action?"

When she put it that way, the answer was obvious.

Action, it was.

5

"I told you this would be useless," I said to Allie on our third walk around the park. "All that's here are some trees and a playground."

"There are a couple of buildings," Allie pointed out.

I glanced around and inhaled the scent of rain that still hung in the air. "Are you suggesting Grace is living in one of the toilets? Because I don't think the bathrooms or the pavilion have been here that long."

Allie spun slowly in a circle, gazing out into the distance. "Maybe we're missing something. Maybe there *was* a building here when the town was settled. Or *maybe* she's buried somewhere beneath our feet."

"Don't you think there'd be a marker? Like a gravestone or something?"

Allie shrugged. "I don't know. Maybe one of these trees marks the spot they left her. Or maybe you were a little off when you threw the dart. She *could* be in the cemetery. That must've been around as long as the town has been here."

"Where's that at?" I asked.

"Just over there." Allie pointed past the playground. "On the other side of those trees."

I sighed heavily. "I don't know. I honestly just feel like going home. We could give our history book a shot, and—"

"Heads up!"

Allie and I jumped out of the way just in time as a Frisbee flew by our heads.

"Holy crap!" Allie cried, holding a hand over her heart. "Are you *trying* to decapitate us, Trenton?"

I recognized the guy jogging toward us. He was the bigger of the two guys who always hung out with Casey, the one in my flying class. Finally, I could match a name to the face.

Trenton pushed wavy blond hair from his eyes and bent to pick up his Frisbee. He shot Allie a sly smile. "So what if I was? Doesn't hurt to scare the competition a little, does it? I hear we're going up against you next week for our first battle."

Allie dropped her hand from her chest. "We're not trying to *kill* each other. Sometimes I think you guys take this competition thing way too seriously. One day, we'll be fighting alongside each other. You know that."

"Relax," Trenton said. "I was only joking. It's Casey who's serious about the competition. You know how she is."

Allie scrunched up her nose like she knew *far* too well.

Trenton turned to me and stuck his hand out. "Hi, I'm Trenton. Ryn, is it?"

I nodded and took his hand. He had a strong grip.

"I hear you've been flying well this past week." A slight smile touched his lips.

Allie's brows shot up. "From who? Casey? I find it hard to believe Casey would give such a compliment to someone other than herself."

"You really hate her, don't you?" Trenton asked, amused. "Actually, Troy was telling me."

I blushed slightly, thinking back to a few days ago when I'd been training with Marek and didn't realize I had an audience. By the time I landed, several groups had entered the valley. I remembered Casey and Troy being among the crowd.

"It's nice of him to notice," I said. "Why haven't you been showing up with Casey and Troy to practice?"

"I've been out of town visiting family," Trenton explained.

Allie glanced around. "Where's your team now?"

"Um... not sure. We don't spend every waking second together."

It seemed like they did. I rarely saw Casey without being followed by her two bodyguards.

Trenton smiled. "It's just me, playing a round of Frisbee golf. Any chance you want to join me? I have a few extra discs in the car."

I was surprised at how kind Trenton seemed without Casey around. I was just about to accept his offer when Allie answered for me.

"Actually, we're kind of busy," she lied. "We have to get home to work on our homework."

Trenton spread his arms wide. "On the first day of school? Blow it off. You'll still graduate."

A little part of me wanted to agree with him.

"Come on, Ryn," Trenton encouraged, nudging me with his elbow. "Don't be afraid of me just because I hang out with Casey." He stared down at me and smiled sweetly.

"I guess we could play *one* game," I heard myself say.

Trenton's smile grew. "Great. I'll go grab my extra discs." He hurried toward his car while Allie and I walked slowly toward the first disc golf platform.

"What are you *doing?*" she hissed.

"I don't know. I figured it wouldn't hurt to have more Davina friends. We might compete during mock battles, but like you said, we're not enemies."

"Yeah, but he's *hitting* on you."

"No, he's not," I insisted.

"He complimented your flying. Plus, did you *see* the way he looked at you?"

"You mean guys can't compliment me without flirting? And I don't think he looked at me in any special way."

"Okay, maybe he wasn't *hitting* on you, but he's definitely acting strange," she said. "It's usually all trash talk with Casey's group."

"Maybe he's different when he's not around her," I pointed out.

"Maybe," Allie agreed with a hint of skepticism in her voice.

Allie and I stopped at the platform and waited for Trenton to return with his discs.

Allie went first. Her disc flew in an arc and ricocheted off a tree. It landed in a mud puddle fifteen yards away. I held back a laugh.

Allie turned to me. She didn't look amused in the slightest. "Let's see *you* do better."

I stepped to the front of the platform and swung my arm around, flicking my wrist at the last second. My disc flew gracefully through the air and landed halfway to the basket. I smiled at her and stepped aside for Trenton.

He drew his arm back for an underhand swing. "Let me show you ladies how it's done."

His strong arm swung around, and his disc flew above the grass with speed and precision I couldn't imagine myself having. The disc landed mere yards from the basket.

My eyebrows shot up. I was impressed.

The game continued like that for the next hour. It turned out I wasn't half bad at Frisbee golf. I wasn't as good as Trenton, but I beat Allie by fifteen points.

"You know," Allie said on our ride back home from the park. "We never checked out the cemetery."

"Sorry," I said. "I didn't mean to get sidetracked. We don't really have time tonight. My mom's going to be on my case as it is since I ran off before doing my chores. We'll check out the cemetery another time."

"Yeah," Allie said slowly, not taking her eyes off the road. "I just hope we figure all this out soon."

6

I woke with dread the following day. Rain gently tapped against my window, which meant another day of torture in first period. I packed my backpack with a change of clothes and extra makeup. Luckily, by the time Allie and I made it to school, the rain had let up. Unfortunately, that didn't make Mrs. Anders's flying class any easier.

We met her at the top of the valley. Below, several groups of students threw white fireballs at foam targets. Another group watched their mentor demonstrate how to block punches.

My jaw dropped in awe. It was like the entire valley had transformed into a training arena since I'd last seen it. Before school started, it was peaceful and quiet. Marek and I almost always had the place to ourselves. Now, it seemed crowded. The extra training equipment scattered around the vast field beneath us only took up more space. My eyes darted between each group of students, trying to take in the wonder of seeing so many Davina in action.

I didn't have long to observe the scene before Mrs. Anders blew her whistle and called us to attention.

Today's exercise involved performing flips in the sky like we were freaking gymnasts. It was supposed to help us learn how to correct our flight if we were ever attacked while airborne. As far as I was concerned, she could shove her whistle and this entire training exercise where the sun don't shine.

Mrs. Anders blew her whistle and yelled at me at least six times. I was sure she'd like nothing more than for me to sulk back to the school and demand to drop her class.

But I didn't.

I was, however, relieved when first period ended.

In second period, Fletcher led our group of nine back out to the valley. He turned to us when we emerged from the forest. "Settle down."

The sophomore girls giggled next to each other, and the three freshman boys whispered amongst themselves. Marek and Kyle had been talking, too, but I didn't catch what they were saying. It took several moments before everyone went silent.

"Today, I will be assessing your skills." Fletcher spoke loudly. "We'll do this several times throughout the year to see how you've improved and to identify which areas our team needs to work on. I want Ethan, Logan, and Dylan to start with conjuring essence. Allie and Kyle, I'd like your help with them."

I could only pray for whichever kid ended up with Allie as their teacher. She was a great friend, but she hadn't exactly been much help when teaching me how to conjure fireballs.

"Emily and Ruby—" he gestured to the two sophomore girls "—you can start on targets. You know the drill. Marek, I want you to help Ryn on her hand-to-hand skills."

Everyone split off in their own directions.

"Why don't *I* get to practice with targets?" I asked Marek as he led me to a clear stretch of grass out of the way of the other Davina.

"Your essence still shines purple sometimes," Marek reminded me. "We don't want to risk anyone seeing that. We'll practice on our own after school."

"Allie and I have plans today," I told him.

Marek frowned. "We already missed practicing yesterday."

I held my hands up. "No need to throw a temper tantrum. I need time to search for Grace. Or would you rather I spend all my time training with you?"

The answer was obvious; I had to be out there doing *something* to find Grace. But I had this strange desire to hear him say he'd rather spend time with me.

"Okay, tomorrow then," Marek decided. "We'll need to find

somewhere else to train, though. The valley's not private enough now that school started. We had a few close calls last week."

"James Marek," I teased, "are you asking me out on a date?"

I could only hope he'd say yes.

"No," he answered too quickly.

My heart dropped. I'd only been joking; I didn't expect the rejection to hit me that hard. Stupid overactive hormones.

Marek leaned into me and spoke softly. "If I took you on a date, it'd be special. Not the same training we've been doing."

And just like that, my heart lifted to settle back in its proper place in my chest.

I elbowed him lightly. "I was only joking, but if the offer for a date ever *is* on the table, I'll take you up on it." I grinned widely.

Apparently, I wasn't being obvious enough, because Marek didn't say another word on the date front. He *had* to know I was into him. We'd kissed! Or maybe that was the problem. Maybe he didn't like the kiss. Maybe he didn't feel the same chemistry I did. Maybe—

Marek's arm swung out and caught my left shoulder.

"What the hell?" I cried, holding onto my arm. I knew he was going easy on me, but dammit, that *hurt*. "I wasn't ready."

"That's the idea," he said with a smile.

And that smile was all it took for my mind to fall back into daydreaming about him. The damn boy was distracting as all hell.

He swung another fist at me. I ducked and then immediately aimed a foot at his abdomen. We weren't trying to hurt each other, but I didn't think it mattered how hard I kicked him. It still felt like kicking a stone wall.

"Good job," Marek encouraged, circling me like he'd felt nothing. "But you'll have to do better if you're going to stand a chance against a demon."

"Give me a break."

Marek raised his brows. "And what happens if a demon attacks you tomorrow? He's not going to give you any breaks."

I held my palm up and wiggled my fingers. "That's why I should be working on my magic. He wouldn't stand a chance."

"Neither would you if an army of demons found out what you were," Marek pointed out.

"Might I remind you that already happened? And I killed them."

Marek hesitated a moment then continued circling me. "You almost killed yourself, too."

He had me there.

Marek jabbed another fist in my direction. I instinctively threw my arm out to block him. His fist cracked into the side of my arm painfully. He had no idea how strong he was.

Almost instantly, his other hand came flying at my head. I jumped backward and put several feet of space between us so he couldn't reach me.

"Impressed yet?" I asked smugly.

"I'm going easy on you," he asserted.

"Sure you are." I rolled my eyes.

Before I knew what was happening, Marek lunged at me. He grabbed my body and whipped me around so that my back was pressed to his front. He pinned both of my arms to my chest. My breaths became shallow, and my heart raced. He breathed in my ear, and for a moment, I thought I might collapse. My knees simply didn't want to hold me up anymore. Every inch of my body heated. He *had* to feel the energy sizzling between us.

"What was that you were saying?" he whispered.

I swallowed, wanting nothing more than for him to hold me in this position forever. Surely by now he could feel my heart trying to beat its way out of my chest.

"I—I don't remember," I said breathlessly.

He laughed lightly. "How are you going to get your way out of this one?"

I twisted my head around to look him in the eyes. My gaze drifted down to his lips, then back up to his eyes. Kissing him would certainly get me out of it.

The sound of a fireball connecting with a target nearby snapped me out of my trance.

"Like this." I threw my hips to the side and wrapped my leg behind him.

He toppled backward onto the grass and released me on the descent. Shock crossed his face, but it only lasted a split second. A smile formed.

He propped himself up on his elbows. "I wasn't expecting that. What's your next move, Ryn?"

I don't know. Straddle you and kiss every inch of your body.

"Um… run away?"

Marek's brows shot up. "So that your opponent can stun you from behind, giving him enough time to kill you?"

I threw my hands up. "I don't know, Marek. Even if I did get on top of you to pin you down, it wouldn't matter how strong I am. I don't weigh enough. You'd just toss me off of you." I paused. "I guess my next move would be to stun you, to immobilize you so I could…" I didn't like how that sentence ended.

"Good," he said.

I offered my hand to help Marek to his feet.

Practice continued for another forty-five minutes. By the time Fletcher told us to head back up to the school, my shirt was soaked in sweat. Stepping back into the air conditioned building was a relief.

"Feel free to talk amongst yourselves until the bell rings," Fletcher said when we returned to his classroom. "Ryn, can I see you at my desk for a moment?"

Nerves knotted in my gut as I made my way to the front of the room. Did he think I did poorly during practice today? Was he going to assign me a different partner because he noticed how distracted I became around Marek?

"What's up?" I asked in a shaky voice once I reached him.

He spoke quietly so no one else could hear. "I wanted to make sure you were okay and not feeling too overwhelmed. I fear you might think I'm expecting too much of you."

The way he said it made it sound like he heard my friends and me talking in the hall the previous day.

I shifted my weight between my feet uncomfortably. "Well, the weight of the world is kind of resting on my shoulders at the moment. Honestly, as my mentor, I thought you'd be more helpful."

I was surprised to hear the words come out of my mouth. I tried not to, but I could be a real asshole sometimes.

"I'm sorry you feel that way," Fletcher said. "See that stack of books there?" He pointed to a pile of books beside his desk. The stack came up to my knee.

I nodded.

"Those are the books I've been looking through to see if I've missed something. I'm hoping there might be a clue somewhere about Grace."

It was official. I *was* an asshole.

And Fletcher was acting all calm like I hadn't just accused him of being totally worthless.

"I'm sorry," I said in a small voice.

Fletcher looked at me seriously. "While I'm going through these books, you might start by talking to Elizabeth Ellington. She's the librarian at the public library here in town. She's quite knowledge-able about the town's history."

I bit my lip. "I thought you were the Davina history expert."

Fletcher nodded lightly. "On ancient Davina history. Elizabeth knows more about the town's history. If my theory is correct and Grace was brought here with the Davina who settled the town, we might be able to find something in the town's records."

"Yeah, I suppose..."

Fletcher stared up at me like he expected me to say more.

"I'll go talk to her after school," I finally said.

That seemed to be all Fletcher wanted to talk about. Without another word, I returned to my seat.

"What was that about?" Allie asked under her breath.

"Change of plans. We're headed to the library after school."

"Okay," she said. "Hopefully we'll find something useful."

I pressed my lips together in uncertainty. "Yeah. Hopefully."

7

"How can I help you?" a woman behind the library's front desk asked as Allie and I approached. She looked about sixty, but her hair had only begun graying. She'd piled it atop her head in a loose bun, and she wore thin black reading glasses.

"Hi," I said. "We're looking for Elizabeth Ellington."

The woman smiled brightly and removed her glasses. "I am she."

"Hi. I'm Ryn, and this is Allie. We're writing a paper for our history class. Our teacher said you might be able to help. The paper's on the history of Eagle Valley."

"Which school do you ladies go to?" Elizabeth asked.

"Galen High," Allie and I answered in unison.

Elizabeth stood and leaned over the front desk. Her eyes darted from side to side to make sure no one was listening. She whispered softly. "So, you're looking for information about *Davina* history?"

"Yes," I answered eagerly.

She held up an index finger. "Give me one moment, please."

Elizabeth walked to a door behind the front desk and stuck her head inside. I could just barely make out what she was saying. "I have some students here I'm going to be helping out. Do you mind keeping an eye on the front desk for me?"

While we waited for her, my eyes scanned the room. It wasn't a large library by any means, but it was beautiful. An area outlined in a rug and several antique-style chairs stood behind us. I could picture myself relaxing in one of those chairs with a good book and never get sick of it.

Above us, the ceiling rose to the second level, where a balcony framed the room. Tall wooden bookshelves reached the ceiling on both levels. Between them, natural light flooded in from high windows. The place reminded me of an old church.

Elizabeth's quiet voice pulled my attention back to her. "Follow me, please."

She led us down a large staircase at the front of the building. The basement air was cool, and the hall was lined in thick stone. Elizabeth stopped at a door near the end of the hall. Her keys jingled in her hands.

"This is our archives room." She pushed the door open and flipped on the light.

We entered a room the size of Fletcher's classroom. Rows of bookshelves lined the walls, and an empty table stood in the center.

"We don't typically let students in here due to the delicacy of the documents, but I like to make exceptions for Galen High students." She gave a sweet smile. "You'll find most of the early history in this section." She pointed. "It's mostly newspapers, unfortunately. Have a seat, and I'll see if I can find some good articles for you ladies to use on your paper."

Allie and I both sat at the table.

"Are there any books that mention the Davina in Eagle Valley?" I asked.

Elizabeth disappeared down one of the rows. "I'm afraid there aren't any specific to Eagle Valley. You'd have to look in your school library for books on Davina history. There aren't many written texts left on the Davina."

"Why not?" I asked.

She poked her head out past the row of shelves and glanced at me above her glasses. "Many of the stories have been lost, unfortunately. Why do you think no one knows about the Davina anymore? They all worship their own gods and goddesses." Her voice became muffled as she returned down the row. "It's better that way, to be honest. Then we don't have people actively seeking us out. Can you imagine what it would be like in this day and age? We'd all be captured for science experiments!"

I looked to Allie. "Why were the stories lost in the first place?"

"I thought they taught you that in your history class," Elizabeth said.

"She's new at Galen," Allie explained before turning to me. "After Praesid put the Originals under protection, people started to question if they were truly still around. Generations passed. Since humans couldn't see the demons, some groups stopped believing they were out there. When the Originals didn't return, they made up their own stories."

"And the Davina let everyone believe whatever they wanted?" I asked.

Allie nodded. "The fewer people who believed in the Davina, the safer the Originals were."

"Here's a good one." Elizabeth returned a moment later and set an old newspaper in front of us. "Be careful with it. The article is on the second page. It explains some of the town's history."

Allie gently unfolded the newspaper and began scanning the pages.

Elizabeth disappeared down the row again. "Many Davina stories are handed down generation by generation the good old way—through oral storytelling." She laughed lightly. "Don't tell anyone I said that. I'm a librarian. I'm supposed to love books."

Elizabeth came back carrying another stack of newspapers. She sat across from us. "What is it exactly that you want to know about the Davina?"

Where they left Grace. If she's still here after all this time.

"Nothing… in particular," I said slowly. "Our paper is going to focus on landmarks and buildings that were here early on. We'd like to give a picture of what the town looked like when it was settled." I hoped that lie would be enough to help us narrow down where Grace might be hidden. "Were there any significant landmarks built at the time? Especially any that could be tied to the Davina?"

"It's all tied to the Davina, so I'm not sure what you mean," Elizabeth said.

All I knew was that if Grace was as important as she seemed, her grave would be marked somehow. Then again, Praesid had been protecting her. They wouldn't make it that obvious.

"I'm not sure what I mean, either," I admitted sheepishly.

Elizabeth turned to Allie. "Did you find anything in that article you can use for your paper?"

"Um… yeah," Allie said, but I heard the lie in her voice. Clearly she didn't think any of it would be useful on our search for Grace. "It says the town was settled in 1857 by a group of men who came from out East and purchased the land with gold earned from their family business."

"That would be the three Haylo brothers," Elizabeth said. "They were Davina."

"Right." Allie glanced back down at the article. "They settled the area for farmland, but once the railroad hit the town, the community expanded."

Elizabeth nodded. "And at that time, it was mostly Davina. The people closest to the Haylo brothers prior to their purchase of the land were the ones who came to settle the town first."

"The article doesn't say much more," Allie said. "It lists which businesses cropped up first."

I immediately perked up. That information could be useful if they'd hidden Grace inside one of the businesses.

"Which ones?" I asked, almost too quickly.

"Um…" Allie bit her lip and scanned the page. "It says there was a blacksmith shop, a grain mill, a lumber yard, and a few department stores."

None of those sounded like plausible candidates.

"What about things like churches?" I asked. If an angel was hiding anywhere, that was as good of place as any to start.

Elizabeth laughed from across the table. "Are you forgetting that the town was settled by *Davina*?"

"So?" I glanced between her and Allie.

They both gave me strange looks.

"The Davina don't associate themselves with any modern religion," Elizabeth explained. "Some Davina communities used to build churches as a way to blend in. Eagle Valley didn't get its first church until thirty years after the Haylo brothers bought the land.

That was shortly after others began moving into the town. You know, people who weren't Davina."

I nodded. So, what did we have? A list of a few old businesses that probably didn't even exist anymore?

"What about other places that *weren't* businesses?" I asked. "Things like government buildings?"

Elizabeth's face lit up. "You're standing in one! This library was among one of the first buildings built by the settlers. It was originally both the library and the town hall, but after they built the new town hall in the thirties, the library expanded to the entire building. And then there was the Haylo brothers' mansion, which of course is now Galen High School."

My heart surged with hope. Why hadn't I thought of that before? Better yet, why didn't *Fletcher* think of that?

It made so much sense. The Davina had retained control of the building for so long. Grace would still be protected, even if no one knew they were protecting her.

"Other than that," Elizabeth said, "the only things I can think of that would've been around in the earliest days of Eagle Valley are the cemetery and a couple of houses."

Right. The cemetery. Allie and I still had to check that one out. Now at least we had two other ideas to add to the list: the library and the school.

"Thank you, Mrs. Ellington," I said with a smile. "You've been a huge help. Can we take any of these newspapers to help with our research?"

Her expression dropped. "I'm sorry, but unfortunately, we can't allow these out of the library. You're free to take any notes you wish, and you can take pictures so long as the flash is turned off. If you don't have any more questions for me, I'll let you girls browse the newspapers alone."

She glanced at her watch. "Please let me know when you're done so I can close the room back up. I'll be at the front desk."

Allie's eyes followed Elizabeth. "Thank you. You've been so much help already."

"No problem, girls," Elizabeth said as she left the room.

Allie turned to me immediately. "Anything jumping out at you yet?"

"I think we definitely need to check out the library and the school."

"After the cemetery, though," Allie insisted. "Your dart landed right next to the cemetery, so I think that has to count for something. We'll go tomorrow when we have more daylight to explore. I don't think we'll have time today once we're done here."

"Okay," I agreed.

Allie reached over to grab half the stack of newspapers in front of us. "I'll take this half."

I slid the second half in front of me.

Allie pulled out her phone and snapped a picture of the article she'd been reading. I thought it was a good idea, so I set my phone on the table beside me.

I sighed heavily and unfolded my first newspaper. I could only hope we weren't missing something important.

8

Several hours later, Allie and I gave up reading the newspapers as it neared closing time. We returned upstairs to tell Elizabeth we were finished and that she could lock the room back up.

When I turned from the counter to leave, I was surprised to see a guy sitting in one of the chairs with his head buried in a book. The sight of Trenton reading made him seem ten times hotter. His eyes darted up from his book for just a moment, and they met mine. He snapped the book shut and set it aside before getting to his feet.

Allie didn't seem to notice his approach until he spoke.

"Hey, ladies." He fell into step beside us.

Allie shot him a suspicious glance.

"Hey, Trenton," I said.

The three of us stepped outside into cool air and stopped on the landing before the steps. The sun had already fallen low in the sky.

Trenton leaned against the concrete banister. "What are you up to?"

"None of your business," Allie said.

No need to be so harsh, I thought.

"We were just researching," I told him, hoping it would make up for Allie's rudeness.

"Oh?" he asked with raised eyebrows. "Researching what?"

"It's for a school project," I told him quickly.

"Yeah, me too," he said flatly.

What school project did *he* have?

"What are you up to now?" he asked.

"Nothing, really," Allie said slowly. "You're being weird again."

Trenton rolled his eyes. "Maybe I'm trying to make up for all the shit Casey's put you through. You don't have to hate me just because I hang out with her."

Trenton had a point. Personally, I had no problem with him, but Allie still had reservations.

She opened her mouth, but nothing came out. When she couldn't come up with a rebuttal, her shoulders relaxed. "Okay, but do you really want to hang out with *us*?"

Trenton glanced around. "I don't see anyone else to hang out with."

"So we're just the most convenient option at the moment?" Allie asked.

I nudged her with my elbow. She didn't have to be so rude.

Trenton smiled. "Basically, yeah. I'm bored. So sue me."

"Don't listen to Allie," I insisted. "It's her time of the month."

Allie let out a breath of air, but I ignored her.

"What did you have in mind?" I asked.

Trenton shrugged. "Anyone up for flying?"

My heart soared at the thought of flying, and I quickly agreed.

Several minutes later, Allie and I rode to the school in her car while Trenton took his own vehicle.

"I think Trenton must like you," Allie said to me on the way there.

"I don't really get that vibe," I told her, though I had to admit the idea flattered me.

"He seems pretty eager to hang out with you," she pointed out.

I shrugged. "I think he's just bored, like he said. It must get exhausting to hang out with Casey all the time. He's probably just looking for a change of pace."

"Yeah, maybe," she agreed when she pulled into the parking lot.

I was glad I'd continued wearing tank tops even when I wasn't sure if I'd be flying that day. It made impromptu flying sessions like this so much easier. I took a mental note to get Mom to order me more tanks online. Which meant I actually had to do my chores and get on her good side.

"Trenton is *so* going down," Allie muttered to me on our way toward the valley. She eyed him from where he walked several paces in front of us.

"Don't be so mean to him," I insisted. *He's not Casey.*

"I wasn't trying to be. He just… has all that muscle, and…"

"Are you checking him out?" I teased.

"What?" She sounded shocked. "No, I just meant… he thinks he's so great because he's strong and all, but I'm a fast flyer. I can beat him."

I tried to hold back a smile. "I can't wait to see you try."

Allie held her chin out proudly. "Watch me."

When we reached the valley, it was completely deserted apart from the training equipment that'd been left out.

Trenton spread his arms out and circled to look back at us. "Check that out. We've got the place all to ourselves."

He reached for the bottom of his shirt and pulled it up over his head. I knew the guy was muscular, but *damn*. I thought for sure I even saw Allie checking him out. He could definitely give Marek a run for his money.

Trenton flexed his shoulders, and white wings sprouted from his back. I'd found that every Davina had a slightly different shade to their feathers. Allie's shimmered a subtle blue, while mine held a hint of purple in them. Trenton's wings, I was surprised to see, had a duller hue. Even in the dimming evening light, they didn't shimmer quite the same way mine and Allie's did.

"What are we doing? Racing?" Allie asked.

"What else?" Trenton replied.

Without warning, they both sprinted to the edge of the hill and threw themselves into the air, spreading their wings wide. I quickly followed behind, digging my feet into the ground and springing upward. My wings spread out behind me. I laughed in exhilaration as I flapped them and flew higher.

Up here, high above the valley, I could almost forget about my troubles. All my cares slipped out the window, like Grace didn't matter anymore.

As I expected, I came in last place. I was so far behind that I couldn't even use their head start as an excuse. Allie had done as she'd promised and beat Trenton. The way she talked about him, I expected him to be a sore loser, but he only smiled and challenged her to a rematch.

The three of us raced several more times. Each time, Allie won and I lost. I eventually grew so tired of flying that I sat in the grass to cool down. My wings spread out behind me.

"You okay?" Trenton took a seat beside me. He leaned back on one hand and rested the other elbow on his knee.

"I'm fine. You guys can keep racing."

"No, it's cool," he told me. "Allie's made her point. Clearly she's a better flyer than me. Always has been."

Allie blushed before she launched herself back into the sky for another flight.

"What about you?" Trenton asked.

"What *about* me?"

"What are your special talents?" He smiled encouragingly.

"Um…" I dropped my gaze and fidgeted with the red stud in my ear.

It might've sounded like I was trying to be modest, but the truth was that I had to think about the question. I didn't really have hobbies. For the first time in my life, this Davina stuff actually felt like something I could stick with, and not just because I felt obligated to. There was a thrill that came along with flying and conjuring essence that I couldn't quite explain. I only wished I'd discovered it sooner.

"Really?" Trenton asked. "Nothing?"

"Sorry," I said. "I don't really have an answer. I'm still new to all this."

"That doesn't mean you're not special."

Well, I *was*, in a way, but I wasn't about to tell him that.

"Thanks." Blood rushed to my cheeks. I did my best to avoid his gaze. Instead, my eyes locked on Allie as she flew around the valley. In the dimming light, it was hard to make her out the farther she flew away from us.

"So," Trenton said after a short silence, "what brought you to Eagle Valley?"

The first time I told Marek it was fate, I'd only been joking around. Now that I'd decided fate actually had something to do with it, it didn't feel right to mention it. Not when Trenton didn't know I had the Power of Grace.

"What brings anyone to Eagle Valley?" I said vaguely, purposely not answering his question.

"Usually family."

I couldn't exactly use that as an excuse. I really should've thought my answer through. It was always one of the first questions people asked when I moved to a new town. I was surprised that Trenton had been the first person to bring it up all week.

I settled with the basic explanation. "My mom likes to move around. I was born in the Midwest not too far from here, and I always loved the area. I convinced her to come back. I just got lucky that I ended up in a town with Davina." I paused momentarily. "What about you? Didn't Casey say you started at Galen sophomore year?"

Trenton nodded. "Like I said, family."

Allie landed a moment later and fell to the grass beside me, exhausted.

"Enjoying yourself?" I asked.

"Yeah," she breathed heavily. "Anyone up for another go?"

Trenton and I both declined.

"It's getting late anyway." I stood and pulled my wings into me. "Mom's going to be mad because the library closed and I'm not home yet."

"Okay." Trenton sounded disappointed. "Maybe we can hang out another time."

"Yeah," I agreed. "You ready to go, Allie?"

She took another deep breath and pushed herself up. Her wings disappeared behind her. "Yeah."

"See you later, Trenton," I said with a wave. I turned to Allie on the way back to the car. "See? He's not so bad, is he?"

Allie's lips turned down. "No, I guess not. Just be careful, okay?"

"What do you mean?" I asked.

"Don't lead Trenton on. I don't think Marek would be thrilled to have competition."

I let out a breath of disbelief. Maybe Marek *needed* competition. He wasn't exactly fighting for my affection lately. Trenton actually seemed like he cared.

I think I'd very much like to see what Marek thought of me spending time with Trenton.

9

"*Y*ou know Trenton?" I asked Marek after school the next day.

Dumb question. Of course he knows Trenton.

The halls had been deserted, leaving Marek and me alone at our lockers. It was my first chance to talk with him alone all day.

"Yeah," Marek answered.

"We hung out yesterday," I stated.

"And?" Marek asked.

That was it? No hesitation? No demanding to know where we'd been and what we'd done? Marek was acting like an entirely different person than the guy I knew.

"And…" I started.

Say you care. Say you're jealous. Say something!

This wasn't how I expected this conversation to go.

"I was wondering what you thought of him," I said.

Marek's features hardened. He shrugged. "He's an okay guy, I guess. But you really shouldn't be hanging out with people when you should be focusing on Grace."

Now he was bossing me around? What the hell?

"*We're* hanging out right now," I pointed out.

"So we can train," Marek said. "If we can get you more in tune with Grace's essence, you might have an easier time finding her.

And Fletcher says you'll need to be in control of your essence to wake her."

"I know," I said with a sigh.

"Should we get started?"

Marek's idea of a private place to practice was in Fletcher's classroom.

Fletcher sat behind his desk, watching my every move. He said he was reading through his stack of history books looking for clues about Grace, but I could feel his eyes on me the whole time.

"Okay." Marek clapped his hands together. "Let's see what you've got."

I held my hand out nervously. I took a deep breath and channeled my energy down my arm. I felt my skin heat as a white orb formed in my hand. I smiled at how effortless it looked, but the moment I let my guard down, the orb darkened to purple.

I closed my palm instantly. "Shit. I'm going to end up killing someone, aren't I?"

So far my uncontrolled essence had only killed demons. Luckily.

Marek placed a careful hand on my outstretched fist. Good thing I didn't still have a fireball in my hand. If my essence reacted the way my heart did, it'd go flying across the room.

"You're not going to kill anyone," Marek promised. "That's why we're getting you to practice. Can you see now why we didn't have you practicing out in the open?"

"Yeah," I said begrudgingly.

"Try it again," Marek instructed. "Concentrate this time."

"I was concentrating."

I focused harder on keeping my magic a crisp white. When I glanced up to Marek's face, his sexy stare distracted me again. The orb flashed purple.

"Damn." I dropped my hand. "What am I doing wrong?"

Marek pressed his lips together. "I'll be honest. I'm not sure. I think it might be a matter of concentration."

Then it's definitely not going to work with you around.

"We just have to find what works for you," Marek told me. "Two weeks ago you couldn't conjure essence by will. Then you realized what it took for you to do it. Suddenly, it wasn't so hard."

"You mean when I realized I could only do it if I was protecting someone?"

"Exactly."

I shrugged uncertainly. "I don't think that's going to help. If I'm protecting someone, my essence is going to turn deadly."

At least, that's what my track record showed.

"I didn't mean that's what's going to help you control your essence," Marek said. "I just meant that we have to find what *does*."

I gritted my teeth. "I'm trying, you know."

"I know." Somehow, Marek kept calm as my frustrations grew. It only made me want him more.

"Try conjuring your purple essence first," Fletcher suggested.

I turned to face him. "What?"

"You're having trouble sustaining white essence," Fletcher said. "Try starting with purple essence to see if that's easier."

I bit my lower lip. "Okay."

I took a deep breath and held my palm out again, this time focusing on the higher charged, electric essence that flowed through me. I wasn't sure how I could tell the difference between the two. It was almost like flexing a separate muscle.

A purple fireball formed. I stared at it intensely, concentrating to maintain the purple hue. I feared it might turn white any second. It didn't.

Marek's voice broke my concentration a minute later. "Great job. What do you say we try the other hand?"

"What?"

"So far you've only practiced with your right hand," he pointed out. "Let's see what your left can do."

I couldn't hold a spoon with my left hand. What made him think I could handle a fireball with it?

"It's okay," Marek encouraged. "You can do it."

I held out my left palm and concentrated on channeling my magic down my arm. My brows constricted, and my jaw clenched. Nothing happened.

"Calm down." Marek gently placed a hand on my shoulder.

I forced myself to listen to him, but it took another fifteen minutes before a purple fireball finally formed.

I jumped in excitement. "I did it!"

"Great." A huge smile formed across Marek's face. "Do it again."

My excitement quickly fizzled.

I tried again, this time succeeding within the first five minutes of trying. Unfortunately, Fletcher's room wasn't big enough to practice much more than that. Another hour and a half passed before we finally called it a day. I pulled out my phone and texted Allie to let her know I was done. Marek said goodbye and slipped out of the room.

"Can I have a word with you, Ryn?" Fletcher asked before I left.

I met him at his desk.

"Did you find the map useful?" he asked.

I dropped my gaze. "I kind of had a feeling about the park, but Allie and I didn't find anything there."

That was a lie. It hadn't exactly been a *feeling*.

Fletcher nodded in thought. "Have you talked to your mother about any of this?"

"No," I answered automatically. "Why would I?"

Even if she *did* believe it, she'd be pissed I'd been lying to her all these years about seeing the demons.

"She doesn't know anything," I insisted.

"That doesn't mean she doesn't deserve to know," Fletcher said. "She may be human, but she's still your mother."

I pursed my lips. Who did he think he was, telling me how to navigate my relationship with my mom?

"With all due respect, Fletcher, I know my mom better than you do. She wouldn't want to hear about any of this."

Fletcher stared at me in shock. "I'd certainly want to know what was going on with my kids—especially if they were in your situation."

I crossed my arms. "You mean being the chosen one? Being hunted by demons for what I am? You don't *have* kids, do you?"

Fletcher shook his head.

"Then you have no place telling me what my mom might feel. She made me feel like I was insane for years. I have no intention of letting her make me feel that way again."

"I'm sorry, Ryn," Fletcher started to say, but I was already out the door.

"How'd the training session go?" Allie asked when she picked me up.

"Terrible," I said in a clipped tone. "Fletcher was meticulously analyzing every move I made. I'd rather practice with Marek alone."

She wiggled her eyebrows. "What happens when you're alone?"

I scoffed. "Keep dreaming. Nothing happens. Especially lately."

Her expression fell. "What's the deal with you and Marek anyway?"

I bit my lip and looked out the window at the passing houses. "I don't know. After our kiss, he seems… uninterested. It's like the only reason he talks to me is when he's trying to teach me something. Maybe he's waiting for me to make another move. I don't know. Forget about me. What about you and Kyle?"

Allie rolled her eyes. "I don't know how much more obvious I can be with him. He still hasn't asked me out."

"Why don't *you* ask *him* out? I thought you *both* had a thing for each other."

"Yeah, I thought so, too. What if he rejects me?"

I shrugged. "What if?"

"It would ruin the whole dynamic of the group."

I frowned. "Yeah, I guess that's the problem with getting too close to the people you spend so much time with. If it doesn't work out…"

I didn't want to think about that.

Allie pulled up to the cemetery just then. We stepped out of the car silently. I glanced around, wondering where to start. I wasn't sure we'd make it through the whole thing by dark.

"What do you think we're looking for?" I asked.

Allie slipped her keys into her pocket. "I'm not sure. I was hoping you'd know. My guess is that we'll know once we find it." She started down the closest row of headstones.

I followed behind her.

"Hmm…" Allie mused. "These dates don't go back far enough. We should start at some older gravestones."

"I agree," I said, "but I don't know if the cemetery was a good idea in the first place."

"What do you mean?" she asked.

"Maybe a headstone would be too obvious of a marker."

"Depends on how they marked it. They maybe didn't put her name on it. I think we're looking for something more subtle."

"Then how do we know she's not in one of the graves we've already passed?" I glanced behind me like I might spot her standing there.

"We don't." Allie stopped and turned back to me. "Didn't you say fate brought you to Eagle Valley?"

I shrugged. "I don't know. That's what Fletcher seems to think. Honestly, it's the only thing that makes sense to me."

Allie turned and continued walking. "Right, so if she's here, the Power of Grace should lead you to her, shouldn't it?"

"I want to agree with you, but I feel nothing. I don't know what I'm *supposed* to feel." This trip to the cemetery felt useless. I wanted to go home, but I had to give the place a chance for Allie's sake.

Allie turned down a row of headstones. "I have relatives buried in this row."

I glanced at the dates. "How long has your family been living in Eagle Valley?"

"I think they came in one of the first groups of Davina after the Haylo brothers bought the town. That's just on my dad's side, though. The other side of my family didn't come to America until later. Mom wasn't from Eagle Valley."

I stopped abruptly.

"What?" Allie sounded concerned.

"I just thought of something. If your dad's family was one of the first to settle here, do you think they could've been part of the secret society that protected Grace?"

She drew her eyebrows together like she was thinking hard. "That would be cool. Now that you mention it, I suppose it's possible."

"Somewhere along the way, they must've stopped handing down the stories about Grace."

Allie nodded. "*I've* never been given any clues that Grace might be here. You think someone else might know where she is? Someone who's still alive?"

I sighed. "I don't know. Even if someone knew, we'd have to figure out who that someone is."

Allie began walking again. "Yeah. It kind of sucks how things are these days. Who knows how many of the stories will be lost over the next few generations?"

"Who knows how much you've already lost?" I asked.

"Here it is." Allie stopped and knelt in front of a grave marker. "This was my great-something-grandma."

I knelt beside her. "It's cool that you're so connected to your family."

"You mean, you don't visit your family's graves often?" she asked curiously.

I shook my head. "I don't even know if some of them are still alive."

I lifted my head and stared into the distance. A tall figure strolled through the other end of the cemetery, but he wasn't close enough to hear us.

"You mean your grandparents?" Allie asked.

My lips turned down at the corners. "I mean my dad."

Allie seemed to realize the mistake she made in prodding for an answer. Her voice softened. "Ryn, I'm sorry."

I shook my head. "No, it's okay. I just think it'd be nice to know where his grave was—if there's one out there for him." I picked at the grass below me. "Mom and I don't know what happened to him. Sometimes… it sounds horrible, but sometimes I *wish* he was dead." I paused. "That came out wrong. I just think it'd be easier knowing that's why he never came back rather than assuming he ran out on us. At the same time, I hope he's out there somewhere and that Mom will find him again."

I lifted my gaze to see that Allie's jaw had gone slack.

"You literally have no idea what happened to your dad?" she asked.

"I literally have no idea." I returned to picking at the grass. "I haven't pressed Mom about it much, either. She doesn't seem to like to talk about him. I think it's too painful for her. Now with all this Davina stuff, I'd like to know more."

"You should talk to your mom about it," Allie suggested.

Ugh. Why were people encouraging me to talk to my mom? She was impossible.

"Maybe knowing more about your dad would help explain things," Allie said. "Like why you have the Power of Grace."

"You think my dad might have something to do with why Grace chose me?"

Allie shrugged. "It's possible. Unless you think your mom's family was Davina, then maybe—"

"There's no way. Mom can't see the demons." My thoughts flew back to one of the most horrifying nights of my life. I'd told Marek about it, but I still hadn't managed to find the right moment to tell Allie.

"Davina powers can skip a generation, you know," Allie pointed out.

I nodded. Marek had told me.

"Even if it skipped my mom, she'd still *know* about the demons. She doesn't. I promise."

Allie seemed to take that as a cue that it was the end of discussion. She got to her feet and glanced around. "Should we try those last few rows and then start weaving our way back?"

I pushed myself to my feet beside her. "Yeah, I think that's best."

I hoped Allie was right and that something would jump out at me, but nothing did. Eventually, we gave up.

"I'm sorry I suggested the cemetery," Allie said on our way back to the car. "I feel like it was a total waste of time."

"Not a *total* waste of time," I said to make her feel better, but it was a lie. "Now we've narrowed the list of places to look."

"Aren't we on a bit of a time limit?" Allie asked. "How long do you think we have now that the Power of Grace has returned?"

I shrugged. That was a question for Fletcher. But Fletcher didn't know I'd had the Power of Grace my whole life—or at least since I was eight and conjured my first purple fireball and killed my first demon. *It's been almost a decade since then. I think the doorway between here and the demon realm can hold out a little longer.*

I tried to convince myself of this, but even the voice in my own head didn't sound believable. I couldn't shake the feeling that I'd been brought to Eagle Valley now because time *was* running out.

"We'll find her," I said with certainty.

I reached for the door handle on the passenger side of Allie's vehicle. Before I could open it, I paused. In the distance, I noticed the same figure I'd seen earlier knelt down next to a nearby headstone.

"What?" Allie followed my gaze.

I didn't take my eyes off him. "Can you give me a couple of minutes?"

Allie opened the driver's side door. "What are you going to say to him?"

I couldn't stop staring at him, as if I could see his grief from fifty yards away. "I'm not sure yet. I think he could use someone to talk to."

I left Allie alone in the car and slowly made my way over to Trenton.

11

"Hey," I said quietly as I approached Trenton.

His face lit up when he saw me, but his expression quickly turned to sorrow again.

"Are you okay?" I lowered myself to the grass beside him and gestured to the headstone he'd been staring at. "Someone you know?"

"Not really," he admitted. "Just a distant relative."

I glanced at the words etched into the stone. *Sarah Spencer.*

"You sure?" I asked. "You seem… sad."

Trenton didn't meet my eyes. "I've just heard stories about her. She was my mom's younger sister."

My eyes scanned over Sarah's birth and death dates. She'd died over a decade before Trenton was born. She'd only been a child.

"I'm sorry," I told him honestly. "The stories must be sad."

He nodded somberly.

I didn't know what to say. All I knew was he could use a friend right now.

"What about you?" Trenton lifted his gaze to meet mine. "Do you have any family buried here?"

"No. My family's not from around here."

"Then what are you doing here?" He sounded genuinely curious.

"Oh, um… Allie and I were goofing around."

Trenton blinked a few times. "I saw you earlier. It looked like you two were looking for someone. Did you find her?"

I swallowed. Sure, Trenton didn't seem all that bad, but I wasn't about to tell him about Grace.

"We weren't looking for anyone in particular," I lied. "Just walking."

"Oh," he said flatly. "Because if you were looking for someone, it doesn't hurt to have an extra pair of eyes out there."

"Wouldn't Casey kill you if she thought you were fraternizing with the enemy in any way?" I teased.

A smile twitched at the corner of his lips. "It's possible, but what she doesn't know can't hurt her."

I laughed. "What is it with Casey, anyway?"

Trenton rolled his eyes. "Don't get me started. You don't want to waste your time talking about her."

"Is there a better way to waste my time?" I was glad I was cheering him up.

Trenton looked away from me for a moment. I could just barely see his face flush through the dimming light around us.

"You could waste your time on me," he said.

I was so shocked by his words that my entire body recoiled. Allie had been right. Trenton definitely *was* flirting with me.

"Oh, I…"

"What's the matter?" he asked. "You don't like my company?"

"No. I mean yes. I just…" What was I supposed to say? That I was already in a relationship? One that apparently didn't involve kissing or hand holding or *anything*?

Trenton's smile widened. "It'd be cool to get to know you better."

I couldn't believe what I was hearing. I tucked a strand of brown hair behind my ear and stared down at the grass. "Are you asking me out?"

At least *somebody* was.

"That depends. Do you *want* me to ask you out?"

When I looked back up at him, all traces of sorrow I'd seen earlier had vanished, replaced by a large—and rather sexy—smile.

My thoughts flickered to Marek. This wasn't fair to him, was it?

To hell with Marek, I thought. *If he wanted a relationship, he would've done something about it.*

"We can hang out," I told Trenton.

"Great. Does Friday work for you?"

I couldn't help it when a smile hit my lips. "Yeah, it should."

Trenton stood. "Cool. So, it's a date?"

I rose to my feet beside him. "I guess so."

He stuck his hands in his pockets. "I'll see you later, Ryn."

"Yeah, see you."

I returned to the car with a smile on my face.

"What was that about?" Allie asked once I slid in the passenger seat.

I shrugged and adjusted my seat belt. "I was just trying to cheer him up, and it sort of turned into him asking me out."

"What?" Allie squeaked about two octaves too high. "What about Marek?"

I could feel the heat rise to my face. "I don't know. What *about* Marek? I figured maybe I should keep my options open. Besides, I like Trenton. He's nice." *And hot.*

Allie started the car and shifted into gear. She pursed her lips but remained silent.

"What?" I asked accusingly. Clearly, she had more to say.

She paused for several seconds but finally caved. "I don't get why you're worrying about boys when you should be worrying about Grace."

"I *am* worrying about Grace," I defended harshly.

"You could worry more," Allie mumbled.

"What am I supposed to do? Put my entire life on hold for her? She apparently led me to Eagle Valley. If she's able to communicate with me, maybe she should be more explicit about it."

Allie breathed heavily and stared at the road.

Say something, dammit!

"You're just jealous I have two guys who want my attention and Kyle still hasn't made a move," I snapped.

Allie slammed on the brakes as we reached a stop sign. She turned to me, fuming. "You think I'm *jealous* of you? Do you know what type of friend I am at all? You *should* be putting your life on hold for Grace. Or don't you realize how important it is to find her? She's the only one with power strong enough to keep our world safe."

"If you worship her so much, maybe she should've chosen *you*!" My voice rose. "I didn't ask for any of this. Would you rather have her power? Here! Take it."

A purple fireball formed in my palm. I shoved my hand toward Allie.

She flinched. "Get the hell away from me!"

"Fine." I kicked the door open and swung my backpack over my shoulder as I planted my feet on the pavement.

"Wait, Ryn!" Allie called. "I didn't mean it like that!"

I slammed the door shut and turned my back to her. She remained at the stop sign for several moments. I wasn't sure if she was contemplating getting out of the car to talk to me or if she was waiting for me to come crawling back to her. Before I had a chance to find out, she applied the gas and sped off in front of me.

I was too angry to feel remorse as I watched her go. After a full minute, I finally gave myself a chance to process what just happened.

It was possible I just lost the first real friend I ever had.

12

$\mathcal{I}$ stormed into the house and pounded up the stairs.

"Kathryn," my mom called from the living room.

I paused with one foot on the landing. I took a deep breath before turning back down the steps.

"What?" I didn't intend to sound so hostile.

"Come here," she demanded.

I gritted my teeth and stopped in the doorway to the living room.

Mom looked at me with a pointed expression. "Where have you been? I texted you three times."

"Allie and I were working on our history paper," I lied.

Mom frowned. Clearly, she didn't believe me. "You've been spending an awful lot of time with Allie lately."

"So?" I crossed my arms. "What's wrong with having friends?"

Mom set her crochet hook and yarn aside on the couch. "There's nothing wrong with having friends. Maybe I just want to spend time with my daughter."

I held back an eye roll. "We never do anything together."

"I still enjoy your company."

She enjoyed when I cooked and cleaned for her.

"Okay," I said. "I'm going to take a shower and go to bed early."

"Hold on," she called before I could make it out of earshot. "What's going on with you lately?"

227

I turned back to her and sighed heavily. *I'm a Davina and still trying to figure out what it means to be one. All my teachers hate me. My best friend might hate me, too. I've been chosen for a destiny I might not be able to fulfill. The future of the world hinges on me—and I'm not even allowed to entertain the idea of boys to distract myself from that fact.*

"Believe me," I said, "you don't want to know."

"Come here." Mom gestured for me to join her on the couch.

I couldn't come up with a viable excuse to escape. I had no choice but to sit beside her.

Mom placed an arm around my shoulder. I couldn't remember the last time she hugged me. It felt awkward.

"What is it, Kathryn?" she asked like she genuinely cared.

"Nothing," I mumbled with a shrug.

"You can tell me anything," she assured me.

Not anything, I thought. Mom would never know I was a Davina. I'd never tell her I still saw the demons or the fact that I killed one to save her life.

"Kathryn," she repeated sternly.

I stared at her without saying anything.

"Is it about a boy?" she asked.

"What? No!" I drew away from her.

Mom sighed and pulled me closer. "Sometimes I forget you aren't so young anymore. You can come to me with questions."

"About *boys*?" I never pictured my mom and I having *that* conversation.

"I'm not completely clueless," she said. "I *have* dated before. Even before your father."

I wasn't remotely interested in hearing about her sex life.

But there was one thing I *was* interested in hearing about. Was my father a Davina? Did he have something to do with the Power of Grace? Could I pass up an opportunity to learn more about him?

"About my father…" I started.

Mom stiffened beside me. "What about your father?"

"What happened to him?" I asked in a whisper.

Her lips curled down at the corners. "Kathryn, we've talked about this."

"I know, but you never told me the whole story. Isn't there more to it?"

Mom shook her head. "Not really. He walked out on us. That's pretty much the whole story."

"How can we be sure he's not dead or something?"

"I tried looking for him after he left," Mom said, "but I never met his family. I didn't know who to talk to. And now it's been so long…"

"Are there any more specifics?" I pressed. Part of me hoped there was some fantastic story behind his disappearance, like that he'd been a Protector and died a hero.

She sighed. "Why are you asking me this now?"

Because everything has changed.

"Because I've always wanted to know. Now that I'm older, I thought you might actually tell me."

Mom's expression softened. "What is it you want to know?"

"I don't know. Did he say anything before he left?"

She shifted uncomfortably. "You have to understand that your father and I hadn't known each other for long. I thought I was in love with him."

Don't kid yourself, Mom, I wanted to say, *you're still in love with him, even though he left.*

"I'd only just graduated from college," Mom explained. "I moved to a new apartment building. Your father lived across the hall."

I knew all that already, but I didn't want to interrupt her.

"When we met, we instantly clicked. It wasn't long after I met him that I found out I was pregnant." She withdrew her arm from around my shoulder.

I didn't dare move or breathe as the seconds ticked by. I only waited for her to reveal more.

Mom's voice cracked. "I thought it was wonderful news, so I was excited to tell him. He said he was happy, but I could tell he was scared." Her face grew red. "That was the last time I saw him."

"You mean, he left because… because he didn't want me?"

I'd suspected it plenty of times, but I'd never gotten Mom to admit it. Suddenly, my chest felt empty.

"All I know is that he said he had something he had to do, left, and never came back." Mom turned toward the window. "He could've come back whenever he wanted. I waited eight years for it. I guess it took me that long to accept he wasn't coming back."

A lump rose within my throat. Was that it? Was my father a coward who didn't want to face the responsibility of raising me? I'd gotten the impression that Davina were stronger than that.

"What was he afraid of?" My voice rose. "Was he afraid I'd end up like him?"

Her gaze flew to mine. "End up like him how?"

I gritted my teeth. "He never mentioned anything to you? You never thought he might be… different?"

Mom tilted her head in question. "You think he might've had mental issues?"

I could hear the last bit she'd left out. *Mental issues like you.* She thought I was talking about my insanity—the craziness that never existed in the first place.

"Never mind," I said quietly. I quickly diverted the conversation. "So, you stopped waiting for him. What have you been doing since, Mom?"

She blinked. "What do you mean?"

I'd never voiced my thoughts aloud to her. "We've moved every year since I was eight. Have you been running away from something or running toward something?"

Mom opened her mouth but quickly shut it. It was like she couldn't believe I'd ask such a question. The way her eyes widened told me she wasn't sure of the answer.

I rose from the couch.

"No, Kathryn," she insisted in a harsh tone. "You don't just get to leave in the middle of an uncomfortable conversation."

I turned back to her. "I'm not, Mom. The conversation is over."

I hurried out of the room and up the stairs. In my bedroom, I fell to my bed. My gaze landed on the map still tacked to the wall across the room. My eyes scanned the image as though something might actually pop out at me this time. One thing became clear the longer I stared. If my father never cared about me, he sure as hell didn't deserve my attention. Right now, I had to focus on Grace and getting my best friend back.

13

No matter how many times I rehearsed my apology speech in my head Thursday morning, I never pictured having to chase Allie down. I expected to apologize to her on the way to school, but she didn't offer to drive me.

I ended up power walking to class and arrived just as the warning bell rang. I didn't have time to find Allie to tell her I was sorry for the way I acted. I waited for her at our lockers between first and second period, but she avoided my gaze and stepped into Fletcher's classroom without a word.

"Allie," I called from behind her.

She slid into a chair in the corner of the room like she hadn't heard me. Kyle took the seat next to her so I couldn't sit by her like usual.

Allie even avoided me during lunch. She and Kyle left the lunchroom with their trays—probably to sit around the fireplace in the common room. Marek had to talk me out of chasing after her. He told me to give her some space and that she'd cool off eventually.

Between Allie giving me the cold shoulder and the mounting stress of searching for Grace, I found it hard to focus on anything. After school in Fletcher's classroom, my essence flickered like a strobe light between white and purple.

"Whoa." Marek backed away like he was scared my magic might explode.

"Something on your mind?" Fletcher asked. I knew he'd been watching me from behind his desk.

I turned to him and crossed my arms. "Actually, yes. Why am *I* the only one who has to search for Grace?"

Fletcher blinked several times. "You're the one connected to her."

"Can't you help, I don't know… look for *clues*?" I threw my arms out in frustration and fell into one of the desks nearby.

"I am," Fletcher assured me, gesturing to the books spread out in front of him.

"Okay, but I mean actively. Elizabeth said the school is one of the oldest buildings in town. Shouldn't we search the building or something?"

"You think she might be here, at Galen?" Fletcher asked in thought.

"Why not?" I said. "This property has been protected by Davina for decades. Whether that was by design or because the rest of you are connected to her somehow, I don't know. I just think it's worth taking a look."

Fletcher pondered the theory for several moments. "Where do you suggest we start?"

I glanced to Marek like he might have an answer. He leaned against one of the desks, deep in thought.

I turned back to Fletcher. He looked at me like I was supposed to magically know the answer, but I was afraid I'd only disappoint him. I wasn't exactly running on instinct here.

I shrugged. "We might as well start on one side of the building and work our way to the other."

"Okay." Fletcher stood.

I quickly realized I had no idea what I was doing. I let Fletcher take the lead, and we strolled slowly from classroom to classroom. Every so often, Marek asked if I knew what I was looking for or if I felt anything.

"No," I told him.

Of course I felt *something*, but it wasn't related to Grace. It was that damn boy next to me sending my heart haywire. When I looked at him, I felt as equally irritated with him as I was attracted to him. Maybe Trenton *was* the better choice. He didn't make me feel so irrational.

By the time we covered the entire first and second floors of the building, I still wasn't ready to give up. That would mean less time with Marek. As much as I hated how confused he made me, I wanted to spend as much time with him as I could.

"Does the school have a basement?" I asked Fletcher.

"Yes," he said. "Good thinking."

Fletcher led us to a door that opened to a dark flight of stairs. When we reached the bottom, it wasn't anything like I expected. I thought we'd find a maze of hallways and storage rooms. Instead, it was simply one vast, empty room interrupted only by support pillars. A musty scent filled the cool air, and the stone foundation looked ancient. The entire space was covered in a thick layer of dust.

"There's not much down here," Fletcher said. "Mostly only maintenance comes down for the furnace."

I pulled my phone out of my back pocket and turned on the flashlight. The small light was almost enough to bathe the large room.

"Hold on." Fletcher returned to the top of the stairs. A moment later, light flooded the basement from overhead bulbs. "That should help." He pounded down the stairs and stopped beside Marek and me.

I glanced around, looking for anything that might draw my attention. "Does it go any further back?"

"No," Fletcher answered.

I began my way around the perimeter of the room.

"You said no one ever comes down here?" Marek asked Fletcher.

"No, not really."

"It seems like so much wasted space," Marek pointed out.

"It can get wet in the spring," Fletcher explained, "so it's not exactly ideal for storage. Finding anything, Ryn?"

"No," I said in disappointment.

"If no one uses the space, maybe we could train down here," Marek suggested.

"That's not a bad idea," Fletcher agreed. "There's enough room, and you don't run the risk of anyone seeing you. I *may* be able to snag an old target from storage that you can start on."

I whirled around. "Really? You're going to let me start using my essence? Like, doing more than just conjuring it?"

Fletcher nodded. "I think you're ready for it."

I smiled. "This is great!"

Fletcher glanced at his watch. "Maybe we should call it a day. I'm sorry we didn't find anything."

He sounded genuinely discouraged, like he might be having doubts about Grace being in Eagle Valley at all. I couldn't say I hadn't wondered the same thing myself.

When we returned to Fletcher's classroom, I gathered up my bag and headed out of the building.

"Hey, Ryn," Marek called, catching up to me.

My heart soared at the sound of his voice. "Yeah?"

"What do you say we head down to the valley?" He wiggled his eyebrows at me. His smile was so sexy; I'd agree to anything he suggested.

Somehow, I managed to keep my cool. "I thought you didn't want to train there anymore."

"It's not for training. It's for fun." His smile widened.

"What kind of fun?"

If he was talking about making out, I was all for it.

Marek nudged me with his elbow like I was being silly. "Flying, of course."

Well, it wasn't making out, but I was still eager to join him.

"Do we get to race?" I asked hopefully.

"Of course we'll race," he said.

"Ready?"

"Huh?" He shot me a questioning expression.

"Set, go!"

I took off running toward the back of the school, but it didn't take long for his footsteps to catch up and his long legs to push forward in front of me. Marek pulled his shirt off his head as he sprinted down the trail to the valley. I just barely caught a glimpse of the scars on his back.

He tossed his shirt aside when we reached the clearing. Without slowing, I dropped my bag to the ground, stripped off my cardigan, and leapt into the air.

For the first time in days, I felt like I wasn't just some girl Marek was forced to teach. We were actually friends.

I hope we end up being more, I found myself thinking.

And then I remembered I had a date with Trenton the following evening. Why was my heart being pulled in two different directions?

14

"Did you find who you were looking for?" Trenton asked when I met up with him at Angela's Café on Friday evening.

"What?" I asked breathlessly.

I'd lost track of the time after school during my training session with Marek. It was thrilling to finally be able to aim my magic at something—and I'd come to find I wasn't a bad shot. I guess being in softball in junior high had paid off. I'd rushed home afterwards to shower. I never told Marek where I was headed.

Trenton's eyes followed me as I lowered myself into the seat across from him. "You said you were looking for someone in the cemetery."

"Did I? No. Allie was just taking me to see her family's graves."

Trenton nodded. "How was the first week of school? Up to anything fun?"

I flipped my menu open. "I wouldn't call homework fun. The training is usually fun, though."

"You're training outside of school?" he asked.

I suddenly realized I'd said too much. "Doesn't everyone? I see you with Casey and Troy in the valley all the time."

"Yeah, but I haven't seen you around."

"I don't like training in the valley," I lied. "I haven't had as much training as the rest of you, so I'd rather not embarrass myself in front of an audience."

Trenton nodded. "Where do you find the time to train between all the other running around you do?"

I glanced up from my menu. "What do you mean?"

"The park, the library, the cemetery… I always see you hanging somewhere around town."

"Are you stalking me?" I accused lightheartedly.

Trenton set down his menu and leaned his elbows on the table. He spoke in a whisper. "So what if I am?"

If he was going for sexy with the way he stared at me, it definitely worked. Something in his eyes hinted at danger, but in a way I wanted to be a part of. It took me off guard, considering Trenton was more like the jocks at my old schools than anything. *Marek* was the one who screamed danger, with his leather jacket, motorcycle, and knack for saving my life.

So why did it feel like I could enjoy the danger in Trenton's eyes just as well?

"Well, it's a little creepy, but flattering." I turned back to the menu and let my brown hair fall in front of me. Hopefully it helped conceal the blush rising to my cheeks.

"At least I have the flattering part down," Trenton teased with a smile. "You know what you want to order?"

I closed my menu. "Yeah, I think I do."

I didn't mind hanging out with Trenton, but every so often, I found my mind wandering back to Marek. What was he up to right now? Did he ever think about me while we were apart?

Trenton was nice. He even offered to pay for my food. By the end of dinner, I thought I might agree to a second date if he asked.

I was smiling when we walked out of the café together, but that smile quickly vanished. Dread filled me the moment I spotted blond hair swaying in the wind. I froze in front of Celeste's, the cute jewelry store I hadn't had a chance to check out yet.

"Trenton!" Casey called from a few shops away. She hurried past a group of five teens I didn't know.

Troy followed behind her.

"Where have you been? Troy and I have been looking—" Her

eyes caught mine, and a hard expression settled on her face. She stopped in front of us and crossed her arms. "Really, Trenton?"

He glanced at me and shrugged like he didn't know what she was talking about.

"You ditched us to hang out with *her*?"

Trenton didn't seem at all fazed by Casey's attitude. "I told you I had plans tonight."

"Oh, Trenton," she said like he was a child. "I didn't think you meant with one of *them*."

"What's your problem with my group?" I snapped. It seemed like she was only mean for the sake of being mean.

She raised her blond brows. "Maybe you should ask your *group*. They're the ones who had a problem with *me* first. I'm only returning the favor."

"Come on," Trenton said with a sigh. "Give Ryn a break."

I appreciated that he was sticking up for me.

Casey looked to Troy like she couldn't believe what she was hearing and wanted him to help her out. Her gaze quickly returned to Trenton. "If you're going to ditch us, Trenton, you should at least date someone who can conjure essence."

"Shh…" Trenton hissed and glanced toward the group of people nearby.

I barely heard him over my own outburst. "Who says I can't?"

Casey scoffed. "Puh-lease. We've run into your team enough times, and I've never seen you conjure essence. All you can do is fly. Based on what I've seen, you're not very good at that, either. What was it Allie said the first time we met? You have amazing powers or something? I'd like to see that one day."

I couldn't stop myself as irritation bubbled to the surface. My brows constricted, and my breaths grew shallow. A wave of heat passed over my skin as anger consumed me. It was like I was watching myself from above, unable to control my own body.

"You wanna see?" I challenged.

I drew my arm back. Inside my palm, a white orb glowed in warning. I aimed for her face. Before I could throw the essence, Trenton's hand caught my wrist.

"She's not worth it," he said.

"Whoa." Casey took a step back and held her hands up. She didn't sound the least bit surprised, only amused.

I closed my fist as my anger subsided. Trenton loosened his grip, and I dropped my empty hand to my side. Shit. I shouldn't have done that. I took several steps back.

The group beyond Casey shot glances our way and whispered amongst themselves. There was no question that they'd seen my outburst.

Casey smiled like she was entertained. "You might be new here, but you should know conjuring essence in public places is off limits."

I swallowed the lump in my throat.

"Come on, Casey," Trenton pleaded. "Don't tell on her."

Casey narrowed her eyes at Trenton. Apparently, she wasn't used to being told what to do.

"You remember how I was when I came here," Trenton said.

Casey paused and then slowly nodded. "Oh, now I see. You like the new girl because you have something in common. How sweet."

I wanted to conjure another fireball and throw it at her head. I couldn't stand the condescension in her tone. Somehow, I managed to keep my fists clenched at my side. I literally bit down on my tongue to keep the nasty words I had for her from spilling out of my mouth.

"Fine, Trenton," she said, turning on her heel. "Have fun. Just be ready for our battle next week, okay?"

Trenton and I remained frozen on the sidewalk as she and Troy distanced themselves from us. I noticed the group nearby staring.

"What?" I snapped. "Never seen a phone before?"

I reached into my pocket and flashed my phone's screen at them. Because they'd *totally* believe that's what was glowing in my hand.

One guy scoffed, and the group turned away from us.

Trenton placed a cool hand on my arm.

I forced myself to lift my gaze. "I'm a freaking idiot. I should have—I can't believe… Thank you for sticking up for me."

He smiled. "What are friends for?" He draped his arm around my shoulder. "Maybe we should get you home."

I nodded. "Thank you."

Trenton led me over to his vehicle and opened the passenger side door for me. My hands shook. That wasn't the first time I'd let humans see my essence. What if people at Eagle Valley High started talking about me and connected the two incidents? Instead of saving the Davina like I was chosen to, I was going to lead them to their destruction by revealing their secret.

Great choice, Grace.

"I'm sorry," I said as Trenton drove down the street. "I just get so caught up in the fight sometimes."

"It's fine, Ryn," he assured me. "It happens. Just don't mention it to anyone, okay? You could get in serious trouble."

"I won't," I promised.

Trenton kept his eyes on the road. "Where do I turn?"

I gave Trenton directions back to my house, and we arrived within minutes.

"Are you up to anything this weekend?" he asked when I stepped out of the car. "We could hang out."

Before I could answer, a second car approached. I looked up to see Allie stepping out of Kyle's red compact car. She stopped in her tracks the moment she saw me. Allie's voice warning me not to get too distracted with boys entered my mind.

"Trenton, I'm sorry. I'm busy."

"Doing what?"

Training. Searching for an ancient Davina. Probably failing at both.

"Homework," I lied. *And I need to talk to Allie.*

"That can't take you *all* weekend."

Allie began walking toward her house. My eyes followed her.

"Sorry, Trenton. I have to go. I'll see you on Monday at school." I closed the door and turned toward Allie. I barely registered the sound of Trenton's car pulling away from the curb as I tried to work up the courage to call out to my best friend.

"Allie!" I heard her name escape my lips.

A strange silence settled over the night as we stared at each other across our lawns.

I took a deep breath. My apology had to come now or never.

15

"Allie," I called as I crossed my lawn onto hers. "We need to talk."

Her jaw tensed, but she didn't object. She crossed her arms, waiting for me to say more.

The whole speech I'd prepared earlier completely fell from my mind the moment I faced her.

"Well?" she prodded.

Silence hung over the lawn as I struggled to find the right words.

"I'm sorry," I managed in a small voice. "I acted like a self-obsessed idiot."

Allie smirked. "At least you admit it."

"I don't want to keep fighting," I told her.

"You could've apologized sooner," she said in a bitter tone.

"I tried!" I defended. "You've been avoiding me for two days."

Allie stared at me without saying anything. I searched her eyes for signs of what she was thinking, but I couldn't read her.

"I still want your help finding Grace," I said.

Allie pursed her lips. "Are you sure? You're not afraid I'll get jealous?"

I sighed heavily. "I didn't mean it about the jealousy thing. I'm just overwhelmed. I'm sorry I took it out on you."

Her gaze dropped to the grass.

After several moments of silence, I spoke again. "I miss you, Allie. I can't do this without you."

A smile crossed her face when she looked up at me. "That's all I wanted to hear. Okay, I'll help you."

That was it? No yelling? No blame? I suddenly realized how lucky I was to call Allie my friend.

"Thank you," I said.

"So, we'll check out the library again in the morning?" she asked eagerly.

Dread filled me. I wasn't looking forward to another failed mission.

"That's it!" I threw my hands up the following day. "I'm completely out of ideas."

Just as I suspected, our search through the library on Saturday morning had been useless. I thought for sure we'd been missing something. I even turned to pulling at books on the shelves to see if they'd open any secret passageways. As cool as that would be, nothing happened.

If I was this close to Grace, I figured I'd feel a pull toward her. The likelihood of her not being in Eagle Valley at all was growing more and more plausible by the day.

I suggested we return to my house around noon. Though Allie was disappointed that our last lead hadn't turned up any clues, she agreed with me.

"I don't get it," she complained as she plopped down on my bed. "Fletcher's theory made so much sense. What else would've brought you to Eagle Valley if Grace wasn't here?"

"I know." I slumped onto the bed beside her. "I've been going through the same thing over and over in my head, too. Maybe..." I bit my lip in thought.

"What?" she asked curiously.

I sighed and stood to pace around the room. "Maybe she's not here at all. What if Fletcher got part of the story wrong?"

"Which part?"

I couldn't believe I was suggesting it. "What if we're not looking for a grave or a body? What if Grace isn't a real person?"

Allie drew her eyebrows together, looking more confused than ever. "What are you suggesting?"

I raised my palm. Inside it grew a purple orb. "What if the Power of Grace *is* Grace? What if they're the same thing?"

She eyed me skeptically. "Are you saying you think you could close the portal to the demon realm on your own?"

Theories and doubts raced through my mind. "I don't know. How do we even know the realm is opening?"

Allie looked at me like I was crazy. "Because the power of the Originals is supposed to return when the world is in danger. Just the fact that you're here, with the Power of Grace, is a *sign*, Ryn."

I stopped pacing abruptly. "What if the stories are wrong?"

"I don't think so, Ryn. I've been hearing these stories my whole life. I mean, I never thought I'd live to see the day, but…"

I fell into the chair next to my desk. "You heard what Elizabeth said. A lot of these stories are passed down orally. The truth could've easily been lost from one generation to the next."

The skepticism deepened on Allie's face. "Just because we haven't found Grace yet doesn't mean the stories aren't true."

"It's not just that," I said.

"What do you mean?" She sounded annoyed.

I took a deep breath. I didn't know if I was ready to tell Allie, but I had to give her some sort of answer. "Because, Allie, I've had the Power of Grace for a long time."

"Wait." Allie shot to her feet. "You knew you had the Power of Grace before you came to Eagle Valley?"

"No! Of course not! I didn't know *what* it was."

Allie's eyes widened. "We don't know how much time we have, but this means we have even less time!"

I calmed my voice. "Sit down, Allie. I think there's something you should know."

She followed my command but never took her eyes off me.

"I was eight the first time I used the Power of Grace," I admitted.

I told Allie about Clinton, the demon who befriended me when I was a child. I told her how he had fed on my mom's essence and convinced her to attempt suicide. I told her how I'd walked in on it, how I saw a purple ball of energy erupt from my palm, and how Clinton had disappeared before my eyes. I told her how I wrapped my mother's wrists in the bed sheet and saved her life.

A lump rose to my throat as I finished the story.

Allie stood from the bed and slowly walked over to me. She wrapped me into a hug before speaking. "Ryn, I am *so* sorry."

"It's okay." My voice cracked. "It happened a long time ago."

Allie squeezed me one more time. "What do you think it means? Do you think after all this time the demon realm could've opened by now?"

"I don't know." I shrugged. "Wouldn't that mean the end of the world? I mean, the demons would flood into this realm, kill us, and feed off human essence. There'd be too many of them."

"Maybe there aren't any demons left in their realm," Allie theorized. "They closed the portals so long ago; they could've died off. We'd have no way of knowing."

I rubbed my hands over my face. "There's so much to speculate about. It's a lot to take in."

Allie raised her brows. "Tell me about it. I've grown up with these stories, and to think that they might not be accurate… It's like abandoning my whole belief system." She paused for a moment. "Maybe there's another explanation."

"Like what?"

Allie's hands rested on the back of my chair. "Well, you've gone nearly a decade without using the Power of Grace, haven't you? It was just the one time when you were a kid and then here in Eagle Valley?"

I looked up at her and nodded.

"Maybe the portals *were* a threat when you were a kid, but something happened and they weren't anymore. And now the risk is there again."

"You think the Power of Grace left me and then came back?"

Allie dropped her gaze. "I don't know. It's just another theory to add to the ever-growing pile."

"It's not a bad one. I just wish someone actually knew the truth. I sure as hell don't feel like I know what's going on here."

Allie laughed lightly. "I'm sure if we found Grace, she could tell us."

I raised my brows. "You still think we have a chance?"

"I think there *has* to be truth to these stories," she said as she returned to sit on the bed. "Even the demons know about them. I think we've missed something important."

I sighed. "So, what? We're back to square one?"

"We *could* try checking out the library and the school again. There are lots of places to look in those buildings. Or maybe we can try a new place, like somewhere that existed during the early settlement but got torn down or something."

I rubbed my fingers across my eyes. "I don't know, Allie." *I don't know what to believe anymore.*

She already had her phone out. "Let's go back through some of those articles we found. Maybe we missed something."

I didn't know what else we could possibly do. It was either follow Allie's suggestion or give up completely and admit the stories meant nothing, that I was just some anomaly rather than the chosen one.

"Kathryn," my mother's voice called from down the hall.

I stood and hurried to my door. "What?"

"You have company."

"Okay, I'll be there in a minute," I shouted back.

Allie placed her phone back in her pocket. "Expecting someone?"

"Not at all." I crossed the room and glanced out the window that looked over the front lawn. Kyle's car was parked near the curb.

Allie peeked out the window beside me. "I hope *he* has good news."

I turned to her. "Let's go find out."

16

We descended the stairs to find Marek and Kyle standing in my front hallway. My heart flipped at the sight of Marek. He looked sexier than ever with disheveled hair and his leather jacket on. His hands were shoved in his jean pockets.

Mom returned to the living room to work on crocheting a third scarf.

"What's up?" I asked.

Marek shrugged. "Not much. We were bored and wanted to see if you guys wanted to…" He glanced toward the living room to check that my mom wouldn't overhear. "Work out?"

I sucked in a breath. "Actually, we were kind of working on something."

"Oh." Disappointment entered his tone.

"You're free to join us," I offered immediately.

He perked up. "Great. What are you working on?"

Allie dropped her voice to a low whisper. "What else? Looking for Grace."

"Should we go back up to my room?" I suggested.

The four of us made it halfway up the stairs before Mom's eye caught mine from the living room.

"You know the rules, Kathryn," she called. "You can hang out in the kitchen."

I sighed heavily. I thought she'd trust me with boys by now. When I turned around and caught a whiff of Marek's scent, I realized even *I* didn't trust myself around boys… at least, not this one.

We headed down the hall and into the kitchen.

Marek's chair screeched across the hardwood floor as he scooted himself closer to the table. "Fill us in on what you've been working on."

"Not much," I admitted in disappointment.

"Mostly coming up with dumb theories," Allie told him.

"They're not *all* dumb," I defended.

Kyle raised a curious eyebrow. "What kind of theories?"

We quickly filled them in on our conversation from earlier, making sure to keep our voices low so my mom wouldn't hear.

"I agree with Ryn," Marek said. "They're not *all* dumb."

I smiled proudly, but that smile quickly faded.

"But I also agree with Allie," he said. "These stories about the power of the Originals returning when the human realm is threatened are too prevalent to dismiss."

"Couldn't they just be old legends?" I argued.

"They're not just *stories*." Kyle sounded offended.

"Yeah," Allie agreed.

I held up my hands in surrender. "Okay. You don't have to gang up on me."

"We weren't," Kyle said.

I shot him a hard glance. "Anyway, Allie and I were going to review some of the news articles we took pictures of when we were at the library. We could've missed something. Unless you had any other theories."

I could tell by the look on the guys' faces that they were just as clueless as we were.

Allie and I pulled out our phones again. Kyle scooted his chair closer to Allie.

Marek rounded the table to stand behind me and look at my screen. He rested one arm on the back of my chair and the other on the table next to me. We nearly touched. It definitely didn't help my concentration. Even the rhythm of his breathing sent my heart summersaulting inside my chest.

Eventually, Marek grew tired of standing and pulled a chair

over beside me. Our knees touched under the table. I couldn't tell if it was intentional or not. Either way, the surface of my skin heated a few degrees. I wasn't quite sure how he didn't notice my heart trying to beat its way out of my chest at his touch. I had to set my phone down between us to hide my trembling fingers.

How am I supposed to function when he insists on distracting me like this?

Marek looked between Allie and Kyle as soon as we finished scanning our final article. "You find anything useful?"

"No," she said in disappointment.

"Maybe we should go back to the library," I suggested. "There could be more news articles we never got a chance to read."

"What do you think we'll find in them if we haven't found anything here?" Allie asked.

She placed her phone into Marek's outstretched hand. He began scrolling through the pictures.

"I don't know," I admitted. "A mention of an old building. Maybe even a mention of Grace."

"I don't think anyone would've risked mentioning her in the paper," Marek said without taking his eyes off the screen.

I knew he was right. I rested my face in my hand and stared at the screen with him. He used two fingers to zoom out of the picture he'd been looking at and then scrolled on to the next one.

My hand shot out and grabbed his wrist. "Hold on. Go back to that last one."

My breath completely left my chest. I grabbed the phone out of his hands to examine the picture closer.

"Why didn't you mention this?" I demanded, turning the screen toward Allie.

"Mention what?" she asked innocently.

"This picture on that page! Don't you recognize that house?"

Allie squinted at the screen. "No."

"Look closer." I shoved the screen toward her.

She eyed the article and drew in a sharp breath. "Oh my gosh! I didn't realize. It looks so different. There are more trees, and the porch is missing. They must've added it on later..."

I looked back at the screen and zoomed in on the article. "Built in 1858, it says. I knew the house was old, but I never would've guessed it was *that* old."

Kyle slowly reached out to take the phone from me. He examined the image. "So it's a picture of your house. What does it mean?"

I gazed at him wide-eyed. Didn't he understand it meant someone from Praesid built this house and lived here?

"It means we found her!" I was unable to contain my excitement. "Guys, we found Grace!"

17

I leapt out of my chair. "Allie, you were right!"

"About what?"

"Everything!" I exclaimed. "About fate bringing me here. You kept saying I should've sensed Grace, and I did. Every time we went looking for her, I wanted to go home. I thought I was just feeling discouraged, but it wasn't that. It's because she's here, in my house!"

I rushed out of the kitchen and took the stairs down to the basement two at a time. Three pairs of footsteps followed behind me.

"Allie, remember when we tried out the dart thing?" I didn't wait for an answer. "The dart landed in the floor at first because it was *literally* showing me where Grace was. Here, take this."

I shoved a paint can into Marek's hands and bent to inspect the carving of the Davina woman I'd found two weeks ago.

"This has to be it," I said.

Allie and Marek both inched closer to view the carving etched into the stone foundation.

"This *means* something," I insisted. "It was only after I found this that I spread my wings for the first time. It's because it *spoke* to me. It *inspired* me. Help me move this stuff."

The three of them went speechless. They stared at me for a moment as I began pulling things off the shelf.

"Come on," I insisted, unable to contain my excitement.

Marek set the paint can aside and began removing random

household items our landlord had left for storage. Allie and Kyle quickly joined in.

"That should be good," I said before situating myself on one end of the shelf.

Marek gripped onto the other side. Together, we slid the shelf across the floor. It screeched along the concrete.

I quickly dropped to my knees to get closer to the carving. A shiver ran down my spine as I grazed my fingers across it. "She's here. I know it."

"How do you know?" Allie asked curiously.

"I just do." I took a deep breath and stood, retreating several steps to get a better look. "There has to be a door or something."

I returned to the wall and ran my hand over the worn stones in search of a seam of some sort. I found nothing.

"She's right behind this wall," I said, more to myself than anyone else.

I closed my eyes and focused on my body. A sensation I'd never noticed before coursed through my veins, like my magic was drawing me toward Grace.

When my eyes opened, a purple glow emanated from my fingertips. I completely forgot my friends were standing beside me as I reached out and placed my glowing hands to the wall.

I held my breath, waiting.

Nothing happened.

"Come on," I said through gritted teeth. I pushed my palms harder against the stone.

I don't know how long I stood there. Eventually, I heard someone shift behind me, reminding me that I wasn't alone. I dropped my hands and turned to my friends. They stared at me with wide eyes.

"How do we get to her?" I asked, as if one of them might know the answer.

"Maybe it's not a door," Kyle theorized. "Maybe it's a clue."

"I don't know…" Marek stepped forward to give the wall his own inspection.

"Hold on." I stuck my arm out and caught him by the shoulder.

Confusion settled on his face, but he stepped out of the way.

"Maybe this'll work." I took a deep breath and opened my palm, concentrating on the magic pulsing through my body. A bright purple orb hovered millimeters above my skin. Pulling my arm back, I heaved the essence toward the carving. It exploded against the wall but did nothing more than wiggle the shelf we'd just moved.

I turned away in frustration. Marek stepped forward again. Beside him, Kyle ran his hands along the stone wall. Allie remained frozen in place.

I glanced around the room like it might hold answers. My eyes fell upon the pile of junk we'd removed from the shelf. I bent to riffle through it until my fingers closed around a cool wooden handle.

"Stand back," I warned.

Marek jumped out of the way just in time for me to swing a hammer at the stone in front of me. It didn't so much as chip away the wall. I pulled my arm back to take another shot at it, but Marek caught my wrist.

"Slow down, Ryn," he ordered.

I was so caught up in finding a way through the wall that I didn't have time to think about the fact that Marek was touching me.

My eyes locked on his, but I felt more annoyed that he'd stopped me than anything. "We have to get through somehow."

"And we will," he promised.

I dropped the hand holding the hammer to my side to show him I was listening, but I couldn't manage to slow my quick, shallow breaths.

"Look." Marek pointed to a small cavity in the stone just below the outline of the Davina woman.

Allie and I both drew closer to inspect it.

I, personally, saw nothing significant about it.

"And?" I asked, looking up at him.

He raised his eyebrows like he couldn't believe I didn't get it. "Look closer."

I did, even going so far as to stick my finger in the hole and feel around. My fingernail caught on a small crack running vertically along the inside of it. I bent to look inside. Realization and disappointment struck me simultaneously.

"A keyhole," I said. It wasn't a question.

Marek nodded.

Kyle knelt next to the hole to take a look.

I paced around the room. "Great. So now that we've found her, we have to find a *key*, too. That could be anywhere!"

I rushed back over to the wall and stuck my finger inside the hole, channeling my magic toward it.

Marek stopped me by taking ahold of my wrist before I could get too far. "Be careful. You don't want to damage the lock, do you?"

"How do you know this won't get us through?" I raised a challenging eyebrow.

"Maybe Kyle was right. Maybe it's not a door. Maybe she's not right here." Marek patted the wall.

"We can at least find out!" I cried.

"That's not what I meant." Marek ran his fingers through his hair like he always did when he became frustrated. I couldn't help but think he was frustrated with *me*. "I meant that maybe the door is somewhere else and this is just the spot that unlocks it."

Marek began pacing along the basement wall like he was looking for a secret passageway. Kyle started on the other side of the room to help look.

"Where?" I asked rhetorically. "I don't see a door, Marek. She's *here*, right behind this carving. I can *feel* it."

Marek tore his gaze from the wall. "Okay, but I still don't think we should destroy the lock."

"What does it matter as long as we get through?" I argued. "I don't see any keys lying around nearby, do you?"

He continued around the room without answering.

I turned back to Allie, hoping she'd agree with me.

It took her a moment to catch me staring. "What? Don't ask me. I don't have any ideas."

"Maybe we should call Fletcher," Kyle suggested from across the room.

My shoulders relaxed slightly. "Fine."

Allie already had her phone out. She snapped a picture of the carving on the wall. While she contacted Fletcher and caught him up on what was happening, I sat on the cold basement floor and stared at the wall in front of me. I still couldn't process the reality of the situation.

"Grace," I mumbled under my breath, "how can you be so close yet so far out of reach?"

~

I managed to get my mom out of the house by convincing her I needed a fluffy purple scarf. I knew she didn't have the yarn for it and would have to make a trip to the craft store. She seemed positively pleased that I was taking an interest in her hobby.

She should've known me better than that.

Marek and Kyle made a show of getting into Kyle's car to leave. Mom wouldn't have let them stay when she wasn't around.

Fletcher showed up a few minutes later. He stood in front of the wall the whole time with his chin rested on his fist and his brow furrowed in deep thought.

"I'll have to go through my history books again," he said.

I knew that meant he didn't have any ideas.

Fletcher, Marek, and Kyle left a few minutes before my mom arrived home. Shortly after, Allie headed home, too.

I returned to the basement and didn't take my eyes off the Davina carving as I lowered myself to the cold floor and crossed my legs. A soothing stillness settled over the basement. Closing my eyes, I tensed my shoulder and felt the familiar sensation of my wings sprouting out of my back. I thought it might help me relax and get in tune with Grace.

I become so consumed in thoughts of how to get through to her that I didn't hear my mother calling for me from upstairs. I didn't hear the door to the basement open or her footsteps descend the steps.

But I heard her audible intake of breath when she saw me sitting there, white wings sprouted from my back and everything.

18

I sprang to my feet and whirled around to face her. I forgot to account for the extra space I took up, and my wings scraped painfully along the stone wall.

"Mom!"

"Kathryn!" She froze.

I pulled my wings into me, but it was too late. Mom's knees shook, and she sank down onto a step in the middle of the staircase. One hand tightened around the railing.

I crossed the basement and climbed the stairs to sit next to her. "Mom, it's okay."

I reached out to place my hand on hers, but she recoiled and stared at me in shock. Her mouth opened, but no sound came out.

"Calm down, Mom," I insisted. "I can explain everything."

Mom finally blinked and dropped her hand from the railing. She brushed her bangs from her eyes, but her gaze never met mine.

"Sorry," she said in a dazed voice. "I don't know what came over me. I just got lightheaded. I think I'm going to go lie down."

Mom rose and started up the stairs.

I shot to my feet. "That's it?"

What the hell?

She stopped at the basement door and finally looked at me. "What?"

"We're not even going to *talk* about this?" I demanded.

255

The time had come to tell her the truth, and she was just going to walk away from it? I could be cruel; I could let her believe she was going insane like she'd done to me my whole life. But this was my chance to finally convince her I wasn't crazy. After all this time, I needed to hear her admit she was wrong.

"I'm just lightheaded is all," she insisted.

"No," I said in a strong voice. "You *saw* my wings."

"What are you talking about?" Her voice shook. I could hear it in her tone; she feared we were sharing in the same delusion.

"I'm not crazy," I said. "And neither are you."

My frustrations grew the longer she stared at me without speaking.

I gritted my teeth and pushed past her into the hallway. "I'll show you!"

I stopped in the living room and tensed my shoulders. White feathery wings sprouted from my back. Mom's eyes widened from where she stood in the doorway. She took a step back and steadied herself against the wall.

"Ever heard of the Davina, Mom?"

"The what?" she asked like she hadn't heard me.

"The Davina," I repeated. "They're like angels. I'm one of them."

Mom shook her head like she couldn't believe what she was hearing. "This isn't happening," she mumbled to herself.

I gritted my teeth. This was happening whether she liked it or not. She was *not* going to make me feel ashamed about it. I had half a mind to slap her across the face and snap her out of her shocked daze.

"Pull yourself together, Mom," I said in a strict voice.

"Don't you use that tone with me," she replied instinctively.

There's the mom I know.

I took a deep breath. "Can you please sit down so we can talk about this?"

She hesitated.

"Please," I begged.

Mom inched along the perimeter of the room like she was trying to keep her distance from me. She sat on the couch and never took her eyes off my wings.

I sank into the loveseat across from her. "Let me explain."

From there, the confessions tumbled out of me. I repeated the stories of the Davina and the demons Fletcher had told me. I told her about Grace and how I had access to her powers. I admitted Grace was in our basement and that it was my destiny to awaken her.

Mom remained silent the whole time I spoke. I had no clue what she was thinking until I finally finished my story.

"Kathryn, this is insane," she said, as if trying to convince us both of that. "Even if it were true, do you really think I'd let you go fight on the front lines of some ancient war?"

She might as well have punched me in the gut the way her words hit me.

"You don't have a choice," I snapped.

"As long as I'm your mother, I do," she argued. "You're not an adult yet."

"What does that matter? This is something I really want to do, Mom."

"You do?" she asked in surprise.

Did I mean it? I contemplated the question for several moments. I wasn't interested in killing demons, but I still wanted to help the Davina. I still wanted to wake Grace.

"Yeah, I do," I said. "It's the first time I've really felt like I was meant for something."

I literally *was* meant to awaken Grace, but it was more than that. There was a passion that came with it that I'd never felt before.

Mom shook her head sternly. "If what you're saying is true, you could be in serious danger."

And I hadn't even told her about Dorian yet.

"We could move far away from here, somewhere you'd be safe," she insisted.

I shot out of my seat, enraged. "All you ever do is run. You've been running away from your past for ten years. I asked you earlier if you were running from something or toward something. I get it now. It's why you always kept us away from the Midwest. It's why you never let me choose where we'd go next. You knew I'd want to come back to this area because it's the only place that's ever felt like home."

Mom's eyes followed me as I paced across the living room. "Kathryn, calm down—"

"Don't you think it's time to finally face your past?" I asked bitterly.

She furrowed her brow. "What do you mean?"

I stopped abruptly. "Maybe it's time we finally talk about the night you tried to kill yourself."

The room went dead silent for ten agonizing seconds.

I took a deep breath and sat next to my mom on the couch. "Mom, there's something you should know about that night."

She fell quiet again as I told her the truth about Clinton. A wave of emotions consumed me. Hot, heavy tears rolled down my cheeks. I sniffled, but I didn't hold the tears back.

Without warning, a second wave hit, this one stronger than the last. I leaned against my mom and buried my face in her shoulder. My sobs grew audible, and my head began to hurt from the tension.

Mom pulled me tighter into her arms. Slowly, she reached out and stroked my wings.

She sighed heavily. "It's so unbelievable—"

"Mom, don't," I said, drawing away from her. "This isn't something I made up. This isn't in my head. It's really happening."

Her expression softened. "Kathryn, I—" She paused for a moment and inhaled a deep breath. "I believe you."

I had the sudden urge to cry again, though this time for different reasons. I'd waited a long time to hear my mom to say those words. I honestly never thought I would.

For one brief moment, all seemed right in the world.

19

It was impossible to sleep that night knowing that just two floors below me lay my destiny. Despite the restless sleep I had, I woke early and headed to the basement in my pajamas. I slowly ran my fingers over the carving again, trying to take in every detail.

"Grace," I whispered into thin air, "how am I supposed to get to you?"

I forced my body to relax. It took an incredible amount of effort when all I wanted to do was smash through the wall. I pictured purple energy flowing through my body and pressed my hands to the stone like I had before. Disappointment washed over me when nothing happened.

Ignoring Marek's instruction, I placed my index finger into the cavity and concentrated on sending my magic down my fingertips and into the lock. That didn't work, either.

A moment later, the doorbell rang. I quickly jerked away from the wall like I'd been caught doing something wrong. I heard my mother's muffled voice from upstairs telling me to get the door.

I didn't know what I expected, but I certainly didn't expect to find Trenton standing on my front porch. He wore a tight black t-shirt that showed off his muscular arms. His blond hair hung in loose waves around his face, and his jaw was outlined in a small amount of stubble. I'd be damned if he wasn't as hot as Marek.

I probably looked like a mess. I hadn't even brushed my hair yet; it was tied in a messy bun atop my head.

"Hey, Trenton. What are you doing here?" I asked curiously.

He smiled confidently. "I wanted to see you."

"Really?" My voice came out several pitches higher than normal.

Trenton stared at me with sexy, smoldering eyes. He spoke softly. "I can't stop thinking about you."

I was struck silent as butterflies danced around in my stomach.

"Who is it?" my mom called from her office upstairs.

"Just a friend," I yelled up to her.

I turned back to Trenton. He had this look in his eyes like he wanted to talk to me about something. I stepped outside into warm, humid air and closed the door behind me.

"What's up?" I asked.

"Here's the thing, Ryn," he said without hesitation. "I like you."

His confession came unexpectedly. I didn't know how to respond.

"I really like hanging out with you. I need to know if you feel something, too." He spoke with a hint of urgency.

I stared up into his dark brown eyes. The more I hung out with Trenton, the more I thought we could work together. But then there was Marek…

"We have fun together, and it was awesome when you stood up to Casey." Trenton reached out to gently take my hand. "Am I crazy, or is there something between us?"

I blinked several times. My hand hardly felt like my own as he ran his fingers across it.

Dammit. I had to say *something*.

Finally, I found my voice. "Trenton, we hardly know each other."

That never stopped me with Marek.

He shrugged like it didn't matter. "What do you want to know?"

"I—I don't know," I stammered. What *did* I want to know about him?

"All that matters is that we have fun together," Trenton said. "It doesn't matter that we don't know about each other's pasts."

I smiled lightly. "You say that like you don't want to talk about your past."

Trenton smirked, confirming he had secrets of his own. "Well, do you want to talk about yours?"

My mind instantly fell upon all the things I *didn't* want to talk about. My mom. Clinton. Dorian.

Trenton spoke quickly. "If you must know, my mother abandoned me because she's the polar opposite of my father; my father basically lives on another planet; and my grandma, who I lived with since I was born, died when—"

"No," I cut him off. I didn't want to have to share all my secrets, too. "I don't want to know all that. It's kind of nice being friends without having to know everything."

"You sure?" he asked with an amused smile. "Because I have plenty of secrets to share. I just need to know if…"

I suddenly felt self-conscious as he stared down at me. I couldn't explain why my cheeks heated under his gaze. "Need to know what?"

Trenton's eyes danced across my face. He reached out slowly and brushed a strand of hair out of my eyes. "I need to know if you're as amazing as you seem."

I couldn't help but smile. But as much as I enjoyed the compliments, it didn't feel right to accept them. Not when I was still hung up on Marek. Not when Grace needed me right now. Not when—

Without warning, Trenton's lips swooped down to meet mine. My entire body tensed. It took a moment for my mind to catch up and realize what was happening. Instinct took over. I relaxed into his embrace and found myself kissing him back. My heart fluttered, but it wasn't the crazy heart-pounding excitement I felt when Marek kissed me.

Trenton's lips parted to deepen the kiss. His lips weren't as soft as Marek's.

I suddenly became aware that my mind was on Marek while I was kissing Trenton. This wasn't fair to him. I drew away.

Trenton's eyes searched mine. I tried to keep my expression neutral, to not give away my thoughts. He smiled down at me as if expecting me to tell him how amazing it was.

But I couldn't lie to him.

My small voice broke the silence. "Trenton, I'm sorry."

He furrowed his brow. "Sorry for what?"

My throat closed up around my words. I didn't want to hurt his feelings.

"I'm not sure I can handle this right now," I said.

Trenton's shoulders dropped. Shit. I was going to be the asshole who broke his heart.

"There's a lot going on in my life," I told him. "I need some time to think about it."

I couldn't watch his heart break in front of me. I did the only thing I could think to do to save us both the trouble. I turned to the door behind me and left Trenton standing on my front porch.

Great. Now I was an asshole *and* a coward.

I breathed a heavy sigh and leaned my back against the front door. I closed my eyes and listened to the stairs creak under Trenton's weight as he retreated. The sound of his car engine reached my ears, but it faded as he drove off down the street.

Tension formed in my head. *Did* I feel something for Trenton? Had I betrayed Marek by kissing him? I hated leaving him hanging like that, but I didn't know what else to do. He deserved better than me.

The next morning, I contemplated how to tell Allie about what happened since I last saw her. I settled on telling her about my mom first.

"I told my mom," I admitted on our way to school Monday morning.

Allie glanced to me from the driver's seat. "Really? How'd she take it?"

I pondered it for a moment. "Better than I thought. It took some convincing, but it's kind of a relief that she knows."

"I bet it was hard trying to keep it from her," she said.

I shrugged. "I never thought I'd tell her, to be honest. I didn't think she'd believe me."

"But she does, doesn't she?" Allie asked.

"Yeah. But *you're* not going to believe what else happened to me yesterday."

"Oh?" Allie's eyebrows rose curiously.

I bit the inside of my lip. "Trenton kissed me."

"*What?*" Allie's foot tapped the brakes.

"Yeah, but I'm not sure about him. It wasn't the same as kissing Marek." I knotted my hands in my lap. "Marek doesn't seem all that interested in me, though. Maybe I should give Trenton a chance. I *do* like him." It sounded like I was trying to convince myself of that.

Allie pulled into the school's parking lot. She cut the engine and turned to me. "No. Here's what you're going to do. You're going to grow a pair of balls and tell Marek you kissed Trenton."

I leaned away from her. "Whoa. When did you become the boss of me?"

"Just now," she said with a smile. "Marek likes you; I know it. Now get your butt into school and make that boy jealous."

I laughed. "And what if he doesn't care that I kissed Trenton?"

Allie shrugged. "His loss."

"Fine. I'll think about it," I said as I exited the vehicle.

Allie and I walked up to school together. We entered the front doors into the common room. My eyes instantly fell on Marek seated at one of the chairs surrounding the mansion's fireplace. Kyle sat next to him in the adjacent chair, and a group of three sophomores sat on the couch across from them. Several other students passed through the room.

Allie nudged me with her elbow.

"Right now?" I hissed under my breath.

Allie wiggled her eyebrows. "Now or never."

A smile lit up Marek's face. He turned and noticed us for the first time. His smile widened when his eyes met mine, and my stomach summersaulted inside my abdomen.

"Hey, Kyle." Allie motioned for him to join her.

He stood, leaving me the seat beside Marek. I gladly sank into it before my legs turned to mush under Marek's sexy gaze.

"Hey," he said. "What's up?"

My eyes followed Allie and Kyle as they disappeared into the hallway behind the grand staircase. I turned back to Marek and shrugged. I wasn't about to admit everything to him with an audience.

"Did you make any progress?" he asked.

"You mean with…" I lowered my voice. "With Grace? No, I don't have any ideas."

Marek frowned. "Fletcher and I came up empty handed, too."

"Don't you think Fletcher's trying a little too hard to find an answer in his history books?" I asked.

Marek leaned an elbow on the armrest of his chair. "I don't know. He's a history teacher. That's kind of his thing."

The warning bell rang, and the three sophomores stood to head to class. Marek shifted his weight, but he didn't get to his feet when he saw I wasn't moving.

"What's up?" Marek asked.

I want you.

My heart pounded wildly in my chest. My throat closed up around my words, forcing them back down my throat.

"Nothing." I tried to sound confident in my answer, but I wasn't sure I succeeded.

"Ryn," Marek said gently. He reached out and took my fingers in his.

My breath hitched.

"Are you okay?" He sounded genuinely concerned.

An intense internal conflict sparked inside of me. I wanted nothing more than to spit out the words yet remain completely silent at the same time.

"I'm fine," I lied.

"No, you're not," he accused. "I know you."

I dropped my gaze and mumbled under my breath. "Hardly."

"Hardly?" he asked like he couldn't believe what I was saying. "Just because we haven't known each other long doesn't mean we don't know each other. I know your secrets. We spend almost all our time together."

"But you still don't want to *be* together." I was surprised to hear the words slip out of my mouth.

Marek's expression quickly turned to confusion. "Is that what's wrong?"

I couldn't bear to look at him. "I—I guess so."

Marek squeezed my hand tighter to get me to look at him. "You can't honestly think I don't want to be with you, Ryn."

Suddenly, the words didn't seem so difficult to find anymore. "Of course I think that. Why would I think otherwise? You've given no indication that you want to be more than friends. Not since we kissed. And I thought that meant something."

"It did," Marek insisted. "It meant something. Every moment I've spent with you has meant something."

I wanted to believe his words, but his actions showed otherwise. "Then why haven't you shown it?"

Marek dropped my hand and raked his fingers through his hair while I spoke.

"Why haven't you done anything?" I asked. "Why—"

"Why haven't *you*?" he shouted.

Two students climbing the stairs gave him a strange look.

Marek seemed just as shocked as I was at his question. He rubbed his hand over his face before dropping it to his lap.

I waited until the common room was empty again before speaking. I didn't care that we only had a minute left to get to class.

"I thought it was obvious," I whispered.

In one swift motion, Marek rose to his feet and pulled me up to stand beside him. Our bodies nearly touched as he tucked a strand of loose hair behind my ear. He closed his eyes and rested his forehead against mine. He smelled familiar—like leather and clean laundry.

For one long moment, it felt as if the world had stopped. My heart rose in my chest, and my breath stopped. We stood frozen, like we were suspended in time.

All too soon, time started again. My heart dropped back down where it belonged and hammered against my rib cage. My breath returned in an uncontrollable, shallow rhythm.

"I'm so sorry, Ryn," Marek whispered.

My knees quivered as his hot breath rushed across my face.

"For what?" I asked in a shaky voice. Now that he was this close to me, it didn't seem like he should be apologizing for anything.

"For leading you on and then just leaving you to read the rest of the signals yourself."

"There were signals?" If it wasn't for my quiet, breathy voice, I was sure the question would've shattered the entire tone of the moment. Somehow, it didn't.

Marek's blue eyes opened and focused on me. "Of course there were. I want to be with you. I just didn't think we should right now, not with everything going on. You needed to focus on your training, not on me."

"And you thought ignoring the topic would accomplish that? If you don't claim me, Marek, someone else will. Trenton kissed me."

Marek's expression hardened. "He did?"

I nodded sheepishly.

"I never meant to let you think I wasn't interested," Marek said. "It was Fletcher's fault. He insisted I leave you alone."

I let out a breath of disbelief. *That jerk.*

"But he lets us train together," I said.

Marek nodded. "He wanted to train you himself, but I talked him into letting me help. He said I could only if I didn't distract you."

I thought about all the times he'd pulled me close during our training sessions. "You didn't make that very easy. You, James Marek, are pretty damn distracting."

Marek brushed his fingers through the ends of my hair. "So are you, Ryn."

Marek bent to brush his lips against mine. Shock riveted through me before I could really process what was happening. One taste wasn't enough for either of us. His arms wrapped around my waist, pulling me into an embrace. His lips pressed against mine with a passion I'd never felt before.

Everything else around us vanished. Even the hardwood floor seemed to evaporate from beneath us. He kissed me like nothing else in this world mattered. Heat rose to every inch of my skin as my body pressed harder against his. I clung to him, never wanting to let go.

Disappointment washed over me when he drew away. I was glad he kept his hands on my shoulders or I might've fallen over from the spell he'd put on me.

"Now do you believe me?" Marek asked.

I answered with a wide grin.

In the heat of the moment, I forgot we were standing in the common room. Marek's face fell as his eyes locked on something —*someone*—behind me.

My stomach dropped to the floor when I turned to find Trenton standing at the base of the staircase. He glared at us with a deeply hurt expression on his face.

Shit. I'd just graduated far, *far* beyond asshole.

"Trenton, wait," I said.

He was already quickly retreating down the hall.

"I'm sorry," I called after him.

The problem was, I wasn't sure that was true.

21

"I can't believe this!" I complained to Allie after school in her bedroom. "Can I see your pillow? I'd like to scream into it."

Allie smiled in amusement and tossed her pillow across the bed at me. I pulled it to my face and screamed, more for show than anything.

"Are you okay?" Allie asked in genuine concern.

I placed the pillow between me and the wall and leaned against it. "I'm overwhelmed. I just broke a guy's heart, and I actually kind of liked him. I've found Grace but can't get to her. Should I go on?"

"We'll get to her," Allie assured me confidently. "We just need to find the key."

I glanced at her skeptically.

"I mean it," she said. "Your instinct led you to Grace. It should lead you to the key, too."

I frowned. "You keep saying things like that, but I don't feel anything."

"Maybe the key is in your house somewhere," she suggested.

"Yeah," I said sarcastically. "Maybe the owners left it on the kitchen counter. I must've missed it when we moved in."

Allie hopped up from her bed and bent to slip her tennis shoes on. "I know what you need."

I eyed her. "What's that?"

"A break," she said.

"No," I objected. "I've already spent enough time distracted today. Between school and practicing my essence with Marek, I hardly had a moment to put more thought into Grace."

"You thought about it *all* day yesterday," Allie pointed out. "Just take a deep breath, okay?"

I reluctantly followed her instruction, but it didn't help. Instead, I shoved my head into her pillow and screamed again. That helped some.

Allie laughed at me.

"Fine," I agreed. "We can take a *short* break."

Allie grabbed her purse. "Let's get something to eat."

On the way to Angela's Café, I noticed for the first time how little I'd eaten over the past two days. I had a ham sandwich earlier that day at lunch. Besides that, I wasn't sure of the last time I ate. I ordered an extra side of potato salad to help fill my belly. My stress eased slightly once we finished eating—though my wallet wasn't pleased.

There was a chill in the air when we stepped outside after our meal. I glanced up the street and noticed Celeste's next door. I had the sudden urge to go inside and check it out.

"Hey." I caught Allie's attention. "Didn't you say you wanted to take me here sometime?"

Allie looked toward the small jewelry shop. "Yeah. You love earrings so much, I thought you'd like it."

I absentmindedly twirled the green studs around in my ears. "Let's check it out."

Allie pulled open the door to Celeste's, and we stepped inside. It was like walking straight into heaven. Unique handcrafted pieces of jewelry hung from the displays. Every necklace I walked by was different from the last. Beautiful stones and gorgeous beads filled my senses, and I caught a hint of rose in the air. The place was perfect.

My eyes fell upon a display of earrings. I rushed over to it.

"I like these ones!" I held up a pair of earrings that dangled with small white feathers.

Allie inhaled a sharp breath. "You should make your own!"

Excitement filled me. I lowered my voice to a whisper even

though we were alone. "You mean, from my *own* wings? That is probably the best idea I've ever heard."

"Do you have the supplies? Because if you don't, I think they have jewelry-making kits over there." She pointed.

"Making jewelry sounds like fun." I grabbed two more sets of earrings and contemplated spending the money on them.

"Come on." Allie led me down the aisle.

I eyed the array of earring hooks, trying to decide on a color.

"Do you ladies need any help?" a woman's voice came from behind us.

I turned to find a thin woman just a few years older than me standing close by. She had long, straight brown hair and a friendly smile. She wore a lot of jewelry, but in a tasteful way. Several rings adorned her fingers, and her ears had been double pierced. A necklace with a key pendant on it hung around her neck.

"No, thank you." I smiled back.

"Okay," she said. "My name's Meg. Let me know if you change your mind. We close in a few minutes, but you're free to browse as long as you like."

"Thank you." I turned back to the hooks and opted for the silver ones. I grabbed one of the jewelry-making kits from the bottom shelf.

Allie and I continued down the row slowly. I couldn't help but take in every piece of jewelry I laid eyes on.

"I swear I could spend a whole week in this store and not get bored," I said. "Oh, look. More earrings!"

By the time we finished browsing the aisles, I'd settled on three pairs of earrings and the supplies needed to make my own. It would eat up the rest of my birthday money, but I'd been saving it for something good.

"All set?" Meg asked cheerfully when we reached the counter.

"Yep," Allie answered for the both of us. She handed over a pretty blue stone necklace for Meg to ring up.

"Do you wear a lot of jewelry?" Meg asked to keep up the small talk.

Allie gestured to me. "She collects earrings."

"Ooh." Meg seemed suddenly interested. "Have any favorite styles?"

I shrugged. "Depends on my mood. I like studs, but if I'm going for cute, I'll try anything unique and dangly."

Meg wiggled her eyebrows. "Anyone you're trying to look cute *for*?" She took Allie's cash from her hand and opened the register.

My gaze dropped slightly as a blush rose to my cheeks. "There's this guy—"

I froze when my eyes fell on Meg's necklace. She didn't seem to notice my words had instantly stopped in their tracks.

"What's he like?" Meg asked.

I hardly processed the sound of her voice over my own pulse pounding in my ears. At first, Meg's necklace had seemed ordinary, like the key had been made to be a necklace—but I knew it had a far greater purpose. It looked old, unlike any car or house key I'd ever owned. I couldn't take my eyes off the angel wing design that spread out at the end of the key.

The key matched the exact pattern of the Davina wings carved into my basement wall.

Meg caught me staring.

"Sorry," I said breathlessly when my eyes met hers. "I like your necklace. Do you have any more like it?"

Meg handed Allie her receipt and then touched her fingers lightly to the key. "Unfortunately, I don't. Most of our jewelry is hand crafted with things we find at flea markets. We aim to make every piece unique."

I swallowed hard, still not sure if I'd breathed at all in the last minute. "What about yours? Did that key come from a flea market?"

"No. My grandpa gave it to me before he passed. My grandma said it'd been in the family for generations, but I never found out what it went to. I figure whatever it unlocked is long gone. It makes a great necklace, though, doesn't it?"

"Yeah, it does," I said flatly. "I guess that means it's not for sale."

Meg frowned. "It's not. But we can keep an eye out for something similar if you'd like and make you a custom piece."

"No," I said. "It's just... I think I might know what it opens."

Meg placed a protective hand over the key. Her voice became defensive. "Like I said, it's not for sale."

Meg rang up my total, but each passing moment felt like an eternity. I barely remembered handing over my money. It wasn't until Allie and I stepped outside, still keyless, that I had a moment to let it all sink in.

"Oh my gosh!" Allie burst with excitement. She hopped up and down as we took a few steps down the sidewalk.

Shock hit me so hard that I had to stop and lean myself against the outside of Angela's Café. My head swam, and my heart raced.

"I was right," Allie gloated, still jumping around ecstatically. "I *told* you that your magic would lead you to the key, and it did. It led you to Celeste's just like it led you to Grace!"

"Shh…" I glanced up and down the street, but no one was nearby to overhear. "Okay, lesson learned. Never question my instinct again, especially when it comes to Grace. I just want to know how we're going to get our hands on that key."

Allie calmed down and leaned against the building beside me. "I don't know. Maybe we could talk to her and tell her why we need it."

"Great idea." I rolled my eyes. "What are we supposed to say? 'Hey, there's an ancient angel buried in my basement. I have the power to wake her and save the world from impending doom. The only thing holding us back is that we need a key to get to her, and you have it.' If you want to go back into the jewelry shop to say all that, be my guest."

"Maybe don't word it like *that*. But if that key has been in her family for generations, she's probably a Davina. She'd know the stories. I'm sure she'd be willing to help."

I pushed myself away from the wall. "I don't know, Allie."

"We could—" she started, but she abruptly stopped when the sound of familiar voices hit our ears.

The door to Angela's Café opened, and Casey stepped out, laughing. Troy and Trenton followed behind her. Trenton's expression immediately fell when he saw me, and I stiffened.

Casey's laughter died, and a look of disgust crossed her face. She took her time eyeing Allie and me up and down individually. I saw it as a blessing that she continued down the sidewalk without saying a word, but the tension in the air was practically suffocating.

Trenton's eyes caught mine as he passed. He scowled.

I wanted to say something to him—to apologize—but I couldn't find the words. He was too far down the sidewalk by the time I found the courage to open my mouth.

"Is it just me, or did it seem like Casey was trying to kill us with her stare?" Allie asked once they were out of earshot.

"Definitely trying to kill us. She knows we're going to beat them in our first mock battle."

"I don't think that's why she was looking at us like that."

I tore my gaze from Casey's retreating figure as she ducked her head into a vehicle. "What's your theory, then?"

"I know why she hates me. The question is, why was she looking at *you* like that?"

I ignored her question. "Why *does* she hate you?"

"I asked you first," Allie challenged.

"I'll tell you if you tell me."

"Fine," Allie agreed. "I'll tell you in the car."

After getting into her car, we sat silently for what felt like a full minute. Allie didn't make a move to start the vehicle, but her hands gripped the steering wheel tightly.

"Okay," she breathed, like telling the story was hard for her. "Something you might not know is that Casey and I used to be really good friends."

"Really?" I asked in shock.

"I know," she agreed. "It seems so unlikely now, but people change. We were practically inseparable until high school."

"What happened?" I asked, dreading the answer.

"Well, for one, puberty hit," Allie said with a tense laugh. "Casey had always been—how do I put this?—bossy. I never really thought much about it. It was just the way she was. Casey was pretty and popular, and if you wanted to be Casey's friend, you did whatever Casey said."

"So," I teased, "she hasn't changed much?"

Allie gave an uncomfortable smile and then continued her story. "Basically, being friends with her was toxic, and it only got worse in junior high."

"In what way?" I asked curiously.

Allie shrugged. "Little things all piling up. She'd tell me I was ugly or dumb or whatever, but then the next day she was all about how pretty and smart I was."

Allie's story reminded me of a friend I'd made in eighth grade. Needless to say, I was grateful to move away from *that* school.

"According to Casey, I could never do anything right, and no matter what I did, she was always *better* at it."

I couldn't help but feel sorry for Allie. "Why'd you stay friends with her?"

A shamed expression crossed her face. "I don't know. I guess I thought our friendship meant something. Then the summer between junior high and high school happened." She took a deep breath. "By the time we started at Galen High, our friendship was over for good."

I waited for her to elaborate, but she'd gone silent.

"What happened that summer?" I prodded.

"It sounds dumb now that I think about it, but it was, like, the biggest deal in the world back then. I fell *really* hard for this guy we used to go to school with."

I could already see where this was going. "Do I know him?"

Allie shook her head. "We went to junior high together, but not high school. He went to Eagle Valley High and graduated last year. He wasn't a Davina."

It was hard to picture Allie having a crush on anyone besides Kyle.

"Anyway, Blake and I—that was his name—spent a lot of the summer talking online. And, of course, I gushed every detail of it to Casey. Then suddenly, *she* liked him, too."

"Ugh, that's the worst," I said.

Allie scowled. "I haven't gotten to the good part yet. Obviously, it annoyed me that she liked him, but I still stayed friends with her. Don't ask me why. But Blake didn't like Casey. When we hung out with him, he didn't really show any interest in her even though she flirted like crazy."

"Good. You're worth way more than she is."

"Thanks," she said sheepishly. "I'd never really had anyone show interest in me because they were always falling all over Casey."

"Boys are stupid," I said. "You're twice as pretty with ten times the personality."

Allie forced a smile. "Thanks. Anyway, since Blake didn't go for her, I thought we had something special. But then I started noticing that he wasn't talking to me online as much. He always seemed to take forever to respond back. Eventually, he told me that he didn't know how he felt about me because he thought he might be falling for someone else."

I drew in a sharp breath. "He did *not* have a crush on Casey."

Allie dropped her gaze. "Well, not exactly…"

"Oh, she *did not*," I said, suddenly catching on.

"She did. She created a fake profile and started talking to him just so he'd stop paying attention to me."

"I'm *so* glad you stopped being friends with her. That's unforgiveable."

"The part that sucks is that the fake profile she made basically *was* me. This fake girl liked all the same music as me, read all the same books I read, even had dark black hair like I do. Casey would steal my statuses and reword them. Like, if I was upset, her fake persona was upset. If I was having a good day, this fake girl was having a good day. It's like she was trying to *be* me in order to get Blake's attention."

"But he wasn't really paying attention to *her*," I pointed out.

"But to Casey, he was. And by that point, she'd distracted him enough that he stopped caring about me. I'm sure that's all she wanted."

"What a *bitch*," I muttered under my breath.

Allie raised her eyebrows. "And you didn't believe me the first time I told you that."

"It wasn't about believing you. I just thought you were being a bit harsh. But now I'm not sure that word does the girl justice."

"I expected better from a friend," Allie said. "I expect better from a *Davina*."

Her words hung in the air for several long seconds.

"So, how'd you find out it was her?" I asked.

Allie's grip tightened around the steering wheel. "She admitted it to me. We were still friends, and I was telling her all about this girl that Blake said he liked. She started laughing and told me *she* was behind the account. She even logged into it on her computer to show me and then bragged about how often they talked."

"I hope you smashed that computer," I said.

Allie smiled. "No, but I did walk out of her house, and I never came back."

"I'm proud of you," I told her. "Casey doesn't deserve a friend like you."

"Thanks. I hate that it took me so long to realize it." She let out a breath and looked at me expectantly. "So, that's my story. What about yours?"

I hated how quickly the conversation changed topics. Quietness settled over the car for several moments.

Finally, I lifted my gaze. "First of all, Casey doesn't like me because I hang out with you and Marek. I think that automatically earns me a spot on her hit list."

"But there's more," Allie said with certainty.

"I should've told you about it sooner, but I thought I'd get in trouble if anyone knew."

The confusion on Allie's face deepened. "What happened?"

I remained silent and chewed on my bottom lip.

"Ryn, nothing you say to me is going to get you in trouble. I'm good at keeping secrets." She paused for a moment. "Unless you think I'll judge you for it... Ryn, I'm not—"

"No, I don't think that," I said quickly. "Honestly, you'll probably be proud of me."

Allie's confusion morphed into curiosity. "Now you *have* to tell me."

I couldn't help the grin that spread over my face. "It's nothing, really. I just... kind of... threatened Casey with a fireball."

"What?" Allie asked like she hadn't heard me correctly.

"Yeah, just over there." I pointed to the front of Celeste's. "It was last Friday, the night Trenton and I went out to dinner. We ran into Casey afterward, and she was being her usual self, and—"

I stopped abruptly when I turned and saw the look on Allie's face. Her jaw had dropped, and her eyes had gone wide.

My face flushed. "I know it was in public and we're supposed to keep all this stuff secret, but Trenton convinced her not to tell on me."

Allie was still frozen in shock.

"You're not mad at me, are you? You know, for showing my magic in public? I know it's risky. A couple people saw, but I don't think they—"

"Are you kidding me?" She reached out to swat me lightly. "I'm not going to tell anyone! I'm freaking *proud* of you for standing up to her."

"But it was in the middle of the street. I really should've controlled my temper."

"Don't worry about it," Allie said. "Casey probably needed that. Explains why she didn't say anything earlier. Probably afraid you'd pull another one on her."

I raised my eyebrows. "If I would've known why you guys hate each other, I might not have been able to hold back this time."

Allie laughed from beside me.

I crossed my arms and feigned disappointment. "At least you get to have fun and try to stun her. I'm thinking I'll sit out of the mock battle. I mean, I'd love to punch that girl in the face, but I don't think my magic is ready."

"You can still participate," Allie argued. "Just don't use your essence. You can practice your hand-to-hand skills."

I shot her a light smile.

"Hey, would you want to do some practice with me? You've been spending all your time training with Marek. Maybe you should shake things up."

"Oh, Allie, that's sweet, but..." How did I tell her she sucked at teaching?

"We'll only spar," she clarified.

I nodded. "Yeah, I think it might help. I'm getting used to Marek's tactics anyway. It'll help to mix things up a bit."

Her face lit up.

"But before we do, we should call Fletcher and tell him about the key," I said.

"Right. The key." Allie pulled out her phone. "Think Fletcher will have any ideas about that one?"

"I hope so," I said. "Because short of stealing it, I don't know how we're going to get our hands on it."

Fletcher sounded proud that we'd found the key so soon. Allie put him on speaker phone and set the phone between us on the middle console.

"I knew you could do it," he said. "You've been touched by Grace, Ryn, and she's going to guide you where you need to go."

"Yeah." Irritation entered my tone. "But just because we *found* the key doesn't mean we *have* it."

Fletcher went silent for a few seconds like he was considering this. "Perhaps it's best if I come along with you to talk to her."

"I think Celeste's already closed today," Allie pointed out.

I followed her gaze past the passenger side window and to the jewelry shop. The open sign that'd been lit when we arrived had been turned off. "Well, that sucks."

"We can try talking to her tomorrow," Fletcher suggested.

I had a feeling getting ahold of the key wouldn't be as easy as he made it sound.

23

"Did you hear what happened?" Allie spoke so quickly the following morning that I barely understood her.

I dropped my backpack onto the floor of her car and slid into the passenger seat. "What?"

"Someone broke into Celeste's. The front window is broken and everything. You should pay more attention to social media. Here."

Allie handed me her phone as she drove.

"Social media is just filled with people from my old schools who I don't care about and who probably don't even remember who I am." In other words, it was a total waste of my time.

I glanced down at Allie's screen. She'd pulled up a picture of the jewelry shop. The displays in the window looked the same as they had yesterday, but the glass on the front door had been shattered. I quickly scanned through the description that went with it. According to the post, the shop had been broken into late last night. Though some of the merchandise had been rummaged through, they had no evidence to suggest that anything of value had been taken.

"Oh my God!" I exclaimed when I finished reading the post. "Who would *do* that?"

"I don't know," Allie said.

"Aren't there cameras or something? They'll catch the person who did it, won't they?"

Allie raised her eyebrows. "Are you kidding me? Do you *realize* how small of a town this is?"

"Do *you* realize we live in a world where cameras are everywhere? Even if the jewelry shop doesn't have cameras, there must be *some* nearby looking out onto the street. Maybe someone saw something. Like you said, it's a small town. Gossip spreads fast."

"The police report made it sound like they were pretty clueless," Allie said. "If any cameras caught the guy, he was probably disguised or something."

I handed her phone back. "We're assuming it's a he?"

Allie pulled into the school's parking lot. "I was just saying that in general." She turned off the engine but didn't get out of the car. "Don't you think it's a little weird?"

"What? A break-in in Eagle Valley? Yeah, I suppose."

"I mean isn't it weird that they didn't take anything. Like, sure, it's just a cute shop and they're not selling engagement rings or anything like that, but wouldn't you think that if someone went through all that trouble to break in that they'd at least head for the cash register or something?"

"Well, yeah, I suppose. What are you getting at, Allie?"

"What if they were looking for something that wasn't there?"

"You think this has something to do with the key?" I asked.

"I think it has everything to do with the key."

Even though school was going to start in a few minutes, I felt rooted to my seat.

"That doesn't make any sense," I said. "Why now? And why not break into Meg's house instead of the shop?"

Allie glanced around the parking lot. "What if someone overheard us talking about it? Did we mention Meg had the key, or were we just talking about how it was in the shop?"

I went completely silent, but my heart beat rapidly against my rib cage.

"How could someone have overheard us? We were in your car practically the whole time." My eyes darted around the vehicle. "This thing isn't bugged, is it?"

Allie looked at me like I was being stupid. Apparently, my question didn't even dignify a response.

"*Practically* is the key word there," she said. "We mentioned the key as soon as we stepped out of the shop."

"But there wasn't anyone on the street."

Allie bit her lip. "I don't know. Maybe I'm just being paranoid. Maybe it has nothing to do with the key."

I suddenly felt sympathetic for her. "Well, I think you're right to be cautious. I still think we should go over there after school and try to talk to Meg. Maybe the break-in will actually help our case."

"How?" Allie looked surprised.

"If someone's after the key, maybe she'll help us."

Allie twisted her lips in thought. "If they didn't get to her first."

"Please tell me I'm making progress," I pleaded with Marek during second period.

Fletcher had paired us up for sparring in the valley again. I was well aware I was distracted today.

"You're doing better," Marek admitted. "I think the extra practice after school has been helping."

I threw a punch in his direction, which he swiftly dodged. "I'm going to have to skip out today."

"Why?" Marek swung his leg around to knock me off my feet.

I landed on my back with a hard thud. He was on top of me a second later, pinning my arms to my sides with his knees. I didn't even try to fight back. Marek stared down at me with desire in his eyes. If we weren't in the middle of class, I'd have kissed him already.

He seemed to notice he'd been on top of me a moment too long. He rolled off of me and got to his feet.

I sat up. "Did Allie tell you what happened yesterday?"

Marek held out a hand to help me up. "Most of it, I think."

"Then you know we have to go back and talk to the girl from the jewelry shop about the key."

"Yeah," Marek said. "And I'm coming with."

"You are?"

"You and Allie are the ones having all the fun lately, searching for Grace and now the key." He looked genuinely disappointed.

"Yeah, but you get to have fun training me every day," I teased. "That's an important job."

"Don't flatter yourself," he laughed.

I told myself he wanted to come because he wanted to spend more time with me. It made the rest of the day bearable, but by the time the final bell rang that day, I wasn't sure what to expect once we went to talk to Meg.

∽

When we reached Celeste's after school, it looked different from the picture I'd seen that morning. The glass had been cleaned up, and two men stood near the open door installing a brand new pane.

Allie and I stepped out of her car. Marek had followed along on his motorcycle, and Fletcher in his own vehicle.

The two men nodded a greeting to the four of us as we approached the door. Inside, a middle-aged woman stood behind the counter and talked to a man dressed in a polo shirt and nice slacks. I heard him call the woman *Celeste* and realized she was the owner. By the look of the logo on the guy's shirt, I guessed he was there to install a new security system. A few displays had been moved since yesterday. I shuttered to think what the place looked like before they'd spent all day cleaning it up.

Celeste looked up when we entered. "I'm sorry. We're closed today."

Fletcher stepped to the front of the group. "We're not here to browse. We're looking for Meg. Is she around?"

Celeste frowned. "I'm afraid not. She's a little shook up about what happened last night. Do you know her well?"

"No," Fletcher admitted, "but we wanted to offer our sympathies."

She smiled lightly. "Thank you, but you'll have to visit her at home."

"Do you happen to know where she lives?" Fletcher asked.

Celeste narrowed her eyes. "I'm not allowed to give out that type of information about our employees. If you don't know her that well, I'm sure it can wait. I can let her know you stopped in, though."

Fletcher leaned up against the front counter casually. Casual didn't work well for him. If he was trying to charm her, he should've left that job to Marek.

"Can't you make an exception this one time?" Fletcher asked softly.

"What did you say your name was?" Celeste's tone was harsh.

"Please," I begged, stepping forward. "My friend and I were in here yesterday just before the shop closed. We know Meg was working and closed up just hours before the break-in. All we want is to check on her."

Celeste eyed me. I must've come across as more trustworthy than Fletcher because she relaxed.

"You were here yesterday?" she asked.

"Yeah," I said.

"You didn't see anything suspicious, did you? No one hanging around or anything?"

My shoulders dropped. "No. The break-in was during the middle of the night, wasn't it?"

"Yes, but it never hurts to ask," Celeste said.

"Did they take anything?" I hoped she'd say yes. I *really* didn't want this to be about the key.

Celeste's brow furrowed. "No, and that's the strange part. I'm not sure they were looking for something of value. I think it was just a simple case of vandalism. My guess is some teenagers playing a prank."

"Do the police have any idea who did it?" I asked.

Her voice grew more irritated, but I couldn't blame her. This had to be a stressful day for her, and people had probably been asking the same questions all day. "Unfortunately, the public knows just about as much as I do. No suspects have been identified yet. I do appreciate you coming in to check on Meg. It was very nice of you."

It was clear in her tone that was the end of the conversation.

"Would you be able to get her a message if I left it with you?" I asked.

"Sure," she said flatly. She glanced around behind the counter and handed me a blank piece of paper and a pen.

I paused for a moment, unsure of what to say. Feeling like I was taking too long, I quickly jotted down the only thing I could think of.

Meg,
The Davina need your help. Please call me as soon as you can.
-The girl who liked your necklace

I wrote my phone number at the bottom then folded the paper into a small square and added Meg's name to the outside.

"We're sorry to bother you," I told Celeste genuinely as I slid the paper across the counter. "Thank you so much."

I could sense everyone's disappointment hit simultaneously when we exited the shop. The unspoken question hung in the air. *What do we do now?*

"I'll poke around on social media," Allie offered. "I'll see if I can find out Meg's last name so we can track her down and talk to her."

"I'll call a few people and see if anyone knows her personally," Fletcher offered.

"I can't believe we were so close!" I complained. "We're better off blasting through that wall than waiting around."

"I don't think that's a good idea." Marek meant it like a suggestion, but it sounded like a subtle demand.

"If something doesn't happen soon, you're not going to be able to stop me," I said.

Marek smiled. "I'd like to see you try."

"How would you stop me? Are you going to start stalking me?" I actually didn't think I'd mind if he did.

"Let's start with making up that training session we missed today," Marek suggested.

I crossed my arms over my chest. "Does it even matter at this point?"

"Yes," Fletcher answered immediately.

"I should be doing something to get that key," I insisted.

"Allie and I can handle that," Fletcher said. "Your training is just as important."

"Why?" I asked. "Once I get to Grace, she can take over from there."

"Only if you manage to wake her first," Fletcher said. "To do that, you need to be able to control your essence."

I opened my mouth to argue further, but Fletcher was right. If I couldn't control my essence to wake Grace, the rest of this didn't matter.

A minute later, I had a helmet strapped to my head and was climbing onto the back of Marek's motorcycle.

Marek pulled into the parking lot behind the school. I slipped off the bike and removed the helmet. He started toward the trailhead.

I glanced toward the school. "What about the basement?"

"We'll get there. I thought we could warm up with a little flying first."

"That sounds like fun!"

Marek stopped abruptly before we made it past the edge of the school. I nearly ran into him.

"What?" I asked in alarm.

He began digging inside his pockets. "I lost my keys."

"You *just* had them on your bike."

"I must've dropped them," he said. "Give me a minute. I'll catch up with you."

Marek jogged back to the parking lot while I continued toward the trail.

Disappointment hit me when I caught the sound of a familiar voice in the distance. Casey's blond hair swayed behind her near the trailhead. Like usual, she was followed by Troy and Trenton. This time, three other people had joined them. Casey turned for a moment. I could've sworn that even from this distance her eyes met mine.

"Maybe this won't be fun," I mumbled to myself.

I continued on and followed her group into the trees. I wasn't about to let her scare me off. I stared down at my feet as I walked, my thoughts racing. Maybe flying would help clear my mind.

The sound of a stick breaking caught my attention. I immediately froze. Before I had a chance to assess my surroundings, a hard object hit my chest and stole the air from my lungs. The ground swayed beneath my feet, and everything went dark.

24

"Are you okay?" The voice sounded like it was coming from under water. Strong hands shook my shoulders. "Are you okay?" the voice repeated, this time coming across more clearly.

I opened my eyes and blinked a few times until Marek's face came into focus.

"What?" I sat up. "What just happened?"

Marek scanned the trees. "You were stunned."

I suddenly felt more alert. "What the hell? Who would do that?"

"I don't know." Marek still didn't take his eyes off the forest. "I could've sworn…"

"Sworn what?" I pushed myself to my feet and dusted the dirt off my jeans.

Marek finally looked at me. "I'm not sure what I saw. I just made it to the entrance of the trail when you fell."

"Did you see anyone?" I squeaked.

Marek squinted into the trees again. "I saw movement, but I couldn't make him out. I threw essence at him, but I missed."

"Is this someone's idea of a joke?" I raised my voice and projected it into the trees. "It's not funny!"

I pushed past Marek and started toward the parking lot. "Forget it. I thought this place was supposed to be safe now."

Marek seemed confused for a moment and then hurried to catch up with me. "It *should* be. I mean, we got rid of Dorian. People

288

are coming and going from the valley all the time now that school's started."

A thought suddenly occurred to me, and I stopped in my tracks. "You don't think it was one of them, do you?"

"One of who?"

"One of the people coming and going all the time! I just saw Casey and her group headed down here."

"You're not suggesting Casey stunned you, are you?"

I gritted my teeth and continued down the trail. "I wouldn't put it past her."

Marek and I emerged from the forest.

"Why would she do that?" He sounded skeptical.

"I don't know. To show me up. To scare me."

"Casey knows the rules. We're not supposed to stun people outside of battles."

"Just because she knows the rules doesn't mean she's not above breaking them," I said. "I kind of pissed her off the other day."

"What'd you do?" He sounded genuinely curious.

I glanced around. Although no one was nearby to overhear, I didn't feel comfortable opening up to him here.

"Can we just get out of here?" I suggested.

"Yeah, sure," he said softly. "Where do you want to go?"

"I don't know. Somewhere where I'm *not* being attacked on a daily basis."

At this point, I was pretty certain I was going to die in those woods.

He glanced behind us once. "Yeah, come on."

Marek took my hand, sending my heart fluttering. A minute later, we were speeding down the street. I felt safer once my arms were wrapped around him.

Marek stopped along the shoulder of the road outside of town. I recognized the pile of rocks that cut through the trees and climbed the hill to our left. He'd taken me here a few weeks ago. It was where we shared our first kiss.

I stepped onto the gravel shoulder and handed him the bike helmet he made me wear. "Thanks for taking me here."

Marek swung his leg over the seat and stood on the road beside me. He took my hand in his and stared down at me. "You like it here?"

I nodded. I liked being anywhere Marek was.

He didn't let go of my hand as we made our way across the road and up the hill. This time, I had a better idea of where to put my feet, so we made it to the top faster. Marek still hadn't dropped my hand when we lowered ourselves to the rocky hilltop and looked out over Eagle Valley. Silence settled as he traced his thumb across the back of my hand.

"I'm sorry about what happened," he said quietly. "I shouldn't have left you for even a second."

"You couldn't have known some idiot was going to attack me— again. What's up with this place?"

"Maybe it comes with being chosen by Grace," Marek suggested like it was supposed to make me feel better.

I stared down at our entwined fingers. "Maybe I don't *want* to be chosen."

"I don't think you have a choice."

It didn't seem like I had a choice in anything lately. I didn't say anything.

Marek finally broke the silence. "You don't really think Casey stunned you, do you? What'd you do to make her mad?"

I sighed heavily. "If I tell you, I don't want any lectures about how stupid I was being, okay? I already know what I did wasn't cool."

"Okay," Marek agreed.

I told him about how I'd threatened Casey. It looked as if agreeing to not pass judgement was causing him physical pain. Knowing him, it took all his strength not to lecture me about using my essence in public.

"I know." I covered my face with my hands. "I was being stupid."

"Hey," Marek said softly. He placed an arm around my shoulder and pulled me into his chest. Somehow he had the power to relax me at the smallest touch. "You're making a bigger deal out of this than it needs to be."

I dropped my hands. "You think so?"

He squeezed me tighter for reassurance.

"But what if Casey thought it was a big deal?" I asked.

"I don't know if that has anything to do with what just happened. I thought I saw someone in the woods, but it didn't look like Casey."

"I thought you said you didn't know what you saw. She could've hung back and waited around for me."

Marek fell silent. I could hear his heartbeat from where my head rested on his shoulder. I closed my eyes and pretended for a moment that everything was normal, that I'd never learned about Grace or the Davina and that I'd come to Eagle Valley to only find romance. Marek shifted, pulling me out of my daydream.

"I don't know what to think," I said quietly. "If it *was* Casey, screw her."

"And if it wasn't?" Marek asked.

"If it wasn't her, who would it be? No one else hates me enough, and it's not like I have a demon after me again." A sudden thought occurred to me, and a sharp breath passed my lips. I straightened up. "What if *she's* after me because of the key? Allie and I thought someone might've overheard us yesterday. It was Casey. It had to be. She was right inside Angela's Café when Allie and I were talking about it."

"Whoa, slow down," he insisted.

I hadn't realized how fast I'd been talking.

"You think whoever stunned you in the woods just now is the same person who broke into Celeste's?"

"Yeah," I said slowly. I mean, there was no guarantee the break-in had anything to do with me, but it seemed like too much of a coincidence to ignore.

"And you think Casey did it?" Marek didn't sound convinced.

"Are you defending her? I thought you didn't like her."

"I'm not saying I like her. It's just, Ryn, she's a Davina."

"That doesn't mean she can be trusted," I pointed out. "Even Fletcher doesn't trust all the Davina."

"Why would she break into the jewelry shop?"

"I don't know." I honestly didn't. "Maybe she wants to find

Grace herself. Or maybe she just can't stand the idea of someone else being the hero."

"But by doing that she'd unleash an army of demons into this realm. Even Casey isn't that stupid."

I pressed my lips together in thought. "But she was there both times, Marek. She must've heard us talking about Grace and the key. And she was in the woods just now. Isn't that a little suspicious?"

Marek and I couldn't seem to come to an agreement over what had been going on these last few days. He tried convincing me that the two incidents weren't related and that I was being paranoid.

All I wanted to do was kiss him to shut him up.

He wrapped me in his arms again. I felt protected and comfortable there, as if nothing could get to me as long as he was nearby. A serene silence settled over the hill. I closed my eyes and focused on the rise and fall of Marek's chest and the warmth of his arms around me.

"Marek," I said softly.

"Yeah?" he asked into my hair.

I didn't know what to say. All I wanted was to enjoy his company.

"What do you want to do with your life?" My voice came out dreamily. The light breeze was putting me to sleep.

"I want to become a Protector."

"Do you feel pressured into it?" I asked curiously.

"No. I didn't grow up with all this. I would've chosen to become a Protector anyway."

"Why's that?"

Marek pulled me closer. "I like the idea of saving people from the evil in this world."

It sounded like there was more behind his words than he was willing to admit.

"You say that like the demons aren't the only evil," I said, still half asleep.

"They're not," he stated flatly.

"What do you mean?" I listened to his heartbeat as I waited for his answer.

He finally spoke in a whisper. "I've seen evil come from other places. Maybe someday I'll tell you about it."

It was clear in his tone that today wasn't that day. I urged to ask him more, to prod for answers, but I held my tongue. I had to respect his secrets and let him come to me at his own pace. He'd do the same for me if I asked him to.

"Can the Davina be evil?" I asked.

He rested his head against mine. "I like to think the Davina are all good, but there's nothing stopping them from doing bad things."

"That makes sense," I said. "Marek?"

"Yeah?"

"I'm glad you want to protect people. You're going to be really good at it."

"Thank you," he whispered.

I remained in his arms for another hour. Unfortunately, the sun began to fall beneath the horizon, and Marek suggested it was time to take me home. Chilly air filled the empty space between us when he pulled away. Disappointment washed over me.

Fifteen minutes later, Marek walked me up to my front door. I turned to him without making a move to go inside.

"Thank you for driving me home," I said.

Marek reached out and tucked a strand of hair behind my ear.

I suddenly didn't register the cool air around me as every inch of my body heated in response to his touch. I didn't think I'd ever get used to the feel of his skin on mine.

"Stay safe, Ryn. Okay?" Marek whispered.

"I'll try," I told him with a smile.

"You better."

Marek bent and pressed a chaste kiss to my lips. His lips were there and gone so fast that I hardly had a moment to enjoy them. Far too soon, he turned and headed back toward his bike.

I wanted to call out and tell him to wait, to rush down the sidewalk and jump into his arms and kiss him with the passion that raged through my veins. But then his bike roared to life, and he was gone.

My heart flipped in my chest as I watched him disappear. In that moment, it became very clear. No other guy stood a chance. My heart would always belong to the boy who saved my life.

My stomach dropped when I spotted Trenton in the hall the next morning. I still hadn't had a chance to apologize to him. I stared at him for what felt like a full minute, contemplating whether or not to say anything. He looked so sad— almost angry. I couldn't help but blame myself.

"Hey, Trenton," I said softly as I approached him.

Confusions settled on his face when he saw me, like he couldn't understand why I was talking to him.

I leaned against the locker next to his. "Do you have a second?"

"I suppose." He didn't sound very enthused.

I took a deep breath. "I wanted to say I'm sorry. I didn't meant to hurt you. I *do* like you, but… not in that way."

The muscles in Trenton's jaw tightened.

I sighed. "Look, Marek and I had a thing going before you—"

"Before I kissed you?" Trenton snapped. "I don't go around kissing just anyone, Ryn. I actually liked you."

My throat closed up. I hated hurting him like this. Before I could say anything else, Trenton started toward his first class. I instinctively reached out for his wrist. It felt unusually cold.

"We can still be friends, can't we?" I asked.

He dropped his gaze. "I'm not sure if we can. Just… be careful out there, okay?"

"Yeah, I will," I said slowly as he distanced himself from me.

I turned to head to class, but I couldn't get his words out of my mind. Was he trying to *warn* me about something?

~

"What do you want to practice today?" Marek asked after school in the hall.

Kissing, I thought instantly. The word nearly passed my lips, but I caught myself before it could. God, I was obsessed.

"Fireballs." *Obviously.*

"How many times do I have to tell you—?"

"They're not fireballs," I finished for him. "I know. But doesn't it make it sound cool?"

"They don't even *look* like fireballs," he argued.

"Speak for yourself. Mine are pretty badass." I reached for the basement door and flipped on the light inside the stairwell.

"I'm not going to argue with that," Marek said. "Just don't go throwing any of them at me."

"I won't." I smiled while I descended the steps.

"I think we should see how your essence performs under pressure today. Let's start with a short warm-up."

Marek wrapped his arms around one of the heavy targets and scooted it back against the wall. His shirt rode up. I caught myself admiring his exposed skin, but then I saw something glisten near his waistband. He quickly tugged down on his shirt, and the object disappeared beneath it.

"What?" he asked innocently when he caught me staring.

"Nothing," I lied.

Except, I knew it was *something*. Marek was carrying around the Davina Blade. That meant he was scared of something. Why hadn't he mentioned it?

"Move back," Marek instructed. "Farther… Okay, that's good. Let's see what you've got."

Marek stood next to me out of the line of fire. He was so close that I could feel his body heat and smell the lingering scent of leather on his skin. If this was the pressure he was talking about, it was definitely a distraction.

The target seemed a mile away, but I formed a white ball of

essence and drew my arm back. The fireball flew forward and crashed into the middle of the foam target. It exploded with a pop.

"Good," Marek said. "Now, step back farther and try it with your left hand."

Marek had me go through every possible scenario he could think of. I shot essence over my shoulder, from the ground, and with both hands at once. He even made me race across the basement while I took shots at the target in rapid succession. Over the next hour, my essence never once flickered between white and purple. I considered it a victory.

"I think I need a break." I sank onto the steps because they were the only place to sit.

"Do you think you're going to get a break during a real fight?"

I glared up at him. "Did you notice how many times I hit the target? Any demon would be dead by now whether I conjured the Power of Grace or not."

"And what if it's an army of demons?" Marek challenged, sitting beside me.

An image of Dorian flashed through my mind. I pictured the demons he'd brought with him to the valley to distract my friends with. If Dorian would've let them have their shot at me, I'd have been stunned within seconds and killed in under a minute. I definitely understood where Marek was coming from.

"I'll have you there to protect me," I teased to lighten the mood.

"That's my goal," he said.

I couldn't help but smile. "How'd I get so lucky?"

Marek leaned into me. His soft breath rushed across my face, heating the surface of my skin.

"I'm the lucky one," he whispered.

His gaze dropped to my lips then back to my eyes. He wanted this. I wanted this.

What the hell?

I went for it.

A split second later, my fingers were tangled in his hair, and his tongue danced across my bottom lip. His hands found the bare skin on my back where my tank top had ridden up. I couldn't help it when the smallest moan escaped my lips. He silenced it with another kiss. And then another. And another.

I hardly caught a breath between each kiss. Oxygen didn't seem to matter in the moment. All that mattered was his lips, his hands, and the fire that ignited in my chest when he touched me.

I shifted to draw my body closer to his. Marek's warm hands settled on my hips, and he pulled me into him until I was on his lap. His strong, comforting arms wrapped gently around my middle. I never felt more like I *belonged* somewhere than I did when I was in Marek's arms. It felt so overwhelmingly *right* that I thought I might cry from the flood of emotions coursing through me.

I wanted more. I wanted to melt into him until we became one. My fingers ran up his shirt and across his bare back, and his did the same to mine. It felt as if we'd never get close enough to each other.

Marek pulled away. Good thing he did before we completely lost control. If we made out much longer, my shirt wasn't going to stay on. And once that happened, his pants were fair game.

We both took a moment to catch our breath.

"We should probably get back to practice," he suggested.

My shoulders dropped. "Yeah. Our first mock battle is tomorrow, and I'm so unprepared."

I didn't want this moment to end. I wanted Marek and his lips, his soft skin, his biceps, his—

"You'll do fine," he assured me.

"Not if I don't get a quick bathroom break and a drink," I teased. *And maybe a cold shower.*

"Okay," he agreed. "I want to sneak some dodge balls from storage anyway. It'll be a good way to step up the pressure. Go take your water break."

"Thank you." I exaggerated my gratitude and pulled myself up using the railing.

Upstairs, I paused to watch Marek retreat down the hall. I couldn't help it when my eyes locked on his backside. I could picture myself stripping off every layer of clothing he wore.

He rounded the corner, and I snapped back to attention. God, I was a creep. Once he was out of sight, I pushed my way into the girl's restroom.

I stopped at the drinking fountain just outside the door when I'd finished. As I bent over it, movement down the hall caught my eye. Thinking it was Marek, I lifted my head, but no one was there.

Out of nowhere, a black ball flew in my direction. Instinctively, I let out a yelp and ducked out of the way. I quickly rose to my feet again.

So this is Marek's idea of training me to dodge fireballs? Sneaking up on me when I'm not ready for it?

I caught a glimpse of someone's arm at the end of the hall as they hurled another dark ball my way. This time, I got a good look at it.

A true scream of terror ripped out of my lungs as a glowing black ball of essence sped toward me. I ducked again, but as soon as I lifted my head, another fireball was flying at me. This definitely wasn't a test from Marek.

This was a demon attack.

26

What the hell was a demon doing in the halls of Galen High?

I took off running. I didn't want to find out the answer to that question. Just as I turned at the end of the hall, a tall figure came out of nowhere and grabbed onto me. I screamed again.

"Shh," Marek demanded.

I quieted instantly. "There—there's someone down the hall… trying to…" I couldn't get the words out.

"Every freaking time I turn my head," he muttered through clenched teeth.

Marek let go of my arms and sprinted down the hall. I hadn't caught up by the time he reached the end of the hall and glanced both ways.

He turned back to me. "There's no one here."

"But there was, Marek! There was!" My voice came out high and shaky.

"I believe you," he said in a breathy voice. "Let's get to Fletcher's classroom. He should still be around."

"Okay," I agreed. My eyes darted around the hall the whole way there.

Fletcher was on the phone when we entered his room in a rush. Alarm settled on his face, and he pulled the phone away from his ear. "Sorry," he said to whoever was on the other end of the line. "I'll call you back."

Marek quickly shut the door behind us.

Fletcher shot up from the chair behind his desk. "What's going on?"

"I—I," I stammered.

"Someone attacked Ryn *again*," Marek said angrily.

"Where?" Fletcher took me by the shoulder and guided me to sit in a nearby desk.

"Here!" Marek's voice rose. "In the school!"

"You can't be serious," Fletcher said in shock.

I managed to find my voice, though my hands continued to shake. "Someone tried to stun me."

Just like they did yesterday.

"Did you see who it was?" Fletcher asked.

"No, but it definitely wasn't a Davina," I said.

Fletcher furrowed his brow.

"It was a demon," I clarified. "Here. At Galen High."

I turned to Marek. "I'm sorry. You were right. This isn't about some stupid drama. Someone's trying to kill me again, but this time they're bolder than Dorian was. I mean... coming into the *school*? They had to be following us, waiting for you to leave me alone."

"You weren't together when this happened?" Fletcher asked with an edge to his tone.

"No," I said. "I was at the drinking fountain when they shot the first fireball at me."

I half expected Marek to tell me they weren't fireballs like he always did.

Instead, he stared forward. "I didn't know what I saw yesterday, but what you're saying confirms it."

"What do you mean?" I asked.

"I couldn't be sure, but yesterday, I thought I saw dark essence hit you right before I saw you fall, but it was out of the corner of my eye. I thought I was being stupid and paranoid. I'm sorry I left you again. The woods right on the edge of town is one thing. I never thought a demon would come into the school."

"What are we going to do?" I asked desperately.

"What happened yesterday?" Fletcher demanded.

Marek quickly explained how I'd been stunned in the forest and apologized for not mentioning it sooner.

"This has only happened when you're alone?" Fletcher asked.

"Yes," I answered.

Fletcher whirled toward Marek and spoke sternly. "I don't want you to let Ryn out of your sight. Not for a moment."

"He'll have to," I said. "He can't exactly stay the night at my house, and we don't have all our classes together."

"Your life is more important," Fletcher insisted. "We'll change Marek's schedule. Allie can stay the night at your house. The way these demons have been working, I don't think you're at risk unless you're alone."

I covered my face in my hands. How much longer did I have to live with being a target for the demons?

"Marek, take Ryn straight home," Fletcher commanded. "I'm going to talk to some people and see if I can't get any news on demon sightings in the area. You're going to be fine, Ryn."

I wasn't sure even he believed his words.

Marek squeezed my hand and led me out of the building to his bike. By the time we reached my house, my fear had turned into anger.

"Are you doing okay?" Marek asked when we reached the porch.

I curled my hands into fists. "I don't know why I ran, Marek. I should've stood my ground and fought."

"You did the right thing coming to find me."

"Next time, I won't," I promised. "I've learned a lot from you in the last few weeks. I think it's time to put that training to the test. Marek, the next time I'm faced with a demon, I'm fighting back."

27

llie stopped by my house that night, and I filled her in on everything that had happened. She didn't seem shocked that I'd been attacked again. It was like it was starting to become a part of my daily routine. Shower, breakfast, school, murder attempt… That was pretty much how my life went these days.

After dinner, I sat on the couch next to Mom. She'd already gotten bored of crocheting and had turned to knitting. At least she was using up the yarn she'd collected.

"What is it?" she asked like she expected me to bring her bad news.

"Allie and I have homework, so she's staying the night."

Mom's lips tightened. "Let me guess. You waited until the last minute?"

I forced a smile. "You know me too well."

Mom sighed. "Don't let this become a regular occurrence."

I left before she could change her mind.

Allie and I hung out in the basement, staring at the Davina carving in the wall. We sat side-by-side on a rug I'd lain across the floor and stressed over every little thing we possibly could.

"I never asked if you found Meg online," I said. "Any chance you got in touch with her?"

Disappointment washed over Allie's face. "No. Sorry. I didn't."

"And Fletcher doesn't know her? If she's a Davina, wouldn't she have gone to Galen High?"

Allie shook her head. "Not if she moved here after high school."

"Good point."

"Are you nervous about tomorrow?" Allie asked.

"What about tomorrow?"

"Our first mock battle."

"You think I'm scared of a little sparring after I've already killed demons? Please. This mock battle is the last thing on my mind."

"Yeah, but it takes place in the woods, in the same place where you've been attacked... how many times is it now?"

"Does it?"

This was the first time anyone mentioned that.

"Tomorrow's battle does," Allie said.

I had to admit, the woods between the school and the valley wasn't exactly my favorite place on the planet, but I wasn't about to let myself get scared over it. I'd been enough of a coward earlier today.

I shrugged. "It's fine. Like I said, I'm ready for anything."

"Are you sure you want to do this?" Fletcher asked the following day during last period. We stood next to the entrance of the trail preparing for our battle. "You don't have to."

"I want to," I assured him. I needed to take my frustrations out somehow. "I'm not going to use essence."

"If you're not going to participate fully—"

"You keep saying I need more training," I pointed out. "Isn't the point of this to put my skills to the test?"

"Yes—" he started.

"Good." I returned to stand by my friends without giving him a chance to respond.

"So, you're going to fight?" Marek asked.

"Yup," I said proudly.

I didn't miss the glance Marek and Fletcher exchanged. The implications of it we're clear: *Don't let her out of your sight.*

"I'll be fine," I assured Marek. "I'm ready for this."

Allie looked uncertain from beside him, but she didn't say anything.

Mrs. Anders blew her whistle, sending my blood pressure skyrocketing. I *hated* that shrill sound.

"Is everyone here?" she called to get our attention.

Our team of five—made complete by one of the sophomore girls, Ruby—stood in a line. Casey's team lined up nearby, opposite us. Unlike other sports I was used to, there weren't any spectators.

"This battle will be a version of capture the flag," Mrs. Anders explained. "Stunning and sparring are allowed. Once someone has captured your flag, you're out, and you must return here. The boundary is marked by the forest. You may go anywhere between here and the valley, but not beyond. You will see orange stakes marking the other end of the boundary. The last team standing wins. When you hear the whistle, the battle is over. This is a split fight, meaning your team members will be split up before the fight starts. You'll have to find each other if you want to team up. Any questions?"

Nobody responded even though a million questions raced through my mind. Apparently, everyone else had done this enough times to understand the procedure.

"Wouldn't it be easy to cheat?" I whispered to Marek. "Like going beyond the boundaries or stealing your flag back?"

"Refs walk around the arena while we fight," Marek explained.

"Okay," I said. "I think I've got this."

I hadn't realized Mrs. Anders had already started handing out flags to the other team. Each of them secured the flags around their waist so that they poked out in the back like a tail.

I turned to Marek again. "What's up with the flags?"

He whispered softly. "The idea is that if you get close enough to steal someone's flag, you're close enough to kill them."

A shiver ran down my spine at his words.

Mrs. Anders reached our team and handed us each a flag. I secured mine around my waist. I was ready to take on anything.

My team entered into a huddle.

"What's the plan?" Kyle asked.

Marek quickly took the lead. "We'll meet up at the middle of our boundary line and go from there. Sound good?"

"Yep," Ruby said.

"Saints Rule on one, two, three?" Allie suggested.

Everyone placed their hands into the center of the circle and shouted *Saints Rule* in unison. Before I realized what was happening, our team was following behind a group of referees in blaze orange t-shirts. Casey's team started in the opposite direction. I felt totally lost.

"We start on either end of the arena," Allie said, noticing the confusion on my face.

"How much does this help prepare for a real fight?" I asked.

Marek shrugged. "It can get intense. You'll see."

We entered the forest near one of the orange stakes. I glanced to Marek, then to Allie. They both had looks of determination on their faces, like they were going into a real battle.

Each of us followed a referee to our starting points.

"Good luck," the referee said before walking away and leaving me on my own.

I stood still, listening to the sound of the wind rustling through the trees. The overcast sky blocked the warm sun, and a chill filled the air.

A whistle blew in the distance, signaling the start of the battle. Instead of heading toward the boundary line like Marek had suggested, I turned with determination toward the heart of the forest. I wouldn't always have a team of Davina at my side. This was as good of a time as any to test my skills and prove to myself I could handle a fight on my own.

Marek was going to be *pissed*.

Leaves crunched under my feet, but otherwise, the woods remained silent. I squinted into the trees, and my heart lurched. At the first sign of movement, I threw myself behind a tree for cover.

I listened intently as the person approached. I stole a glance toward the sound and saw blaze orange moving between the trees. It was only one of the refs keeping an eye out for injuries and cheaters. I breathed a sigh of relief and stepped out from behind the tree.

My senses remained on high alert. At one point, I heard a grunt followed by shuffling feet in the distance, indicating that someone had been stunned. I formed a white fireball in my palm when I spotted a girl from Casey's team approaching, but she held her hands up to show that she was already out.

I was quickly starting to get bored.

A stick broke nearby under somebody's weight. My head instantly jerked in the direction of the noise. A white fireball flew toward me, and I ducked instinctively. It hit one of the trees behind me. I stood up straight in a defensive stance.

Casey advanced. "You're all alone, I see."

I formed white essence in my palm, though I didn't intend to use it. "You, too. You could've stayed with your own team, you know."

Casey stepped around a tree and crinkled her nose. "Nah, it's more fun this way. What's taking you so long? I thought for sure you'd be eager to use your essence now. Don't you want to show me what you've got?"

I swallowed. "I'd rather not hurt you."

"Didn't anyone tell you that's the *point* of this?" she growled.

"I thought the point was to capture the flag."

Casey smiled. "It doesn't hurt to have a little fun doing it."

I gritted my teeth. If Casey wanted a real fight, I'd give her one.

28

I stepped toward Casey, ready for anything she threw at me. Turned out, the first thing she threw was a punch. Pain shot through my cheek bone.

I quickly retaliated. My fist met her jaw with a satisfying *thud*.

That one's for Allie, I thought.

"We're supposed to be sparring, not boxing," I snarled.

"Relax," Casey said, apparently not fazed by the punch. "We both heal fast."

Casey's fist flew out again. Though I made a move to duck, I wasn't quick enough. Her fist hit the side of my head. I barely felt the pain as a fire ignited inside of me. What was this bitch's problem?

Casey kicked her foot out in a swift, controlled motion. I jumped back just in time. We began circling each other.

"What's your problem with me?" Casey asked with a smirk.

I raised an eyebrow. "I could ask you the same question. It wouldn't happen to have anything to do with my boyfriend, would it?"

Casey's expression faltered momentarily.

It didn't take a genius to realize I'd guessed right. Never mind Marek's preferences or that he had plenty of opportunities to go out with Casey and never took them. None of that mattered in the moment. It was like a silent mutual agreement existed between us that said the last girl standing would win Marek's affection.

I threw another punch in Casey's direction, but she successfully blocked it. It took all I had to keep my fireballs at bay.

"Are we just going to stand here all day?" Casey asked as we continued to circle each other.

I took her question as an invitation and lunged toward her. Her arms instantly came out to block my attack, but it didn't matter. I'd tossed all my weight on top of her, and we tumbled to the forest floor together. She grunted when we landed.

I managed to get in another punch. I was sure she'd end up with a black eye from the blow. An instant later, her hand was in my hair, tugging at the long strands. I cried out in pain and clawed at her face.

"Ow!" she shrieked. "You *bitch*."

"Me?" I asked in disbelief, still trying to struggle away from her grasp. I was a lot of things, but I'd never measure up to Casey's level of bitchiness. It didn't matter that she was a Davina. The girl was evil.

No matter how much I scratched at her face, she didn't loosen her hold on my hair. I did the only thing I could think of and plunged my fingers into her long blond locks. She let out a cry of pain, and her fingers loosened just enough on my hair that I was able to pull back and free myself. I managed to drag a good chunk of her hair with me in my fist.

Casey got to her feet quickly.

I backed up several paces and opened up my hand to let her hair fall to the earth.

"Don't tell me you're scared," she challenged.

"Oh, believe me, I'm only getting started," I threatened.

I threw my body forward again. My knee connected with her ribs. Suddenly, arms and feet were flying faster than I could process them. Casey landed another punch to my jaw and kicked me hard in the thigh. I got a second kick to her ribs and a third to her shin.

Just as another fist swung in my direction, I dodged out of its path. Instead of pulling away from Casey, I spun toward her. My elbow connected with her nose while my other hand reached around her body and plucked the flag from her waist.

Only then did I take several steps back. Casey had fallen to her knees, with both hands pulled protectively to her face. When she withdrew them, I saw that a crimson red liquid coated her palms.

"Whoa. What's going on here?" an unfamiliar voice came through the trees.

Casey and I looked toward the newcomer in surprise. It was one of the refs who was supposed to be observing the arena and making sure this very thing didn't happen. We were only supposed to practice our skills, not hurt each other.

The ref's eyes flickered between the flag in my hand and Casey's bloody face.

Casey held up a hand to stop him. "It's okay. It was an accident."

My jaw nearly dropped. Casey wasn't trying to protect me, was she? Or maybe she was protecting herself, considering she started the fight.

Casey stood, holding onto her bleeding nose. "Ryn won fair and square."

The ref frowned. He didn't believe us.

Casey wiped the blood from her face. "I have to hand it to you, Ryn. You fight better than I thought you would. Just don't think you'll get lucky every time."

Then she turned to head out of the trees.

I could hardly believe my ears. Had Casey *complimented* me? It almost sounded that way, but there was more to it. There'd been a threat in her tone that told me she expected to—or at least wanted to—fight again.

"You two behave yourselves," the ref warned before he headed off to find other fights to observe.

I shoved the flag I'd taken from Casey in my pocket and smiled as she disappeared through the trees. Still high on adrenaline, I started forward quickly in search of another fight.

I stopped abruptly when I saw Marek standing just yards away with his arms crossed over his chest. He did *not* look happy.

"What?" I asked innocently.

"Well, I have some ideas on where you need improvement."

How long had he been watching?

"Improvement?" I asked. "But I won."

Marek looked like he was trying not to roll his eyes. "You won a catfight."

"A catfight?" Truth be told, I couldn't exactly deny that's what it had been. "Okay, maybe I won a catfight, but only thanks to what you've taught me."

Marek raised his eyebrows. "And we have a long way to go."

I shrugged. "I'll get there."

Marek frowned. "You weren't supposed to run off."

"You ran off, too!" I accused. "Where's everyone else?"

"They teamed up like we planned. I came to find you. Should we go find the rest of Casey's team?"

"Fine."

A moment later, another sound reached my ears.

Marek placed himself in front of me. "Let me take this one."

I had to peek around his muscular form to see what was going on. Troy was closing in on us—and quickly.

Marek pushed me. "Run."

I followed his instructions and sprinted away from the oncoming attack. I was starting to see the fun in these mock battles.

I slowed and then turned, expecting Marek to be right behind me, but he was gone.

"Damn it, Marek," I muttered under my breath.

I remained on high alert. I began back the way I came, hoping to join up with Marek. If I was lucky, I could sneak up on Troy from behind and get a little sparring in before I stole his flag.

I didn't make it very far before movement caught my eye from straight ahead. I didn't have time to process the object coming at me. I threw my body to the earth not a moment too soon. Dark essence whizzed by my head.

Reality hit me a split second later. This was no longer a mock battle.

It was the real thing.

29

*J*umped to my feet and stretched my palm out. I could already feel the white electricity pulsing through my arm. I scanned the trees for movement. My eyes met nothing but bare tree trunks and undergrowth.

"Show yourself!" I demanded.

The air grew still while I waited, but my heartbeat pulsed loudly in my ears. This was nothing like when Casey and I fought. Casey wanted to hurt me, but she didn't want to kill me. A demon wasn't about to offer me the same courtesy.

"I said show yourself!" I yelled.

Another dark fireball sped toward me. As I threw my body behind a nearby tree, I caught sight of motion out of the corner of my eye. The attacker sought cover behind one of the largest trees in the forest.

"What kind of demon are you if you can't face your opponent?" I shouted.

"I'm the kind you don't want to mess with!" he called back.

My breath hitched. I knew that voice, but it definitely didn't belong to a demon.

I didn't have a chance to ask for an explanation before a tall, shirtless figure stepped out from behind the tree. White wings rose out of his back. Though he looked entirely Davina, there was no mistaking that something was amiss. In his right hand glowed white essence, indicating his Davina blood. In his left hovered a black ball of essence I'd only seen demons conjure.

Agony filled my chest at the betrayal.

"What do you think you're doing, Trenton?" I demanded.

"I'm stopping you," he said before he hurled two balls of essence at my head, one light and one dark.

I spun behind the tree again for protection. A moment later, I threw my own white fireball toward him. I knew I told Fletcher I wouldn't use my essence during this fight, but I didn't have a choice but to defend myself.

I just need to stun him, not kill him.

"Stopping me from what?" I yelled from where I crouched for cover.

A twig snapped in the distance under Trenton's weight.

"I know what you're up to." He said it like it was a threat. "I know what you are."

My entire body tensed. How could he possibly know? And why would another Davina want to stop me from awakening Grace?

I need answers.

I sprang up to throw essence toward him again, but I acted too quickly and missed him entirely. He was on the move and closing in on me fast. I hurled another fireball toward him, this time with better aim, but I didn't stick around to see where it landed.

I took off, dodging around trees and jumping over fallen branches to put distance between us. I hardly noticed that I'd passed the boundary marker. Another black orb flew by my head as I ran. I quickly ducked behind another thick trunk.

"We can talk this out, Trenton!" I called. "I thought we were friends."

"We could've been. But not anymore." He stalked toward me with a hard expression on his face. He definitely looked like he was out for blood.

"Maybe tell me why you want me dead," I suggested. "I thought you were going to become a Protector after graduation. You know what it means to protect, don't you?"

Trenton was closing in on me fast. I took my chances and sprinted away.

In the distance, the sound of twigs breaking reached my ears, but it came from a different direction than where Trenton stood. Something in the sound of those footsteps filled me with a sense of hope.

Marek.

He didn't know this mock fight had turned into a real one. I thought about calling out to him, but I realized the moment I opened my mouth that calling him over could get him stunned—or killed.

I have to take Trenton out first.

I stopped behind a large tree for cover. Trenton paused for a moment and looked out toward the sound of approaching feet.

The distraction was a blessing. I hurled three white fireballs toward him in quick succession. The first flew by his ear and pulled his attention back to me just in time for the second to hit his shoulder and the third to hit his chest.

Trenton's tall, muscular body crumbled to the ground. I hurried over to him and fell to my knees. Marek arrived a second later.

He gazed down at Trenton in confusion. "I thought you weren't going to stun anyone."

"I wasn't," I said flatly. "Marek, it was Trenton."

His brows came together. "What do you mean?"

"I think it's safe to assume he's the one who's been trying to kill me."

"What are you talking about? Trenton's a Davina."

I looked down at Trenton's face and shook my head. "I'm not sure he's entirely Davina."

Marek crouched to my level. "Ryn, what are you talking about?"

"Doesn't matter," I said.

I whirled to my right and then my left in search of anything that might immobilize Trenton before he woke. My gaze fell upon my shoes. I instantly began untying my laces.

"We have to get him to talk. Here, help me." I wrenched the shoelace from my tennis shoe and held it out to Marek before turning to the second one.

Marek took the lace but didn't make a move.

"Marek, I'm serious. Trenton can conjure dark essence. He said he wanted to stop me. He said he knew what I was up to."

"You don't think he was talking about Grace, do you?"

"I do."

"Why would he want to stop you?"

"My question exactly. Now hurry up!"

Marek seemed to catch the urgency in my tone. He rounded Trenton's unmoving body and hoisted him into a seated position against a nearby tree. Marek began securing one of my laces around Trenton's left wrist. I did the same to the right.

Trenton made a small noise, indicating that he was waking up. Marek tugged at the laces to confirm they were secure. I wasn't sure they'd hold, but they were the best thing we had.

"Give it to me," I demanded, stretching my palm out toward Marek.

"Give you what?"

"The Davina Blade. I know you have it."

Marek took a step back. "What makes you think I have it?"

"You're wasting time," I snapped. "You've been carrying it around. I know it."

Marek sighed and reached into the back of his jeans. "Be careful with it."

"Thank you," I said as I snatched the weapon from his hands.

I crouched next to Trenton and pressed the blade to his throat. At the cool touch of metal, he inhaled a deep breath. I thought for a moment I read fear in his expression, but it quickly turned to anger when he realized what was happening.

"Holy shit!" Trenton cried.

"Yeah, that's a knife against your throat," I assured him. "Unless you want to see what it's capable of, you'll answer my questions. What are you?"

"I'm a Davina," he answered quickly.

I pressed the blade tighter against his skin. "Do *not* test me. I've killed demons before. I'm not afraid to kill you if I have to. Let me ask this again. What *are* you?"

"Ryn," Marek whispered. He placed a hand on my shoulder like he thought I was being too hard on Trenton.

I shrugged him off.

"Fine," Trenton said through gritted teeth. "I'm half Aedes."

Marek shifted beside me. I probably wouldn't have believed it either if I hadn't witnessed it myself.

"How do you know what I am?" I asked harshly.

Trenton didn't answer at first. He only stared back at me.

I applied more pressure to the blade. "How do you know?"

Trenton pressed the back of his head against the tree to relieve as much pressure as he could on his neck. "I saw it!"

"When?" I demanded.

This was exactly what Fletcher had been talking about. He didn't want us to tell anyone about my power because he didn't want the wrong person finding out. I thought we'd been careful. I was terribly mistaken.

"When you were fighting those Aedes in the valley before school started," Trenton admitted. "Casey, Troy, and I were there earlier that night. Not long after we left, I saw the light coming from the valley. I ditched Casey and Troy and came back to check it out. I saw you fighting the Aedes. I was going to join in, but I didn't…"

"Didn't what?" I demanded.

Trenton gritted his teeth. "I didn't know which side to fight on! It's one thing to talk about killing the Aedes. It's another to see it in person. Then you conjured purple essence. I'd heard the stories. I knew what it meant."

"Then what happened?" I asked.

"Are you *trying* to kill me?" he snapped.

I realized I'd drawn a small amount of blood. I glanced at it for a second to see that it was a darker shade of red than it should've been. Trenton might've had white Davina wings, but he definitely had demon blood running through his veins.

I pulled back slightly, but not enough to make him think he was safe. "What. Happened. Next?"

"I was supposed to follow you for information," Trenton said.

"That's why you tried to befriend me," I accused.

My heart broke at the thought. My instinct had failed me with Trenton. I should've at least listened to Allie.

"You *were* stalking me!" I realized. "You were always trying to get me to tell you what I was up to, always trying to coerce a bit of information out of me. You even tried to get me to admit I was different!"

I recalled the day we flew together and how he'd asked me about my talents. The whole time, he'd been trying to get me to tell him about Grace. I couldn't believe I thought he was just being nice.

"I actually believed you liked me," I said in disgust. How could I have been so gullible?

"I did like you," Trenton admitted. "I almost backed out of the whole plan for you."

"What exactly *was* your plan?" I narrowed my eyes.

"I knew you were searching for Grace," Trenton said. "I was supposed to let you lead me to her."

"*You're* the one who overheard Allie and me talking about her." It wasn't a question.

I thought back to Monday afternoon and the conversation Allie and I had outside the jewelry shop. I wondered how much we'd given away, how much Trenton had heard.

"Yeah, I overheard you," he snapped. "Once I knew where Grace was, they said I could take you out. Once you were gone, there was no chance of awakening her. And if we knew where she was, we could destroy her, too."

"Who's 'they?'" Marek asked from beside me.

Trenton closed his eyes like he was in agony. "The Aedes."

"Which ones? Is there a group of them?" Marek's voice became harsh.

"There will be," he admitted with a grimace.

"What do you mean?" I asked. "Someone's building an army? Who?"

Trenton didn't answer.

I dug the blade deeper into his skin. "Who?"

Trenton burst. "My father!"

30

The forest went silent. Trenton's words echoed in my mind.

"Start from the beginning," I told him sternly. "How do you go from being good one moment to evil the next? Tell us *everything*."

Trenton's eyes remained closed, like he was truly scared I might slit his throat. "Fine, but you're in for a long story."

I leaned in closer. "I have time."

Trenton looked so pale I thought he might puke. "The first thing you should know is that my mom was a Davina, and my dad was Aedes. If you think my dad was the evil one just because my mom was an angel, you're wrong. She abandoned me the second she gave birth. I needed food and shelter, but my dad couldn't provide any of that. So I got dropped off at my Davina grandmother's house. She, of course, knew what I was. She let my dad hang around. Despite being Aedes, he still cared. Oh, don't look so surprised."

Trenton narrowed his eyes at Marek before turning his gaze back to me. "My grandma died when I was fifteen. I had no choice but to turn to my mom's brother. I met him a couple of times, and he knew what I was. But he was ashamed."

By the tone of his voice, it was clear he had some pent up anger he needed to get out.

"That's what brought me to Eagle Valley. My father wasn't welcome here. If he even tried to step into town, he'd be killed on the spot. So there I was, completely unwanted in a town of people who would kill me if they knew my secret."

"They wouldn't have killed you," Marek argued.

Trenton's brows shot up. "Sure about that? Who's the one with the knife to his throat?"

"I wouldn't have to if you weren't trying to kill me," I said. "Finish your story."

Trenton breathed heavily. "I had to play along and pretend I was completely Davina even though I'd grown up being both. Turns out Galen High wasn't as bad as I thought it'd be. I mean, at least the hottest girl in town was willing to fool around with me. Couldn't be too bad, could it?"

He had to be talking about Casey. The thought made me want to hurl.

"She changed my mind about things. I started to think that maybe this was where I actually belonged. I *wanted* to become a Protector. I convinced myself my Aedes side meant nothing, that my father was just an anomaly."

"Changed your mind pretty quickly, didn't you?" I snarled.

"When I saw you fighting those Aedes, it was like…"

"Like *what*?" I demanded.

Trenton's words poured out of him quickly. "It was like watching you kill my father!"

He took a deep breath before continuing at a normal pace. "I realized then that I'd lived in Eagle Valley so long without Aedes that I forgot what it was like for one of them to actually *care* about me. My uncle sure as hell didn't. Casey only cared when it worked in her favor."

Did he have to put that image in my mind *again*?

"Then what?" I asked. "You just decided that because no one cared, it was a good idea to kill me?"

The anger in Trenton's eyes intensified. "No. I left town for a couple of days to find my father."

"And?" I asked.

"And I already told you the rest! I told him about you, and he told me to come back and find out where Grace was. I was supposed to prevent you from awakening her and then wait for him. I've done a pretty good job so far, haven't I?"

I ignored his question. "So he's building an army?"

"Yes," Trenton said. "I already told you. He can't exactly stroll into Eagle Valley on his own. He's going to be coming with all the Aedes he can round up."

Marek scoffed from beside me.

"What?" I asked him without tearing my gaze from Trenton.

"Demons aren't exactly a community race," Marek explained. "How many will he be able to round up? A dozen?"

More than that. I instantly thought of Dorian and the six other demons he managed to round up in a day.

"No, they're not," Trenton agreed. "But that's only because they've never had anything to come together for before. Now they actually have something to fight for."

"Why would you want to fight with them?" I asked.

"Because—ow—would you get that thing off my neck?"

"No," I snapped.

"Because the Aedes deserve this world as much as the Davina do," Trenton answered.

"What about the humans?" Marek said with an edge to his tone. "An influx of demons will destroy the humans more than your race already has."

Trenton scoffed. "I won't even try to explain it to you. You'd never believe the truth anyway."

I gritted my teeth. "Tell us—"

"What's going on here?" a stern voice called.

I tore my gaze from Trenton's face to find Fletcher walking toward us. We'd been so engaged in conversation that none of us noticed his approach.

"This isn't a real battle!" Fletcher exclaimed.

Marek stepped forward. "It's more real than you might believe."

Fletcher's eyes darted between mine and Marek's. "What are you talking about?"

I glared at Trenton. "It's been him all along. He overheard us talking about the key outside of Angela's. He's been trying to kill me ever since."

"That's absurd," Fletcher said.

"He's half demon," I stated flatly like that would explain it all.

Fletcher opened his mouth, but I was already speaking to Trenton before he could say anything.

"You didn't get the key, though, did you? You never heard where it actually was."

"Didn't matter," he said like it amused him. "At first, I was going to get the key so that you couldn't. When I didn't find it, I figured it was better to kill you before you could get to it first. I didn't need you after I overheard where Grace was."

He smiled like he was proud of himself.

It took all my strength not to dig the blade deeper into his throat. "You didn't do a very good job of that, did you?"

"I hadn't planned on anyone finding out it was me! Marek kept showing up and getting in the way."

"Yeah, he has a thing for saving my life," I said before turning to Fletcher. "What do we do with him?"

"He's a demon," Marek said in a harsh tone. He didn't have to say the rest for me to understand what he meant.

He's a demon, and it's our job to kill demons.

"It doesn't matter what you do to me," Trenton cut in. "My father will be here soon."

Marek and Fletcher exchanged a glance. I made the mistake of turning my eyes away from Trenton to watch their exchange.

Trenton's body moved quickly, faster than I could process it. My heart leapt into my throat as his hand snapped to my wrist and squeezed tightly. In a swift motion, he spun me around and pinned me to his chest. His hand gripped my fingers so that I couldn't drop the blade.

I was surprised by my strength as I struggled against his attempt to bring the blade to my throat. In a split second, I managed to wiggle my other arm free of his and swing my elbow back into his face. He loosened his grip just enough that I was able to dig my heels into the ground and distance myself from him.

Marek and Fletcher acted quickly. Two white fireballs sped toward Trenton. He dove to the side just in time for both fireballs to explode against the tree we'd tied him to.

Trenton sprang to his feet and spread his white wings. He launch himself upward and disappeared above the canopy before anyone had a chance to stun him.

31

"Shit," Marek said. "I knew those laces weren't going to hold."

"Of course they weren't," I snapped. "They were just to hold him there for a bit. The Davina Blade did the rest."

"The blade didn't kill him," Marek replied.

"He was a student!" Fletcher sounded horrified.

"He's a demon!" Marek roared. "He tried to kill Ryn. He's probably flying off to tell the demons everything he knows."

Fletcher breathed heavily. "We have to wake Grace now. No matter what it takes to get to her."

I handed Marek the blade, and he slipped it into the sheath hidden beneath his waistband.

Fletcher led us out of the forest near the trailhead. Casey looked at us smugly, clearly thinking we'd both lost our flags. Three of her teammates lined up beside her. On our team, Kyle and Ruby had returned flagless, which meant Allie was still out there in the trees somewhere.

"What's going on?" Mrs. Anders asked. "Did I just see a student fly out of the trees?"

Fletcher frowned, clearly no longer interested in this game. "Trenton forfeit, but we have bigger problems."

"He just left?" Mrs. Anders asked.

"Yes," Fletcher confirmed. "Call everyone back, please."

Mrs. Anders raised her eyebrows like she couldn't believe a student would just leave in the middle of a battle. She brought her whistle to her mouth to call Allie and the referees back.

"Wait!" Casey cried. "This isn't fair. If a member of our team dropped out, that means they had an advantage."

I didn't bother pointing out that three of our teammates remained standing. It didn't matter.

"We'll get a rematch, won't we?" Casey demanded.

I couldn't hold myself back. "Is that all that matters to you?"

"*What?*" Casey bit back like she couldn't believe I was speaking to her.

"You *have* to win every time, don't you?" I strode toward her swiftly until she was only an arm's length away.

"I'd be careful if I were you," Casey warned. "We had plenty of time for this during the mock battle, and—"

"Life isn't a mock battle!" I yelled.

I was vaguely aware of Marek and Fletcher insisting I calm down, but I ignored them.

"We're Davina," I stated. "We're fighting a real war. When you get out there in the real world, you're not going to be keeping score with *flags*."

I ripped my flag from my waist and threw it at her feet to make a point. My breath became shallow as anger coursed through my body.

"You're going to be keeping score by how many people you lose!"

Casey blinked a few times, shocked by my outburst.

I lowered my voice to a normal level. "Trenton left. By my count, you've already lost one person."

Casey didn't say anything as I headed back to my team. Allie had made it out of the woods and saw my exchange with Casey.

"We need to go," I insisted when I made it back to my team.

I didn't know how much time we had left before Trenton's father arrived with his army of demons. *Soon* could mean anything between a few hours to several weeks. I didn't like the uncertainty.

"What's going on?" Mrs. Anders asked.

Fletcher turned to her. "There's no time to explain."

He gestured for our team to follow him. Even though Mrs. Anders shouted questions in Fletcher's direction, he ignored her.

"Mr. Fletcher," Ruby said, sounding confused, "what's going on?"

"I'm sorry, Ruby," he said without looking at her, "but this doesn't concern you. Go home and get some rest. I'll try to explain when this is all over."

She's too young for this, I thought. *He's trying to protect her.*

Ruby drew her eyebrows together. She hesitated momentarily, but she agreed. Ruby left before we made it back to Fletcher's classroom.

Fletcher paced back and forth in front of the whiteboard, thinking.

"Will someone please tell me what's going on?" Allie blurted.

"Yeah," Kyle agreed.

I opened my mouth to explain, but Fletcher cut in before I could.

"We've run out of time. I thought we had more."

"We've never had time!" I blurted before I could stop myself.

Fletcher's eyes locked on me. It was clear what I was saying; there were things he still didn't know.

"No more secrets, Fletcher. I've had the Power of Grace for a long time," I explained quickly. "The first time I used it, I was eight. That must mean the portal has been a threat longer than you thought."

Fletcher's brows constricted.

I turned to Allie and Kyle. "Fletcher was right. We can't trust all Davina. Trenton found out, and now there's an army of demons on their way into town. They want to stop us from awakening Grace."

Allie's jaw dropped, and Kyle's eyes widened.

"Trenton has something to do with that?" Kyle asked.

"He has everything to do with it," I said.

"But why would—" Allie started.

Marek quickly cut in. "Trenton's half demon."

He proceeded to give them a condensed version of what we'd discovered in the woods.

While he spoke, my phone began vibrating.

"Shit," I muttered under my breath. I didn't have time for a phone call.

I slipped the phone out of my pocket. I didn't recognize the number, but instinct told me to answer.

I pulled the phone to my ear. "Hello?"

"Um, hi," a woman's voice came over the line. "This is Meg."

"Meg!" I exclaimed in excitement.

Everyone stopped to look at me.

"Yeah, I'm calling to let you know I got your message."

"I know what your key goes to," I told her. "Would you be interested in testing it out?"

"How do you know what it opens?" She sounded genuinely curious.

"I found a carving that matches the design," I explained.

"You said it has something to do with the Davina?"

"Yes. If we meet up, I can explain everything."

"Um… okay. Where do you want to meet?"

"My house."

"Where do you live?" She didn't sound like she was committed to the idea yet.

I gave her the address.

"You're kidding," she said in shock.

"No."

"That was my grandpa's house! We sold it after he died."

"So, can you meet me there?" I asked.

"What time works for you?"

"Right now," I answered eagerly.

"Okay. Give me a couple of minutes and I'll be on my way."

I hung up.

"Okay. Let's go," Fletcher said with determination.

"No," I said sternly.

Eyes widened around me. Everyone seemed shocked that I'd speak to Fletcher that way.

I was the one who'd been touched by Grace. It was time I started taking that role seriously. I was in charge now.

"We're done with the secrets," I said. "You can't protect me anymore. You need to round up as many Davina as you can and tell them what's going on. Eagle Valley needs to be prepared for an attack."

Fletcher relaxed and rose his head proudly. "I'll do my best."

"Good." I turned to my friends. "As for the rest of you, it's time to wake Grace."

32

$\mathcal{I}$ burst through front door of my house minutes later. My friends followed closely behind. I quickly kicked off my loose shoes at the door and slipped on my mom's since we were the same size.

"Kathryn?" Mom called from the living room.

"Sorry, Mom," I said in a rush. "Don't really have time. Ancient Davina in the basement that needs awakening and all that."

Mom called my name again just as my hand hit the doorknob to the basement. She stepped into the hall. "What's going on?"

"Sorry, Mom. Totally forgot to tell you that a demon tried to kill me a few weeks ago. Now an army is on their way to try to do it again. We need to get to Grace as soon as we can."

A horrified expression crossed her face. "And you think I'm just going to let you walk head-first into danger?"

"Try to stop me," I challenged.

Mom's eyes glistened at the threat of tears.

"Everything will be fine once I wake Grace," I assured her. "You have nothing to worry about. The demons can't touch you."

"But they can touch *you*." Mom sounded scared. "I thought you didn't know how to get to Grace."

"We know the person who has the key. Speaking of which…" I hurried into the living room and looked out the window. "Where is she? She should be here by now."

"Let's just cool down and be patient," Kyle said.

I whirled toward him. "We don't have time for patience! We've run out of time!"

Marek placed his hands on my shoulders to calm me, but I shrugged him off.

"Come on, Meg..." I pulled my phone from my pocket and punched my fingers at the screen.

How long will you be? I texted.

Several agonizing minutes passed without her response. I paced around the living room, unable to sit still. Finally, I heard the sound of an approaching vehicle and stole another glance out the window. A blue sedan pulled up to the curb. I raced to the front door and opened it before Meg was even on the porch.

"Hi," I greeted her quickly.

Meg stepped inside and glanced around. "I have so many memories here. It looks so different, but some things will always be the same, like the stained glass window." She turned to my mom and smiled. "Hi, I'm Margaret."

"Oh," Allie said, dragging out the word. "I thought Meg was short for Megan."

"Nope," Meg said. "Margaret, like my grandma."

That explained why Allie couldn't find her online. She'd been searching the wrong name.

"Yeah, that's great and all, but we—"

The sound of Marek's ringtone cut me off.

"It's Fletcher." Marek answered immediately and put him on speakerphone.

"Is it done?" Fletcher's voice came over the line.

"Not yet," I said desperately.

"Hurry up," Fletcher demanded. "A group of Aedes have been spotted flying just outside of town. We're luring them to the valley. Get there as soon as you can. It's time to fight."

Shit. We really were out of time.

Meg's eyes widened. "The Aedes are *here*?"

"Yes, but we need—"

"My parents will want to fight, but my dad..." Meg's eyes widened in horror. "I'm sorry. I can't let him fight. I have to go."

"Wait, Meg!"

She didn't wait for an explanation. She spun around and sprinted back to her vehicle.

"Stop!" I called, chasing after her. "We need the key to—"

She was already in her vehicle. The engine roared to life.

"The Davina need you here!" I cried.

She never heard me.

"God dammit!" I whirled around to see my friends had followed me outside.

"Shit," Marek muttered through clenched teeth. He stared after Meg's car with an expression of disbelief on his face.

Kyle and Allie exchanged a worried look.

I hesitated for only a moment. "Screw this. We're going to help."

"Wait!" Marek stopped me. "You shouldn't go. We need you to stay safe. If you get hurt—"

"You think you're going to be able to keep me away?" I challenged.

Marek's shoulders dropped in defeat. He knew he couldn't.

I started across the lawn toward Allie's car. Everyone followed, including my mother.

I stopped abruptly. "You're not coming, Mom."

"Like hell I'm not!" she argued.

"You can't even see the demons!"

"We've already been through this," she said sternly. "I may not be able to see them, but they can't touch me."

"Not unless they get their hands on our Davina Blade. That thing exists across all planes and could hurt any of us." It was a long shot, but it was the only argument I could come up with.

"Don't worry," Kyle said as Marek handed him the blade. "I'm not letting any demons get their hands on it."

I reached out and pulled my mom into a hug. "You're not going to stop me from doing this. Please stay here and be safe."

Mom stared after me speechlessly as my friends and I climbed hastily into Allie's car.

Allie fumbled with the keys for a moment and then whipped out of the driveway.

"I love you!" my mom called after me.

Allie put the car into gear and tore off down the street, blowing through the stop sign at the end of our block.

Tires squealed as she slammed on the brakes in front of Galen High. I kicked the car door open and raced across the grass. My breath caught in my chest as my eyes turned to the sky. A dense black cloud of smoke rose above where the valley hid in the forest. It was in motion but didn't follow any particular pattern. I slowed momentarily.

"Oh my God." Marek stopped beside me.

The trees weren't on fire. It wasn't a black cloud of smoke.

It was a flock of winged demons.

"I hope Fletcher rounded up enough reinforcements," Kyle said under his breath.

I took off running again. Before I made it to the trees, I flexed my wings and launched myself into the gray sky. I was aware of three other sets of wings flapping behind me. I dove straight into the middle of the fight, aiming white essence at demon after demon. Black wings flapped all around me. Occasionally, white wings appeared.

Once I was directly above the valley, I was finally able to take in the sheer number of people fighting. Black cloaks dominated up here in the sky, but white wings were most prevalent on the ground. Some Davina fought hand-to-hand while others stunned demons out of the air. The entire town must've been here—at least, the Davina portion of it. There had to be hundreds of us. But we were still outnumbered.

Dark essence flew by my head, pulling my attention from the ground and back to the sky. I turned to face my attacker, but there were so many bodies flying through the air that it was impossible to tell who it'd come from. I threw several more fireballs toward the demons closest to me and then dove to join the Davina on the ground.

Marek landed beside me and shot essence into the air. It hit a demon in the head. He spiraled out of the sky and landed a few yards from us. A sickening *crunch* met my ears as the demon's neck broke upon impact. He disappeared in a puff of black smoke, leaving behind nothing but his cloak.

I shot a white fireball at an approaching demon. More and more demons landed in the grass to fill the valley. Nearby, I noticed a young girl with red hair taking on two demons at once. Fletcher told her to go home only half an hour ago. It seemed like an entire lifetime since our mock battle ended.

Ruby kicked one of the demons in the gut and then spun and threw a white fireball at the other. He collapsed, stunned. She made the mistake of taking a split second to relish in her victory before the other demon caught her and wrapped a strong arm around her throat. Somehow, through the deafening sound of shouts and flapping wings, I could hear her gasping for air.

I didn't take a moment to think about it. I formed white essence in my palm and aimed it at the demon's face. It hit him square on, and he crumbled to the ground.

Ruby was momentarily confused, like she couldn't figure out where the demon had gone. Then her eyes fell on me.

"What the hell are you doing here?" I demanded as I abandoned Marek and raced over to her. I shot another fireball at the demon running up behind her. "I thought Fletcher told you to go home."

Ruby held her head up proudly. "Yeah, and then I came back. I heard you needed all the help you can get."

"But you're only fifteen!" I grabbed onto her shoulders, and we ducked another attack. The dark essence fizzled out behind us.

"So what?" Ruby asked. "Fletcher thought I was good enough to fight with you earlier."

"That was a stupid exercise! It's nothing compared to this. You could die out here!"

Another white fireball left my palm when I spotted a demon too close for comfort.

"So could you," Ruby said stubbornly. "Besides, I've been training longer than you have."

It was clear there was nothing I could say to convince her to leave.

"Don't let your guard down," I instructed.

"I won't," she assured me before sending a fireball toward a demon behind me.

I left her on her own and sprinted through the crowd, knocking out as many demons as I could along the way. Nearby, I spotted Kyle with his blade.

"Kyle, duck!" I shouted just in time for him to barely miss being stunned.

Allie fought beside him, working with him as if they were a single unit. She reached out for the blade just as another demon swooped down out of the sky. She spun and sliced the blade across the demon's throat. Blood spurted, and a line of deep red liquid covered Allie's white wings. It didn't even slow her down.

I stopped in my tracks. The sound of battle faded around me as I spun to take in the scene.

Troy tackled a demon to the ground, but a second demon jumped on top of him a moment later. He took Troy's wing in his hands and wrenched on it. Troy cried out in pain. Casey shot a fireball at the demon, and he fell to the ground. Troy's wing hung at an odd angle, the bones in it broken.

A man who looked strikingly similar to Casey fought beside her. I watched in shock as his hands clamped around a demon's head. He twisted. I didn't hear the crack, but I saw the demon go limp and vanish a second later.

This entire battle was a blood bath.

All of this happened in mere seconds, but it was enough to momentarily distract me. I just barely caught sight of a demon flying toward me from out of the corner of my eye.

The demon landed and faced me. His hood had fallen, displaying his skeleton-like features and black irises. In one swift motion, I swung my leg out and knocked him off his feet.

Marek rushed over to me and threw himself on top of the demon before I had a chance to blink. Marek's strong fist crashed into the demon's trachea. The demon gasped for breath.

Marek didn't wait around to watch him die. He sprang to his feet and took my hand. We only made it a few more feet before another black fireball flew by my head.

When I glanced toward the source, my eyes didn't meet the sight of a hooded figure as I expected. Instead, a shirtless man with white wings stalked toward me.

Apparently I hadn't scared him off earlier. Trenton still wanted me dead.

<h1 style="text-align:center">33</h1>

Trenton drew his arm back again, and I kicked myself into the air. His essence exploded where I'd just been standing. I flew up into the swarm of demons, hoping to lose him. When I glanced back, I saw he was closing in on me. I quickly shot a white fireball at him, but he dodged it. It disappeared into the crowd.

Marek found his way between me and Trenton, using his own body as a shield to protect me.

I wove between bodies, flying upward then diving down, dodging wings from left to right. Marek stayed close behind me. No matter how hard we tried to disappear into the crowd, Trenton kept up with us.

I didn't know how this was going to end, but I knew it wasn't going to end up here. Flapping my wings as hard as I could, I dove toward the upper edge of the valley. My feet landed hard in the grass. I ignored the pain and grabbed Marek's hand when he landed beside me. We raced into the trees. I skidded to a halt behind a thick stump and pulled my wings into me, breathing heavily. Marek took cover behind the tree beside me.

"What are you screwing around for?" he hissed. "Use the Power of Grace!"

I didn't answer.

In the thickness of the forest, the sound of flapping wings and screams grew quiet. I could almost pretend nothing was happening past the edge of the trees.

I sensed Trenton land nearby.

"That was quick," I shouted toward him. "Didn't take you long to find your dad and call him into town, did it?"

"He was already on his way." Trenton's voice grew closer and closer as he spoke. "Told you he'd bring an army."

"You don't even understand what you're fighting for!" I accused. "Demons don't even fully exist here."

I flinched when the tree I leaned against shook as Trenton threw another fireball toward me.

"I'm sick of listening to you talk," Trenton sneered. "Why don't you come out and face me?"

"I don't want to kill you," I said truthfully.

Marek shot me a look. *He's a demon.*

But he's a Davina, too, I wanted to argue.

Trenton laughed. I could tell by the sound of his voice that he was only ten yards away.

"You think I'm scared of you?" he asked.

"You should be." It wasn't a threat. It was simple fact.

A white fireball was ready in my hands. I leapt out from behind my tree, but before I could aim at the tall, muscular figure before me, Marek sprang forward and knocked Trenton to the ground. Trenton rolled away from him and quickly got to his feet.

"Leave her the hell alone!" Marek shouted.

"Screw you!" Trenton roared.

"Marek! Trenton!" I yelled.

Marek had already tackled Trenton to the ground again. Trenton tried to get back up, but Marek threw another kick. Trenton was back on the ground in under a second. Marek swung his foot at Trenton's face over and over again.

All I could do was watch in horror. I didn't want to be a part of this, of the fighting, the bloodshed.

Dark blood rushed from Trenton's face, splattering onto leaves beneath him. Without warning, an angry roar burst from Trenton's chest. He rolled just outside of Marek's reach, giving him enough time to jump to his feet. Trenton lunged forward, and his body slammed into Marek's. He pinned Marek against a tree as his strong fingers wrapped around Marek's neck and sought to strangle the life out of him.

Marek's hands clawed at Trenton as he struggled to free himself, but Trenton was just as strong, if not stronger.

"Let him go!" I growled. I threw myself onto Trenton's back. My fingernails scraped across his face repeatedly.

"Get off of me." With one hand still pinning Marek to the tree, he reached behind him with the other. His cold fingers tangled in my hair, and he tugged. Hard.

I landed on my side in the dirt, my skull aching.

Trenton turned back to Marek with fury in his eyes. Marek's face had gone purple from lack of oxygen. He gasped for breath that never came. He flailed, but most of the fight had already drained out of him. He was on the brink of passing out.

"NO!" I screamed.

I scrambled to my feet and wrenched at Trenton's strong arms, but they didn't budge. Trenton swung an arm out. His elbow slammed into my chest and sent me stumbling backward.

As Trenton's fingers tightened around Marek's throat and he gasped for breath, one thing became very clear to me. Trenton had spent a lifetime fighting between his demon and Davina instincts. His demon side had won. He'd find pleasure in watching the life drain from Marek's eyes.

"Trenton," I begged.

Trenton's lips curled back, and his eyes narrowed, filling his expression with rage.

My time for apologies was over. There was no more reasoning with him. I had only one option left to save Marek.

I don't want to do this, I thought.

I had no other choice.

I pressed my eyes shut tightly and lunged at Trenton. My palm slammed into his bare chest as a flash of purple erupted from my hand. Trenton's body flew backward and crashed to the forest floor several yards away. I flinched.

Marek slumped down the tree onto his back. He inhaled deep, audible breaths.

"Marek!" I cried. I fell to my knees beside him and placed my hands on the side of his face.

"I'm okay," he said in a raspy whisper.

Marek's eyes widened. I followed his gaze and shot to my feet. A purple fireball formed in my hand in a split second. A demon stood several yards past Trenton's unmoving form. But he didn't stick around for a fight. He jumped into the air and flew out of the forest through a break in the trees.

I drew my arm back to aim my fireball at him, but I never took the shot. I lowered my hand to my side and dropped to my knees again. I didn't want to fight anymore.

Slowly, I lifted my gaze and turned my attention to Trenton. He lay sprawled out on the ground with his white wings stretched wide. His arms lay limp at his side.

A lump so large rose to my throat that I struggled to breathe. Unlike the demons that disappeared as soon as their life energy could no longer tether them to a stable plane, Trenton's body remained. His lifeless eyes stared up into the canopy above us.

I couldn't bear to see him like that. Slowly, I crawled over to him and gently closed his eyelids. And then I threw my body over his chest and wept.

"Ryn!"

I was vaguely aware of someone calling my name. I didn't know how much time had passed, but when I raised my head to identify the source of the voice, I noticed that dusk had settled over the forest.

Marek sat beside me with a comforting hand rested on my shoulder.

A chill breeze brushed across my arms and sent a shiver down my spine. I sat up to wipe at the tears on my cheeks, but they'd already dried.

"Ryn! Marek! Oh my God." Allie skidded to a halt beside us and dropped to pull me into a hug. "We couldn't find you. We thought that maybe you—you…"

Hot tears rose to my eyes again at the sight of Trenton's body. "I—I killed him, Allie. We were going to die. It was the only way to stop him."

No, I told myself. *I could've stunned him instead. Stunned him and walked away. That's what I should've done.* All I wanted to do was turn back time and take back what I'd done.

Allie squeezed me tighter, and I buried my face in her shoulder. "It's okay, Ryn. You had to."

"Is it over?" I whispered.

"It is for now," Allie said gently. "The demons retreated."

I pulled away from her. "They'll be back with more."

"Yeah," Marek agreed in a quiet voice. "There'll be plenty who want to see that portal open."

"We should get back and let everyone know you two are all right," Allie said.

I dared to steal a final glance at Trenton. In the dimming light, he was only an outline.

"What do we do with him?" I asked.

Allie took a deep breath. "We'll have to bury him with the others."

I thought I might hurl. I didn't have to ask for confirmation. Allie's sorrowful tone said it all.

We'd lost others. A lot of them.

"Come on," Allie encouraged.

I could hardly think straight as we distanced ourselves from Trenton's body. We broke through the trees, giving us a clear view of the valley below us.

Nausea slammed into my gut at the sight. Black cloaks littered the valley as if they were the ghosts of the demons lost today. Dozens of unmoving Davina lay beneath us. Those who were still alive moved slowly and solemnly, taking in the devastation. Stillness settled over the valley as if nature itself mourned our losses.

A pained shriek reached my ears. Somehow, it seemed more appropriate than the silence.

My eyes quickly found the woman who'd screamed. She dropped to her knees beside a man's body and took his hand in hers.

I forced down the lump in my throat and summoned my wings. Marek and Allie followed behind me as I flew down to land in the center of the battlefield. Closer up, I had a better view of everyone's faces.

Tears rolled down my cheeks as I took note of the Davina we'd lost. Some I didn't recognize. Most I did.

The woman who'd screamed knelt above a dark-skinned man with broad shoulders. *Mr. Collins.* Beside him, a woman's neck twisted at an odd angle. *Mrs. Banks.* Mrs. Presley, our principal, lay next to her with her lifeless eyes turned to the sky.

I abandoned Marek and Allie and rushed from body to body, praying the familiar faces would end. They didn't.

I saw Troy, with his white wings mangled beneath him. A long bruise lined his neck where he'd been strangled.

Then I noticed Ruby knelt over another young girl's body. Tears fell down her face and splashed onto the other girl's shirt.

"Emily," I whispered.

The second sophomore girl on our training team had somehow found her way to the fight. And it cost her her life.

Gently, I lowered myself to Ruby's side and wrapped an arm around her. "Ruby, I'm so sorry."

She didn't answer past the tears.

Through the darkness, I could see Marek and Kyle carrying Trenton's body out of the trees and down the stairs. They placed him at the end of the row that'd been started to gather our dead.

Scanning the crowd, I noticed that several people nearby had sustained serious injuries. One guy's arm bent in the wrong direction, and another woman's nose was broken. Two girls from my flying class sat wrapped in each other's arms. One girl's wings were twisted. I wasn't sure she'd ever fly again. Nearby, I spotted Casey and her father arguing in hushed whispers about her decision to join the fight.

And then my eyes fell upon another familiar face. Her friendly smiled had vanished, but I recognized her porcelain skin and long brown hair. Her eyelids were closed, but it didn't make her dead body any easier to look at.

I slowly inched my way over to Meg, not really feeling my legs move beneath me. My fingers involuntarily reached out to take her limp hand. Agony twisted in my gut. It felt a lot like guilt, like her death and the carnage surrounding me was somehow my fault.

If I found Grace sooner... If I tried harder to get to her... If I explained things to Meg faster... Maybe all this could've been prevented.

I pushed Meg's hair out of her face. Her skin was still warm. I could almost pretend she was only sleeping.

The key we needed hung loosely around her neck. I leaned forward and undid the clasp. It didn't feel right claiming the key as my own, so instead of placing it around my neck, I slipped it into my pocket.

"Rest in peace, Meg," I whispered.

"Ryn." Someone placed a gentle hand on my shoulder, making me jump.

I turned to find Marek standing next to me. He'd retracted his wings, but he remained shirtless from the battle. Without thinking about it, I got to my feet and flung my hands around his neck. He gently wrapped me in his warm arms. Neither of us spoke. It was easier that way.

Minutes later, Fletcher approached us, and we were forced to part.

"How are we going to explain all this?" I asked, gesturing to the bodies lying in the grass nearby.

Fletcher's face fell. "This is going to be a terrible loss for the town. The Davina will all know what happened. As for everyone else… we'll have to explain it away as a mass accident."

"The demons will be back," Marek said quietly. It sounded as if speaking caused him pain.

"I know," Fletcher agreed. "We'll be contacting the Davina Council and bringing in as many Davina as we can. Everything will be easier once we wake Grace."

My stomach dropped. I couldn't explain the feeling in my gut that told me Grace wouldn't be able to fix this. Things would only get worse before this war was finally over.

END OF BOOK TWO

AWAKENED BY GRACE

DIVINE FATE BOOK THREE

1

I thought I could learn to live with killing the demons. Marek kept telling me that's what it meant to be a Davina. More than anything, I wanted to be a Davina. But I didn't want to be a killer.

And that's exactly what I was. A killer.

A murderer.

I sat alone on the cold concrete steps in front of Eagle Valley High School and stared across the full parking lot. Dense fog and silence filled the air, as if the town itself was mourning with the rest of us. I'd just abandoned my friends inside the gymnasium, which was the only place in town big enough to hold the memorial service for the Davina we'd lost three nights ago.

I crossed my arms to ward off the chill in the air. A heavy weight settled on my chest, but my stomach felt empty. I couldn't remember the last time I ate. I didn't feel hungry. I didn't feel much of anything. Only cold, empty, and broken. I wasn't sure how I was going to piece myself together after what I'd done.

A flash of purple entered my memory. I saw Trenton's face—the moment of shock that hit right before his heart gave out. Right before I stopped it. On *purpose.*

Trenton. My friend. A person I truly cared about.

A person.

Demons. Angels. Aedes. Davina. The labels meant nothing. We were all *people*.

Footsteps approached. I knew without looking that it was Marek. He didn't say anything as he lowered himself to the step beside me. Although he was only inches away, it felt as if a ghost of Trenton's essence lay between us, turning those few inches into an expansive ocean.

"Are you okay?" Marek asked softly, yet his voice still sounded too loud.

My gaze dropped to my feet. This was the part where I was supposed to tell him I was fine. But I couldn't lie, especially to Marek.

"Ryn," Marek pressed, like he thought I hadn't heard him.

He reached out and took my hand. I didn't pull away, but I didn't entwine my fingers in his, either.

I closed my eyes and took a deep breath. "I'm… alive." At least there was that. "What about you, Marek? Are you okay?"

He stared out into the fog, contemplating the question.

"It's a hard question, isn't it?" I asked flatly.

He nodded. "I've heard so much about this demon war. I've spent the last three years preparing to fight in it. But now that it's actually happening to me—to *us*—it doesn't feel real."

"I know what you mean," I whispered.

A beat passed before Marek spoke again.

"Why'd you walk out of the memorial service?" he asked curiously.

I shook my head. I didn't want to talk about it, but the words escaped my lips anyway. "I couldn't listen to them lie. The people we lost deserve better than that."

The whole town believed the deaths occurred in an accident at the community center. They thought Galen High students, parents, and staff were there for a fundraiser meeting. The Davina told them the building had a leaky section of roof that was never inspected properly, that it'd taken on too much water damage over the years and collapsed, killing dozens. The Davina even staged the whole thing while the town slept. They'd closed the streets surrounding the community center to keep people away from the demolished building.

The Davina Council had come into town under the guise of law enforcement personnel to conduct an "official investigation." In other words, they came to cover up the massacre.

"Why can't we just be honest?" My voice came out smaller than I intended.

Marek's lips turned down. "There are a lot of reasons the Davina keep secrets."

I'd heard every excuse in the book. Exposing ourselves would lead to mass panic. We'd be captured and studied by scientists. Keeping our secret was the safest way to protect the Originals, to protect Grace.

And still, I felt like the people of Eagle Valley deserved the truth. They *knew* the Davina we'd lost. They'd been business owners, cops, waiters, hairdressers, librarians, politicians... The list went on. Humans and Davina didn't live separate lives here in Eagle Valley. They were *friends*. Even those who didn't know the secrets of the Davina felt the loss and the sorrow.

"Do you want to talk about it?" Marek asked. "I mean, about him."

Him. That one simple word was enough to make my guts feel as if they were trying to force their way up my throat. I swallowed hard to keep the lump at bay.

"I'm sorry I couldn't fight harder," Marek whispered. "I'm sorry I couldn't prevent what happened."

I didn't regret saving Marek's life. I only regretted that I had to kill Trenton to do it.

The damn Power of Grace. That's all it was good for. Killing. So far, I hadn't seen it accomplish anything else.

"I thought I was meant for something greater than this, Marek," I said. "I mean, Grace must've chose me for a reason."

Marek shifted to drape his arm around me. It was hard to feel comforted in the wake of everything that happened.

"I'm sure she *did* choose you for a reason," he assured me.

His words hung in the air. I didn't care to discuss it any further, and Marek didn't push it. We sat in silence until the front doors banged open and people began flooding out of the school. Marek and I stood. I watched as faces passed—familiar and unfamiliar. Most people kept quiet, with their gazes locked on their feet as they headed to their vehicles. I finally caught sight of Allie and Kyle as they exited the building at the back of the crowd.

"Hey," Allie said somberly when they reached us.

"How are you doing?" Kyle asked me.

People needed to stop asking questions I didn't want to answer.

I sighed. "I don't know what to do anymore."

Allie stepped forward to wrap me in a hug. "You can't give up. Not when we're this close."

I shook my head. "I'm not giving up. I'm…" What *was* I doing? I certainly didn't feel hopeful. Was that the same thing as giving up?

Allie drew away from me. "I know how hard this is, but there's still work that needs to be done. We need to awaken Grace now more than ever."

My stomach sank. I didn't think I was ready for this. I wasn't sure I'd *ever* be ready for this. I'd managed to put it off while everyone grieved, but I'd promised to wake her as soon as the memorial service ended.

Allie noticed my fallen face. "What is it?"

I bit the inside of my lower lip. I wanted honesty, which meant I had to open up to my friends. "I don't want to use the Power of Grace again."

"It's just one last time." For once, Kyle was trying to be reassuring.

"Yeah," Allie agreed. "Once you wake Grace, you don't have to worry about her power anymore. Grace will be able to end all of this. Things will go back to normal."

It was a relief to think about, but Allie was wrong. Things would never go back to normal. Maybe it'd be *her* normal, but *my* normal set sail a long time ago.

"Look." Allie gestured to the people quietly climbing into their cars. "These people need hope. Grace can bring them that."

I continued to chew on my lip without replying.

"We can wait until you're ready," Marek offered, but I knew he didn't mean it. None of us could afford to wait any longer.

"No," I said. "I think you're right. It's time to wake Grace."

My legs felt like noodles as they carried me back to my house. The silence between my friends was agonizing. I half expected someone to speak up and explain to me how this had all been an elaborate prank, but no one did.

I took a deep breath and descended the flight of stairs to my basement. The sound of my friends' footsteps behind me should've been comforting, but it only made me more nervous. It felt like I should be doing this alone.

I stopped in front of the Davina carving I'd found weeks ago. I could hardly believe the moment had finally come. All that stood between me and my destiny was a wall. My heart pounded so loudly in my ears that if any of my friends said anything, I wouldn't have heard them. My mouth grew dry, and my fingers quivered.

"What's wrong?" Allie asked softly.

"Ryn." Marek reached out and placed a hand on my shoulder.

I cleared my throat. "I just—what if…"

How did I tell them I was freaking terrified that something might go wrong? What if Grace wasn't here like we thought? What if I couldn't wake her like I was supposed to?

You won't know unless you try, I told myself.

I shook my head. "Never mind."

Somehow, I managed to steady my shaking fingers long enough

to pull Meg's key out of my pocket and slip it into the lock beneath the Davina carving. I closed my eyes and twisted.

A horrible noise like crunching gravel filled the basement, and a large puff of dust exploded around me. I took a step back, coughing. Everyone else lifted their hands to shield their faces from the dust cloud. When I opened my eyes, I noticed a seam that followed the outline of stones. A section of wall had popped inward to reveal a door.

When no one made a move, I realized they were waiting for me. I stepped forward and pressed my palms to the cold, hard stone. The door swung open under my weight. The overhead light behind me illuminated a small section of dusty floor. Beyond that, I found nothing but darkness.

I reached for my phone in my back pocket, but before I could use it to brighten my way, a light shone from behind me. Marek had pulled a flashlight from the shelf nearby and handed it to me.

"Thanks," I said before turning back to the room.

The room was barely bigger than my bathroom. The light from my flashlight reached the back wall. A large rectangular stone took up most of the space.

I inched my way inside and circled around the stone, keeping the flashlight fixed on it. A large carving of the same Davina woman that we'd found outside the door had been etched into the top. Instead of her hands at her sides, however, the woman held her hands together at her heart. A crack ran between them, like that part of the stone had deteriorated over the last century and a half.

She's here! She's really here! Excitement fluttered in my chest, and my worry melted away.

I barely noticed everyone else filter into the room. Allie and Kyle stood on my left while Marek stopped on my right.

Allie ran her fingers over the top of the stone. "It's a tomb."

Marek pressed his hands up against the decorative lip that ran along the perimeter of the concrete grave. "Let's open it."

I quickly slipped the flashlight under my arm and mimicked his stance. Allie and Kyle joined in.

"On three," I instructed. "One… two… three."

I pressed my feet to the floor and put all my strength into lifting the stone, but the top of the grave didn't budge. Everyone seemed to realize at the same time that our efforts were useless. We all stepped back.

There goes my excitement. We're going to need a freaking jackhammer to get through to her.

"Maybe it opens somewhere else," Allie suggested. "Like on the sides."

I shined the flashlight on the side of the smooth stone and found nothing. Everyone pulled out their phones and used them as lights to inspect the area they were closest to. I quickly rounded to my right and squeezed past Marek to see if there was anything. There wasn't.

I passed by Kyle, who was crouched near the door in search of clues. Past him, I found only smooth stone on Allie's side. I returned to my spot at the head of the grave and ran my fingers over the wings carved into the top.

My jaw tightened. How were we going to get to her? "Maybe we need to use the key again."

"Where would it go?" Marek asked.

"I don't know," I answered. "Kyle, can you grab the key out of the door?"

He hadn't stood from where he crouched. "Um... you should come see this."

I pressed my body to the cold wall to pass by Marek again. "What is it?"

Kyle moved out of the way so I could make out what he was looking at. I was vaguely aware of Allie and Marek squeezing in behind me to get a good look.

I shined the flashlight on the words carved at the foot of Grace's tomb.

Here lies Grace, a Davina of old.
The time will come when legends unfold,
When Grace will walk the earth once more,
Protecting from a demon's war.
To awaken her, you'll need a key,
An ancient object old as she.
Be wary; take not this task so light.
When Grace awakes, prepare to fight.

Kyle broke the silence. "A key as old as Grace? It can't mean Meg's key. Grace is thousands of years older than this tomb."

I didn't take my eyes off the words as I read them through a second time.

"Is it talking about the Power of Grace?" Allie theorized.

I shook my head. "I don't think so. It says *object*."

Kyle sighed. "We have to find *another* key?"

I shook my head, but Marek spoke before I could.

"*An ancient object as old as she*," Marek emphasized.

I pulled myself up from the floor. "Good thing we already have one of those."

Realization crossed Allie's face as I held my hand out to Kyle.

"Ooh." Kyle pulled the Davina Blade from the sheath hidden beneath his jeans. I traded him my flashlight for the blade.

I rounded back toward the head of the tomb. "There must be a lock built to the blade's unique shape."

Allie glanced around in search of a keyhole, and Kyle followed the blade with his light. My gaze flickered between the Davina carving and the blade. It was clear to me what I had to do. I placed the tip of the blade in the crevice between the palms of the Davina carving, hovering it just above where her heart would be. Then I plunged the blade into the stone.

A satisfying click filled the otherwise quiet room.

Allie gasped. "A perfect fit."

I removed the blade and handed it to Marek. Everyone returned to where they'd stood before and placed their hands on the tomb. With a large heave, we managed to slide the heavy stone aside.

"Quick, the flashlight." I eagerly held my hand out to Kyle.

I inhaled an audible breath when I saw what was hidden inside. A beautiful woman with skin dark as night lay motionless beneath me. Tight black curls framed her flawless face, and she wore a long white dress. Her hands lay folded over her heart. She looked as if she might simply be sleeping, but she didn't breathe. My heart hammered so hard I thought perhaps the sound of it might wake her.

"She's so pretty," Allie whispered.

Marek and Kyle drew their heads closer to get a better look. It was a long time before anyone spoke.

"How does this work?" Kyle asked.

I blinked several times, still mesmerized by the sight of the Davina in front of me. I'd heard so much about her, and here she finally was—in the flesh. I wasn't sure I ever truly believed we'd make it this far.

"Ryn?" Marek spoke my name with a hint of curiosity.

"Sorry, I just…" I didn't look up. Instead, I shoved the flashlight back in his direction.

"You have the Power of Grace. Shouldn't you—?" Marek started.

"I know what to do," I stated confidently.

I didn't know how I knew, but in the same way Grace's power led me to Eagle Valley, it told me how to awaken her. I lowered my hand into the stone casket and placed it upon hers—directly over her heart. Inhaling a deep breath, I relaxed to let Grace's magic flow through me.

A deep purple glow traveled down my arm, continuing from my hand to hers. Color returned to her body, leaving her dark ringlets shinier and her skin more vibrant. It was like watching something from a movie. An intense electric current filled me as I pulled more and more of Grace's power from the earth and returned it to her body, restoring their connection.

The intensity quickly dissipated as the last remaining threads of Grace's essence left my body into hers. It felt strange. I'd become so used to feeling that electric energy inside of me that it felt like something was physically missing. It was also a relief, like I'd gotten rid of a tumor, a burden I never wanted in the first place.

Grace's eyes sprang open, and she drew her first breath. I jumped away, stunned by her sudden awakening. Grace looked shocked at first, but after blinking her purple eyes several times, she seemed to finally focus on the faces above her.

My friends stared at her in awe. I didn't know if I should be impressed or freaked out.

Grace pushed herself to a sitting position.

Freaked out, I decided. It was like watching a zombie rise from the grave, only without the dead flesh hanging off her bones.

Grace turned until her gaze landed upon me. "Kathryn?"

I stepped forward. "I'm Ryn—Kathryn." I didn't sound particularly confident.

Grace reached out toward me. I wasn't sure what she wanted, but I gave her my hand. She took it and squeezed it lightly. Everything about the gesture felt cold.

"I knew you had what it took," she said.

I returned an uncertain smile. "Thanks."

Grace looked around the small, dark room again. "It's quite cramped in here, isn't it? Should we go somewhere more comfortable?"

I couldn't believe how casual she was being. This lady had been asleep for millennia and was talking to us like we were old friends. Except, I didn't feel like I knew her at all. I expected a smiling, happy goddess, but Grace seemed… different. Maybe that was what happened when you spent thousands of years in a deep slumber.

Marek rushed to Grace's side and helped her out of her tomb. We filed out the room, still in a complete state of shock.

In the main area of the basement, Grace stopped and closed her eyes. "Just a minute."

I recognized the concentration in her expression and the way she flexed her shoulders. Two large white wings rose up from behind her. She took advantage of the space and spread her wings as far as they could go. Though hers were much bigger than mine, the white feathers shined a similar purple.

Allie inhaled an audible breath. I half expected her to drop to her knees and bow down before Grace.

Grace opened her eyes. "That's much better."

Allie managed to pick her jaw up from the floor, but her eyes remained fixed on Grace. "Can I just say what an *honor* it is to meet you?"

Grace smiled like she agreed her very presence was an honor.

"Um…" Kyle said, like he wasn't sure he was allowed to speak. "I'm just curious… Maybe this is a stupid question, but how do you know English?"

"There are no stupid questions," Grace said. "Though my body has been resting for a long time, my essence and consciousness have been part of the earth for just as long. I have been watching, observing the world I was meant to protect."

"So you're aware of what's been happening?" I asked. "You know what happened here in Eagle Valley?" I wondered if she knew how many people her powers had killed or if that responsibility fell on me. I wasn't sure I wanted the answer, so I didn't bring it up.

"Yes," Grace said. "I'd like to start making preparations to retaliate right away. But first, I'd like to visit the injured."

Grace's suggestion sounded noble, but there was something about her that rubbed me the wrong way. I couldn't explain why, but I just had a bad feeling about her. Perhaps it was her eagerness to fight, or maybe it was the smug smile on her face.

All I knew was, I wasn't sure I'd awakened the goddess everyone was expecting.

3

The dense layer of fog from earlier hadn't lifted when we stepped outside several minutes later. Grace insisted she needed to spread her wings, so we took flight and led her to Galen High. It wasn't far, but I still worried we'd be seen.

Though Grace had been observing all this time, it was like she couldn't believe it was all real. She seemed intrigued by one of the neighbor's dogs, and she couldn't take her eyes off a car driving along the street below us.

"We're here!" Allie exclaimed when we landed in front of Galen High. Her gaze flickered toward the mansion, like she expected people to start rushing out to give Grace the red carpet treatment.

I stared at the back of Grace's head as we walked toward the doors. I wasn't sure what I was supposed to do at this point. Should I be kissing the ground she walked on? Racing out of Eagle Valley now that my part was done?

Marek paused at the front door. "Grace, welcome to Galen High School."

He twisted the doorknob and pushed the door open before stepping aside for Grace.

All conversation died. A small group of a dozen people were gathered around the fireplace in the common room. I recognized Fletcher and Casey's dad—Mr. Harris—among the group. The others were complete strangers, who I figured were part of the

354

Davina Council. Most of them wore suits, like we'd just stepped into a business meeting for a big corporation. The usual scent of lemon cleaner was masked by the distinct smell of shoe polish and arrogance.

All eyes turned toward Grace. She didn't need an introduction; they'd been expecting her. Her white dress, flawless skin, and purple eyes gave her away.

The front door clicked shut behind us, startling me.

A guy with white hair and a bald patch was the first to compose himself. He fell to one knee and bowed his head. "Grace," he said in a breathy voice.

Several others moved to bow as well, but Grace raised a hand to stop them.

"That's really not necessary," she objected, but a smile spread across her face, like she gladly welcomed the gesture.

A tall guy with short black hair rose from a bow and stepped forward. He held his head high. If I had to guess, I'd say this guy was in charge.

"Grace." He reached out to shake her hand. "I apologize that we couldn't arrange a better introduction. We didn't expect you awake just yet. I'm Anthony Lucas, head of the Davina Council. Welcome."

I didn't like the way he said *welcome* as if he owned the mansion. This guy had probably never even been here before.

Anthony glanced between Allie and me. "One of you is Kathryn, I presume?"

I took a step forward. "You can call me Ryn."

He looked down at me past his nose. I read judgement in his eyes, like he couldn't believe *I* was the one who woke Grace. Or maybe he was just pissed he'd missed it.

Anthony stuck his hand out in my direction. "I've heard a lot about you. We planned to meet you as soon as possible, but I only just arrived."

Just in time to miss the memorial service, I thought.

Anthony's handshake lasted only a moment before he dropped my hand and turned back to Grace. "Can we get you anything?"

"I'd like to see the injured." She spoke with confidence, like she knew no one would refuse anything she asked.

"Of course, of course," Anthony agreed. "This way."

He led Grace to the staircase on our left. Conversation broke out again, and the other councilmembers quickly followed. My friends and I were pushed to the back of the group, like we were a mere afterthought.

Ever since I learned what I was, it was all about finding and awakening Grace. Now that she was here, I didn't have a clue what to expect. I didn't know where I fit in to all this anymore.

"Everything went well, then?" Fletcher asked as we ascended the stairs.

"Yeah," I answered. "Just great."

Except, it didn't *feel* great. I should've been jumping in excitement and shouting for joy, just like the rest of them. Instead, I felt like I was only going through the motions, but no one told me what the next move was.

We climbed the stairs to the third level. A set of double doors opened to a vast room with a slanted ceiling and hardwood floors. The sounds of chatter and the occasional groan of pain spilled out into the hallway.

We entered a makeshift hospital, a refuge for the Davina who'd been severely injured in the recent battle. At least two dozen Davina lay on cots that lined the long room. Volunteers and family members sat at bedsides changing bandages or keeping the injured company. Not a single person smiled. Even the volunteers looked as if they were in pain just being in this room where sorrow leaked from the walls.

"Donations are still rolling in," Anthony explained to Grace. "We had to keep everyone here, or it would arise suspicion. We couldn't bring this many Davina to the hospital at once. We heal too fast. And, as you can see, some of the injuries are Davina-specific."

He gestured to a girl my age, who sat propped upright on a cot. Her wings were spread out behind her. One hung in a sling attached to one of the wooden frames we used to prop up foam targets. I remembered her from the battle. The broken bones in her wing had been set since then, but I still wasn't sure she'd fly again.

Beside her, a man struggled to push himself up so he could take a sip of water. Judging by the way he held onto his side, I guessed he had broken ribs. Beyond him lay a guy with a broken leg and a girl with a broken arm, both wrapped in casts. Across the room, a woman applied ointment to a large gash on a man's abdomen. It looked as if a demon had used one of our blades to slice his skin open. It'd been sown back together with at least two dozen stitches.

Grace stepped farther into the room and spun in a circle, taking it all in. Sorrow crossed her face, like she couldn't believe what she was seeing. Her enthusiasm from earlier had vanished, and her eyes glistened at the threat of tears.

Conversations slowly died out as more and more people noticed the noise in the room decreasing.

Grace's voice cut through the silence. She sounded more confident than she looked. "Please don't worry. I'm Grace, and I'm here to help."

Whispers broke out around the room.

Grace?

An Original?

I can't believe it.

For the first time, I saw someone smile. Allie had been right. These people needed hope, and Grace was their answer.

"Grace?" The girl with the hurt wing rose her voice.

Grace slowly approached her and knelt beside her cot.

"Is it really you?" the girl asked. She stared up into Grace's purple eyes.

"It is," Grace replied with a nod. She sounded kind, but her lips curled down at the corners. "How can I help you, child?"

The girl reached out toward Grace. When Grace didn't take her hand, she let it fall limply off the side of the cot. I glanced to Marek to see if he'd noticed Grace's cold greeting, but he only stared at her in wonder, just like everyone else.

Grace continued her way around the room, stopping at each bedside but not touching a single patient. It was like she was afraid their ailments were contagious.

My friends and I stood forgotten in the corner as Grace paraded around the room and soaked in the glory of her return. I thought about pointing out my observations, but Allie and Kyle spoke so highly of her that I knew I'd only offend them.

"Are you okay?" Marek asked me.

I forced my lips into a smile. "Grace is back. Why wouldn't I be okay?"

Marek slipped his fingers into mine. "You're being so quiet. I thought you'd be…"

"Be what?" I shrugged. "I don't know what to say, Marek. I'm not the hero anymore. Grace is."

"Does that bother you?" he asked.

"What?" I recoiled. The accusation felt like a slap to the face. "I'm not jealous of Grace, if that's what you mean."

I'm just not sure I like her.

I caught Fletcher's gaze from beside Marek. He quickly looked away, but I could tell he'd been listening.

I lowered my voice so only Marek could hear. "Don't you notice how she's being a bit… cold?"

"Cold?" Marek's eyes followed Grace.

"She won't touch anyone," I pointed out.

Marek shifted uncomfortably. "She's been asleep for a long time. She probably just needs some time to warm up to being around people again."

I frowned. Could that be why she rubbed me the wrong way? Or, maybe Marek was right, and I *was* jealous of her.

Another hour passed before Grace finished making her rounds. My friends hadn't made any suggestions to leave, so I stayed with them in our corner of the room. Eventually, the chatter returned to normal levels. It sounded happier and more upbeat than before.

Grace moved to the center of the room. Silence settled once again as all eyes turned to her.

"Thank you for allowing me to visit you today," she said. "It has been a great honor. I want you to know I will do everything in my power to ensure nothing like this ever happens again. You have my word."

Her words sounded calculated and stale to my ears.

She continued. "To the injured, you have nothing to worry about. All I want you to do is focus on getting well. To everyone else, please go home and get some rest. Spread the word that we'll meet back here at sunrise." Grace took a breath, then rose her voice. "Tomorrow, we will begin preparing for war!"

My stomach sank the same moment cheers broke out around me. Even my friends joined in on the clapping. Marek was the only one to notice I remained quiet, but he didn't say anything.

I stayed silent even as my friends and I walked back home.

"I'm not going to get *any* sleep," Allie said.

"Me, either," Kyle agreed. "How does Grace expect us to rest after we just met her? I'm ready to start preparing for war tonight!"

My gut twisted. How could war *excite* him?

Relief washed over me when we reached my house and Allie and Kyle continued across the lawn toward hers. I didn't know how much longer I could listen to them talk about how great it would be to fight the demons again.

Marek walked me up my front steps. "I'm sorry this is so difficult for you. I know it's hard feeling hopeful after what happened the other night, but with Grace here, things are already turning around."

I wrung my hands together. "Are you sure?"

Marek placed a finger under my chin and forced my gaze up to his. "I'm certain. You don't have to worry anymore."

Marek's warm arms wrapped around me. I tried to relax into him, but the doubt in his voice made me uneasy. Or was I imagining his doubt, too?

It's my paranoia, I told myself.

It was the same paranoia that told me no matter how hard she tried to disguise it, Grace was hiding something from us. It was only just a matter of time before I figured out whether or not my fears were justified.

4

My heart pounded as a figure moved through the trees. Something about his footsteps sounded familiar—but dangerous.

"Ryn!" his voice called.

Guilt slammed into my gut.

"Trenton?" I stared out into the dark, dense forest in the direction his voice came from. "Trenton, please. Let me explain."

"There's nothing to explain," he growled.

I whirled around and slammed into his bare chest. Trenton towered six inches above me and was a solid wall of muscle. His long blond hair hung in front of his hostile eyes. A large scar the shape of lightning cut across his torso.

I took a cautious step back. "Please. I'm sorry I—"

"Sorry for what?" he spat.

My hands shook at my sides. I slowly distanced myself from him, but he followed.

"Sorry for breaking my heart? For choosing Marek over me? For killing me?"

My heel met the base of a tree. I pressed my back against it, cowering away from him.

He didn't give me a chance to answer. "You should be sorry—about it all. About never giving the Aedes a chance to explain! I thought you were special, but you're as bad as the rest of them."

A fireball with a dark center and red outline formed in his palm.

"I don't know what you mean!" I cried.

Trenton's dark essence was already speeding toward my chest. I didn't have a chance to get out of the way before the impact stole the air from my lungs.

∽

I woke in a cold sweat. My sheets had been kicked to the foot of the bed, and my heart pounded in a quick rhythm. The street lamp outside my window cast a sliver of light across the room.

I closed my eyes and forced my breathing to slow. What had Trenton meant about giving the Aedes a chance to explain? Explain what?

"Bad dreams?" a deep voice asked.

A yelp escaped my lips. I instinctively grabbed the first thing my hands found and threw it at the intruder.

Because my *pillow* was totally going to save me during a home invasion.

The mystery man caught the pillow and stepped forward into the light. My muscles relaxed when I saw it was Marek.

"Are you insane?" I hissed, listening intently to make sure I hadn't woken my mom. "What are you doing here?"

Marek crossed the room and handed me my pillow. I sat up in bed and curled my legs under me so he could sit beside me. I wore sweatpants and a tank top, but Marek was still dressed in his normal attire—jeans, a t-shirt, and his leather jacket.

"I couldn't sleep," he said. "Turns out, it's really easy to climb onto your porch roof and into your bedroom. The window wasn't locked. You were practically inviting me inside."

I swatted at him. "Don't flatter yourself. I keep it unlocked for my other boyfriend."

Marek laughed quietly, and I smiled back. I realized it was the first time I'd smiled in days.

"I can leave if you don't want me here," he offered.

"No." I reached out for him before he could stand. "I want you to stay. It's just… I'm dead if my mom finds out."

Marek wrapped an arm around me and placed a gentle kiss on my forehead. "Then we'll have to make sure she doesn't find out."

His soft, warm lips left my skin. I ached to have them touch me again.

What was I thinking? He was in my bedroom in secret, and all I wanted was another kiss on the forehead? I could do anything I wanted with him right now.

"We can talk if you want," Marek suggested. "Or not. It's up to you."

That was it? He wanted to *talk*? What kind of guy was he?

A gentleman, I thought.

I snuggled into his chest and took a deep breath, inhaling the fresh scent of his t-shirt. I didn't know where to start. "I just keep thinking about the people we lost. I don't know what I'd do without you."

"I'm not going anywhere," he whispered into my hair. "I promise."

I frowned. "You can't promise that."

"I'll always be there in spirit," he said, like that was supposed to make me feel better. It only made me think of death. "How about this?"

Marek stood. He stripped off his leather jacket, then reached over his shoulder and grabbed his shirt. He pulled it up over his head and tossed it to the floor.

My heart hammered in excitement and fear. Maybe he wasn't a gentleman after all. I think I preferred his wild side.

Marek flexed his shoulders, and two massive wings rose from his back. He turned to his left wing and pinched a white feather between his fingers. He winced when he tugged on it and it broke free from his skin.

Marek stepped forward and handed me the delicate feather. "Now you'll always have a piece of me with you."

I stared down at it. For a brief moment, my heart felt full.

"Marek, I—"

He reached out and curled my fingers around the feather. "You don't have to say anything."

I pulled it to my chest and spoke softly. "Thank you."

My words weren't enough to show how much I truly appreciated the gesture. I only wished I had a good place to keep it.

An idea suddenly struck me. I stood from the bed and summoned my wings, then plucked a feather out like he'd just done to his.

Marek smiled and held his hand out to accept his gift.

"Hold on." I turned and crossed over to my desk, where I dug in the bottom drawer for my jewelry-making kit. Once I found it, I sat in my desk chair and began twisting wire around the end of the feather.

Marek sat on my bed and eyed me through the darkness. "What are you doing?"

"I said hold on." I smiled while I worked.

Marek fidgeted as he waited, and I could tell the suspense was killing him. I quickened my pace, then turned to him when I finished. A necklace with my feather attached dangled from my hand. Marek reached out slowly and took it.

I undid the clasp on mine and secured his feather around my neck. "Now we'll always have a piece of each other close to our hearts."

Marek placed the necklace around his neck and slipped his t-shirt back on, hiding my feather beneath his shirt. "Thank you, Ryn. It's perfect."

Marek reached out and gestured for me to join him on the bed. I lowered myself to the pillow and curled up next to him. My muscles relaxed, helping me forget the horror of the past few days. Marek pulled the blankets up from the foot of the bed and draped them across us. His body was like a furnace—warm and comforting. His hot breath passed across the back of my neck, and his arm rested over me with our fingers entwined.

Beyond a gentle kiss on the back of my head, nothing happened. Part of me yearned for more, but another part was simply grateful he was here and that he cared. All I needed right now was someone I could count on.

I didn't want to face any more nightmares on my own.

∾

I woke the next morning feeling more relaxed than I had in weeks. Marek's heavy arm draped over me and weighed me down. I managed to wiggle free of his embrace and climb out of bed without waking him. A yellow glow filled the room as the first signs of daylight touched the sky.

At my dresser, I gathered a change of clothes and then tiptoed out of the room to take a shower. I sped through washing my hair and shaving my legs. I was dried off and dressed within minutes.

I poked my head back into my room to see Marek's forearm covered his eyes while he slept. I quietly shut the door and turned down the hall to the stairs. I was surprised to find my mom in the kitchen, already starting on her coffee.

"You're up early," she said without turning from the coffee maker.

Shit. She knows.

"I have stuff to do today." I tried to sound as innocent as possible.

Mom finally looked at me. She brought her coffee mug to her lips and took a sip. "You mean Davina stuff?"

I grabbed a banana from the counter and began peeling it. "Yes."

Mom frowned like she always did when we talked about the Davina.

"Grace is awake," I stated flatly.

Mom took another sip of coffee but didn't say anything. We both knew it'd just turn into another screaming match and I'd run off and help the Davina anyway. It's not like she could keep me from going to school, even though I had no idea what school would be like now that Grace was back. Would classes be canceled?

I snatched up another banana and left the room before we started fighting again. Marek was awake when I made it back to my bedroom.

"It's not much, but I snagged you some breakfast." I handed him the banana. "If you don't want my mom to slit your throat, you'll have to sneak out the way you came."

Marek raised an eyebrow. "You think your mom can take me?"

"You'd be surprised what she's capable of when she's pissed. Besides, we're late." I glanced out the window to see the sun had risen.

"My bike's parked outside," Marek said. "I'll meet you downstairs."

Minutes later, I was climbing on the back of Marek's motorcycle, and we were headed to school.

Marek pulled into a full parking lot, but the walk up to the school felt strangely quiet, which was weird because the weather was decent and first period hadn't started yet. When we entered the common room, my stomach sank. We were met by complete and utter silence.

Everyone was gone.

5

"Oh my god, Marek!" I glanced to the clock above the mantel and confirmed we were on time. Where was everyone? Had they rushed into battle without us?

Marek took my hand. "I'm sure everything is fine."

If everything was fine, where were Allie, Kyle, and Fletcher?

"Let's check upstairs," Marek suggested.

My knees shook as we ascended two flights of stairs to the makeshift hospital wing. Relief washed over me when a volunteer told us everyone else was in the valley.

Marek and I hurried down the trail near the back of the school. The morning air was chilly for just a tank top, but I knew it would get warmer as the day wore on.

When we broke out of the trees, the valley was full of Davina. There must've been hundreds. Grace stood in the middle of the swarm with her wings spread out in all their glory. Excited chatter reached us from where we stood at the top of the hill.

Marek's face lit up when he saw the crowd. "Finally, we're getting somewhere. Let's get down there before we miss anything."

Marek pulled off his jacket and t-shirt in a flash. He held onto them as wings grew from his back. I followed his lead, and together, we glided down to the base of the valley and landed at the back of the group.

Grace cleared her throat. The crowd responded by quieting and turning their full attention toward her.

"I think we're ready to get started." Grace projected her voice to the people in the back.

While she spoke, my eyes scanned the crowd. Davina of all ages had gathered to hear Grace speak. I even noticed Dylan, Ethan, and Logan, the freshmen in our mentor group.

It didn't seem right that they were here. They were too young.

My eyes landed on Allie and Kyle standing next to Fletcher and Allie's dad, Jay. I gestured to Marek, and we quietly made our way over to them. Allie smiled at me but quickly returned her eyes back to Grace.

"Our biggest advantage in fighting the Aedes is our numbers," Grace continued. "That is why I have decided to train Davina of all ages in battle tactics."

My stomach twisted uncomfortably. She wanted children to fight with us?

Nobody objected; they just stared at her in awe. I was stunned by their silence.

"I have recruited active Protectors to assist in this training." Grace gestured to a group of Davina behind her.

At least fifty young men and women held their heads high and stared straight ahead, looking like perfect soldiers. I shuddered to think that this was what Galen High was preparing me for.

I turned to Marek and kept my voice low. "I thought our people were already trained in this kind of thing."

Marek shifted his weight between his feet and nodded. "I'm sure it's just a refresher. Plus, Grace knows things we don't. She'll want to teach us."

"What about Ethan and them?" I argued. "They've hardly trained at all."

Marek didn't have an answer for me. He just bit the inside of his cheek and stared straight forward.

What the hell, people? Don't you care about your kids?

Where were the protesting parents? The ones demanding to call in more Protectors so their kids wouldn't have to fight?

I continued to eye the crowd while Grace spoke. Her instructions seemed like they were meant to inspire, but to me, they didn't sound authentic.

I wanted to slap the Davina and tell them to pull themselves together, to *think* for themselves. I couldn't believe no one was speaking up about throwing fourteen-year-old children into this war.

Chatter erupted around me following something Grace said that I missed.

Well, damn. I'd remained quiet for too long. If no one else was going to say something, I would.

"Shall we get started?" Grace asked the crowd.

"Hold on!" I shouted from the back.

All eyes turned toward me. I felt like a zoo animal on display.

I cleared my throat. "Shouldn't there be an age limit?"

Grace didn't have a chance to answer before Ethan spoke up.

"What does age matter?" he asked, clearly offended.

"Sorry, Ethan, but you haven't trained enough for this," I said sympathetically.

"Neither have you," he argued.

It felt like a slap to the face. He wasn't exactly wrong.

"Two weeks ago, you didn't want to become a Protector," I pointed out, trying to talk some sense into him. He'd even made it sound like his parents were skeptical. "Now you're going to race head-first into battle without any clue what you're doing?"

Heat rose to the surface of my skin, and I clenched my hands into fists. This wasn't right.

"That's what we're training for," Logan retorted from beside Ethan. "Grace is here now. We don't have any reason to be afraid."

The crowd murmured in agreement.

Grace rose a hand, and the Davina quieted. When her eyes fell on me, the crowd parted to create a path between us. I shifted uncomfortably under her stare.

"We can use as many Davina as we can get," Grace said. "I can't stop anyone who wants to fight. The best I can do is prepare them for what's to come."

"Do we even know what that is?" I asked.

People around me scoffed. Whispers broke out, and I swear I heard someone call me an idiot. For a brief moment, my eyes met

Casey's. I was surprised when she shot me a sympathetic expression instead of joining in on the skeptical stares. I wasn't sure Casey was buying any of this shit either.

"We can discuss that as part of our practice," Grace said.

My shoulders fell when I realized there was no point in arguing with her. When Grace saw I had nothing more to say, she turned her attention back to the other Davina and began splitting them into training groups.

"Seriously?" I turned to my friends and kept my voice low. "No one has any problems with this?"

"Grace knows what she's doing," Allie said, defending her.

"Does she, though?" I asked.

Kyle frowned. "At least she's doing something and taking action."

"This isn't action!" I gestured to the Davina around me, who were still trying to decide which groups to break off into. "It's not even organized. It's chaotic."

"Be patient, Ryn," Marek encouraged. "Grace is only one person trying to guide all these Davina. Give her a chance."

I waited for Grace to share some sort of battle secrets or for something grand to happen, but it never came. As groups formed, all they did was conjure essence and spar each other. It was the same boring crap we'd been doing for weeks. The only useful thing I noticed was Mr. Harris demonstrating to a group of teens how to snap a demon's neck. My group listened to a Protector tell the story of his first kill. It was totally useless.

I couldn't sit around and watch this nonsense any longer. I abandoned my group. Marek's eyes followed me, but he didn't protest as I approached Grace.

"Grace, can I have a minute?" I asked.

Her eyes never met mine as she strolled from group to group, observing. "What is it?"

I took a breath. "I'm just wondering why we're wasting time doing all this while the Aedes are out there, probably gathering new recruits. Doesn't it make sense to strike right away while they're still weak? Or at least try to gather intel on their next move? Why are we practicing when most people here already know what they're doing?"

I noticed Casey in a group nearby watching me, listening. Her expression remained neutral. I couldn't read her.

Grace finally stopped and looked at me. "I'm not sure why you continue to question me like this. I'm doing what has to be done. Why can't you just trust me?"

That was a good question. Maybe it was because I didn't grow up with the stories of the Originals. Everyone else saw her as a goddess before they even met her. No one else was about to question her.

I bit my lower lip. If I started a fight right here in the midst of her loyal followers, they'd tear me to shreds—perhaps literally.

"Return to your group, Kathryn," Grace ordered. God, she sounded like my mother. "You need to be as prepared as everyone else, and frankly, you have a lot of catching up to do."

My teeth ground together.

Screw this. This whole thing was ridiculous.

I turned from her without another word. Back at my group, the guy was going on about his third kill. It sounded more like he was bragging than teaching, but Allie and Kyle were eating it up. Marek and the rest of them didn't notice me breeze past them and take flight. I didn't look back to see if Grace saw me, either.

I landed at the top of the hill and started down the trail back to the school. I wasn't sure where I was headed or what I was going to do at this point. All I knew was that I couldn't stand around and watch the circus Grace was running.

I decided to head up to the hospital wing and see if they needed any help there. Even if I was just keeping someone company, at least I'd be helping. I hurried up the concrete steps at the back of the school and reached out for the door handle.

Before I could twist the knob, a cold hand clamped around my mouth. My heart leapt inside my chest as my feet flew out from beneath me.

A moment later, an electric shock slammed into my back, and everything went dark.

6

Confusion clouded my mind. I was being carried. Or was I flying? Every so often, I caught a glimpse of color as my eyes peeked open. Then, that shock would hit my chest again, and I would lose consciousness.

My body dropped onto a hard surface with a *thud*. Strong hands propped me up. I hadn't gathered enough strength to peel my eyes open yet.

Slowly, the world came back into focus. I found myself in an unfamiliar room, lit only by the daylight seeping in through the curtains in the adjoining living room. A worn hardwood floor stretched out in front of me and met a door with a splintered frame. The living room split off in one direction from the entrance, while the kitchen sat on the other side. Stairs rose to a second level behind me. To my right, a small table below a cracked mirror had been knocked over. A vase lay shattered on the floor, but the flowers had withered away to almost nothing. A thin layer of dust coated everything. It didn't look like anyone had lived here for years.

Panic immediately set in when I noticed my hands were secured together behind me. I scrambled to get to my feet, but before I could, a foot connected with my gut, and I fell to the floor again.

"There's no point in struggling," a deep voice said.

My head snapped upward. A tall figure in a black cloak stood above me with his arms crossed over his chest. The room was too dark for me to see his face.

Fricking demons.

"You're too late," I snapped.

"Too late for what?" He sounded genuinely curious.

"Hurting me won't accomplish anything. Grace is already awake." Maybe that'd convince him to let me go. I doubted it.

The demon shook his head. "I don't want Grace. I want *you.*"

"I don't have the Power of Grace anymore. I'm useless to you."

"No, you're not," he said in a cold voice.

"Then what *do* you want me for?" Fear didn't come across in my tone—only anger. I'd had enough of this demon shit to last me a decade.

The demon reached for his hood and lowered it before squatting to my level. I kept my eyes on his to show I wasn't afraid, but the truth was, his dark eyes and thin, pale features made me uneasy. Behind his angered expression, something about him looked familiar… and dangerous. Maybe that was just a demon thing.

"Allow me to introduce myself," he said. "I'm Malcolm. I believe you've met my son."

The air left my chest.

"You're Trenton's dad?" I didn't know why I said it like a question. The answer was obvious.

Malcolm's lips pressed together. "Rumor has it you killed my son."

"I didn't mean to!" I said desperately.

"*Didn't mean to?*" Malcolm threw my words back at me in disgust. "You don't kill people on accident!"

"He was trying to kill my friend!" I tried to justify.

"And you thought your friend's life was worth more than my son's?" Malcolm roared. His face came so close to mine that I had to turn away from him to keep our noses from touching.

My heart pounded, and my breath wavered. I spoke in a whisper. "I didn't want him to die. Please believe me."

Malcolm rose to his feet. "Believe you? You're a Davina! I don't *trust* Davina."

I couldn't keep the words from escaping my lips. "You trusted Trenton."

"Don't you talk about him like you knew him!" Malcolm shouted.

Pain shot across my cheek as his hand cracked against the side of my face.

"You think the Davina are all *high and mighty*. You're not! Every Davina I've ever met had to *take* something from me. First it was Sylvia—Trenton's mother. We were in love, you know. Apparently, she didn't love me enough to bear the thought of others knowing she had my child. She ran away and took my heart with her. *Her* mother wasn't much better. She didn't want me around Trenton, but I didn't give her a choice."

While he spoke, my eyes scanned the house in search of an exit. I didn't feel the familiar weight of my phone in my back pocket, so I couldn't even entertain the idea of calling for help. The only exit I found was the front door. Even though the wood was splintered around the handle, and it was probably just hanging loosely from its hinges, I didn't think I could get it open while my hands were out of commission.

"When *she* died," Malcolm continued, "the Davina Council found out I'd been hanging around. They raided our house to get to me. Look at it. It's despicable." He glanced around the disheveled home.

"So this is where Trenton grew up?" I had to keep him talking to give myself a chance at escape. Not that I had much of a chance. I needed to figure out how to get untied first.

"It *was* our home," he spat. "Before the Davina destroyed it."

Davina wouldn't do that... would they?

"Killing me isn't going to help you get your revenge on the rest of them," I said. "They don't care about me now that Grace is back. It's not going to bring Trenton back, either. Believe me, if there was a way to bring him back, I'd do it myself."

Malcolm scoffed. "I told you before. I don't believe anything the Davina say. You don't trust us. Why should *we* trust *you*?"

"Why *would* we trust you?" I snapped. Was he actually suggesting demons were worth trusting? "You feed off human essence and play your stupid games with them."

My mind flickered to Clinton and the horrible things he'd done to my mom. Maybe there was a reason my friends wanted to rip the head off every demon they saw.

"We do what we need to do to *survive*," Malcolm snarled. "If that means borrowing a bit of essence, taking human lives, or killing Davina to protect ourselves, we'll do it."

What did he mean *to survive*? I thought the demons fed on human essence for fun—because they'd been oppressed for so long that it was the only way for them to feel they had any power. Was there more to it than that?

"What do you—?"

The air left my lungs as Malcolm's foot slammed into my stomach again.

"All I wanted was a life with my son, and you killed him!" he roared.

Malcolm kicked me again, sending me tumbling to my side. The right side of my face connected with the hardwood floor.

"Help!" I shrieked, hoping someone would hear me. "Help me!"

"No one's coming to your rescue," Malcolm taunted.

"Please," I begged. "Can't we—"

Malcolm shoved his fingers into my hair and wrenched my head upward. "Your time for begging is over. You think I'll give you a second chance when you didn't allow the same for my son?"

I couldn't hide the fear and desperation in my voice now. "I told you, I—ow!" I screamed as Malcolm slammed my face into the floor.

Malcolm's fist rushed toward my jaw, but I kicked my feet into the air to block him. My feet sank into his stomach, and he stumbled back. I used the split second I had to roll over and get to my knees. I wasn't on my feet before Malcolm's weight crashed into me. Without my hands free to catch myself, my forehead knocked into the wall. The room spun around me as I rose to my knees again.

"Please, Malcolm. You don't understand." I didn't know what else to do but beg.

"If you think putting on an innocent little girl act is going to spare your life, you're wrong," he growled. "It won't work on me."

While he spoke, I channeled essence into my palm. I wasn't sure what I was going to do with it, but it was the only option I had left.

Something was wrong. I felt the electricity run down my arm, but it didn't sizzle with the same charge I was used to. Had Malcolm's beating drained me that much?

It suddenly occurred to me that wasn't the case at all. I didn't have the Power of Grace anymore. My essence wasn't as strong. I was... *normal*. At least, normal for a Davina.

The realization distracted me. I didn't have time to duck out of the way of his next attack. Malcolm shoved me backward. My legs twisted under me, and I fell onto the stairs. The edges dug painfully into my spine. Malcolm stood above me with a dangerous look on his face.

"Why are you doing this?" I screamed. "Stop dragging it out and kill me already!" I didn't mean it. I didn't want to die.

Malcolm's nostrils flared. "That'd be too easy. I want you to *suffer.*"

Malcolm could hurt me all he wanted. Maybe I even deserved it for what I'd done. But one way or another, I was going to make it out of here alive—even if it meant I came out broken.

I narrowed my eyes at him. "Bring. It. On."

Malcolm welcomed my challenge and bent over me. A moment later, my skin turned cold.

Malcolm's anger turned to curiosity. "I've never fed on Davina essence before. I'm not sure anyone has. It's different. Stronger."

Is that what the chill was? Was Malcolm stealing my essence?

Fear slowly fell to the back of my mind as a new emotion overcame me. It began as desperation, melting away the terror that consumed me. It left behind a strange, almost comforting feeling. This new sensation tingled its way through my body, offering me strength when I couldn't seem to find it myself.

What was this? It was almost like the Power of Grace had returned, but it was different. It was my own. Instead of pulsing through my body the way Grace's power did, it flowed smoothly.

I concentrated on my essence energy and pulled it back, resisting Malcolm's gross invasion. My muscles tensed, and heat returned to my skin as I tried to block him out.

Malcolm gritted his teeth. "There's no need to fight it."

"Please... stop..." I struggled to say. I could feel my essence being pulled away from me.

At the same time, that strange new power grew as my struggle for survival intensified. It suddenly occurred to me that maybe I could use it to my advantage.

This was my way out. I knew how I was going to survive. It didn't matter that my hands were tied. I'd killed five demons at once without my hands. Malcolm would never see it coming.

And so, I let my defenses fall. I freely let my essence flow from me to Malcolm. It was the only way I could access my essence myself. It was the only way I thought I might survive long enough to get out of this house. And I *had* to survive.

The channel opened between us again, and that strange tingle across my skin grew more prominent. The hairs on my arms stood. Instead of channeling my essence to my hands like usual, I brought the energy to my heart, holding back only slightly so it wouldn't be too much for my body to handle.

Before I could see what this new power was capable of, the front door burst open.

7

*G*race stopped abruptly in the doorway to take in the scene. Several men in suits quickly filed in behind her. Malcolm took one look at the group and shot to his feet. He sprinted away, passing straight through the wall leading to the kitchen. The group of men who'd arrived with Grace immediately raced after him.

I noticed Fletcher in the group as he rushed to my side and knelt beside me.

"Ryn, are you okay?" His voice filled with worry.

I let out a breath of relief. "I am now."

Fletcher helped me sit up and began untying my wrists. I knew Malcolm had used fabric from a demon's cloak because I'd seen demons use the trick before. It was the only tool he had to bind me.

Grace took a slow step forward. "We're glad we found you before you were hurt."

That depended on her definition of *hurt*. The long stretch of black fabric fell from my wrists, freeing my hands. I lightly touched my swollen face. It was tender, but Malcolm hadn't broken skin.

My eyes turned toward Grace. She stood awkwardly, like she wasn't sure what to do.

"How'd you find me?" I asked.

Fletcher offered a hand to pull me to my feet. "Someone in the hospital wing saw you get taken. One of the volunteers flew after

377

you but lost you. Another came to get us. Luckily, one of the councilmembers remembered this place from a few years ago. It was a hunch considering the direction the Aedes took you."

One of the guys returned, huffing. "We lost him, Grace."

"Don't worry," she said without looking at him. "We rescued Ryn, and that's what's important."

Her words sounded more like a formality and left a bad taste in my mouth. She shouldn't have been the one to save me. She should've let me save myself. At the very least, she should've let Marek come along. He was probably worried sick about me. And I didn't even have my phone to call him and tell him I was all right.

"Should we get back to the school?" Fletcher suggested. "There's a car waiting outside."

Fletcher led me through the front door. Trees surrounded the house on all sides, and a long gravel driveway stretched out to a quiet road. No wonder no one had heard me. We were in the middle of nowhere.

Two big black SUVs, no doubt courtesy of the Davina Council, sat parked in the driveway. Fletcher ushered me into the back seat of the first SUV.

Fletcher and Grace lectured me on the twenty-minute drive back to Eagle Valley.

"You shouldn't have wandered off," Grace scolded.

"I didn't!" I defended. "I was right outside the school."

"How many times have I told you to stay with someone else at all times?" Fletcher said.

I expected sympathy from Fletcher. Why was he treating me like this?

Because he's siding with Grace, I thought.

"Something happens to you every time you're alone," Fletcher pointed out.

I stared out the window at passing corn fields. "Yeah, I know."

Why were they acting like it was my fault I'd been abducted? Maybe they should be blaming themselves for not having decent security at the school. We were at war, after all.

I held my tongue.

Several minutes later, someone's ringtone cut through the silence. The councilmember who was driving answered his phone.

He nodded his head along to the person on the other end of the line.

"Okay," he said. "We'll be there shortly." He hung up and turned to Grace, who sat in the passenger seat. "They found it."

She nodded once. "Good."

"Who found what?" I asked.

No one answered. It was like they hadn't even heard me.

We pulled up in front of Galen High several minutes later.

"Everyone else is still in the valley," Grace said to the driver. "We'll meet them there and let them know."

"Let who know what?" I asked Fletcher as we stepped out of the vehicle.

Fletcher led me in the direction of the valley. "You'll find out soon enough."

I huffed but followed him without another word. Why did it seem like the adults around me no longer wanted me to be a part of this war? It was like they'd only rescued me to keep their reputation intact.

When we arrived in the valley, the Davina were still split into groups. I wasn't sure they'd even realized anyone left to find me. I figured I was safe enough here, so I spread my wings and abandoned Fletcher at the top of the valley. I landed beside Allie and Kyle. They were taking lessons from Mr. Harris on the quickest ways to kill a demon using a Davina Blade. At least that lesson was useful.

Allie rushed over to me when she saw me. "Oh my god! Ryn…"

First things first. "Where's Marek?" I asked.

"Looking for you," Kyle said as he hastily followed behind Allie. "He headed up to the school, like, an hour ago. I thought he would've found you by now."

"Yeah, well—"

"Ryn!" The sound of Marek calling my name distracted me.

I turned to see him soar out of the sky and land in the grass fifteen yards away. He pulled his wings into him and quickly closed the distance between us.

"Ryn, where have you been?" He gripped onto my shoulders, and his eyes danced across my face. Worry filled his expression. "I looked everywhere for you—up at the school, at your house... What happened to you?"

Long story. I guided his hands off my shoulders, hoping it'd show him I was all right and he could calm down.

All around us, Davina training slowed. The valley quieted as more and more eyes fell upon me. Whispers filled the training area.

"Shit." I nervously ran my fingers through my tangled hair. "Is it that bad?"

"Bad is an understatement," Allie said under her breath. Her eyes darted between the Davina who'd stopped to stare. "Ryn, you have two black eyes and blood under your nose."

I swiped my finger across my upper lip. A small amount of dry, crusted blood flaked off.

"What are you looking at?" Kyle snapped at the closest group. "You should be training."

A couple of guys from my physical combat class scoffed and rolled their eyes. Davina returned to their practice, but I could still sense eyes on the back of my head.

"I was going to help the volunteers in the hospital wing," I started in a low voice so only my friends could hear. "But then..."

"Then what?" Marek's expression hardened.

I resisted the urge to roll my eyes. "What happens to me every time I'm alone?"

Kyle inhaled an audible breath. "You were attacked? *Again?*"

I crossed my arms. "Kidnapped is more like it."

Allie's brows drew together, and disbelief crossed her face. "You're serious?"

"I'm serious," I deadpanned.

Marek leaned in closer to inspect my injuries.

Allie's expression fell. "You were attacked with all these Davina here? Or *was* it a Davina?"

"It was a demon," I said. "He must've been watching for me."

A muscle popped in Marek's jaw when he drew away from me. "What'd the bastard do to you?"

I gave them the condensed explanation.

Marek's fists tightened. "I'm gonna kill—"

"No," I stopped him. "He's gone for now. I'm fine."

"And he'll be back," Marek growled.

"I can protect myself if he gets close to me again," I stated confidently.

"How?" Kyle's voice filled with concern and skepticism. "I mean, you don't have Grace's power anymore, do you?"

"No," I answered, "but I think I have something similar."

My friends leaned in curiously, and I told them about the strange power I'd felt earlier.

"I think I might be different than other Davina," I admitted. God, I sounded full of myself, but it was the only explanation. "Maybe it's why Grace chose me in the first place."

"Can you show us?" Allie asked.

I glanced around at the Davina around us, but no one was watching. I held my hand out in the middle of our small huddle. I concentrated on that strange energy I'd felt earlier, but I couldn't find it. All that glowed in my hand was a normal white orb.

"Maybe it doesn't work unless I'm in danger," I theorized. "Kind of like how the Power of Grace didn't work for me at first unless I was protecting someone."

"Davina," Grace called from where she stood at the center of the valley.

My friends and I turned our attention toward her, as did everyone else. She gestured for the group to come in closer so everyone could hear.

"We can talk more about this later," I whispered under my breath.

"I have great news!" Grace said with a gleeful smile. "We've found an Aedes camp outside of town."

Several people gasped.

"These are the Aedes who recently led the attack on Eagle Valley," Grace continued. "I believe they are gathering more Aedes to launch another strike on your town. We must stop them before they have the chance."

"Yeah!" someone shouted in agreement gent.

"That's why tomorrow, we—the Davina—will attack first." Grace sounded optimistic. "Anyone who is able to fight is expected to arrive here at sunrise. We will continue to train today so that we can go into battle tomorrow prepared. Everyone will have a chance to rest. And then tomorrow, we will win this war!"

The crowd erupted into cheers. Allie jumped up and down excitedly, and Kyle shot his fist into the air. Marek glanced between me and Grace, like he didn't know whether to join in or not.

I didn't like this. Did Grace really think a single day of training would prepare us for battle? I knew most of the adults in Eagle Valley used to be Protectors, but they weren't in the same shape they were during their twenties.

Then again, maybe Grace was on to something. Maybe striking first was our only chance to end this war. Maybe—with Grace's guidance—we could finally eliminate the demons and bring peace to this realm.

I just couldn't shake the feeling that we were going about it all wrong. Something in my gut told me we were about to make a terrible mistake.

8

"I'm staying the night at Allie's," I told my mom when I arrived home that night.

I was already up the stairs and halfway to my room when she stopped me.

"Hold on, Kathryn." Mom stopped at the top of the stairs with her hands on her hips. "Do you mind telling me where you've been all day?"

I paused in the hall. I didn't want to look at her. Allie had enough makeup in her locker to help cover up the bruises, but I still feared Mom would notice the swelling.

I sighed and turned to her. "I was at school."

"And after school?" she asked.

I shrugged. "I told you this morning I was doing Davina stuff."

"But you never told me when you'd be home," she pointed out. "You *need* to start answering my text messages."

My thigh heated where my phone sat in my pocket. Someone had found it at the back doors of the school, where Malcolm had attacked me. Fletcher returned it to me when I'd gone to help in the hospital wing after Grace's announcement, but the screen had been cracked beyond repair.

"Sorry," I said. "I didn't get any of your messages. My phone broke."

Mom frowned. "You need to be more responsible."

My mouth hung open. She wouldn't be saying that if she knew what happened to me earlier.

"Mom, I'm fine," I insisted. "I'll just be next door tonight. It's not a big deal."

Mom crossed her arms. "No, I think you can stay home tonight."

I let out a breath. I wanted to stay at Allie's so we could head straight to the battle together in the morning. I didn't want to be alone the night before we went to war. Of course, I couldn't tell Mom that. She'd mentioned more than once that she didn't want me fighting at all. I'd never make it out of the house if she knew.

"But, Mom—"

"No *buts*. I'm sick of you *telling* me what you're going to do instead of asking my permission. You can stay in your room tonight and think about what it means to respect your mother."

Was she serious?

Mom looked at me with a pointed expression, waiting for my reaction.

"Whatever. I can't wait to get out of here for good." I turned to my bedroom and slammed the door behind me.

In my room, I fell onto my bed. I couldn't believe how controlling my mom could be sometimes. Didn't she realize I was old enough to make my own decisions? I had half a mind to follow her downstairs and tell her just what I thought of her stupid rules.

The sound of voices outside caught my attention. I stood and looked out my window to see Marek and Kyle heading up the walkway to Allie's house.

Great. They were all going to hang out without me, and Mom wanted to keep me trapped in here.

To hell with her.

I grabbed my backpack from the foot of my bed and hurried to my dresser to grab a change of clothes. I slung the bag over my shoulder and opened my window. I was *so* going to get in trouble if Mom found out. But I didn't care. I stepped out of the window onto the shingled porch roof.

"Hey!" Kyle called across the lawn when he saw me.

"Shh…" I hissed as I quietly slid my window shut.

"Whatcha doing up there?" Kyle asked.

"Shut up!" I whisper-yelled. "Unless you want to alert my mom."

I hurried across the roof and lay on my stomach at the edge. My legs found the porch support, and I shimmied my way down it onto the porch railing. I jumped onto the grass and then stole a glance in the front window to see that my mom was occupied in front of the TV. Hopefully, she wouldn't check on me.

I turned away and raced across the lawn to Kyle and Marek. Marek laughed and held his arm out toward me. I wrapped my arm around his waist.

"I'm a bad influence, aren't I?" he teased.

I shrugged. "I think I can figure out how to sneak out on my own."

"But you wouldn't have snuck out if you didn't want to hang out with me," he said lightheartedly.

"Very true," I agreed, smiling up at him.

"Hey!" Allie greeted enthusiastically at the door.

I sniffed the air, and my stomach twisted in hunger. "Is that pizza I smell?"

"Yep," Allie said with a smile. "And ice cream for dessert."

This totally beat another bowl of cereal for dinner with my mom.

Allie put in a dumb slapstick comedy while we ate. Kyle stretched out on the couch, while Allie lay on the floor beneath him. Marek and I sat cuddled on the loveseat together.

Kyle was the last to finish his ice cream. He stood and headed back into the kitchen for another bowl. While he was gone, the rest of us burst into laughter at one of the jokes in the movie.

Kyle raced back into the room at lightning speed, his empty bowl still in his hand. "What'd I miss?"

"You wouldn't have missed it if you weren't such a glutton," Allie teased.

"I'm not a glutton!" Kyle exaggerated his offense. "I *need* to eat a lot. I'm a growing man."

Allie's hand slapped over her mouth as she tried to hide her laugh. "Man? You should be a comedian."

Kyle dropped his bowl on the end table and bent to swipe the throw pillow out from under Allie's head. A *thud* came as her skull connected with the carpet.

"Ow!" she complained, springing to her feet. "Give it back, Kyle."

She reached for the pillow, but Kyle held it high above his head. She punched him so lightly in the ribs that he probably didn't feel a thing. "Jerk."

Marek's shoulders shook next to me in laughter. The movie continued in the background, forgotten.

"Are they always like this?" I whispered.

"Only when they're flirting," he teased.

Allie stood on the sofa and jumped onto Kyle's back. She could've easily reached the pillow, but instead, she used her weight to throw Kyle off balance and tackle him to the couch.

"This is how they flirt?" I asked.

"Yeah," Marek said. "How do you flirt?"

I batted my eyelashes to demonstrate. "Is it working?"

Marek bit his bottom lip, like he was trying to hold back a smile. "Maybe…"

Something in his eyes told me he wanted to kiss me. Nerves fluttered in my gut. *I should just kiss him. He's my boyfriend. I can kiss him whenever I want.*

A high-pitched screech across the room stole my attention. I looked toward Allie and Kyle, thinking Allie accidentally got hurt. Then I realized the noise had come from Kyle.

Growing man my ass. This guy had the falsetto of a ten year old.

Allie sat on top of Kyle and dug her fingers into his ribs. He squealed but made no effort to push her off, even though he was twice as strong. Kyle continued to hold the pillow out of Allie's reach.

"A little help here," Kyle begged between giggles.

I exchanged a smile with Marek and hopped out of the loveseat. I stood at the edge of the couch and ran my fingers across Kyle's bare feet.

"Not like that!" he cried.

While I had Kyle momentarily distracted, Allie lunged forward and snatched the pillow out of his hands. She rolled onto the floor and pulled the pillow to her chest.

Kyle kicked his foot out and narrowly missed my nose.

Without warning, my legs swooped out from under me, and I was suddenly four feet off the ground.

"Whoa there," Marek said into my ear as he cradled me in his arms. "We don't need a broken nose."

"Hey, put me down," I demanded.

Marek only took it as an invitation to toss me over his shoulder.

"*You're* going to end up with a broken nose if you don't put me down." The words escaped between laughs, making me sound anything but serious.

"Am I?" he feigned innocence. The next second, his fingers were tickling the soles of my feet.

"Unfair!" I giggled. My legs flailed, and I beat my hands against his back, but it didn't seem to faze him. "Put me down."

"As you wish." Marek dropped me onto the loveseat, but my hands tangled into the fabric of his t-shirt. He lost his balance and caught himself a split second before he crushed me.

I breathed heavily. His body hovered above mine, his lips only inches away. His t-shirt had ridden up, displaying his hard abs. If Allie and Kyle weren't in the room, I might've ripped the shirt the rest of the way off.

Marek's eyes traveled down to my lips. He was probably thinking the same thing I was.

"This part is hilarious," Allie said, pulling our attention back to the TV.

I reluctantly sat up so Marek could sit beside me. Curling my legs under me, I snuggled into his arms. I inhaled his familiar scent and focused on the soothing rise and fall of his chest. My body completely relaxed into his. I couldn't remember the last time I felt this happy.

As the night wore on, my happiness faded. Soon, images of battle invaded my mind. I squeezed my eyes shut and forced down the lump in my throat. Marek's delicate feather sat between my fingers, close to my heart. It was in that moment that I realized that one day, this feather might be all I had left of him. This happy night with my friends was only an illusion—a distraction.

Tomorrow, any one of us could die.

9

I woke in Marek's arms the next morning, feeling more refreshed than I had in a long time. Thank god Allie's dad hadn't kicked the guys out last night. I really needed those hours curled up in Marek's arms.

Marek's head rested against the plush armrest of the loveseat we cuddled on. He stirred and cleared his throat. "Good morning, beautiful."

I smiled and sat up straighter. "You think I'm beautiful?"

He placed a kiss on my nose, sending my heart fluttering. "Of course I do."

I stared into Marek's blue eyes. I could lie here for hours just looking at him.

Something soft bounced off my head. I whirled around so fast that I almost fell off the loveseat. The pillow Kyle had thrown at my head lay on the floor. A light from the kitchen cast shadows over the living room.

"Snap out of it, lovebirds," he said as he bent to tie his shoe. "It's almost time to go."

Tension immediately returned to my shoulders. Right. The fight.

My friends and I were ready to go before sunrise. Allie's dad joined us outside, where the air was cold enough to cause goose-bumps to break out over my arms. Marek wore nothing on his upper body but my feather necklace. He must've been freezing. Kyle and Jay were also shirtless.

Wings grew from Jay's back.

"Are we flying?" I asked.

Jay shrugged. "Grace flies everywhere. I don't think she minds."

Everyone else seemed to agree with him and shifted into their Davina form. I felt like they should be a little more wary of exposing themselves, but it was like they didn't think there would be any consequences now that Grace was around. I summoned my wings and followed behind them.

We arrived just as the first rays of sunlight began to light the cloudy sky. There were already at least a hundred Davina in the valley, and more were flooding in. Everyone was dressed to fight. Most guys had their shirts off, and the women wore tank tops so it'd be easy to fly at a moment's notice.

I noticed several guys from school had painted white wings across their bodies. Some had black strips under their eyes like football players. They stood in a circle chanting *Da-vin-a, Da-vin-a.*

I stopped in my tracks. Did they think this was a *game*? This was nothing like the mock battles we had during school. This was real life. People were going to die today. *They* might die today. And they were treating it like some sort of sporting event. My gut twisted.

I turned to Marek. He watched the group of chanting guys, almost like he wanted to join them.

"What is it now, Ryn?" Kyle sounded annoyed.

I realized my brows were tight, giving away my uncertainty. I forced myself to relax.

"I—" I didn't know what to say. Yesterday, it seemed like a good idea to strike first. Now, I wasn't so sure. We should be worrying about the people we were going to lose, not cheering for the ones we would kill.

"I'm just wondering if this is the right answer," I said.

"What other answer is there?" Kyle asked. "Think of all the demons you've met. Dorian. Trenton. Malcolm. Each one's just as bad as the next."

I sighed heavily. "Maybe… but—"

"Don't you want this war to end?" Allie sounded genuinely curious.

"Well, yeah," I answered.

"Then let Grace do her job," Kyle said.

"Lay off her, Kyle," Marek defended. "She hasn't been preparing for this as long as you have."

I shot Marek a grateful expression then turned back to Kyle. "I just don't get it. All the stories you told me said Grace would wake when a portal was opening and threatened our realm—and that she'd be able to close it. None of the stories said anything about her rising up against the demons and killing them off."

"They attacked us first," Kyle pointed out.

"I'm sure Grace *is* worrying about the portal," Allie said. "But these demons are a bigger threat right now. We need to fight them before they attack Eagle Valley again."

If they're such a threat, why'd we waste a whole day "training"?

"I want peace just as much as any Davina," I stated. "I was just saying, maybe there's an alternative. Are you actually *excited* about killing them?"

"Who wouldn't be excited?" A deep voice came from behind me.

I turned to find the group of guys from school making their way over to us. Half of them were in my combat class. The guy who spoke was at least three inches taller than Marek, and his biceps were as big as my head.

Marek's jaw tightened. "No one asked you, Gabe."

I slowly reached out for Marek's fingers.

"Ryn's just scared," Gabe accused without sympathy. "Mr. Collins was right to be skeptical about you."

I narrowed my eyes. "I'm not *scared*. And I think I proved myself a time or two in his class."

"You need to stop having such a big head," Gabe jeered. "So you woke Grace. Big deal."

The guys around him nodded in agreement.

My expression momentarily faltered. "I didn't realize everyone knew it was me."

Gabe crossed his arms. "Secrets don't stay secret for long here in Eagle Valley. You don't realize how many people talk about you, do you?"

I glanced to my friends. Guilt settled on Allie's face, like she knew and just never told me.

"What are you talking about?" I demanded.

Gabe scoffed. "Everyone knows you've conjured essence in front of humans more than once. We know you were kidnapped yesterday."

Freaking small towns.

"So?" I challenged.

Gabe smirked. "So, it's clear you have a thing or two to learn about being a Davina."

Marek stepped forward. "Seriously, Gabe. Back off."

Gabe ignored him. "Face it, Ryn. You're not important anymore."

I gritted my teeth. That's what Gabe thought this was about? That I wanted *attention*?

"That's not what—" I started, but Grace's voice cut me off.

"Davina," she called.

Everyone quieted and turned to her. Her large white wings rose up behind her.

"Thank you for joining us today," Grace said. "I hope that everyone has had a chance to rest, because it's time to give the Aedes what they deserve. They killed your friends and family. And now, we will do the same to them!"

"*Da-vin-a!*" Gabe shouted beside me.

The crowd joined in until the word *Davina* echoed throughout the valley. All around me, wings sprung out of people's backs in preparation for flight.

Marek gazed down at me and squeezed my hand. "Don't worry. This is what Galen High has been preparing us for. We've been training to become Protectors. It's time we finally get our chance to protect."

Marek's words echoed in my mind. At the mention of protection, my thoughts wandered to my mom. If I didn't do this, she—and everyone in Eagle Valley—would be in danger.

"Are you ready?" Marek asked.

Grace spread her wings and shot into the air. All around us, Davina followed.

Nerves fluttered in my gut, but Marek was right. We had to protect Eagle Valley, no matter what it took. I stretched out my wings and joined my fellow Davina in the sky.

Wings flapped all around me. No one seemed to worry about being seen as we flew over the corn fields and treetops outside of Eagle Valley. Something about flying with so many other Davina was empowering. Up here, moving as one unit, I had to believe that, together, we were capable of anything.

Up ahead, a patch of forest lay between two corn fields. Just as I spotted it, the Davina at the front of the group dove toward the trees. The rest of our group followed in a spiral, as if warning the demons of the impending danger we sought to bring down upon them.

Screams filled the air when the Davina landed and immediately jumped into combat. Some were shrieks of warning, others of pain. Most sounded like the cries of eager Davina pumped for battle. Demons scattered.

Marek stayed close to me, and together, we raced through the thin forest, knocking out demon after demon. Several Protectors followed behind us and quickly finished off the demons we'd stunned. Some turned to snapping necks. Others used the Davina Blades they'd brought with them.

Ahead of us, I spotted Fletcher engaged in combat with a tall demon. Beyond him, a flash of purple caught my eye. I paused, momentarily distracted by Grace's essence. It was nothing like the essence I'd used when I had access to her power. Purple lightning blasted out of her hands like a stream of water shooting out of a firehose. She shocked four demons at once. Before I could process what just happened, they were gone.

"Ryn, come on!" Marek grabbed my hand.

I sprinted behind him, deeper into the middle of the fight. Without warning, a demon jumped out from behind a tree straight in front of me. I rammed into him and fell to the ground.

Marek didn't miss a beat. He knocked the demon to the forest floor and slammed his head against the ground. I quickly got to my feet and readied myself for whatever came next.

"Behind you!" Marek called.

I whirled around and sank my foot into a demon's stomach. He stumbled back a few feet and fell to the ground. His hood dropped.

All around me, the sound of battle faded, and it felt as if *I'd* been kicked in the gut. I stared, shocked and horrified, into the demon's face. It wasn't a man at all.

A young girl looked up at me, her dark eyes filled with fear. She couldn't be more than twelve years old. An image of Emily's face flashed across my vision as I stared down at the girl. Emily, the fifteen-year-old training partner we'd lost in the last battle. It suddenly occurred to me that the demons weren't all like Clinton, Dorian, and Malcolm. Some of them were like Emily—young, scared, and innocent.

The girl hesitated for a moment. I could see it in her eyes. She thought this was the end for her, that I was going to beat the living shit out of her until her final breath.

And I knew I wouldn't touch her.

When she saw I wasn't about to pounce on her and snap her neck, she scurried to her feet and raced away. But she only made it a few yards before a strong male Davina gripping a blade crossed in front of her and slit her throat.

"No!" My knees grew weak.

The Davina continued fighting like it didn't even faze him.

I rushed over to the girl and caught her as she collapsed. She wheezed, struggling to suck air into her lungs. I pressed my hands to her throat to try to stop the bleeding, but it was too late. Dark blood spurted from her throat and coated my hands.

"No, no, no," I mumbled under my breath. "I'm so sorry. This isn't fair to you."

The girl looked up at me but gave no indication that she heard my apology. Her eyes glistened with tears and the pain of war. In her terrified expression, I could read what she'd say to me if she could.

Why?

And then she went limp. Her weight in my arms vanished the moment her body disappeared in a puff of black smoke. Her cloak draped over my arms. It remained the only reminder that she had, in fact, been real.

I sat there for far too long, staring down at the empty cloak in my hands. If any demon had noticed me amidst the chaos, they could have easily snuck up behind me and killed me on the spot.

But no one seemed to care about the Davina girl mourning for one of her enemies.

My hands shook as I used the girl's cloak to wipe my skin clean of her blood. The forest slowly came into focus again. By now, the screams and chaos had died down. I glanced around me to see that only Davina remained. The demons had either run off to save themselves or had died trying.

Marek rushed over to me and dropped to his knees. "Ryn, are you okay?"

I swallowed hard. "It's over already?"

It almost seemed unfair how much devastation we could deliver in such a short amount of time. Black cloaks lay scattered across the forest floor, and Davina trampled over them like they were of no consequence.

And then I spotted the bodies. The Davina bodies, the people the demons managed to kill before they scattered. I rose to my feet and started toward the closest body. It was a small figure with dark black hair.

Please don't let it be someone I know. Don't be Allie.

Relief and pain washed over me all at once. It wasn't Allie, but I was all too familiar with the young boy's face.

Ethan.

My chest felt empty. Another member of our training team… gone.

"I told him he was too young for this." My voice cracked.

Marek stared down at Ethan and spoke quietly. "I know. But this is war, Ryn."

I had a feeling he was saying that to reassure himself. It was like convincing himself it was all worth it to eliminate the Aedes was the only way he'd be able to stomach it.

I buried my face in Marek's chest. "I don't want to lose anyone I love."

"I don't, either," Marek whispered. His strong hands ran up and down my back. "Let's go find Allie and Kyle, to make sure they're all right."

I opened my mouth to agree, but before I got a word out, cheers erupted toward the other end of the forest. I turned to see a large group surrounding Grace, celebrating our victory.

As Marek and I stepped closer to the crowd, Grace struggled to push her way out of the group. Finally, she broke free, but celebration around her continued. Grace stumbled forward and caught herself against the trunk of a nearby tree. Color had drained from her face, and she looked as if she might vomit. Grace kept her eyes on the ground without regarding the dead bodies she passed.

An invisible force tugged at my heart. I felt for her. She acted like she didn't think we should be celebrating when we had yet to mourn for our fallen Davina. I felt the same way.

I rushed toward Grace to offer my sympathies. Marek followed behind me but didn't say anything.

"Grace," I called when I was several paces away from her.

She lifted her head, and her eyes met mine. Her expression remained neutral, like she was trying to hide her true feelings.

"Grace, are you okay?" I asked.

What am I saying? Of course she's not okay. She just led a handful of her own people to their deaths. That's not something you come out of feeling *okay* about.

Grace straightened and held her head high. She took a breath to say something but sighed instead, as if contemplating how to express her feelings. "This will all be over soon, Ryn. Then, we will finally be at peace."

Grace turned away from me without another word. I stared after her speechlessly. The way she said it, it almost sounded like she was already at peace. Something told me she'd accepted that her death would come sooner than later.

A scary thought hit me. Maybe this battle wasn't the first step in winning this war after all. Maybe it was a test for Grace.

And maybe she found her answer.

Following the battle, Davina slowly began to return to Eagle Valley. Several stayed to assist the injured, and a group of Davina came back with vans to help transport the fallen home. Allie, Kyle, and Marek lifted dead bodies into one of the vans. I couldn't take looking at their lifeless faces.

Instead, I walked through the forest, gathering the cloaks that lay forgotten. The metallic scent of blood filled my nose. Allie shot me a somber expression, but other Davina eyed me skeptically, wondering why I bothered. I wasn't sure I had an answer. It just didn't seem right to leave them, like the Aedes we killed didn't matter. I tried not to count the cloaks draped over my forearm.

I dropped the pile of cloaks at the edge of the trees and then headed back into the forest to gather more. Once I collected all the cloaks I could find, I laid each one in a line beside each other. I didn't know if the Aedes would return here or not, but if they did, at least they wouldn't have to do this themselves. I hoped it would be easier for them to mourn their lost this way.

By the time I finished, the vans had pulled away from the shoulder of the road, and only my friends and I remained at the scene of the battle.

"How many did we lose?" I asked as I slumped over to my friends.

Allie dropped her head. "Too many."

I was glad she didn't give me an exact answer.

"Should we head back?" Marek suggested.

I nodded solemnly and flexed my shoulders to summon my wings. The flight back to Eagle Valley took a good ten minutes at top speed. We landed in the valley and walked the rest of the way back to the school. Davina swarmed the lawn behind the mansion, dancing, singing, and celebrating our hard-won victory.

I didn't know how they did it. No one acted like this after our last battle. It was like they were already becoming immune to it, like they were losing a piece of their humanity.

Kyle joined the group celebrating, and Allie followed behind him. Marek hesitated beside me.

"Go ahead," I told him. "I need to find Fletcher and talk to him."

"I don't want to leave you alone," Marek said.

"I'll be fine," I assured him. "There are enough Davina here."

"There were plenty of Davina around last time, too," Marek pointed out. "At least let me stay with you until you find him."

"Okay," I agreed.

Marek and I walked through the crowd for fifteen minutes without spotting Fletcher. When we couldn't find him outside, we entered the mansion. Marek stopped at his locker to grab an extra t-shirt before we headed upstairs to check the hospital wing.

Several more cots had been added to provide rest for the newly injured Davina. My heart sank when I saw volunteers rushing around the room, trying to treat the injured as fast as they could. While everyone else was outside celebrating, our injured were in here suffering, and the volunteers were swamped.

I spotted Fletcher across the room, holding onto a woman's hand as two others tried to stitch up a large gash across her swollen face.

I didn't want to bother Fletcher while he was busy. Instead, Marek and I helped where we could. We filled patients' water bottles and adjusted pillows. I helped a girl with a cast on her leg to the bathroom.

It was several hours before things calmed down enough that I felt confident bothering Fletcher. Nerves twisted in my gut when I approached him.

"Hey, Fletcher," I said. "Can we talk?"

Fletcher looked exhausted, but he nodded anyway. "I heard they put out a salad bar a few hours ago in the cafeteria. Should we go get something to eat?"

Marek was too noble to stop volunteering, so he stayed in the hospital wing while Fletcher and I headed downstairs. The cafeteria was empty, but there was still food out at the salad bar. I filled up my tray—even though the lettuce had wilted slightly. Fletcher and I sat across from each other at the table farthest from the doors.

Fletcher stabbed into his salad. "What is it you want to talk about, Ryn?"

I poked at my food, but I couldn't bring myself to eat it. "Here's the thing…"

I couldn't find the words.

"Yes?" Fletcher prodded.

I took a deep breath. "I feel awful about what we did. There were *kids* fighting in that battle. We killed children. I watched an Aedes girl die, Fletcher. She looked *terrified*. I'm not sure if she was that much different from the innocent Davina we lost today."

"The Aedes *are* different, Ryn," Fletcher stated.

"But maybe they're not as bad as everyone thinks they are," I argued. "Maybe we can…"

I trailed off. I suspected Fletcher would only laugh at me if I suggested we could make peace with the Aedes.

Fletcher rested his fork on his tray. "Ryn, I realize that you don't have a lot of experience with the Aedes and that you view them through a different lens than the rest of us do. But, perhaps the lens in which you view them is misguided."

My brows came together. "You think it's misguided for me to believe there has to be an alternative to all this?"

Fletcher sighed heavily. "The Aedes can't be reasoned with."

"No one's tried—"

"Let me tell you a story," Fletcher cut in. He rested his elbows on the table and brought his fingers together in front of his face. "Like most Davina, I was a Protector in my early twenties. I was very good at what I did. I killed a lot of Aedes, but it only takes one moment, one mistake, to change everything."

I fell silent and listened to what he had to say.

"I was married then. We were both Protectors and fought alongside each other. I was a Protector, but I wasn't able to protect *her*—or our son."

Fletcher's confession was like a slap in the face. I had no idea something so terrible happened to him.

"I thought you said you didn't have any kids," I pointed out.

Fletcher shook his head. "Not anymore. My family died at the hands of an Aedes."

My heart sank. After all this time, it was clear the topic still caused him pain to speak about.

Fletcher paused for a beat before continuing. "I wanted revenge, to hunt down the Aedes that killed her, but instead, I gave up being a Protector. I came back to Eagle Valley and started teaching. I thought that by doing so, I could help future generations from making similar mistakes."

"What was her mistake?" I asked curiously.

Fletcher's gaze dropped. "It wasn't her mistake. It was mine."

An inaudible gasp passed my lips.

"I let an Aedes go," Fletcher admitted. "He was the first one to beg me to spare him, and I fell for it. He repaid me by killing my family."

We both fell quiet. The only sound I heard was the hum of the freezers in the adjoining kitchen.

"Fletcher," I whispered. "I'm so sorry."

He straightened up. "It was a long time ago."

"That doesn't make it any less significant," I told him.

Fletcher didn't meet my gaze. "No, I suppose it doesn't. I just hope that you, Ryn, will not keep yourself from recognizing the threats out there."

I wasn't sure how to respond.

"Most of us have lost people we love to the Aedes," Fletcher said. "Perhaps now, with Grace back, we can finally end it."

"Maybe," I said flatly, "but how many people are we going to have to sacrifice in the process? We're losing people we love as we speak."

Fletcher's lips tightened. "And we'd lose more if we left this alone."

"I wasn't suggesting—"

"The Aedes are evil," Fletcher declared. "We finally have a chance at exterminating them."

Fletcher didn't seem to be listening. That, or he didn't care. Grace was supposed to return when the line between the realms was thinning. If that was the case now, it wouldn't matter how many Aedes we killed first. They'd quickly outnumber us.

It sure felt like I wasn't the only one who was misguided around here.

I found Allie sitting on the back steps of the mansion, staring out into the distance. It'd been a long day, and the sun hung low in the sky. The group from earlier had thinned, but others stuck around, still looking positively pleased with the victory. I sat beside Allie, but she kept her eyes on the lawn, never looking at me.

"Hey, Allie. How's it been going out here?"

She shrugged and looked down at her feet.

"What's going on?" I asked.

Allie shrugged again.

"I can tell you're not okay. Please don't shut me out." I scooted closer to her and wrapped my arm around her shoulder. "With everything that's happening, we need each other now more than ever."

Allie shook her head, like she didn't want to tell me. "It's nothing. I'm just… not feeling very much like celebrating."

Did I detect a hint of regret in Allie's tone?

I spotted Kyle with a group of guys shooting essence at each other and dodging it like it was a game. They didn't even seem to care they were out here in the open, like they knew the end of the world was coming and so the secret of our magic didn't matter anymore.

I wondered if that's why they acted so cheerful—because they weren't certain if they'd be the ones to die in the next battle and they were trying to have as much fun as they could.

When I finally spoke again, my voice came out small. "Do you think we did the right thing?"

"What do you mean?" Allie asked.

"Attacking the Aedes," I clarified.

"Of course," she answered. It sounded like an automatic response. "If we didn't kill them first, they'd kill us. That's how they work." She swallowed. "That's what happened to my mom."

I didn't say anything further. Allie was hurting right now, and I knew she wouldn't listen to what I had to say.

I sensed Marek's approach before he sat beside me on the concrete steps.

"Hey," he said lightly. "How are you two?"

Allie glanced at him and shrugged.

"I think everyone's just really tired," I said. I knew I was.

Marek kept his eyes on Allie's fallen face. "You okay?"

"Yeah," she replied, but it didn't sound genuine. "Like you said, I'm just tired. I think I'm going to go get Kyle and head home." Allie rose to her feet.

I stood beside her. "I'm ready to go, too."

"I'll take you home," Marek offered. The way he looked at me told me he wanted us to talk alone.

"Okay," I agreed. I turned back to Allie and pulled her into a hug. "I'll see you later. Make sure to get lots of sleep."

"Thanks. I'll try." She offered a half-hearted smile then headed across the lawn toward Kyle.

I turned back to Marek just as he pulled his t-shirt over his head. His wings grew behind him.

"We're flying?" I asked.

He nodded, and a slight smile touched his lips. "Come on."

Marek pumped his wings and launched himself into the air. I hesitated only a moment before following.

11

We landed outside of town on a rocky hilltop, the hill where Marek and I shared our first kiss. The sun touched the horizon, and most of the cloud cover had disappeared. A light breeze rustled through the trees surrounding the small clearing.

Marek pulled his wings into him and put his t-shirt back on. He sat on the large slab of granite and reached an arm out to me, inviting me to join him. The tension in my shoulders eased when I snuggled into his warm chest. The nighttime was peaceful in contrast to the bloody day that came before.

Eventually, Marek broke the silence. "What's wrong, Ryn?"

My mouth grew dry. "Nothing," I lied.

How could he tell?

"You know that's not true. Today was hard on you." There was no question in his voice. "Do you want to talk about it?"

I dropped my gaze to my feet. "Not really."

He'll just brush me off like Fletcher did.

Marek tightened his arm around me. "You can tell me anything."

I wanted to believe that so badly. I pulled away from him, and his arm dropped from around my shoulder.

I knotted my hands together. "I know that, but I can't always predict how you'll react."

"Please talk to me," he pleaded.

I couldn't refuse the look in his eyes, but my heart began to hammer as I prepared for the confession. "Okay… The thing is, I feel uneasy. Everyone's acting like the battle meant nothing, and they're using Grace to justify killing. But Marek, I'm not sure we should trust her."

His brow furrowed. "Why wouldn't you trust her?"

I sighed. "See, this is why I didn't want to say anything. You're acting the same as everyone else. And now you think I'm being stupid."

"I don't think that at all." He placed his arm around my shoulder again, but I didn't lean into him.

"I don't get why we have to *kill* them," I said. "Can't we compromise?"

Marek's lips turned down. "I think it's a little unrealistic."

"Is it, though?" I asked. "Has anyone ever tried? You said they're not a community race, but now they've finally come together. Maybe if we could talk to their leader, the rest of them will listen."

Marek stared out across Eagle Valley. "Maybe Grace could—"

"No," I said too quickly.

Marek shot me a questioning glance.

"I'm not sure Grace *wants* peace," I explained. "It feels like… like she's up to something."

Marek eyed me skeptically.

I pressed my lips together. "Isn't it a little strange that she hasn't mentioned the portal at all? I thought she came back because the Aedes's realm was about to open. It's like she's distracting us with training and ideas of war when none of it matters. So maybe she doesn't know where the portal is. Or maybe she *wants* Aedes to flood our realm."

"Or she's just trying to help us eliminate the most immediate threat—the demons that attacked Eagle Valley," Marek suggested. "Or maybe she never came back because a portal was opening. She said she's been observing all this time. Maybe she came back to help us win this war."

"Then why not return sooner?" I argued.

Marek thought about it for a moment. "Maybe she knows things she doesn't want to talk about publicly."

I sighed. "This is why I didn't want to talk about it. You won't listen to me."

"I *am* listening," Marek assured me. "I'm just trying to understand better."

My jaw tightened. "I don't know what else to say, Marek. I just don't get why everyone's mindlessly following Grace. I watched an Aedes girl die in my arms today. I can't believe everyone is okay with murdering children."

Marek sat still for several minutes, considering my words. We were both silent for so long that I thought maybe that was the end of the conversation.

Finally, he spoke. "I think you might have a point."

Excitement rushed through me. Finally, someone actually listened!

"About which part?" I asked.

"That we should try negotiating peace first," Marek answered. "I just don't know how we'd do it and how we'd get Grace to listen to us. And I'm not sure it would solve all our problems anyway. After all, the demons aren't the only ones who are evil."

A sense of *deja vu* hit.

"You've said that before," I said gently. "What do you mean by it?"

Marek's features hardened, like he suddenly realized he'd said too much. "I just mean… anyone can be evil."

My heart dropped. Was Marek *ever* going to open up to me? I'd told him all of my secrets. But I knew better than to push it or guilt him into telling me, so I didn't say anything.

"Let's forget about it for tonight. Right now, it's just you…" Marek placed a light kiss on the top of my head. "…and me… alone."

I titled my head up to look into his eyes. His warm breath rushed across my cheek, awakening the butterflies in my stomach. What was he suggesting?

His lips brushed across my forehead. "I hate seeing you like this. I wish I could make it better."

My face heated, and I shied away. He was trying to distract me. And dammit, it was working.

He bent and touched his lips to the side of my mouth. Worries fell from my mind as I surrendered to his touch. I didn't have a chance to breathe between each kiss he placed on my lips. My hands tangled in his hair, and I pulled him closer to me.

I wanted more. I wanted all of him.

I never took my lips off his as I got to my knees and climbed into his lap. His strong hands settled on my hips. I reached for the hem of his shirt and pushed the fabric out of the way so my hands could run along the hard muscles in his abdomen. I'd seen him shirtless plenty of times, but it was different to touch him, to feel him.

Marek's shirt rode up above his pecks as I ran my hands up his chest and then across his back. He pulled away momentarily and lifted his arms, inviting me to strip the shirt off from him.

I gladly complied. I tossed his shirt beside us and began trailing kisses down his neck. My lips touched the necklace I'd given him.

Marek wrapped a strong arm around my middle. He whirled me onto the ground and kissed me like he couldn't control himself. His hands rode up my tank top, and I wrapped my legs around his hips.

You can touch me if you want, I wanted to say to him, but I was afraid I'd ruin the moment if I spoke. Instead, I let him explore my body at his own pace.

Marek's fingers grazed across the underwire of my bra.

Take it off already, I begged silently.

My heart hammered violently against the inside of my rib cage, like it was trying to pound its way out of my chest and into Marek's hands. I squeezed my legs tighter around his hips to let him know he had my permission to take things as far as he wanted.

A moment later, he pulled away.

"What's wrong?" I asked in a rushed, breathy voice.

Marek reached for his shirt and balled it into his hand. "It's getting late. We should get you home."

"My curfew isn't for another few hours." I reached out for him, but he pushed my hands away.

What the hell?

After everything we'd been through and all the sacrifices I made for him, he was still holding back from loving me? I'd *killed* for him! Didn't that count for something?

I pushed myself to my elbows and spoke softly. "Did I do something wrong?"

He shook his head, but it was hard to see his expression through the darkness.

"Then why'd you stop?" I asked.

Marek reached out a hand and helped me to my feet. "It's just..."

Cool air brushed across my exposed midsection. I tugged down on my tank top to settle the fabric back into place.

What part of this wasn't perfect for him?

"Marek?" I reached out to lace my fingers through his.

He turned away and summoned his wings, like he hadn't noticed. "Let's get you home."

That's how this is going to go?

My lips tightened, but I followed his instructions. It was clear I wasn't going to get a real answer from him.

We landed in the shadows on my back lawn several minutes later, but it felt like hours of silence had passed between us.

"Marek," I started, but my throat closed up around my words.

Marek stepped forward and took my hand. "Get some rest. I'll see you tomorrow."

He bent and placed a chaste kiss on my cheek. I was sure it was meant to make me feel better, but after the moment we shared at the top of our hill, it felt like an insult.

Marek turned and launched himself into the air, leaving me standing alone in my back yard. My chest tightened with each passing moment that I stared after him. I didn't know why Marek was shutting me out.

In that moment, I realized that I had no idea what my future with Marek held. All I wanted was for him to open up to me, but I knew with certainty that if he couldn't be honest with me, our relationship was doomed for failure.

I'd never be ready for the moment we eventually crashed and burned.

12

After Marek's disappointing departure that night and another pointless argument with my mom, I'd just about had it with everyone's shit.

It didn't matter that I was still exhausted from the sleepless night I had. I rose early and dragged my tired ass to Galen High, intent on finding Grace. One way or another, I'd get her to listen to me.

The school was unusually quiet for a Wednesday morning. After yesterday's battle, we were supposed to start a more rigorous training program, but so far, a new schedule hadn't been issued. In my book, that meant school had been effectively canceled until Grace and the Davina Council figured things out.

When I didn't find Grace in the hospital wing, I tried the valley. Three small groups of Davina practiced their skills below me, but I didn't see Grace anywhere.

I turned to head back to the school but rammed straight into someone. I stepped back a few paces and looked up to see Gabe staring down at me. Several Davina from school stopped behind him. My eyes caught Casey's for a brief moment. Apparently, she'd found a new group of Davina to hang out with.

I tried to step around Gabe, but he moved to the side to block my path.

"Where ya going?" Gabe taunted. "You're not headed to cry over another demon, are you?"

Several people laughed behind him. I didn't look to see if Casey was one of them. I wouldn't put it past her, though.

I gritted my teeth. I was *so* not in the mood. "Let me through."

"Why don't you come practice with us?" Gabe's tone was anything but inviting. "It'll help toughen you up. Davina don't cry over demons."

I swallowed hard. "Maybe there's something wrong with that."

I spread my wings and shot myself above the tree line. *To hell with Gabe. And the rest of them.*

"They're only demons," Gabe called after me.

I hardly heard him as I flew over the trees between the school and the valley. I pumped my wings harder and soared above the top of the three-story mansion. I planned to circle around and land near the back doors, but something caught my eye. A dark-skinned woman in a white gown sat in a chair on one of the school's balconies.

I glided down to her. I came in faster than I intended and slammed into the railing. My abdomen caught the bulk of the blow, and I thought for a moment I might puke.

Grace slowly lifted her gaze. Apparently, my horrible landing wasn't as bad as I thought, because she hardly noticed my arrival. I gripped onto the top of the railing and swung my legs over it until I stood on solid ground.

"Hi, Grace," I said like we were old friends.

Her eyes met mine, but it felt as if she was looking through me. Her gaze returned to look out across the empty lawn.

"What can I help you with, Ryn?" she asked softly.

Good to know I'm not invisible.

I leaned against the railing and crossed my arms. I hadn't exactly planned what I was going to say to her. I just knew I had to reason with her *somehow*. If she wasn't going to listen to me, the Aedes sure as hell wouldn't.

I forced my voice out past the lump in my throat. "There's something I want to talk to you about."

Grace didn't respond.

I cleared my throat and continued. "I think we should arrange a meeting with the Aedes to try to come to a peaceful solution."

Grace still didn't say anything. I expected her to object, but it was like she hadn't heard me.

"You were around when the Davina tried to make peace with the Aedes before," I continued. "Maybe we can learn something from your experience and try again. These are different Aedes. Perhaps this time, they'll listen."

I waited several moments for Grace's reply, but she was completely checked out. Just as I was about to snap my fingers in front of her face, she spoke.

"Do you feel that, Ryn?" She closed her eyes and inhaled a deep breath.

I narrowed my eyes. "Feel what?"

"Just hold still and concentrate," she instructed.

I chewed the dry skin on my lower lip but eventually caved. I closed my eyes and listened to my body. All I felt was far too much tension in my shoulders.

I peeled my eyes back open. "I don't feel anything."

"I feel everything," she said without opening her eyes. "I feel the heat of the sun on my skin. I feel the light morning breeze passing though my hair. I hear the birds chirping in the trees and the sound of wind chimes down the street. The heartbeat of every patient in the hospital wing pulses across my skin."

I furrowed my brow. That last part couldn't be true, could it?

Had she heard me at all? What did any of this have to do with the war we were facing?

"What's your point?" I struggled to keep the irritation out of my tone.

Grace finally opened her eyes. "My point is, if you look for it, you'll find peace. Peace is out there, in nature."

"Okay… but that's not going to help us with the Aedes."

Grace tilted her chin toward the rising sun. "No. I never said it would."

This woman was impossible. When did she start speaking in riddles?

I turned to the glass doors beside us. Clearly, she wasn't going to listen to me. Would anyone?

After I abandoned Grace, I found Allie and Kyle in the hospital wing. I was relieved to see several cots were empty and the rest of the injured Davina seemed to be doing better. Our healing abilities weren't anything short of a miracle.

"Can I get you anything else?" Allie asked as she handed a water bottle to the lady with stitches on her face.

"No, thank you," she answered. "You've helped immensely already."

Allie noticed me for the first time.

"Can we walk?" I suggested.

Allie nodded and left the hospital wing with me. I eyed her as we headed down the stairs. Bags had settled under her eyes, and she hadn't even bothered with makeup today. Allie used to be so excited to become a Protector. Now that day was here, and I wasn't entirely convinced she was cut out for it.

"How are you doing?" I asked her.

"I'm fine." She couldn't hide the lie in her tone. "What about you?"

We reached the bottom of the stairs. Several Davina sat around the fireplace in the common room.

I didn't speak until we passed them and entered the hall behind the grand staircase. "I tried talking to Grace about meeting with the Aedes, but I'm not sure she heard a word I said."

Allie gazed down at her feet while we walked. "I'm sure Grace has a reason for whatever it is she's doing."

It didn't sound like Allie truly believed what she was saying. It was like she said it only to reassure herself because she was so desperate to believe in Grace the way the rest of the Davina did.

"Sure, she has a reason," I said. "But her reason may not be as noble as everyone thinks."

Allie bit the inside of her lip. "Maybe not…"

"Ryn," a familiar voice called.

I stopped in the hall and retreated a few steps before glancing into Fletcher's classroom. My eyes first fell upon Marek standing near Fletcher's desk, but it was Fletcher who had called my name.

I purposely avoided Marek's eyes and looked to Fletcher instead. "Yeah?"

"Come in." Fletcher gestured to Allie and me.

I glanced warily between Marek and Fletcher. Marek's expression remained calm. Was he even bothered by what happened between us last night?

"The Davina Council is looking for people to fly the outskirts of town to watch for any threats from the Aedes," Fletcher said. "I thought maybe you'd be interested in helping out."

I exchanged a glance with Allie. Her face lit up, like she couldn't be happier to get out of here.

"I thought we weren't supposed to fly where humans could see us," I pointed out.

Fletcher frowned. "We shouldn't be, but the Davina Council doesn't seem to care now that Grace is back. She's the one who said she wanted Davina flying out there to guard from another Aedes attack. I'm asking you three—and Kyle, if he wants—to volunteer, because I know you four are competent enough to keep an eye out without making a scene."

Marek nodded. "We'll do our best."

I didn't like how Marek answered like he spoke for the entire group, but I knew I'd follow him anyway. Flying totally beat sitting around Galen doing nothing all day.

~

Several hours passed as we circled the outskirts of Eagle Valley without spotting a single threat. We flew high above the cornfields near the clouds, where the air was thin and cool.

"How much longer should we patrol?" I shouted toward Marek, who flew several yards away from me.

I couldn't help it when my eyes traveled over his exposed torso. I wanted so badly for him to hold me against his chest, but I didn't know at this point if he *wanted* to hold me. He hadn't given me a clue how he felt all day.

Marek shrugged. "Fletcher never said, but if you're getting tired—"

"Don't be a wimp!" Kyle called out from in front of us. He flipped in the air and quickly caught himself. "I thought you liked flying."

"I do like flying." I quickened my pace to catch up with him.

Kyle raised his eyebrows and sped up to distance himself from me. A challenging look crossed Allie's face as she pushed ahead of him.

"Hey, guys—" Marek started.

His voice was drowned out by the sound of wind rushing past my ears. I pumped my wings harder and passed by Kyle.

"Guys!" Marek called again.

Allie and I exchanged a mischievous glance and sprinted beside each other, swaying one way and then the other to block Kyle from passing us.

"Not fair!" he called.

We dropped lower when he tried to fly beneath us. We weren't racing as much as trying to keep Kyle from getting in the lead. We had no destination and weren't paying attention to where we were going. I was sure Marek yelled at us at least five more times, but it was hard to hear him. The farther we went, the more tuckered out I got. Allie noticed me slowing down.

"Do you need a break?" she called.

I nodded.

Allie turned back to Kyle and Marek and gestured toward the ground. She quickly changed direction and dropped out of the sky. I dove after her. We landed in a large grassy clearing with trees on all sides, and I fell onto my back with my wings spread wide beneath me. Laughter filled my chest.

Marek fell into the grass near my head and reached out to touch my fingers. My initial reaction was to pull away, but I didn't. My eyes met his, and he stared back with an apologetic expression.

"I'm sorry," he whispered. "About last night."

A smile touched my lips. It was a relief to know he wasn't mad at me.

"I'm sorry, too," I replied. "I don't want to fight."

Marek ran his thumb across the back of my hand. "Me, either."

"That was fun!" Allie exclaimed breathlessly, breaking the spell between Marek and me. She hadn't noticed our exchange.

Kyle sat with an elbow rested on his knee. "Ready for another go?"

I lifted my head to look at him. "Give us a second to cool down, would—?"

My voice stopped dead when my eye caught something across the clearing. The air rippled, interrupting the stillness in the clearing and distorting the landscape beyond it. The tree trunks themselves seemed to sway in slight motion. Something was amiss, as if the threads in the fabric of reality as we knew it were unraveling.

"What?" Allie looked at me, then glanced to where my eyes were locked.

Was I imagining it?

Everyone stopped to follow my gaze. If they said anything else, I didn't hear them. I rose to my feet and inched closer to the disturbance. A strange energy grew inside of me the closer I got to it.

"Whoa," Allie said in awe beside me. I hadn't realized everyone else had gotten to their feet and followed.

We stopped mere inches from the ripple. It was hardly visible, but I noticed a swirling of colors in the air the longer I stared. It was the size of a doorway, rising only a foot or two above my head.

Kyle wet his lips and reached out to touch the visible air.

Marek grabbed his wrist before he could make contact. "Don't touch it."

Kyle listened, but I didn't. I felt nothing but air when my fingers connected with the strange phenomenon. The only reason I knew I'd touched it was because of the small ripple that spread out from my fingertips. The air waved in front of us like the surface of a pond.

"You don't think…?" Allie started.

She didn't need to finish her question. I was sure we were all thinking the same thing.

"That it's a portal to the Aedes realm?" I whispered. "*The* portal. The one Grace came back to protect us from? Yeah, I think it is."

Kyle turned to me. "But if a portal has opened, then—"

"I don't know if it's fully open yet," I said.

"How can we know for sure?" Allie asked.

"We could try to step through it," Kyle joked.

"We're not doing that," Marek replied seriously. "We don't have any idea what it could do to us."

"Or what could be waiting for us on the other side," Allie pointed out.

I walked the length of the ripple to view it from every angle.

"This is really strange," Kyle stated.

Allie swatted at him. "Obviously."

"No, I mean, it's strange that there's a portal so close to Eagle Valley," Kyle said.

"It *is* a strange coincidence," Marek agreed.

Or not a coincidence at all, I thought.

"Maybe we're wrong," Allie suggested. "Maybe it's just some strange natural phenomenon."

I stopped pacing. "It's not. This is where the realms touch, and that line is thinning."

Excitement surged through my body. Finally, we were getting somewhere. We could take action.

"We need to get Grace out here before this thing breaks open," I said.

Marek spread his wings wide. "Let's go tell her."

"There's no need for that," a voice said from behind us.

We all whirled around in unison to find Grace standing mere yards from us. What were the chances? There was no time to waste.

"Grace!" I exclaimed. "This is where the realms touch, isn't it?"

Grace nodded.

"You can secure it, can't you?" I asked desperately. "That's why you had me wake you. We can destroy this portal now, before it has a chance to open."

Grace frowned. "I'm afraid I can't do that."

What?

She was the one leading this war against the Aedes. Did she *want* the rest of them to flood this realm and destroy us? A terrifying thought occurred.

"You're on their side!" I accused. "You don't care how many Aedes we kill, as long as you can distract the Davina long enough for a portal to open. Then you'll have enough Aedes to take over this realm! Why would you do that?"

Grace remained calm. "You're terribly mistaken, Ryn."

"Then why won't you destroy this thing?" I yelled.

Grace looked down at her bare feet and stepped toward us. "Ryn, I think it's time that you finally knew the truth."

13

$\mathcal{G}$race promised we were in for a long story and invited us to sit in the grass while she explained. My friends and I exchanged wary glances before joining Grace on the ground.

I didn't like this. I should be standing, with my wings spread out, so I could take flight at a moment's notice. But I feared Grace wouldn't talk until I did as she instructed.

Grace took a deep breath. "The truth is, the stories you've heard are wrong."

I eyed Grace skeptically. Allie gasped beside me, and Marek and Kyle exchanged a questioning glance.

"The Davina today fear a portal to the Aedes realm because they fear what is on the other side. The Originals feared the portals themselves," Grace explained. "We believe the realms were always unstable but that they became more of a threat after The Great War that killed the gods."

She dropped her gaze. "The gateways between the earth and Vehena were the first to go. Davina began pouring back into our home realm when we realized the portals were collapsing. The sixteen of us didn't choose to stay behind as your stories say. We were just the last to make it."

I could hear the heartbreak in her tone.

Grace continued. "By the time we reached the last remaining

portal, we saw that our realm had turned into a wasteland on the brink of falling completely apart. Our world was dying. The other Davina were already gone. To protect our demolishing realm from affecting the others, the sixteen of us sent our essence into the portal and collapsed it, sealing off the realm. To keep the remaining two realms from destroying each other, we pushed the Aedes back for their own protection and sealed the portals."

"How?" Marek asked curiously. "How did you seal them?"

"Think of the portals like an archway," Grace said. "If you apply enough pressure—essence, in this case—they will collapse."

"How is there one here, though?" Kyle asked. I could tell he was burning for the answer. "How is it this close to Eagle Valley?"

"Long ago, Praesid had records of where the old portals were located," Grace told us. "They used these locations to predict where the new portals might open. Praesid spread the Originals across the globe to the most likely locations. Over time, several portals opened. They were able to plug those locations into the equation and better pinpoint where the next would occur."

"Wait," Marek stopped her. I could tell by the look on his face that we were thinking the exact same thing.

"You mean… the portals have opened before?" I asked in disbelief.

"Yes," Grace answered. "It has happened many times throughout history. On several occasions, other Originals were awakened to protect this realm, but that was before the rest of them died. This is my first time being awakened. It appears that Praesid and the Haylo brothers calculated the next portal properly."

Silence hung in the air as we all considered her story. Marek's uncertain gaze caught mine. Could all of this be true?

"What happened after you sealed the first portals?" Allie asked.

"We knew we wouldn't be safe forever," Grace replied. "The realms had previously been sealed off and reopened when the gods were still alive. The realms touch, and they can create cracks between them. We had an idea of where they might strike next, but we couldn't be sure. To monitor the earth for these events, we sent our consciousness and essence into the earth, freezing our immortal bodies."

I couldn't miss the disbelief that fell over my friends' faces. Her story made so much sense, but it also meant that all the stories they'd grown up believing in were laced in falsehoods. The Davina had lost so much of the truth throughout time.

"Now what do we do?" I asked Grace.

"When this portal opens fully, the realms will collide. It will destroy them both." She spoke without emotion, like the threat didn't bother her one bit.

Panic spread throughout my body. If what Grace was saying was true, we didn't even have a chance—not unless she took action immediately.

"Why aren't you *doing* something about it?" I shot to my feet. "You have all this knowledge and power, and you're just *sitting* here." I whirled toward the portal behind me. "Let's do something! Let's close it!"

Grace dropped her shoulders. "I'm afraid I can't."

"Can't? Or won't?" I asked with an edge to my tone. "What are you even here for? Why'd you have me wake you if you weren't going to do something about this? You've been distracting everyone with fighting against the Aedes when you *should* be trying to destroy this thing before the realms destroy each other!"

Marek stood beside me. "Ryn is right. We need to do something."

A silent beat passed over the clearing.

"Answer me, Grace!" I shouted.

Grace's soft expression never faltered. "Please. Calm down, and I'll explain."

Anger pulsed through my veins, but I fell silent and waited for her to continue.

"I called out to you in order to stop the portals," Grace said. "But now that I'm here, I've seen the damage your races have caused. The truth is, I've lost my will to fight."

I narrowed my eyes. "I thought you'd been observing all this time. None of this should surprise you."

Grace frowned. "Yes. It's one thing to observe. It's another to see it firsthand. I am the last Original. I'm… alone. And I'm not sure I have the heart to restore this world. The best thing I can do is to distract the Davina and the Aedes with the war and allow the portal to destroy the realms."

"What?" Allie cried.

She and Kyle were on their feet in less than a second.

"You can't do that!" Kyle objected.

"You're just going to let us die?" I cried.

Grace took a soothing breath. "I believe our essence will live on as always."

What a bitch! How can she act so calm when the fate of our world rested in her hands?

"Whatever remains of the ashes of our realms will bring about new life," Grace continued. "Everything will start fresh. There will be no more war, no more pain and suffering. Everyone will finally be at peace."

My hands balled into fists. "And you just thought you'd let the rest of us die without any say in the matter? We're not going to let you do this!"

A hint of amusement crossed Grace's face. "You can't stop me. Only I have enough power to stop the portal, and I'm not going to."

"I'll report you to the Davina Council!" I threatened.

Grace's brows shot up. "And you think they'll believe you? Four teenagers over me, an Original?"

I kept my narrowed gaze on her, but I knew she was right.

I crossed my arms. "Why tell us, then?"

"Because I want you to stop poking around and asking so many questions." There was an edge to Grace's voice as she rose to her feet and spread her wings. "You need to accept this is your fate, Ryn. And you need to accept that there's nothing you can do to stop it."

Grace shot into the sky, leaving my friends and me alone at the foot of the portal.

My stomach dropped.

"Wait!" Marek called after her.

Grace continued flying away from us without missing a beat.

"Shit." Marek raked his fingers through his hair. "What are we going to do now?"

Kyle's mouth hung open, like he wanted to give an answer he didn't have.

"Maybe..." Allie started.

We all turned to look at her.

Allie bit her lip. "Maybe there's something to what Grace was saying."

I let out a breath in disbelief. "You can't actually agree with her, can you?"

Allie shrugged. "I don't know. Maybe starting over is what the world needs."

"This isn't a fresh start for any of us!" I shouted. "This is a *death sentence!*"

"I know—" Allie started to say, but I cut her off.

"I'm not ready to die yet," I stated. "Are you?"

Allie averted her gaze. "No."

"What Grace wants to do is wrong," Marek said through clenched teeth. "There are too many innocent people."

"Yeah." Kyle's lips pursed. "It's wrong on so many levels."

I struggled to steady my heavy breathing. "Then there's only one option."

"What's that?" Allie asked curiously.

My jaw tightened. "We go against Grace."

I couldn't believe it'd come down to this. A group of four teenagers had become the world's last hope.

Since Grace wasn't going to do anything to save the earth, we'd have to figure out a way to destroy the portal ourselves.

14

It was late afternoon by the time we returned to my house. I paced around my bedroom, unable to sit still. I could feel my friends' eyes on me.

"Here's what we're going to do." I spoke confidently, but I didn't feel very enthused about my plan. "We're going to find Malcolm."

"No," Marek objected from where he stood near the window.

A skeptical expression crossed Kyle's face. "You want to go *looking* for him after what he did to you? Are you insane?"

"Don't call me that," I snapped. "I'm not insane."

"Kyle's right," Allie protested. "We can't go looking for Malcolm."

"Yeah," Marek agreed. "It's not a smart idea."

I raised my eyebrows. "Do you have a better idea? Because right now, we're desperate."

I glanced between the three of them. They all stared back silently.

"I say we try to come to some sort of peaceful agreement with Malcolm on our own," I suggested. "From there, we can try to get more Davina on our side. We're wasting time fighting the Aedes. We need to stop this fighting and get everyone on common ground. With enough supporters and enough essence, maybe we don't need Grace at all. We could collapse the portal ourselves."

"What if—" Kyle started to say, but I cut him off.

"The least we can do is try." I wasn't taking no for an answer. "The only thing we know for certain is that if we don't try, we—and everyone we love—will die."

~

Night fell before we landed on the front lawn of Trenton's old house. In the dark, it seemed even more eerie than the first time I was here. The chipping paint, curtained windows, and splintered front door frame screamed *Go Away!* Perhaps in some ways, this house truly was haunted.

I thought it was best if I approached Malcolm alone. Otherwise, he might think it was an ambush. My friends snuck around the side of the house to hide in case I needed them.

My knees shook as I walked toward the front door and reached for the door knob. Before my hand could close around it, a light breeze pushed the door open on its loose hinges, as if inviting me inside.

Freaky.

The hardwood floor creaked under my weight, and a strong dusty scent met my nose. I glanced around the abandoned home, but I couldn't see more than four feet in front of me through the darkness.

"Malcolm?" I called. His name didn't come out as strong and commanding as I intended it to. I cleared my throat and repeated his name.

Only silence returned my call.

I stepped farther into the house and peeked into the kitchen. It was strangely quiet without the hum of the appliances filling the air. I crossed the entrance hall and carefully stepped over the broken vase into the living room.

"Malcolm," I called again. "It's Ryn. I want to talk."

My heart leapt inside my chest as a loud *bang* filled the air, like the sound of a close-range gunshot. I whirled around. My heart slowed when I realized the bang was just a gust of wind slamming the front door into its frame.

I took a deep breath and turned. I practically leapt out of my skin when I rammed into a tall figure cloaked in black. I stumbled back several steps and almost tripped over the coffee table. My pulse quickened at the sight of him.

I expected Malcolm to leap forward and attack me, to lunge for my throat or throw a fireball at my face, but he stood as still as a statue.

My heart rate slowed, and I took a cautious step forward. "Malcolm?"

He lowered his hood. I could just barely make out his expression in the darkness. His lips turned down at the corners, and his shoulders slumped. He looked like the kind of man who'd lost all hope. He put up no fight... almost as if he'd resolved himself to letting me take the first shot.

"What are you doing here?" He made it sound like I was the last person in the world he wanted to see. I probably was.

I cleared my throat. "I want to talk."

"You didn't come here to fight?" He sounded surprised.

"No," I assured him. "I want to negotiate peace. The Aedes will listen to you."

Malcolm frowned. "You think we'll agree to peace after what the Davina did to us? You've killed hundreds of our recruits in the last few days."

"We've lost people, too," I pointed out. "Look, there's something bigger going on here. If we don't do something about it, all of us are going to die."

"What are you talking about?" he demanded.

"The line between the realms is thinning," I explained. "A portal to your realm is opening."

"Yeah," Malcolm said like it was obvious. "That's why Grace has returned, isn't it? She wants to keep the portal closed so we can't return."

"No, she—" I stopped abruptly.

Why hadn't it ever occurred to me that all the Aedes wanted to do was return to a realm they could call their own? Everyone always made it sound like all the Aedes wanted was power and that they wanted to take over the earth.

"Grace was *meant* to keep the portal closed," I told him, "but it's not why you think. The portals themselves are the threat."

Malcolm seemed intrigued. He let me continue.

I explained what Grace had told us earlier, how the realms would destroy each other if we didn't do something about it first. I told him about how Grace had given up and wanted to wash our slates clean, to give birth to a new realm where none of us survived.

"Grace is using you as a distraction," I explained. "If you retreat and stop fighting the Davina in Eagle Valley, then maybe everyone else will see Grace's true colors and we can convince them to help us prevent this."

A hard expression crossed Malcolm's face. "Even if what you're saying is true, peace between our two races will never work. The Davina and the Aedes have never listened to each other. Maybe if Sylvia hadn't left me, she could've convinced them, but now..."

"Maybe the Davina will listen this time if we—"

"You don't get it, do you?" Malcolm exploded. "Your people have made us out to be monsters when all we ever wanted was to survive!"

I froze, momentarily dumbstruck. "Survive?"

"Yes!" Malcolm shouted. "I learned a lot living around Davina for the last two decades. Most Aedes don't get why you hate us so much. The way our stories go, *you're* the power-hungry monsters."

"So—"

"So you think we feed off human essence for fun!" Malcolm roared. "Some abuse their power, but the rest of us only access human essence because it's the only way for us to survive."

Malcolm might as well have dropped a brick on my chest. How could the Davina have had it so wrong all this time? Unless Malcolm was lying to manipulate me...

"You mean... human essence keeps you alive?" I asked.

"Of course it does! We're not immortal. How else would we survive?"

I didn't have a decent answer. I'd assumed because they were direct descendants of the gods, their healing abilities kept them alive until old age. I'd never given it a second thought. I was an idiot.

"We have the unique ability to borrow—access—another being's essence," Malcolm explained.

"So the Davina can't—?"

"No," he answered before I finished the question. "Not modern-day Davina, anyway. The Aedes, however, can borrow essence and transform it into life energy. We use it to grow and stay alive."

"Can't you pull your essence from the earth?" I asked.

"Yes," Malcolm answered. "But it has its limits—for all races. Borrowing essence from another being provides an easier channel than taking from the earth. It allows us to access enough to stay alive."

My jaw hung slack. "Why don't the Davina know about this?"

Malcolm crossed his arms, but his tone softened. "I suspect some of them do and have decided to keep it from the rest of you. It's a good way to keep you believing we're worth killing."

He couldn't be telling the truth. Was Malcolm really more trustworthy than the Davina Council?

Probably, I thought.

"If the Davina Council knows, why would they let us keep killing you?" I asked.

Malcolm's jaw tensed. "There are Aedes who've given the rest of us a bad name."

Like Clinton, I thought.

"Perhaps the Davina don't realize some of us only take what we need," Malcolm continued. "They lump us all together as monsters and won't entertain the truth."

I don't believe this! Though, the truth was, I believed every word, and it broke my heart.

"This racism has to end," I stated. "The hatred needs to stop."

Malcolm eyed me like I was a poor helpless little girl who just didn't understand. "And I suppose you're going to lead the charge?"

I held my head high. "Yes. If I have to."

Malcolm sighed heavily. Obviously, he had no faith in me.

"Why would I help you?" he asked. "You killed my son."

Guilt slammed into my gut at the mention of Trenton.

My gaze dropped to my feet, and my voice came out small. "He was killing my friend. I tried to stop him, but—" My words caught in my throat. "I wouldn't have hurt him if I thought I had any other choice."

Malcolm's lips pressed into a thin line, as if contemplating whether or not to trust me. "How do I know you're not lying?"

I sighed. "Would I be here if I trusted Grace?"

Malcom still looked skeptical.

"We've all had to make sacrifices in this war," I said. "But the fact is, we want the same thing—to survive. And that's not going to happen unless we band together."

Silence momentarily settled over the house.

"All you want from me is to retreat?" he asked.

"Yes," I answered. "We need the Davina to focus on the real issue. They need to know Grace isn't on their side."

Malcolm paused for what felt like a whole minute.

"Okay, I'll give you a chance," he finally said.

Hope soared in my chest.

"But—" Malcolm's word came out harsh, softening my hope. "If you can't convince them of the truth and they attack us again, we will do what we have to in order to defend ourselves."

I nodded. "That's fair. I will do what I can to keep them from attacking your people again."

I didn't know *how* I was going to do that, but one way or another, I would figure it out. If I didn't, time would eventually run out for all of us.

I reached out my hand. "Truce?"

Malcolm hesitated before shaking it. "Truce."

"Where can I find you if I need to contact you again?" I asked.

"Right here," he answered.

I turned to leave, feeling optimistic. As I stepped out the door, something caught my attention out of the corner of my eye. I did a double take, but the flash of white I'd spotted was gone.

My mouth went dry. I could've sworn I spotted white feathers disappearing around the side of the house—and I wasn't sure those feathers belonged to any of my friends.

15

y opponent grunted as I sank my foot into his gut. What he had in strength, I made up for in speed. His thick arm swung out, reaching for me, but I ducked and threw myself forward. I tackled him to the ground like a football player.

Kyle coughed. "Jesus, Tyler. Where'd you learn to fight like that?"

I offered him my hand and helped him to his feet. I shrugged. "I didn't think I was that good. Maybe don't take it so easy on me next time."

"He wasn't taking it easy on you," a familiar voice said.

I turned to see Marek standing nearby, observing us. I hadn't realized he and Allie had finished sparring.

Yes. Sparring. Again. Like useless maniacs.

A new training schedule had finally been issued, and we'd been *required* to report to the valley for training. All around us, groups of Davina fought one another, but it felt more like we were playing games than actually preparing for anything.

"This is pointless," I complained to Marek. "If Malcolm was being honest with me—and I think he was—we're not going to need to know all this. We *should* be trying to convince everyone we can of the truth."

Fletcher was the first person on that list, but I hadn't seen him all day. We needed to talk to him first. If we couldn't even convince

Fletcher, we had no hope of convincing anyone else. When Allie and I went to go find him earlier, one of the councilmembers followed us back to the school. We had to fake using the restroom so they wouldn't get suspicious.

Someone cleared their voice from behind me. "Miss Tyler."

I whirled around to find Anthony Lucas, head of the Davina Council, glaring at me from several feet away. Three other guys in suits stood behind him, like they were the freaking secret service. I recognized Mr. Harris among them.

"Yes? Can I help you?" I tried to sound sweet and innocent, but it didn't really work for me.

"Why don't you and your friends come with us?" Anthony suggested. It sure didn't sound like we had a choice.

All three of my friends came to stand beside me. Marek's shoulder crossed over my own protectively.

"Why?" I demanded.

Anthony cleared his throat and glanced around at the other Davina, like he was afraid I was about to make a scene. I wasn't, unless he gave me a reason. The look he gave me told me he had plenty of reasons.

"We can discuss this further in private," Anthony said.

I crossed my arms. "I'd like to know what I'm getting into first."

Anthony's jaw tightened. "It wasn't a suggestion. You and your friends are to come with us. Now."

It looked as if he was trying to physically restrain himself from dragging me behind him by my hair.

I glanced to Marek. I'd never seen him look so uncertain and scared before.

"We should go with them," Marek said under his breath.

Allie and Kyle both wore the same look Marek did. Reluctantly, I gave in.

I held my shoulders back, trying to appear strong as I followed behind Anthony. The truth was, I was terrified of what he might want.

Anthony and the three secret service guys led us up to the school and into Mrs. Presley's old office. The room wasn't much bigger than my bedroom.

The first thing I noticed was Grace seated behind the large desk near the window. The surface of the desk was empty, like they'd already removed Mrs. Presley's memory from the room.

"Please sit," Grace said sweetly, gesturing to the two seats opposite her.

My friends and I exchanged a wary glance, but eventually, Allie and I claimed the two chairs. Marek stood behind me with his hands on the back of my seat. His knuckles touched my shoulder in a comforting gesture. Mr. Harris shut the door behind us, and silence settled over the room.

"Is something wrong?" I asked innocently.

Anthony crossed the room to stand next to Grace. He placed his hands on the surface of the desk and leaned toward me. His eyes narrowed, and his lips tightened. "Where were you last night?"

My expression never faltered as I met his stare, but inside, I was screaming. *How do they know?*

Grace had the Davina Council wrapped around her little finger. I wasn't inclined to admit the truth in front of any of them. We needed more time to share the truth with the other Davina before Grace found out what we were up to.

"What do you mean?" I asked, like I had no clue what he was talking about. "I was at home last night, like every night."

"I didn't ask for attitude," Anthony barked.

"But it's the truth." I mean, technically it *was* true. I'd gone home after we met up with Malcolm.

"We know you went to see that scum demon last night," Anthony growled. "What we don't know is *why*."

I leaned back in my chair. "I don't know what you're talking about."

I looked to my friends. They all quickly denied it as well.

Anthony gritted his teeth. "I'm going to ask you one last time. What did Malcolm want?"

I sat up straighter. "And I'm going to tell you again; I don't know what you're talking about."

Anthony let out a heavy breath. Grace just sat there looking content, like she was happy to watch Anthony yell at us.

"You're working with that demon," Anthony accused. "What are you planning?"

Anthony took one quick step around the side of the desk.

Before he could get up in my face, Marek stepped between us. Their noses were inches apart.

"She said she doesn't know anything," Marek snarled. "Leave her alone."

Anthony's nostrils flared. "Fine. If *she's* not going to talk, maybe *one* of you will."

One of Anthony's three henchmen lunged for Kyle. Allie shrieked, while I gasped.

"Hey!" Kyle struggled away from the guy. He quickly broke free and straightened his sleeve.

Anthony pushed past Marek and faced Kyle. "Spread your wings."

"What?" Kyle demanded.

Anthony leaned in closer. "Spread. Your. Wings."

Kyle looked to me, then to Allie. I wished I could help him, but what were we going to do? Overpower the most powerful Davina alive and her four trolls?

"Do as he says," Grace instructed.

Kyle stood still for several more seconds before giving in. He pulled his shirt over his head, and large white wings slowly grew from his back.

Anthony reached for Kyle's shoulders and forced him onto his knees. "You have one last chance. What are you planning with Malcolm?"

"Stop!" Marek shouted. "We told you we don't know anything. You must be mistaking us for someone else."

A smirk spread across Anthony's face. "Wrong answer."

In a flash, Anthony ripped a handful of feathers out of Kyle's wings.

Kyle cried out in pain. I winced at the same time Allie's hands slapped in front of her mouth. I thought I even saw Mr. Harris flinch from where he stood in the corner of the room. Marek's fists clenched beside me. I bit down hard on the inside of my lip to keep from spewing insults at the Council.

Allie looked to me with fear in her eyes, begging me to tell the truth.

"Still don't want to talk?" Anthony taunted.

He crossed in front of Kyle, grazing the handful of feathers across his cheek. Kyle turned his face away, and a wild expression entered Anthony's eyes. The Davina Council had officially gone mad trying to win this war.

A moment later, Anthony's fist connected with Kyle's jaw. Blood spurted from Kyle's mouth and across the hardwood floor.

Allie stared down at the blood in horror. When her eyes met Kyle's, he shot back the smallest shake of his head. He didn't want her to speak.

"Tell us!" Anthony thundered a moment before his foot sank into Kyle's groin.

Kyle grunted, and his hands shot between his legs protectively.

Anthony shoved his hand into Kyle's dark hair and smashed his face against the side of the bookcase near the door.

I yelped. Beside me, Marek's knuckles turned white as his hands curled into tighter fists.

Anthony dragged Kyle upward by his hair and shoved him across the room. Kyle's wing twisted under him when he landed.

Allie shot to her feet. "Let him go!"

Anthony paused. "Are you ready to tell the truth?"

"Yes!" Allie cried. "Just stop!"

Well, shit. We were all going to die.

I quickly cut in before Allie could say more. "You're making a bigger deal out of this than it needs to be! We went to find Malcolm because we wanted to fight him after he kidnapped me. But when we got there..."

Crap. I needed a good lie—and fast.

"When you got there... what?" Anthony prodded.

Marek jumped to my rescue. "He was gone by the time we got to his house."

Anthony narrowed his eyes. "Why didn't you say that to begin with?"

"Because our mentor would be mad at us for trying to deal with him ourselves," I lied. It was the best I could come up with.

Anthony didn't look like he believed me.

"Let them go." Grace's bored voice cut through the momentary silence.

Anthony hesitated. "What?"

"Let them go," she repeated. She never tore her gaze from the window.

It took Anthony another moment, but he finally gave in. "Fine."

Marek rushed to Kyle and helped him to his feet.

"Please return to training with the rest of the Davina," Grace instructed.

I didn't see the point, but I also didn't think we had a choice. I stood and breezed past the councilmembers without making eye contact. I swung the door open and stopped dead in my tracks. Allie nearly rammed into me.

Casey straightened immediately from where she leaned against the wall. Her eyes widened like a deer in the headlights.

"You!" I accused.

Casey took a cautious step back. "Me, what?"

"You turned us in. You followed us last night and tried to get us in trouble!"

It was *her* feathers I'd seen outside Malcolm's. It had to be.

"I don't know what you're talking about," Casey said flatly.

I stared at her in disbelief. I barely noticed Marek drag Kyle past me toward the hospital ward.

"I think you know exactly what I'm talking about," I snapped.

Casey held her hands up in surrender. "Seriously, I'm just waiting for my dad."

"Right," I said with an eye roll. "This is fun for you, isn't it?"

Casey crossed her arms. "No, actually, it's not."

So she was sticking to her story.

"You're such a liar." I lunged for her.

Before I could get my hands on that pretty little face of hers, Allie caught me and dragged me away. I struggled out of her grip, but she dug her fingernails into my arm.

"Stop it, Ryn," Allie hissed. "We have bigger problems than Casey. We need to be on our best behavior."

Allie's words struck me, and I stopped struggling. Allie was right. If the Davina Council figured out that we were trying to make peace with Malcolm, we'd all be killed for treason.

And I was determined to save the world before I died.

Training ticked by slowly, but I was able to channel my anger into it and knock a huge Protector on his ass twice. Apparently, I wounded his pride, because he gave up trying to teach me and asked Allie to spar with him instead.

I was relieved when training ended and we were given permission to go home. I still hadn't seen Fletcher all day, so I headed back up to the school to see if he was in his classroom. Marek took my hand and followed, insisting that I shouldn't be left alone.

When we turned down the hall to Fletcher's classroom, I was surprised to see Grace headed our way. I kept my head down, but we didn't make it past her unnoticed. Grace stepped in front of us, blocking our path. She stood with her hands crossed in front of her and a smile on her face.

Shit. What did she want now?

"Ryn," Grace said pleasantly. "Can I have a word with you?"

I glanced to Marek warily. Could I say no to her?

Grace's eyes traveled the length of Marek's body. "Alone?"

I couldn't for the life of me imagine what she wanted to talk about—unless Casey had overheard everything with Malcolm and told Grace the truth. Maybe she wanted to walk me to my execution.

"It's okay," Grace said sweetly.

I didn't trust her.

"Actually, we're kind of busy." I tried to step around her, but Grace blocked my path a second time.

Marek's hand tightened in mine, like he was physically trying to restrain himself from lashing out at Grace.

"I'm sure whatever it is can wait." The way she said it implied anything could wait for *her*, like the pleasure of her company was the most important thing in the world.

I shifted my weight between my feet. "Um…"

"All I want is a moment of your time," Grace pushed. She hadn't dropped the motherly façade. "It'll only take a few minutes."

Marek could no longer contain himself. "She said no."

Grace narrowed her eyes at him.

"It's fine," I cut in before a fight broke out. "We can talk."

Marek looked uncertain, but I squeezed his hand to let him know that I would be all right.

"Anything you say in front of Ryn, you can say in front of me," Marek argued.

Somehow, I knew Grace wasn't going to go for that.

"I'll be okay," I assured him.

Marek's face fell, but I dropped his hand and followed behind Grace.

She led me down the hall and up the stairs. My fingers shook against the railing. What could she possibly want from me?

Grace stepped into Mr. Collins's classroom and shut the door behind us. I glanced around the room cautiously, as if waiting for one of the Davina Council members to jump out and attack me, but we were alone.

I swallowed hard and crossed my arms over my chest. "What did you have to drag me away from my boyfriend for? He was right, you know. Anything you say in front of me can be said in front of him."

Grace walked around the student desks to the front of the room. She leaned against Mr. Collins's desk and pursed her lips. "I want you to tell me the truth of what you were doing at Malcolm's."

Grace's tone came out friendly but stale. She reminded me of my old therapist, who seemed friendly enough, but you knew under that fake smile, she was judging you.

My jaw tensed. "I told you. We went to get revenge. We didn't find it."

Grace's expression remained cold. "We've known each other for a long time, Ryn. I thought by now you could be honest with me."

She might've been watching me my whole life, but I'd only just met Grace. Whatever connection she thought we might have, I didn't feel it.

"If that's all you wanted from me, I think I'll get back to my boyfriend now." I turned, but before I could twist the doorknob, Grace spoke again.

"I think honesty is best for both of us, Ryn."

I whirled around. "Then why weren't you honest with me to begin with?"

Grace dropped her head. Holy crap. Had I made her feel bad?

"Perhaps I can make up for it," she said.

"How?" I was actually curious to know the answer.

Grace took a long, deep breath. "Would you like to know what really happened to your father?"

What did she just say?

Her offer struck me like a punch to the gut. My breath stalled. I wasn't sure if it was out of fear or excitement. I hesitated. Grace couldn't actually know what happened to my dad, could she? She was only saying it to keep me here—for whatever reason. Then again, Grace had been observing the world all this time. It was possible she knew much more about what happened in our world than she let on.

"You actually know what happened to him?" I asked, my voice low.

Grace nodded. "Take a seat."

I stepped closer to the desk she'd gestured to.

"It's a long story," she said, like that would make me feel better about accepting her invitation to sit.

I sank into the chair. "What do you know about him?"

"There's a reason I chose you to wake me, Ryn."

"Because of my father?" I asked.

She dropped her gaze. "Because of your father's mistake... and mine."

What could she possibly mean by that?

"Before I chose you," Grace explained, "I chose your father."

I gasped. This couldn't be real. *Grace is lying to me.*

"The line between the realms has been thinning for many years," she told me. "I led your father to Eagle Valley, but I made the mistake of leading him to the site of the portal before he could wake me. He must've felt my urgency in reaching it because it was close to finally opening fully. Then your father learned he was about to have a child."

Me. And then, poof, he was gone.

"He became desperate," Grace continued. "But he hadn't found me yet. Communicating with him—as you're very familiar with—was difficult."

You can say that again.

"Unlike you," Grace said, "he knew he'd been chosen because he grew up hearing the stories of my powers. He knew he was running out of time. To save you—and the rest of the world—he tried to use my powers on his own. However, a mortal like your father was unable to access all of my powers at once. He couldn't collapse the portal by himself. But he didn't give up. Your father threw himself into the portal with a portion of my essence."

A lump grew in my throat. Could this be true? Or was she just telling me what I wanted to hear?

More than anything, I wanted it to be true. It meant that my father had died a hero. He hadn't walked out on us because he didn't want me. He wanted me so much that he sacrificed himself to save me.

Grace cleared her throat. "The portal partially collapsed, but it only delayed the threat. The same portal your father sacrificed himself to eighteen years ago has been rebuilding itself. I spent many years searching for a new Davina to share my powers with. I had to be selective so that I could build a connection with whoever I chose. That way, they could find me first, instead of the portal. I searched many years for the perfect person, but I kept coming back to you."

"Because of my strange essence?" I asked.

Grace's brow furrowed. "Your essence? No. You were only a child, but already, I could see that you had a good heart. You couldn't be manipulated by the Aedes as others could."

I thought of Clinton and how he'd manipulated my mom but never manipulated me.

"The more I thought about it, the more I realized that perhaps choosing a child was the best option," she said. "It would allow us to grow a stronger connection so I could lead you to me."

And our connection had still sucked. But then again, I *had* found her before it was too late. But it was too late for my father…

"So you're the reason my dad's dead?" My voice cracked.

"I—" Grace paused a moment, as if carefully considering how to word her answer. "Your father acted by himself."

My fingers tightened around the corner of the desk until my knuckles turned white. "And he'd still be alive if you hadn't chosen him and messed up!"

"Ryn, I—"

"Unless… unless he's still alive…" I thought out loud.

Grace shook her head. "No, he's gone."

"How can you know?" I bit back. "Maybe he made it to the other side. Or maybe he's trapped inside the portal."

"It's not possible," Grace insisted.

I shot to my feet. "You don't know that for sure! You never tried to save him, did you?"

The portal was opening again. If he survived, maybe I had a chance to save him. I'd never know until I tried.

"Ryn," Grace started, but I didn't listen.

I whirled around and raced out of the room.

I didn't care if it was a long shot. I had to save my father.

17

I sprinted down the hall and descended the stairs to the front of the building. Footsteps followed behind me, but I pushed forward. My fingers just barely grazed the door handle when strong hands grabbed my biceps and spun me around.

"Ryn, what's wrong?" Marek's voice filled with alarm.

"My dad—Grace said—there's a chance—" I sputtered between heavy breaths.

"Slow down," Marek demanded.

The words spilled out of me. "Grace said my dad went into the portal. What if he's still in there, Marek?"

I didn't give him a chance to respond. I spun back toward the door and raced outside. Before my feet touched the grass, wings had sprouted from my back. I flapped them hard and launched myself into the sky. Cold wind rushed by my face, tangling my hair into a giant knot.

Marek followed closely behind. Up here, he didn't have a chance to ask any more questions.

The flight to the portal seemed to take hours. My father had encountered the portal almost two decades ago, but it felt like if I didn't get there now, I'd miss my chance at saving him.

I landed in the grassy clearing with a hard *thud* and stumbled forward. My heart pounded, and I inhaled deep breaths as I approached the portal. The ripples in the air were bigger and more prominent today. The portal was getting stronger.

"Ryn," Marek said softly, as if afraid he might startle me. His fingers grazed across mine, but I barely felt them.

"Dad?" I projected my voice into the rippling air.

Nothing met my ears but the light breeze passing through the trees.

"Dad, are you there? It's your daughter, Kathryn."

No response.

I realized that if my dad had survived the portal, he wouldn't even know my name. How freaking sad was that?

"Daniel," I tried instead. "I'm Gloria Tyler's daughter! I'm here to help."

Seconds ticked by. I waited for a strong, deep voice to call out from within the portal—the voice I'd always imagined.

The weight of Marek's hand settled on my shoulder. "Ryn, I don't think he's—"

"He could be!" I snapped my head in Marek's direction. "We don't know what it's like inside the portal or on the other side! He could've survived."

Marek bit his lower lip, like he wanted to say more but was trying to restrain himself.

I turned my gaze back to the portal. I had to believe my dad was still there. All I ever wanted was to hear an explanation, to reunite with him. I wanted him to tell me he didn't leave because he didn't want me but because he had to, that he thought of me every day since and regretted that he never had a chance to tell me he loved me.

"Maybe he can't hear us," I theorized.

I stepped closer to the portal. Marek's arm wrapped around my waist, holding me back.

"Don't touch it." A hint of alarm entered his tone.

I pushed his protective arm away from me. "Why not? If he's in there—"

"If he's in there, it means you could get stuck in there, too."

"So, what do we do?" I asked desperately.

My eyes darted across the portal in search of a weak spot. If we could somehow widen the portal, perhaps my father could find his way out.

Before Marek had a chance to stop me, I conjured a white fireball and hurled it at the center of the ripple. My essence passed through the rippling air, like it'd been swallowed up. Then it expanded like an explosion, as if there was an invisible brick wall just behind the rippling air.

"Dad!" I yelled again.

Silence.

My blood began to boil the longer we waited. Tension grew in my head. I drew my arm back to throw another fireball.

"Ryn." Marek's voice stopped me. "You could end up doing more harm than good."

"We have to try something!" I cried.

I sent another ball of essence into the portal. It did nothing but expand rapidly like the last one had.

"Help me, Marek!" I begged.

Marek opened his mouth but only sighed. Finally, he spoke in a whisper. "I don't know what to do."

"Don't just stand there! Do something!" My hands shook at my sides as the urge to punch something—anything—overcame me. I shot another fireball at the portal, and then another and another.

Marek just stood there watching me freak out. An expression of hopelessness settled on his face.

Help me! I wanted to scream.

I reached out a hand to plunge it into the portal, but my fingers just barely grazed the center ripple before Marek grabbed my elbow and whirled me around. I struggled away from him, wanting nothing more than to dive into the portal to save my dad. Marek only caught my wrists and restrained me tighter.

"Let go of me!" I objected.

"Please, stop." The look in his eyes begged me to comply. "You're going to hurt yourself."

My bottom lip quivered.

Say something more, I thought. *Tell me he's in there. Tell me we can save him. Please let me go so I can save him.*

But I realized Marek was right. There was nothing more I could do.

I sank to my knees and bit the inside of my cheek. A tear rolled down my face and fell into the grass. Marek knelt behind me and pulled me into his arms.

"He's really gone, isn't he?" My voice cracked, and I squeezed my eyes shut.

This wasn't right. All this time, I thought my dad might be dead, but I wasn't sure I actually believed it until now.

"There's no saving him, is there?" I sobbed.

Marek buried his face in my hair and kissed the top of my head. "I'm so sorry, Ryn."

I covered my face with my hands. "How can Grace do this? My dad sacrificed himself to save the world, and now she's just going to let it end. She has no right to do this. It's her fault my dad is gone. It's her fault for everything."

My shoulders heaved uncontrollably. I didn't want to cry here in front of Marek, but that thought only caused me to sob harder.

"Grace isn't going to let this portal destroy the world," Marek said. "I won't let her do it."

I drew away from Marek to look him in the eyes. "You won't?"

"I won't," he emphasized. "I am *not* going to let your father's death be in vain."

Fresh tears rolled down my cheeks as a new wave of emotions overcame me. Marek's strong arms wrapped around me again. I pressed my face into his bare chest and stayed wrapped in his arms until my tears dried and the sun set.

I was on the verge of falling asleep and couldn't find the strength to stand. I would stay out here under the stars in his arms all night if I had to. I just didn't want to move. It would only make all of this too real and remind me of the heartbreaking truth.

Eventually, Marek rose to his feet, cradling me in his arms. I clung to him, but he didn't say anything as he launched us both into the sky and flew me home.

18

Marek landed softly on my front lawn and carried me up the front steps. The porch swing swayed beneath me as he set me down. I blinked my eyes open to look at him. The porch light created a halo around his head, but his face was cast in shadows.

"Thank you for bringing me home," I whispered.

He bent to push my hair from my face. "It's what I'm here for."

I struggled to sit up. Somehow, my high emotions had translated into physical pain in my muscles.

"I should probably get inside," I said. "I'll see you tomorrow."

I stood and wrapped him in a hug. All I wanted was to invite him inside and spend the night in his arms, but I knew it'd be wrong to ask. I'd been in enough trouble these past few days with my mom. I held onto Marek a minute longer and then peeled my body off his and said goodbye. It broke my heart to step inside the house without him.

"Kathryn?" Mom called from the kitchen.

I didn't want to face her, but I didn't want to fight, either. I headed down the hall and stopped in the kitchen doorway. "Yeah?"

Mom looked up from the sink, where she was rinsing a bowl after the dinner I missed. I could only imagine what sort of mess I looked like. I was sure my hair was disheveled from flying and my eyes were still red and puffy from crying.

"Kathryn, what's wrong?" She sounded genuinely concerned.

Lie to her, I thought. Mom didn't need to be dragged into this. Then again, it wasn't fair for me to keep this a secret, either.

"It's Davina stuff again, isn't it?" She turned off the faucet and turned to me. "Are you ever going to tell me what's really been going on? The lady at the bank says people are talking about giant birds and angel sightings. I thought it was all supposed to be a secret."

It is, I wanted to say. *But no one cares anymore because our world is colliding with another realm, and they'll inevitably collapse in on each other. What do secrets matter anymore?*

Somehow, I couldn't bring myself to share *that* secret with her. I wasn't sure I was going to say anything, but she continued to stare at me. I knew she wouldn't let me leave without some sort of explanation.

My throat tightened, and tension grew in the air. I was surprised to hear my quiet voice break the silence. "I know what happened to my father."

Mom gasped. "What—how?"

"Maybe we should sit down," I suggested.

Mom's hand gripped the back of the nearest chair to steady herself. After a moment to digest what I'd just said, she sank into it. I sat across from her at the table.

"You can't know what happened to him," she stated.

It wasn't that she didn't believe me. It sounded more like she didn't *want* to believe me, like she was afraid of what I might tell her.

I cleared my throat. "I think it's pretty obvious by now that my dad was a Davina."

Mom nodded.

"Well, he was involved in this war," I said. "Another Davina knew him, and she told me..."

I lifted my gaze to meet my mother's. Her fear was clouded with an expression of hope. She was finally going to get an answer to the one question that had plagued her all these years.

I didn't know how much I could tell her without devastating her beyond belief. How would she feel if she knew like I did that my father's sacrifice had been in vain?

I settled for the easiest explanation. "He sacrificed himself for a lot of people. He didn't leave because of you or because he didn't want me. He left to save us. He was very brave."

I didn't know what I expected from her—perhaps an outburst or for her to call me a liar—but she just sat there.

Mom bit her lower lip. Her voice came out so gentle that it didn't sound like her own. "Can't you see this is why I worry about you, Kathryn? I already lost your father to a Davina battle. I don't want to lose you, too."

I didn't bother correcting her, that he hadn't died in battle, nor could I deny that she might lose me, too. I simply didn't speak. It was easier that way.

"Thank you for telling me," Mom said.

It was strange to hear her talk so softly. Usually, all we did was yell at each other.

"You're glad I told you?" I asked.

Mom thought about it for a moment and then wiped at her eyes. She nodded. "Yeah."

"Mom, I'm sorry—" I started.

"No," she replied with a sniffle. "It's okay. It's good to finally know. I—I think I'm going to go to bed early."

Mom stood and exited the kitchen before I could say anything more. I thought about following her upstairs to comfort her, but I decided to give her space.

I rose from my chair and poured myself a bowl of cereal. It was hard to eat when I didn't have much of an appetite lately. After I finished, I left my dirty dishes in the sink and climbed the stairs.

The door to my mom's bedroom creaked when I peeked my head inside to check on her. She didn't stir as the light from the hallway crossed her bed. Seeing that she was okay, I shut the door and turned to my own bedroom.

I lay in bed and stared up at the ceiling. Since my phone was broken, I didn't have a clock next to me to check the time. No matter how hard I tried to fall asleep, I kept tossing and turning.

After what felt like hours, I kicked back the covers. I wrapped a robe around my body for warmth and tiptoed down the hall. Downstairs, I checked the clock above the TV. Only an hour had passed since I'd gone to bed. Why did it feel as if time was slowing down?

I was careful to not make any noise when I opened the front door and stepped out onto the porch. I sat on the lowest step and stared up into the sky while I held onto Marek's feather that hung around my neck. The nearby street lamp drowned out most of the stars, but I could still make out the brightest ones. I inhaled deeply and released the tension in my shoulders while I counted each star I could see. I knew I might not have much longer to enjoy all of this.

I was so preoccupied with staring up at the stars that I didn't notice a figure approaching from down the street. I only saw her when she started up the sidewalk toward my house. At first, I couldn't see who it was. Instinct told me to hurry to my feet and lock myself inside. Then a familiar voice came past the shadows.

"Hey, Ryn."

"Casey?" I pulled my robe tighter around me. "What are you doing here?"

Was she here to pick another fight? Something in the cautious way she approached me told me that wasn't the case.

"I was just out walking." I heard the lie in her voice.

"Really?" I eyed her skeptically.

"Okay," she caved. "I came to see you. Mind if I sit?"

I shook my head. As much as I hated Casey, I honestly didn't mind. I actually preferred her company over the empty step beside me. I caught a whiff of Casey's floral perfume as she sat next to me.

"Anyway, I saw you out here and thought…" She trailed off.

"Thought what?"

She shrugged. "It just looked like maybe you could use someone to talk to."

I raised my eyebrows. "And you thought you'd be the perfect person?"

Casey held her hands up in surrender. "Hey, if you don't want me around, I'll leave." She got to her feet.

"No," I said. "Stay."

Casey relaxed back onto the step. Neither of us said anything. But this was Casey. What was I supposed to say to her besides *'Get off my damn lawn'*?

"I hope you don't mind me being so forward about this," Casey said, "but I have to ask… What *happened* earlier?"

I frowned when I looked at her. "You really don't know?"

Innocence crossed her face. "I know you think I turned you in to the Davina Council for something, but you should know that I didn't."

I wasn't sure I believed Casey. If she hadn't followed us to Malcolm's and ratted us out, who did?

"Something big is going on here, isn't it?" Casey asked. "Something bigger than our recent battles with the demons."

"Believe me," I said, "you don't want to know."

"I heard part of the conversation earlier," Casey blurted. "You went to see Trenton's dad?"

My cheeks heated. "Why do you care?"

Casey paused for a moment, like she wasn't quite sure of the answer. "Because I want to help."

Casey sounded honest, like she'd be willing to go against the Davina Council and Grace with us if it meant doing the right thing. But still, it was *Casey*.

My brow furrowed. "You want to help *me*? I thought you'd be more willing to help the Davina Council fight their war."

Casey scoffed. "My dad is Eagle Valley's rep. He hardly wants me in Eagle Valley right now with things the way they are. He's not exactly interested in my help."

I could hear the disappointment in her voice.

A brief silence settled between us before I changed the subject. "Can I ask you something?"

"Sure, but I might not answer," Casey said with a light laugh.

I'd been burning with this question for days. "Did you know what Trenton was?"

Casey lips turned down. She definitely didn't like the question. "You mean, did I know he was half-demon? No, I had no clue. The whole thing… It feels like a betrayal."

I twisted the fabric of my robe in my hands. "You two were close, weren't you?"

Trenton had hinted that they'd been a little more than friends at one point or another.

Casey nodded. "It's hard not to get attached to your training partners. I just can't believe Trenton and Troy are both gone."

"I'm sorry," I whispered. I'd forgotten she'd lost so many people close to her.

Casey shook her head, like I shouldn't be sorry. "I just can't get what you said to me out of my head."

Confusion crossed my face. "What do you mean? What did I say?"

Casey shifted to face me. "You said that one day we'd be fighting together, and we'd be keeping score with how many people we lose. You counted Trenton as the first one lost."

I swallowed hard. I'd been in a state of high emotions when I'd said that. "I didn't mean—"

"You were right," Casey interrupted. "We've lost so many people recently, and that's more important than my petty drama."

I was shocked to hear her admit it. I always thought she had too much pride to ever say she was wrong.

"What's with the drama in the first place?" I asked. "I mean, why do you hate me?"

Casey laughed, like it was a long story she didn't want to get into, but she answered anyway. "You have everything I want."

"*What?*" I had nothing. I didn't have a real home or a father. Hell, I didn't even have half the boobs she had.

"You have Allie, and we used to be best friends," Casey pointed out. "And you have Marek. I always thought that we'd eventually end up together, but then you came along. I don't even have a chance anymore."

Good, I thought. *Marek's mine.*

"I'm going to be honest with you," Casey continued. "I'm a little jealous of how everyone fawned over you when school started. *I* used to be the center of attention at Galen."

I blushed, but I hoped she couldn't see it through the darkness. "People did not *fawn* over me."

"Maybe not to your face, but they sure talked about you a lot."

"What?" I squeaked. "I'm not even interesting."

Casey rolled her eyes. "Tell that to all the guys constantly checking out your ass."

I laughed. "Please. You're the one with the ass worth looking at."

Casey held back a smile. "True."

Silence filled the air between us, but I was surprised to find that it wasn't awkward. I felt almost comfortable sitting next to Casey with no obligation to speak up.

Casey eventually broke the silence. "So, you're not going to tell me what's really happening?"

I bit my lower lip. "Depends. Who sent you here to coerce an answer out of me? Grace? Your dad?"

"No one," she answered like she was offended by the accusation. "I swear."

I couldn't deny the honesty laced in Casey's tone. She was telling the truth. My internal bitch that hated Casey screamed for me to keep my mouth shut, to keep Casey in the dark.

But the rational part of me told me that if she was willing to side with us, she deserved to know the truth. The more Davina we got on our side, the better.

"Okay," I caved. "I'll tell you."

And I did. I told Casey about the portal and how Grace had given up hope and wanted to let the realms destroy each other. I told her the truth about why we'd gone to visit Malcolm and that we couldn't tell the Davina Council of our peace treaty before we had a chance to convince others of the truth.

"Why haven't you told everyone else yet?" Casey asked curiously.

I frowned. "Most of them will side with Grace no matter what she says. I don't want her locking me up before I have a chance to convince at least a few people of the truth."

"We have to destroy that portal," Casey stated. "No matter what it takes."

Finally, someone understood.

"I know," I said, "but Grace is the only one with enough power, and if she isn't willing to help—"

"Then we'll find another way." Casey sounded like she truly believed we could.

I smiled half-heartedly. It was hard to believe Casey was taking my side.

"Whatever we have to do," Casey said, "I'll stand behind you. I'm not going out of this world without a fight."

My jaw tightened. "Neither am I."

19

I woke early the next morning and rushed through a shower and breakfast before flying to Galen. Dawn was only just breaking, and the streets were quiet.

After talking with Casey last night, I came up with two options. The first was to convince Grace to help us, no matter what it took.

The second… well, I didn't want to think about that.

I soared over the mansion, and my eyes landed on a figure sitting on Galen's rooftop. Her massive white wings were spread out on either side of her, and she had her knees pulled to her chest.

Grace didn't look up when I landed beside her. She continued staring out toward the horizon, like she never heard me.

"Hello, Ryn," she said in a cold voice.

She didn't seem upset to see me. It was more like she was upset that the world hadn't collapsed yet.

I approached her slowly. "Mind if I sit?"

"Go ahead." She sounded like she didn't care either way.

The shingles were rough on my hands as I lowered myself beside her. "What are you doing?"

Grace waited a breath to answer. "Watching the sunrise. I'm not sure how many more we'll have."

I stared out toward the horizon with her. The sun was just beginning to peek up over the trees, casting a yellow glow across the sky.

"You have a thing for nature, don't you?" I asked.

Grace nodded lightly. "Being asleep all this time, I've missed it. You don't realize how much you miss the sun on your skin until it's gone."

I wrapped my arms around my knees and spoke softly. "Then why don't you want to save it?"

Grace finally pulled her gaze off the sky and looked at me. "I think it's time for a fresh start."

"For you, or for all of us?"

My words hung in the air. I didn't mean for the accusation to come out like a slap across the face. I was honestly curious to know what she was feeling. I had to understand her before I could change her mind.

"I don't expect you to understand," Grace finally said.

"I can try," I offered.

Grace pressed her lips together, as if fighting a harsh internal battle. She sighed heavily. "I was in love once."

What? When? I wanted to say, but I kept my mouth shut. I wasn't about to interrupt her.

"After the Davina created humans, we lived with them for many, many years. I fell in love with one of them." Grace swallowed hard. "We had children together, but neither him nor my children shared my immortality. I had to watch everyone I loved age and die."

My heart broke for her. I couldn't imagine losing Marek the way she lost her husband.

"I stayed behind as long as I could to watch my grandchildren and my great grandchildren grow," Grace continued. "But I couldn't keep watching them die while I continued to live. Many Davina had already returned to Vehena by then. But, by the time I was ready to go, only sixteen of us remained."

A lump rose in my throat. "Do you think Vehena is still out there somewhere?"

Grace shook her head. "I don't think our realm survived."

"And the Aedes realm?" I questioned.

She cleared her throat. "We begged the Aedes to return. We forced those who didn't comply, but obviously, some of them remained. We sealed off their realm. We feared the earth would die if they remained connected. Without the gods' powers to stabilize the realms they created, it just wasn't possible for them to naturally coexist."

"Then what happened?" I was completely engrossed in her story now.

"We watched over the world while we rested. The whole time, I thought I could save it again, but now…"

"Now?" I pressed.

Grace frowned. "Now that I've been awakened, I see how terrible it's truly become. There are so many people suffering. I've seen war after war break out. I've watched humans wipe out entire populations. It's so much worse seeing the cost of war up close. Not to mention poverty, abuse, rape… There's so much cruelty in this world."

I carefully considered Grace's words. She was right about this world being cruel. But she had to believe the world had more to offer.

Grace let out a long breath. "It wasn't always like this. The world used to be good. People actually cared about each other."

"And that's why you want to destroy it?" I asked lightly.

"Yes," she whispered. "I'm the last Original left, and I'm not sure I can do this alone."

"You're not alone, Grace," I pointed out.

She looked at me with uncertainty.

"You have the rest of the Davina behind you."

She dropped her gaze. "It's not the same."

Sympathy filled my heart. "Maybe if you try, you'll find more of what you've been missing."

Grace tilted her head in question. "What do you mean?"

I gestured to the horizon. "You missed the sunrise, and here you are, enjoying it. There are other wonderful things in this world that aren't worth giving up."

"Like?" She sounded skeptical.

"Like community, music, and art," I answered. "Like compassion and joy and love. As long as love still exists in our world, we can survive the rest of the bad stuff together."

The corners of Grace's lips turned down. I still hadn't convinced her.

"Don't give up, Grace," I begged. "There's still good in the people around us. You have the power to inspire and bring out the best in people. The world needs you, and even though it's hard, I believe you can make it a better place. You can show us how things used to be and teach us so much. Maybe our fresh start doesn't begin with death. Maybe it starts with *you.*"

She had to believe this was possible.

"You really think I can be this world's new beginning?" Grace asked.

I nodded. "I really do."

"But—"

"You can't doubt yourself, Grace," I interrupted. "This will only work if you believe in yourself."

Damn. Where was all this wisdom coming from?

Silence stretched between us for what felt like a full minute.

"You must believe there's still good in this world," I stated. "You mentioned the sunshine. Can't you think of at least one more thing?"

Grace contemplated my question for a moment. "I—I guess... laughter."

I smiled, and a small laugh escaped my lips. "Laughter's great. See? There's plenty of beauty in the world if you just look."

Grace bit her lip. "I haven't laughed since I last saw my family."

"Family is another wonderful thing to be grateful for," I pointed out. "Think of all the other families out there, watching the sunrise and laughing together."

Grace nodded.

"If you can't do it for us," I said, "do it for your family. Help us restore the world that was once their home."

Another stretch of silence followed.

Finally, Grace sighed. "Maybe there *are* some things in this world worth saving."

I'm getting through to her!

"Maybe..." Grace paused. "Maybe we *can* set things right again."

"Really?" I couldn't contain my excitement. "You'll help us, then?"

Grace smiled. "I'll help. For my family."

I squealed and leapt to my feet.

Grace stood and held her head high. "I will bring the Davina hope. Once the Davina arrive for training this morning, I will lead them to the portal so they can witness me close it."

Grace is going to help us! I felt more optimistic than I had in a long time.

I only hoped it wasn't too late.

My eyes scanned the clearing. There were so many Davina that some had to stand back in the trees. The crowd buzzed in curiosity. Davina stood on their toes and craned their necks to get a better look at the portal in front of us.

Marek placed his arm around my shoulder, and I leaned into him. Allie and Kyle stood beside us. Next to them, Fletcher stared at the rippling in the air in wonder. Nearby, Casey shot me a smile. Hope surged in my chest.

"Davina!" Grace called.

The clearing quieted.

"I have led you here today to reveal the truth. You have all heard the stories of the portals and know that danger would come to you if one opened." Grace gestured to the rippling air behind her. "This is a tear between the realms, a place in space where the earth and Malum have collided. Each passing day, the portal grows wider. *This* is what I have returned to protect you from."

Whispers spread throughout the crowd.

Can you believe it?

How long has it been here?

She's going to save us!

"What you don't know is the truth about *why* this portal threatens your home," Grace continued. "You fear a portal to

Malum because you fear the Aedes on the other side. The truth is, the realms themselves have the power to destroy each other."

A woman gasped behind me.

Grace continued her story, repeating what she'd told me about the Originals losing their home. She went on to tell the Davina about how they pushed the Aedes back to Malum and how they'd been protecting our realm ever since.

"And now," Grace said with her head held high, "I must sever this connection between the realms. I have brought you together to witness this historic event so that you can tell your children and your children's children that the Davina are the hope in this world. The Davina will live to see another day, and together, we will heal this world!"

Applause spread across the clearing. For the first time, I joined in on it.

Grace slowly spun toward the portal, and the crowd fell silent. My heart pounded in excitement, and sweat rose to my skin. The moment we'd all been waiting for was finally here. I couldn't believe I was a part of it.

Grace took a deep breath to collect herself. A moment later, purple essence shot from her hands. It was even more fantastic than the first time I saw it. Purple waves of essence danced across her skin and lit up her body as if she was made of electricity. She directed the essence in a massive stream straight into the portal. Her essence expanded inside of it, and the clearing became cast in a purple tint. It was so bright that I had to tear my gaze away from the portal. I looked to Marek instead.

Above us, the clouds darkened, and a crack of thunder vibrated throughout the clearing. I cursed under my breath.

"What?" Marek gazed down at me.

"A thunderstorm, right now?" I said.

Marek nodded toward Grace. "Can't you tell? Grace is doing it. Controlling the weather is one of the powers of the Originals."

My disappointment quickly turned to wonder. Suddenly, a thunderstorm didn't seem at all like a bad thing.

"I didn't know that." I almost had to shout to be heard over the wind that had picked up.

Leaves began to break off the trees, and I had to gather my hair at the nape of my neck to keep it from tangling. Marek rubbed his warm hand up and down my arm to help ward off the chill brought on by the strong winds. The portal changed from rippling to swirling.

This is it, I told myself. I rose to my toes to look over the shoulder of the Davina in front of me. *This is the moment we make history.*

In the blink of an eye, a lightning bolt came down from the sky and struck the portal. Before I could truly process it, the air expanded around us rapidly and slammed into my chest. The force blasted my body backward into the Davina behind me.

I gasped for breath and stared up at the sky. The dark clouds began to lighten.

Finally, the air returned to my lungs, and I sat up.

All around me, Davina had been knocked off their feet. Confusion crossed everyone's faces as they tried to piece together the events of the last few seconds. Had Grace done it? Had the portal been destroyed?

I looked back toward Grace, but my heart immediately sank. I expected the air to be clear where the portal once stood.

Instead, the rippling was more prominent than ever.

Grace propped herself up on her elbows. From where I lay in the grass, I could see the look on her face. Her eyes widened in horror as she stared at the air in front of her. Grace knew as well as I did that she hadn't destroyed it at all. She'd only widened it.

Our end was about to come sooner than we thought.

I rose to my feet and hurried over to Grace.

"Are you okay? What happened?" I asked in a rush.

Grace's eyes flickered between mine and the portal. She opened her mouth to speak, then closed it.

"Are you hurt?" I asked, frantically searching for any signs of injury.

Grace shook her head, but her eyes remained wide. "I—I waited too long. The portal is too powerful."

I helped her to her feet. "We can still fix this, can't we? Tell me we can save everyone."

The answer I dreaded fell from Grace's lips. "There is nothing we can do."

"But—" My throat felt like it was lined with sandpaper as it closed up around my words.

"I'm sorry," Grace whispered. "I let everyone down. I'm not the hero they thought I was. I am alone now without the other Originals' help. I am powerless to close this portal."

I felt the blood drain from my face.

Grace turned back toward the crowd of Davina. They were all getting to their feet now. She paused, as if the words were too painful to speak, but she pushed on… because she knew she had to.

Grace projected her voice into the crowd. "Please forgive me, Davina."

Tension grew in my jaw. This couldn't be it. Were we truly hopeless?

"You can try again," I encouraged.

Grace shook her head and spoke so only I could hear. "That was all my power."

It was true. We *were* hopeless. Grace had tried her hardest. And it wasn't enough.

"Try again!" I cried, desperately glancing between Grace and the portal.

Grace turned back to the crowd, like she hadn't heard me. "Our final hours have come. It's only a matter of time before this portal breaks open completely and your realm is destroyed. There's nothing more we can do. You should return home and say goodbye to your loved ones."

Murmurs spread across the crowd.

"No! Grace!" I screamed, but she ignored me.

People began moving, pushing other Davina out of the way. Screams filled the air as people were knocked to the ground. Others spread their wings and shot into the sky.

I paused to take in the chaos. Then the reality of what was truly happening sank in. I rushed over to Marek, but the crowd was in a panic. Someone rammed into me, and I fell to the ground.

"Marek!" I screamed. I could no longer see him through the crowd.

Strong hands gripped my arms and pulled me to my feet. I pushed away from whoever had ahold of me until I turned and saw it was Marek. I flung my arms around his neck.

"This can't be happening," I cried into his shoulder.

Marek wrapped me in a protective hug. "I can't believe it, either."

Allie and Kyle pushed through the panicked crowd and found us. I kept one arm around Marek's neck and placed the other over Allie's shoulder, pulling her in to me. Kyle wrapped an arm around her, and my friends and I joined in a group hug.

Davina continued to rush out of the clearing until we were the only group left.

Fletcher approached slowly. I dropped my hands from Marek and Allie. I didn't see Grace anywhere.

Fletcher's gaze dropped to the grass. "I'm sorry. I was wrong not to listen to you, Ryn. I put all my faith in Grace, and... and this happened."

Allie bit her lower lip. "Now what do we do?"

"We do as Grace said," Fletcher replied, as if he'd given up hope. "We say goodbye and enjoy what time we have left."

"There has to be *something* we can do," I insisted. "Grace could've tried harder!"

Fletcher shook his head. "I'm not sure if she could've. She used a lot of power, and it didn't work."

I wouldn't give up yet... not until I breathed my last breath.

There must be another way, I thought. The longer I stared at the portal, the more the conversation around me faded.

Eventually, the sound of Allie's voice calling my name pulled me from my thoughts. "Ryn. It's time to go."

"Actually," I replied, never taking my eyes off the portal. "I... I'd kind of like to be alone right now."

"Ryn." Marek sounded hurt. He reached out to take my hand.

I finally looked at him. "I'll be back to say goodbye," I promised.

Marek's expression softened. "Are you sure?"

"Yeah." I nodded.

My friends glanced between each other, like they weren't convinced it was safe to leave me alone. I didn't give them any other choice.

"I'll be fine," I assured them. "You guys go have fun. I'll be there soon."

"Come on," Marek encouraged my friends. "She has someone else to say goodbye to."

It occurred to me that Marek thought I wanted to stay to say goodbye to my dad.

My eyes followed my friends as they took flight. I waited until they were out of view before I turned back toward the portal. I stepped toward it cautiously.

A strange tingling filled my body and spread across my skin. It was the same kind of magic I felt when I was defending myself from Malcolm. I stopped just feet from the portal and focused on the new energy flowing through my body.

What was this strange feeling? Why hadn't anyone mentioned it before when they told me about essence?

Maybe because none of them had experienced it before. Maybe because, like Grace, I was different for some reason. I just didn't know why.

I closed my eyes and focused on this energy and brought it to the surface. When I felt it reach my fingertips, I finally peeled my eyes open. White mist rose out of my palm and swirled in the air above my hand.

I pictured the smoky essence forming into an orb like the fireballs I was so used to conjuring. To my surprise, the magic complied with my demands. In that moment, I realized I could direct and control this new essence.

I aimed my palms toward the ground and directed the essence away from me. It stretched out of my hands like a ghostly snake and slithered a foot above the ground. My eyes followed the wispy magic in awe, as if I wasn't the one controlling it.

I wasn't sure what I was doing when I sent the magic to wrap itself around the portal. It spread out above the portal like a force field. Through the strange fog, I saw the rippling in the air pause for a moment, but it was back a second later, as though the portal was flickering on and off.

Could this new, unexplored essence be the answer to saving us all?

It seems too easy.

Just as the thought crossed my mind, a powerful wave shot me backward. My body flew into the air, and I landed on my ass a good fifteen feet from the portal.

I cursed and rolled over, rubbing my tailbone. Finally, I lifted my gaze only to see that I hadn't done a damn thing to destroy the portal. The air rippling across the clearing continued.

But I had done something, I thought. The portal had flickered under the power of my essence.

This new essence couldn't help us like this, but maybe it could help us in another way. There was only one option left.

That can't be the only answer, I thought.

But it was. We'd run out of time.

My chest compressed, and my legs shook. Hot tears rushed from my eyes and fell into the grass. My fingers sank into the dirt as I curled my hands into tight fists and ripped the grass roots from the earth. It didn't help stifle the agony ripping through me.

"I don't… want… to die…" I whispered between heavy breaths.

But more than that, I didn't want my *friends* to die. I wouldn't let them.

I had to follow in my father's footsteps in order to save the earth. Whatever magic I had inside of me, it was strong enough to buy my friends more time.

It took all my willpower to blink away the tears and rise to my feet. I took one last glance at the portal. I didn't want to accept what was going to happen here, but I had to. Swallowing down the lump in my throat, I spread my wings and launched myself into the air.

I had to say goodbye before I made my sacrifice.

21

I landed on Marek's front lawn. The street was quiet, like everyone was in their own homes saying their goodbyes.

I approached the front door and raised my hand to knock, but before I could, the door swung open.

"Ryn!" Marek threw himself forward and pulled me into an embrace.

I laughed lightly, though it didn't feel like I should be laughing right now. "Did you miss me? I wasn't gone that long."

"I know," he said into my hair. "But I did miss you."

Marek let me go, and I stepped into the house.

I glanced around the empty living room. "Where is everyone?"

Marek raked his fingers through his untamed hair. "Allie and Kyle are with some people from school planning an end of the world party for tonight. I wanted to stay here so you knew where to find me."

"Where's your family?" I asked.

Marek dropped his gaze. "They've been gone for a couple of days. I told them to leave after the first attack on Eagle Valley. It was the best way to protect Bailey."

I inhaled a sharp breath. "And they just left you behind?"

Marek bit the inside of his cheek. "I didn't give them a choice."

Why did Marek always have to be so noble?

"I kind of regret it now," he said. "I'm not going to be able to say goodbye to them properly."

My heart broke for him.

"Marek." I stepped forward and placed my hands in his. "You don't have to be alone tonight. I'll stay with you." I rose to my toes and placed a kiss on the side of his face. "I promise."

A smile slowly touched his lips. "I'd like that."

Somehow, we ended up lying in Marek's bed, snacking on pretzels and fruit snacks.

I tossed an orange fruit snack toward the ceiling. Marek stretched away from me to catch it in his mouth. It bounced off his eyelid and onto my chest. I quickly snatched it up and popped it in my mouth with a smile. Marek frowned, like I was being unfair. I dug into my bag of fruit snacks for another, but they were all gone.

"Sorry," I told him as I tossed the wrapper on the floor.

Surprisingly, it was the first piece of trash I saw on his carpet. I wasn't sure what I expected to find in Marek's room, but I didn't think it'd be so clean. Weren't guys supposed to be sloppy pigs?

I still couldn't get over the fact that I was in Marek's room. This was where he slept and did his homework. He probably spent his nights lying in this very bed staring up at this very ceiling thinking of me. Or so I liked to believe.

His navy blue comforter smelled like him. I wanted to take it home and put it on *my* bed. Then I remembered I'd never sleep in my own bed again, so it didn't matter.

"What's wrong?" Marek asked, noticing my sudden change of mood.

I snuggled into his chest and ran my fingers along the veins in his arms. My fingers trailed up to his chest before settling on my feather that hung around his neck. "Do you really have to ask that question?"

Marek sighed. "No. I guess not."

"I just wish we could've had more time together," I said honestly.

Marek pulled both arms around me and squeezed me tight. "I know. I wasted so much of the short time we had."

I drew away from him just enough to look into his eyes. "What do you mean?"

"I shouldn't have let Fletcher persuade me to leave you alone and treat you as only a training partner," he replied. "I should've told you how I felt right away. I shouldn't have been so caught up in my duty and been so scared."

My brows came together. "You were scared? Of me?"

Marek's eyes fixed on the ceiling. "I wasn't scared of you. I was scared… to love you. I told you before, I have a hard time opening up to people."

I nodded. I remembered.

Marek took a long breath. "There's something you should know about me."

I immediately perked up.

Marek swallowed hard, but he didn't speak.

"What is it?" I prodded.

Marek fidgeted with the feather around my neck. "I'm sorry. It's just… hard. It's been so long since I talked about it."

I laced my fingers through his and waited for him to look at me. "You can tell me anything."

"I know," he whispered. "The thing is, my mother came from a Davina family, but she didn't develop Davina powers like her parents or sisters had. For all intents and purposes, she was entirely human."

I remained still, listening intently.

He paused for a beat. "She was resentful of her family and eventually cut herself off completely from them. That was before I was born. My dad was human, but he wasn't around much, so my mom was left to raise me by herself. She never mentioned her family, and I never asked."

Marek cleared his throat. "I always saw the Aedes, but my mom never acknowledged them. I told her about them once, but she made me swear I'd never mention them again. That should've been my first clue that something was out of the ordinary. Things didn't really change until I was ten."

"Change how?" I asked.

Marek continued slowly, like he wasn't sure how to tell the story. "We lived next to this big lake. There was one spot with a huge rock that stood about fifteen feet out of water. There was a rope swing tied to a tree above it. I never had any interest in jumping in. Honestly, I was afraid of heights as a kid. Seems ironic now, doesn't it?"

He didn't wait for an answer. "One day, I was walking alone on the rock. I slipped and fell, but I never touched the water. That was when I first discovered my wings."

I couldn't imagine what it was like for him to discover his wings on his own.

"I ran home and into the kitchen, thinking my mom would be able to help," Marek continued. "When she saw me, wings and all, she dropped the glass in her hand, and it shattered all over the floor. I tried to help her clean it up, but I cut my hand. It was so deep I thought we should go to the hospital, but she started yelling about how I wouldn't need stitches, that it was going to heal on its own because I was cursed. We started fighting. She mentioned the Davina, but obviously, I didn't know what she meant at the time."

Marek's tone softened. "To this day, I'm still not quite sure what we said to each other to make it escalate so far. But I remember how it ended."

His voice cracked, and I could already tell I wasn't going to like the rest of the story. "My mom reached out and grabbed one of my wings. With my wing in one hand and the piece of glass I cut myself on in the other, she sliced my wing clean off."

I inhaled an audible breath. I couldn't imagine what kind of monster would do that to anyone, let alone their own son. It made me sick to my stomach to think about.

Tension grew in Marek's voice as he recounted the memory. "After she removed the second one, she stood and looked down at me. She didn't even seem to care that I was all bloody and crying. She said, *'There, James. I've fixed it. You're not a Davina anymore.'*"

It took everything I had to hold the tears back. I couldn't believe what Marek had been through.

"Marek, I'm *so* sorry," I whispered. I didn't know what else to say. There just weren't words for this kind of thing.

A muscle popped in his jaw. "She actually thought she was doing me a favor. Can you believe it?"

I couldn't bear it any longer. Silent tears began to fall down my cheeks as I stared, horrified, at the man beside me. For a moment, I thought I could spot the helpless ten-year-old inside of him.

Marek's eyes grew red. "That was only the first time she did it."

"Oh my god." I couldn't help but say *something*, even if I couldn't find the right words to tell him how sorry I was he had to go through that.

"Do you think I'd have these scars if it only happened once?" Marek asked, clearly not expecting an answer. "It wasn't long before the cut on my hand had healed and my wings started growing back. I wish I knew at that time that I could make them go away, but I didn't. Even if I could, I'm not sure now if I would've been able to hide them while they were healing. Anyway, I wasn't able to hide them from my mother. They weren't even healed completely before she cut them off again, yelling about how she couldn't believe she'd given birth to a Davina. I tried to get her to explain, but she never would."

"She sounds horrible," I said in a whisper.

Marek's expression hardened. "She was. It was three more years of hell with her. She wouldn't let me outside, and every time my wings grew back, she'd *'take care of them for me.'*"

"I can't even imagine."

"Good," Marek said in a clipped tone. "I don't want you to. No one should have to live through what I did."

He sighed again. "As I grew up and grew stronger, I eventually started fighting back. Then one day, I guess my mom gave up. She packed up the car with a bag of my stuff and drove me here, to Eagle Valley. She dropped me off at my aunt's house with a note, and that was the last I saw of her."

Marek balled his hands into fists. "The bitch didn't even have the courage to walk up to the front door and talk to her sister."

I couldn't believe this had really happened to him. It sounded like something you only saw in horror movies, not something that happened in real life. No wonder Marek talked so much about the evil in the world.

Marek's tone shifted. "I'm not scared to love you anymore, Ryn.

You're the polar opposite of my mother. You're everything she wasn't. You're *good*."

"I am?" I couldn't stop the words from spilling out of my mouth.

"Yes," Marek said. "I knew it when Dorian attacked you in the woods. When I tried to kill him, you said there had to be an alternative. You said, '*You can't fight evil with evil.*'"

Did I really say that? I didn't remember.

Marek pushed a strand of hair from my eyes and spoke softly. "I knew there was something special about you because no one had ever thought of it like that with the demons. No one ever tried to make peace with them like you have. This whole time, you've been trying to see the good in them."

I blinked back tears. I hadn't realized how much of an impact I had on Marek.

"I wish I would've loved you fully when I had the chance," Marek said.

I pushed myself up to sit. "What do you mean, Marek? We still have time."

He shook his head. "I'll never be able to take you on a nice date or to a dance or anything."

I rose to my feet and pulled at his arm. "This isn't a date?"

Marek followed my lead and stood. I wrapped my arms around his neck, and his hands settled on my waist.

I swayed my body. "We can dance right here."

Marek closed his eyes and rested his forehead on mine. He shifted his weight from one foot to the other. "There isn't any music."

"We don't need music to dance," I whispered.

Marek didn't seem to agree with me. He began humming the soft, slow tune to one of my favorite songs while we swayed in a circle.

"How'd you know I loved that song?" I asked.

Marek shrugged. "I didn't."

His melodic voice filled my ears and warmed my heart. How had it taken me this long to learn Marek had an amazing voice?

His humming turned into lyrics.

We don't have to talk.

The tears don't have to fall.
Lie down next to me;
We'll forget about it all.

I melted into him, pressing my body against his while he sang to me. A wave of conflicting emotions consumed me. I was beyond happy to be here in his arms but devastated that it wasn't going to last. It wasn't fair that we didn't have more time. It wasn't fair that we weren't going to grow old together.

All we had was tonight. And my body burned to make these last few hours we had count.

My lips crashed into his, silencing the music coming from them. Marek tensed in surprise but quickly relaxed.

I gasped when he swept my feet out from under me and tossed me onto the bed. My body trembled as Marek climbed on top of me. My hands locked on the side of his face, and I guided his lips up to meet mine again.

Marek kissed me gently. Too gently.

I wanted more. I wanted him. Every last bit he'd share with me.

I ran my hands across his back. My fingers momentarily crossed the scars along his shoulder blades, and I was instantly reminded of the story he'd just told me. Now, more than ever, I wanted to share myself with him, to heal his emotional scars, to make everything better.

I knew I could never do that, but the least I could do was try. Because I loved him.

The thought struck me hard. Did I *love* Marek?

Yes, I told myself instantly.

There was no question about it. I loved this man with all my heart, and I'd be damned if I didn't show him just how much he meant to me.

I drew away from him.

Marek propped himself up and looked down at me. "What?"

I stared into his eyes, burning the beautiful blue color into my mind. By now, I'd memorized the pattern of brown flecks in his irises.

"I just wanted you to know I love you, Marek," I whispered.

A wide smile brightened his face. "I love you, too, Ryn."

I knew with every fiber of my being that he meant it. I flung my arms around him again and pulled him back onto me. Our bodies collided like magnets.

Marek's hands found the thin line of exposed skin between my tank top and jeans. He slowly inched his fingers up my body, exposing more and more skin.

Finally, they reached the fabric of my bra. Marek pulled away.

I bit my lower lip and stretched my arms above my head.

Marek hesitated. "I—I've never—"

"Me, either," I told him.

"Are you sure?" he asked gently.

"I'm sure," I whispered breathlessly.

My heart hammered against the inside of my chest as the cool air touched my skin. If at any moment I thought my heart might stop out of fear or excitement, it was nothing compared to this.

I was going to die of a heart attack for sure.

It didn't matter how I died, as long as I got to spend this night with Marek.

Somehow, tonight felt like my first—and my last—night on earth.

22

$\mathcal{M}$arek stirred next to me, waking me. I blinked my eyes open to see the morning sun filling the room and illuminating his gorgeous body beside me. Happiness filled my chest, but it quickly disappeared when reality hit me.

My time with Marek was already over.

The smile that had started creeping across my face faded before it had a chance to fully form. Tears welled in my eyes.

Marek suddenly became alert. "Ryn, what's wrong?"

"Nothing," I lied.

I sniffled involuntarily. Dammit. Now was *not* the time to let him see me cry.

"I'm just not ready to go home yet." I reluctantly peeled myself away from him and sat up in the bed. The comforter we'd been cuddling under covered my chest.

Marek touched my shoulder. "You don't have to go."

I reached for my clothes on the ground and began pulling them on. I didn't look at him; I couldn't bear to right now.

"I do have to go," I insisted. "I have to say goodbye to my mom."

I stood and reached down to slip my shoes on. Marek sat up straight. His exposed chest distracted me momentarily, but I forced my gaze back up to his eyes.

"Is that *all* you're going to do?" he asked.

"Mm-hmm," I lied again. How did he know me so well?

"You're sure?" he pressed.

I took a deep breath and forced the tears away. After last night, it didn't seem fair to lie to him. But I knew if I told him the truth, he'd only try to stop me.

"Yes." My chest compressed. I was a bad liar.

Marek frowned. He didn't believe me.

He pushed back the covers and reached for his jeans. "I'll come with you."

"No," I said, almost too quickly. "I'll be fine. I want to talk to my mom alone."

"Okay." It still didn't sound like he was buying it.

I bent over the bed to place one last kiss on his lips. I swallowed down the lump in my throat. It took everything I had to keep the tears from spilling over the edge. I didn't want to leave him.

My fingers remained on the side of his face a moment too long. I wanted to tell him I'd see him later, but that was one lie I couldn't bring myself to spit out.

Instead, I told him the truth. "I love you."

Before I left the room, the last words I'd ever hear Marek speak reached my ears.

"I love you, too."

I raked my fingers through my hair on the walk to my house. Maybe Mom would believe I was out flying all night and not getting tangled in Hot Stuff's sheets.

I laughed internally. She could probably sense the teenage hormones from here.

The old wooden porch steps creaked under my weight. I opened the front door and quietly stepped into the house.

Mom stood in the hallway with a hand on her hip and her lips pursed. She'd been waiting for me.

"Mom, please," I said. "Can we not fight right now?"

"Are you going to be honest with me?" She tapped her foot. She actually *tapped her foot*.

"Depends…" There were things I couldn't tell her.

"Where were you last night?" she demanded.

Okay, that one I *could* tell her. I just didn't *want* to.

"Don't play the silent game with me," she warned. "I already know where you were."

What the hell? How did she know?

"Then why are you asking?" I replied.

Ugh. Did we really need to do this *again*? All I wanted was to snuggle up next to my mom like I did when I was five. Now that I was facing her, I wasn't sure that would help anything.

"I was hoping you'd be honest with me," she said. "I know you went to that party with Allie last night."

Oh. Well, she could think that all she wanted. I wasn't going to correct her.

"Who told you that?" I asked, partially out of my own curiosity.

Mom crossed her arms. "When you didn't come home last night, I went over to Allie's to see if you were there. Her dad said you two were at some party. I just can't believe you never called or anything."

"My phone is broken," I reminded her.

"I know," she said, "but you could've used Allie's phone to call. I just wanted to hear your voice. I wanted to know you were all right and not lying in the ditch somewhere after being thrown off the back of your boyfriend's motorcycle."

I was so shocked that I actually took a step back. Mom wasn't *mad* at me. She was *worried*. And unfortunately for both of us, her worry manifested in anger. Why hadn't I realized that until now?

A silent beat passed between us. I couldn't take it any longer. I stepped toward her and flung my arms around her neck.

Mom's body tensed in surprise. "Kathryn, what's wrong?"

I shook my head. The truth was too overwhelming. "I'm just sorry. I never meant to make you worry."

Mom rubbed my back. "You're my daughter. I worry about you all the time."

"I'm okay, Mom. I promise." I drew away from her. "Did you have breakfast yet?"

She shook her head.

"What do you say we make some pancakes?" I suggested.

Mom brushed her fingers under her eyes. "I'd like that."

Life had been so hectic lately that I hadn't had many chances to cook. It was nice to be back in the kitchen again. I spent extra time getting the pancake recipe just right. I knew it would be the last meal I ever ate.

Mom pulled orange juice from the fridge and set the table while I cooked. Silence settled over the kitchen, but for the first time in a long time, there wasn't tension in the air between us.

"Hey, Mom," I said as I flipped a pancake.

She sat in one of the kitchen chairs. "Yeah?"

"I was just wondering... Which phase was your favorite?"

"Phase?" she asked with raised eyebrows.

"Yeah." I shrugged. "You know how you go through phases. Which one did you like best?"

"What do you mean, phases?" She looked completely baffled.

Oh my god. Mom didn't know she went through phases. Something about jumping from one hobby to the next must've seemed so natural to her. Maybe that was why she never encouraged me to choose something and stick with it.

"You really don't know?" I asked.

Mom shook her head.

"You're always changing hobbies," I pointed out. "You work through them almost as fast as we move. I thought you realized."

"Ooh," Mom said in realization. "I just like to try new things, Kathryn. There's nothing wrong with that."

I poured more pancake batter into the pan. "I never said there was anything wrong with it. I just wanted to know what you liked best."

Mom shrugged. "Well, I like all of my hobbies."

"Including sewing?" I tried to hide my teasing smile.

Mom rolled her eyes. "Okay, maybe not sewing. What were my other phases?"

I didn't even have to think about it to begin listing them. "Martial arts. Running. Photography. Scrapbooking. Cooking—"

"Cooking," Mom cut me off.

"Cooking?"

"Yeah, that one was my favorite."

Huh. Mine, too.

"Why?" I asked.

Mom stood and reached out for the spatula in my hand. "Because that's the one I had the most fun doing with you."

She flipped the pancake and smiled at me. I couldn't help but smile back.

It felt eerie sitting across from my mom and watching her eat without her knowing this was the last time she would ever see me.

After we finished and I helped her wash the dishes, Mom took a look at the clock on the stove. "What are your plans for the day?"

I hesitated. I had no choice but to lie to her. "I have some training scheduled for today."

My feet remained grounded in the kitchen. I wasn't ready to go. I didn't know what Mom would do without me. But I had to do it—for everyone else.

I pulled Mom into a hug. This time, she didn't seem surprised by it.

"I love you, Mom."

"I love you, too, Kathryn."

We embraced longer than any sane mother and daughter would've. I didn't care if it meant Mom could tell something was up. I just wanted to keep her in my arms and inhale the scent of her strawberry shampoo for hours. I wished I could make up for all the nights we fought instead of snuggled up in front of the TV like we should've.

I squeezed her tighter. "Mom, I want you to know that I admire you for how strong you are."

She opened her mouth to speak, but I didn't let her.

"Whatever happens with this Davina stuff, I want you to keep fighting no matter what," I said. "You always have to keep fighting."

"I wish you didn't have to do this," Mom whispered.

For a moment, I thought she might know what I was planning, but then I realized she meant she wished I didn't have to fight with the Davina. She didn't want to lose me like she had my father.

"I'm sorry."

Those two simple words held so much more meaning than she could possibly know.

～

Nerves hit my stomach when I stepped out of the house. Cool air touched my skin, and a thin layer of clouds covered the sky. It was starting to feel and smell like autumn.

It was almost time.

Almost.

There was still one more person I had to see.

I crossed my lawn and headed up Allie's front porch steps. I held my breath and knocked on the door. I wasn't sure if I was ready to see Allie for the last time. Saying goodbye to her would be harder than saying goodbye to my mom—or even Marek.

No answer came, and I wasn't sure if I was upset or relieved. I was just about to knock again when the sound of voices reached my ears.

Allie and Kyle.

I followed the sound of their voices around the side of the house and stopped when I finally saw them. They swayed in the swings on Allie's old playset with their backs to me. They moved back and forth in sync with their fingers entwined.

I had the sudden urge to step back around the corner of the house unseen. I couldn't ruin their moment. I pressed my body against the vinyl siding.

"I'm not ready for this, Kyle." Allie's voice traveled through the light breeze toward me. "I've dreamt of becoming a Protector my whole life. I never imagined I wouldn't make it that far."

"I know," Kyle's deep voice replied.

"There are other things, too," Allie said in disappointment. "I always thought I'd have kids and that we'd—"

Her words stopped in their tracks.

"We'd what?" Kyle asked.

Allie tucked her dark hair behind her ear. "I can't believe I'm saying this, but I always thought that one day we'd get together and... I always pictured us growing old together."

Kyle dug his heels into the dirt and stopped swaying. I expected him to say something to her, but instead, he reached out for her and caught her mid-swing. She gasped in surprise, but before she had a chance to say anything, Kyle's lips were on hers.

I resisted the urge to start cheering from where I hid. *Finally* they'd gotten together! I was so happy for Allie that it was almost as if her own happiness filled my heart.

I forced my gaze off the happy couple and returned around the side of the house. It wasn't fair of me to watch their happy moment unfold without their consent.

"Allie," I whispered under my breath. She'd never hear my words, but for a moment, it felt as if the wind could carry them over to her for me. "I can't believe we've only been friends for a few months. It feels like a lifetime."

I took a deep breath. It felt silly to talk out loud to myself, but I needed to say these words, even if she'd never receive the message. "I wish we'd met sooner and had more time together. I wish Marek and I could've grown old alongside you and Kyle. I wish… I wish for a lot of things, but honestly, I'm just glad I got the time with you that I did. You're my best friend, Allie. And I hope that what I'm about to do gives you the chance to live your dreams—for a few more years, anyway."

I swallowed down the lump in my throat. "I love you, Allie."

I couldn't bear to look back. If I did, I might not be able to bring myself to leave.

And so, I flexed my shoulders and leapt into the air.

I was finally ready to make my sacrifice.

23

The town was quiet today as I flew above it. It was like Eagle Valley itself had given up hope with the rest of the Davina.

Someone see me. Stop me, I begged internally.

No one did.

An audible breath passed my lips when I landed in the clearing and looked up at the portal. The ripples in the air had grown so large that they looked like waves. The trees behind the portal were so distorted that it was impossible to make them out.

As I stepped forward, a strange breeze passed across my arms. It was warmer than the air around me, but something about it chilled me to the bone. The hairs on my arms stood, and a burnt scent hung in the air. It wasn't the pleasant scent of a burning fire during winter. It was more like the smell of a hot car or burnt rubber—the scent that told you to stop whatever the hell you were doing before something exploded.

Could that strange air be coming from the portal? From Malum?

I stopped two yards from the portal and steadied myself. My head swirled as I stared into the distorted air. I closed my eyes so it wouldn't distract me and called upon my white wispy essence. I felt it rise from my toes and up into my shoulders. It flowed smoothly down my arms, reaching my elbows, then my wrists.

Before it reached my fingertips, something hard slammed into my side. The air left my lungs as I crashed to the ground. I didn't have time to catch myself. I landed on my shoulder before the side of my head smacked into the ground.

I opened my eyes to try to make sense of what had just happened, but the sky swam above me. Had I been sucked into the portal?

No. Some asshole had tackled me.

Anthony Lucas's face came into view above me.

Yep. Some asshole.

"What the—?" I started to say.

Before I could get the words out, Anthony's shiny black shoe connected with my face.

Everything went black.

~

Deep voices met my ears, but I couldn't focus long enough to make out what they were saying. My head lolled to the side.

Where was I? Was I moving? It felt like my body was bouncing. Over potholes?

No. I was being carried. And we were descending a flight of steps.

I gathered what strength I had and peeled my eyes open. Wherever I was, it was dark. I could just barely make out Anthony's face above me. We reached the bottom of the steps, and I felt Anthony drop me onto a cold, hard surface. His footsteps retreated and then stopped.

The sound of a door swinging shut was like an alarm to my ears. Suddenly, I was alert. I shot up to a sitting position. Bad idea. My head pounded like a bass drum.

I blinked several times, and my eyes finally adjusted to the darkness. I looked up to see a flight of wooden stairs above me. They rose to meet a dark wood door. A click sounded.

I scrambled to my feet and scurried up the stairs. "Hey!" I shouted as I wrenched on the door handle. "You can't just leave me here!"

I pounded my fists against the door, but no answer came. My

heart dropped from my chest, down the stairs, and straight onto the concrete floor below me. At least, it felt like it.

I screamed in frustration as I twisted on the door knob and kicked the door. My foot throbbed now, and the screaming didn't help my headache.

I stopped abruptly and quieted, though my chest continued to heave as I inhaled deep breaths. My eyes scanned the stairwell I stood in. It looked familiar. I descended several steps and looked out into the vast room they'd locked me in. A low ceiling was held up by support pillars, and small windows lining the top of the walls allowed a slight amount of light to filter in. Across the room, I spotted the old foam targets we used for training in the corner.

I was in the basement of Galen High School.

And somehow, the Davina Council had found time to switch the door knob so it locked from the outside.

There must be a way out. I had to find it and get back to the portal before it destroyed us all.

I went with my first instinct. I turned back to the door and conjured a white fireball, aiming it toward the new door knob. The fireball smashed into the door and exploded like a firecracker. When I stepped forward to see if it'd done any damage, the door looked perfectly fine. I cursed under my breath.

"It's no use," a voice said.

I jumped back and almost tripped down the stairs. I caught myself and peered across the dark room.

"I thought I was alone," I said, like that would explain my madness. "Who's there?"

A feminine voice cleared her throat. The last person I expected to see stepped out of the shadows and into the dim light.

"Casey?" I asked in surprise.

Of course it's Casey, you dimwit.

She stood just feet away from me. I could make out her features clear as day. Bags had settled beneath her eyes, and her lips were chapped. Her face was bare of makeup.

"How long have you been down here?" I asked. "You look like hell."

Casey sighed and sank onto one of the lower steps. "I've been down here since last night."

"Why would they—?"

"I followed my dad and tried eavesdropping on their council meeting." Casey stared forward into the darkness without looking at me. "Grace wanted the council to surround the portal and keep an eye on it."

In other words, Grace didn't want me trying anything. After yesterday's catastrophe, she still believed the world needed to end.

"So Grace changed her mind again," I said under my breath as I lowered myself beside Casey.

"I was going to go find you and tell you before they had a chance to get out there. I thought maybe you had an idea to save us." Casey eyed me curiously. "You do have an idea, don't you?"

I bit my lip. "I have something worth trying. What happened after you overheard the council?"

Casey's expression hardened. "Anthony was there—like, right behind me—watching me eavesdrop. He grabbed me by the hair and dragged me down here."

I gasped. *That dick!*

"He said he couldn't let me out with all the stuff I heard."

I crossed my arms—and not just because it was chilly down here. "So, Grace has them all wrapped around her little finger?"

Obviously.

Casey pursed her lips and nodded. "I've spent all night trying to get out of here to warn you they'd be there. I figured you'd try to go back, but nothing I've done has worked."

"Lovely," I said flatly. "What are we supposed to do? Just sit around and wait for the realms to collapse?"

Casey dropped her gaze. "What other choice do we have? Unless you have your phone on you to call for help. They took mine."

I shook my head and got to my feet. "No, I don't, but we can't just give up."

Casey chewed on her thumb nail. "What are we supposed to do?"

"I don't know," I sighed.

The sound of a key in the door reached my ears. My head snapped in the direction of the door.

"Maybe we can seduce this one to let us out," I whispered under my breath.

Casey's eyes fell on the man who opened the door. "Uh, sorry, but that's not going to work on him."

Mr. Harris took one look at Casey and rushed down the steps. Casey got to her feet just as he reached her. He wrapped her in a hug. A moment later, the door slammed shut, making me jump. I heard the audible click of the lock slipping back into place.

"Dad!" Casey cried. "What are you doing here? I thought the Davina Council wouldn't trust you—"

"They don't," he interrupted.

I stood there awkwardly, watching this family reunion I wasn't a part of.

Mr. Harris drew away from Casey. "I convinced them to let me visit you. I wanted to stay with you until the end."

Casey shook her head. "No, Dad. You can't give up! You have to get us out of here."

Mr. Harris looked hopeless. "I—I can't."

"Can't? Or won't? You still agree with Grace, don't you?" Casey stepped away from him, as if she'd been betrayed.

Mr. Harris rubbed his eyes, like this had all become too much for him. "Grace has watched the history of the world. She knows things the rest of us don't."

"And you're just blindly following her!" Casey yelled, taking another step away from him.

Mr. Harris frowned. "I don't understand why you don't have any faith in her. I thought I raised you differently."

I inched away into the shadows. This didn't seem like the kind of family fight I should be involved in.

"You *raised* me to think logically," Casey bit back. "I can think for myself, and I don't think Grace's plan is a good one."

"Our essence will survive," Mr. Harris pointed out, but it sounded more like he was trying to convince himself of that.

Casey shook her head. "You don't know that. Our essence lives inside the earth. If it's destroyed—"

"I know." Her dad cut her off. He dropped his shoulders and took a long breath before speaking again. "I know. Some of the councilmembers have their doubts. But Casey, there's nothing we can do."

"Then what is Grace protecting the portal from?" Casey asked.

"I—" Mr. Harris stopped mid-breath, like he hadn't considered the question until now.

"Ryn has a plan." Casey's eyes traveled over to me.

Mr. Harris's gaze followed.

I shifted my weight uncomfortably between my feet.

Mr. Harris sighed. "Even if I wanted to let you go, they locked me down here with you."

"Then at least help us find a way to escape," Casey begged.

Mr. Harris's jaw tensed. "There *is* one thing we can try."

Casey and her dad exchanged a look, as if they shared some telepathic conversation I wasn't a part of.

"What?" I asked. "How are we going to escape?"

"Just watch." Casey smirked. "And be ready to run." She turned back to her dad and erupted in anger. "What are you doing here? I don't want to see you!"

I recoiled in shock.

"I came because I love you." Mr. Harris's voice rose.

Oh. They were putting on a show.

Casey screamed again. "It's too late for that! You let them throw me down here. I was hungry and thirsty and scared!"

Okay, maybe it wasn't *all* for show.

Mr. Harris huffed and turned back up the stairs. His fists pounded on the door. "Let me out, Harold! I've changed my mind. My daughter is being a *brat*, and I have better ways to spend my time."

"No can do," came a voice on the other side of the door.

"What are you talking about?" Mr. Harris demanded. "I told you to let me out!"

"Boss said I'm not to open this door for anyone," Harold replied, sounding uncertain.

"Surely Grace didn't mean me," Mr. Harris snarled. "I came down here voluntarily."

Harold didn't answer.

"Harold!" Mr. Harris shouted with a tone of authority. "The world is ending, and I have better people to say goodbye to than an ungrateful teenager."

I leaned over and whispered to Casey. "Does he really think you're ungrateful?"

She shrugged. "Probably, but if he saves our lives, he can apologize later." She raised her voice and projected it up the stairwell. "Seriously, Harold. Let my dad go. I'd rather die down here alone!" She threw in a couple of heavy sobs for show.

Damn. What was this girl doing training to become a Protector? She should've been training to become an actress.

"Where are the girls?" Harold called through the door.

"At the bottom of the stairs," Mr. Harris answered. "Why?"

"Everyone step back," Harold instructed. "I want the girls as far away from the door as possible."

Mr. Harris winked over his shoulder. "Okay," he answered. "You can open the door now."

My knees shook in anticipation. I heard the lock on the other side of the door click. Slowly, the door handle twisted.

Mr. Harris sprung straight into action. He rammed his shoulder into the door, knocking the guy on the other side of it down. Mr. Harris shot two fireballs straight into Harold's chest. Harold crumbled to the ground.

Ouch.

"Come on," Mr. Harris hissed, gesturing for us to follow him.

Casey and I rushed up the stairs side-by-side. Her dad placed his index finger over his lips and stepped over Harold's still body. We followed behind him, careful not to make too much noise.

"This way," he whispered, leading us to the back of the building. His eyes darted around the hall.

My heart slammed against my rib cage. *They're going to catch us. There's no time. We're not going to make it out of here alive.*

Mr. Harris carefully looked around the corner before gesturing that it was safe. The sound I'd been dreading reached my ears when we turned down the hall. A door creaked open, and then—

"Hey!" someone shouted. "What are you—?"

My heart leapt in my chest.

Mr. Harris turned around, almost ramming into us. "Go! I'll hold them off."

Casey's feet moved under her, but she hesitated. "But, Dad—"

"No arguing!" he roared. "Run!"

24

*T*wo… Three… Five… I couldn't keep track of how many pairs of footsteps followed behind us. Shouts echoed down the hall as more Davina Council members joined in on the chase.

What are they all doing here? I thought. *They should be saying goodbye to their loved ones, not hanging out at the school.*

Maybe they didn't have loved ones. That, or their duty to Grace came first. I wasn't interested in sticking around to find out which it was.

I heard the familiar sound of essence exploding against the ground, but I didn't look back to see what was going on. Casey and I turned down another hall, and I instantly felt my body being jerked to the side.

"In here," Casey hissed as she dragged me along behind her.

Casey and I raced through the library, the dark mahogany bookcases blurring together as we sped by. She led me down a narrow hallway and through another door. She quickly swung it shut behind us and secured the lock.

I glanced around while trying to catch my breath. White overwhelmed my senses—white walls, white tile, a white toilet, and a white sink. There was even a white radiator in the corner of the small bathroom.

Casey cursed under her breath. "We shouldn't have left my dad out there. The Davina Council is going to kill him."

I caught Casey before she could reach the door. "You don't know that. They'll probably just lock him up again."

Casey struggled out of my grasp.

"Stop it!" I whisper-screamed. "We have no chance of saving him if we get caught, too."

Casey relaxed slightly. "Then we have to get out of here before they find us."

She quickly crossed the bathroom and reached for the lock on the window. She grunted as she tried to push it open. I hurried over to help her. We pushed up on the window together, but even with all our strength, it didn't slide open.

"The damn thing's been painted shut." Casey turned away from it and sank down onto the closed toilet lid. I noticed her knees were visibly shaking. "We'll wait it out for a couple of minutes. Just to make sure."

I raised my eyebrows. "And if they find us?"

"We'll break the window." She paused for a moment. "So, what's your plan?"

It felt awkward to open up to Casey, but I knew she was on my side. Still, I struggled to swallow my pride and admit it.

I leaned against the window sill. "I discovered this… strange essence. I don't know if I'm the only one who has it, but it seems powerful enough to affect the portal. I already tried it, and it did something, but it wasn't enough."

Casey raised her eyebrows like she didn't believe me. "A new kind of essence?"

I nodded and held my hand out. I narrowed my eyes at my palm, concentrating hard. It was like the first time I discovered essence and couldn't conjure a basic fireball to save my life. I knew I had it in me, but I couldn't seem to access it at will. I concentrated harder and harder, until I thought my head might explode from the tension. Casey must've thought for sure I was talking shit. The tingling sensation in my body grew, until finally, white smoke escaped my fingertips and swirled into an orb above my palm.

Casey straightened and eyed the essence in wonder. Slowly, she reached out with her index finger, but before she touched it, she jerked away like she'd been shocked.

"Have you ever seen anything like it?" I asked.

She shook her head, never taking her eyes off the orb. "What is it?"

I shrugged and let the essence dissipate. Holding it there for that long was draining. "I don't know. I could only do it after I woke Grace."

Casey never took her eyes off my hand, even though the essence wasn't there anymore. "You're sure it's essence?"

I furrowed my brow. "What else would it be? It feels like essence. Just... different."

"What do you mean, different?"

I didn't have a chance to answer. I fell silent the moment male voices met my ears.

"You go that way," one of them called to the other.

Casey and I both held our breath as footsteps passed by the door we hid behind. We breathed a collective sigh of relief when the footsteps continued down the hall.

Casey turned her eyes back to me. "What are you going to do with this new essence?"

I bit my lower lip. I didn't know how it'd sound to admit the rest out loud. Probably crazy. Maybe I was crazy.

I took a breath. "I thought if I entered the portal and used the essence inside it, it might collapse—even partially—and buy everyone a little more time."

"No." Casey shook her head in protest.

"What do you mean, no?" The surface of my skin heated involuntarily. I had the urge to throw another fireball at Casey's face when she blatantly dismissed my plan, but I had to remind myself that we were on the same side. It was still weird to me.

"You're talking about *killing* yourself!" Casey hissed.

Her words should've tore at my heart. I should've felt sick to my stomach and begged her to talk me out of it. Instead, I felt a strange sense of peace wash over me.

"Yes, I am," I answered.

"You can't!" she objected under her breath.

I raised an eyebrow. "Do you have a better plan?"

Her shoulders fell. "No. But even if your plan worked, you can't exactly go sacrificing yourself when the Davina Council is watching the portal."

"Maybe you can distract them," I suggested.

She looked at me with an unamused expression. "How?"

"I don't know." I shrugged. "Strip naked and run around the clearing."

Casey rolled her eyes.

"It's the end of the world," I pointed out. "There's no time to be modest."

"You just want to watch me make a fool out of myself," she said lightheartedly.

I smirked. "Maybe."

Casey turned serious again. "Let's just take a breath, and we'll figure something else out."

I shook my head. "We don't have time."

"We don't know how much time we have," Casey pointed out. "It could be days or—"

"—or hours," I finished for her. "Let's get out of here, and then we'll figure out how to distract the Davina Council."

Casey frowned. "You're going to do this with or without my help, aren't you?"

I nodded.

Casey hesitated but eventually rose to her feet. Slowly, she unlocked the door and peered out into the hall.

"It's clear," she whispered.

We slipped out of the library unnoticed, but my footsteps sounded like cannons going off. I was sure I'd alert the Davina Council. The back door of the school stood at the end of the hall. We were so close, but it felt like a mile away.

Almost there.

Someone was going to jump out and get us. I knew it.

Except, by some miracle, we reached the end of the hall and broke out into the cool autumn air without being spotted.

"Ryn!" a voice shouted my name.

Shit. I spoke too soon.

Wait… no. I knew that voice. I stopped, and Casey skidded to a halt beside me.

Marek jogged down the steps behind the school to catch up with us. Allie and Kyle followed behind him.

"Marek, I—" I started.

"Where have you been?" Concern was etched into his tone. He reached for my hands and inspected my arms and then my face, searching for signs of injury. "You said you'd be back. We've been searching everywhere for you."

I inhaled a heavy breath. "Marek, I'm sorry. I—"

"We don't have time for this," Casey said in a rush.

I followed her gaze to see two Davina Council members in one of the windows pointing across the lawn at us. They quickly turned away from the window and rushed out of the room.

"They're coming!" Casey cried.

Marek glanced over his shoulder.

"Who?" Allie demanded. "What's going on?"

I didn't have time to explain. "We need to get out of here—now."

Casey spread her wings beside me, and I quickly followed. I heard Marek's, Allie's, and Kyle's wings flapping behind me. I pumped my wings harder and pushed ahead of Casey. I wasn't sure where I was going until I spotted a rocky hilltop and dove for it.

I landed on the granite without stumbling. *Finally* someone saw me land like a proper Davina.

I paced along the top of the hill. I wasn't sure why I brought everyone here. This was *mine and Marek's* hilltop. Marek landed next to me, and without thinking, I fell into his arms.

Marek squeezed me but drew away far too soon. "Ryn, what's happening?"

"I wanted to—I tried to—the Davina Council—" I couldn't manage to choke out the words.

"Take a deep breath," Kyle suggested. He looked genuinely concerned for me.

"Maybe you should sit down," Allie said.

I gladly complied with her invitation and sank to the ground. Marek knelt beside me.

Casey placed her hands on her hips and tried to catch her breath. "The Davina Council locked Ryn and me in the basement. They don't want anyone trying anything with the portal."

Marek's head snapped in Casey's direction. "What were you trying to do with the portal?"

Casey huffed. "It wasn't me. It was Ryn."

"Casey, don't—" I started, but the words were already flying out of her mouth.

"She's going to sacrifice herself to buy us time."

"No!" Marek objected at the same time Allie's hands shot over her mouth. Kyle stared at me speechlessly from beside her.

"Casey's lying," Marek accused.

She frowned. "I wish I was."

"You can't!" Marek roared. He shot to his feet and paced in front of me. He raked his hands through his hair, and his face contorted in pain.

"Marek, I—" I started.

"You were just going to leave me?" he shouted, cutting me off. "You lied to me!"

"I had to!" I cried. "I knew you'd try to stop me. Marek, if I don't do this, everyone will die. The least I can do is give the rest of you a chance."

"If you do this, *you'll* die!" Marek growled.

I dropped my gaze. My voice came out as only a whisper. "I know that, and…"

Marek stopped pacing and lowered himself to sit beside me on the ground. His fingers grazed the side of my face, and I was forced to look at him. His tone softened. "If you're going to die, we're going to die together."

He doesn't mean that, I told myself.

I spoke softly. "You're the one who said you wouldn't let my father's death be in vain. This is the only way."

"But it won't work," Allie protested.

I looked up to see a deeply hurt expression settled on her face.

"You don't have the Power of Grace anymore," Allie pointed out. "Your essence isn't strong enough."

"I have something else, though," I said. "Remember?"

Kyle glanced to Allie in uncertainty. "You said you felt something when Malcolm kidnapped you, but Ryn, you couldn't even control it when you tried to show us."

"It's still inside of me," I argued.

"It doesn't matter!" Allie burst. "You can't sacrifice yourself!"

"Why not?" I asked. "My dad bought us eighteen years. I can buy the rest of you a few more. Maybe it'll give you enough time to figure out a permanent solution."

"We can't lose you!" Allie declared.

Marek's eyes glistened with tears. "Allie's right. We can't lose you." He took my hand in his and brought it to his lips. "*I* can't lose you."

Didn't they realize they'd lose me either way?

"See?" Casey said. "I'm not the only one who thinks you shouldn't sacrifice yourself."

"Maybe there's something else we can do," Allie suggested.

"Like what?" Casey asked.

Allie looked uncertain. "What if we turned to Malcolm?"

Kyle eyed Allie like she was crazy. "What's that going to accomplish?"

Allie bit her lower lip. "Maybe the Aedes have some insight. Maybe they can help."

I could hardly believe she was the one suggesting it. All this time, Allie had been lecturing me about how evil the Aedes were. Now she wanted to side with them?

I thought about how Malcolm had mentioned that the Davina never listened to the Aedes. Maybe they had stories—knowledge— about their history they never shared. Maybe they *did* have something we could use against the portal, against Grace.

I straightened. "I think we should do it. At the very least, he and the other Aedes might be able to help us reach the portal before it's too late."

~

The air felt eerie and cold when we arrived at Malcolm's house. I knew we'd established a truce, but I still approached the house with caution.

"Malcolm?" I called out, peering into the slit between the curtains.

No response.

"Malcolm?" I raised my voice and entered the house. "Are you here?"

I peeked into the dark living room while Marek checked the kitchen. Kyle headed to the end of the hall and poked his head into a bedroom, and Allie followed Casey upstairs. They returned a minute later, and we all exchanged a look of disappointment.

My shoulders dropped. We didn't have time for this. "He said this is where I could find him if I needed to."

"Maybe he was lying," Kyle theorized.

"He wasn't," I said with certainty.

"Well, he is a de—" Kyle started.

"An Aedes?" The sound of Malcolm's voice cut Kyle off before he could finish the insult.

I whirled around to see Malcolm standing in the front doorway with his hood down.

The look Malcolm gave Kyle could've cut glass. "I thought we had a truce."

"We do," I assured him. "And we need your help."

I quickly explained to Malcolm what was going on. His expression softened the more I revealed.

"Can you help us?" I asked hopefully.

Malcolm pressed his lips into a thin line. "There might be something I can do, but it's a long shot."

Without another word, Malcolm turned from the doorway. Then he spread his dark, feathery wings and gestured for us to follow him.

25

e landed on the gravel outside of an old building at the edge of the small town Malcolm lived near. Trees surrounded the property, but I noticed a cluster of run-down houses up the road.

The building in front of us was at least six times bigger than my house, and most of the white paint had chipped away. The concrete walkway leading to the front doors heaved at odd angles and had thick grass growing up between each slab. The sidewalk twisted around the side of the building and ended at a small cemetery. I lifted my gaze to view the bell tower above us.

I noted how strange it was that demons were taking refuge in an old church. Except, they weren't demons any more than we were angels.

I took a cautious step forward. Malcolm approached the church like he was completely comfortable here, but the twisted trees above my head and the cemetery just a stone's throw away gave me the creeps.

"Come on," Malcolm hissed.

I quickened my paced and followed behind him. He didn't stop at the front doors like I expected him to. Instead, he headed around the side of the church.

"We settled here after the last attack," Malcolm explained. "We needed somewhere the Davina couldn't see us from the sky, and this seemed like the least likely place you'd look for us. It's been abandoned for decades. There's a broken window in the back you can get through."

Tall windows lined the side of the building. Most had been covered by wood from the inside. Malcolm stopped at the one on the end and gestured for us to follow. He phased straight through the wall as if he were a ghost. The window had been broken in the lower right-hand corner, but the opening was hardly enough to crawl through.

Marek apparently thought the same thing. "Stand back," he warned.

I jumped aside just in time for him to swing a fistful of rock at the remaining half of the window, shattering it.

We all stared at him in shock.

Marek shrugged. "It was already broken." He turned back to the window and hoisted himself up and through it. I followed behind him.

"Careful," Marek's voice came through the darkness.

I stepped onto a wooden floor in a large room with a high vaulted ceiling. I expected to find rows of pews lined up throughout the chapel, but they'd all been removed. Glass crunched under my feet, and a pile of beer bottles and cigarette butts lay just a few feet away.

Then there were the eyes. Hundreds of pairs of Aedes eyes stared back at us. They all had their hoods down, like they always wore them like this in private. Despite their thin, pale features, I felt like I was looking into the faces of humans—not the evil creatures the Davina made them out to be.

Silence fell over the church. The only sound I heard was the brush of Kyle's jeans against the window frame as he crawled into the chapel.

"*Davina*," one of the closest Aedes hissed through clenched teeth.

As soon as he said it, three of the Aedes lunged for Marek and me. I instinctively yelped and jumped backward.

Malcolm raised a hand, stopping the Aedes in their tracks. "Please don't alarm our guests."

"Guests?" the first Aedes snarled.

Malcolm nodded. "Yes, Rob. These Davina are my guests."

"And you've shown them where we're hiding!" Rob yelled back.

Malcolm shook his head but replied calmly. "I already told you we've negotiated peace with a small group of Davina. These are the Davina seeking an alliance with us, and they've come to ask for our help."

"They're just kids!" someone shouted.

"Why would we help them?" someone else asked at the same time.

"QUIET!" Malcolm roared.

His voice was so commanding that I stumbled backward into Allie's feet. There was a reason these people respected him.

"Just listen to them," Malcolm instructed.

Malcolm looked to me, and I realized it was my turn to speak. I warily stepped forward, making sure to keep enough distance between myself and the closest Aedes in case anyone felt like attacking me.

"Look." My voice came out stronger than I felt. "I know you want to see the portal open. Malcolm told me that you'd like to return to Malum, but it's not possible."

Whispers traveled around the room.

"Shut it!" Malcolm snapped.

The church fell silent again.

"There's a reason the Davina closed the portals long ago," I explained. "It's because the realms are a threat to one another. If the portal opens all the way, the realms will collide. They'll destroy each other. It's why the Davina sealed off the portals in the first place."

"She's lying," someone accused.

"I don't think she is," Malcolm replied.

Several curious gazes met mine, but most Aedes narrowed their black eyes at me like they didn't believe me.

"The Davina no longer have the power to close the portal and protect our realm," I concluded. "We've come to ask if the Aedes have any ideas how to stop this."

"How would we know?" Rob snarled.

I tried to keep an even tone without snapping back at him. Now was *not* the time to get into an argument. "We thought maybe you'd heard stories that the Davina hadn't."

"Why should we listen to her?" a woman asked Malcolm. "We should get to the portal and cross over to Malum as soon as possible!"

Echoes of agreement spread throughout the church.

"There's no guarantee you'd survive," I argued. "The realms could destroy each other before the portal opened enough to allow you to pass through. I know it's hard to view the earth as your home when you've been treated the way you have your whole life, but my hope is to help you make a home here if we survive this together."

"But you're a Davina," Rob pointed out. "Davina have never helped us before. Why should we trust you now?"

"I may be a—" I started, but several voices cut me off.

Soon, so many people were shouting that I couldn't make sense of what they were trying to say.

"SILENCE!" Malcolm roared, quieting the crowd once again.

I took a deep breath. "I may be a Davina, but I'm also human, and where I come from, we help each other out. I don't want to live in a world riddled with war and bloodshed any more than you do."

I expected an uproar again, but I was only met with silence. Rob's gaze turned to the ground. I waited… and waited.

"Please," Marek pleaded. "If anyone knows anything, now is the time to say something."

Someone cleared their throat at the other end of the church. All eyes fell upon the man. I stood on my toes to see him, but I couldn't get a good view from this distance.

"Ayden," Malcolm said, welcoming the man to come forward.

The crowd slowly parted until an old man reached the front. He stood slightly hunched, and his pale skin hung off his bones. He looked like he should be lying in a nursing home rather than fighting in this war.

Ayden's voice came out hoarse when he spoke. "I may have some information, but I don't know if it's true."

"Anything you might know can help us right now," I assured him.

The old man cleared his throat. "Long ago, there were rumors that the Aedes could unlock the powers of the Davina. It was said it was as if the gods themselves had been reincarnated. Perhaps there is truth to the rumor."

I glanced to Marek in uncertainty. This couldn't be the answer we were looking for, could it?

Marek caught my gaze then turned back to the old man. "Do the legends say how the Aedes do it?"

Ayden shook his head. "That is all the legend said. I do not know how they did it, only that somehow, the Aedes could make the Davina more powerful. As I said, I do not know if it is true. Our ancestors wouldn't have gone seeking the answer to making our enemies stronger."

I chewed my lower lip and thought about what he said. *Somehow, the Aedes could make the Davina more powerful.*

I was more powerful. And it only happened the first time when Malcolm fed off my essence.

I drew in an audible breath. "Malcolm, you did it once before."

His eyebrows drew together.

"Try it with me again," I demanded. "Feed off me."

"What?" Malcolm asked like I was insane.

"Feed off my essence, like you did before. I think that's the key."

Malcolm eyed me skeptically. "All that would do is unbalance your energies. It would weaken you."

"I insist," I told him.

Malcolm smirked and placed his hands on my shoulders. His eyes widened, and he inhaled a deep breath.

My skin chilled as fear overcame me. It was like I was in his house again, back to that moment when I thought this might be the end.

Then suddenly, a warm and comforting sensation consumed me. Essence tingled through my body, rising up from my toes and filling my heart. With each passing second, my body grew stronger. The essence inside of me felt as if a dam was opening, allowing me to pull magic from the earth and into my body.

It was as if Malcolm was helping to open the channel that my essence flowed through. I pictured that channel opening wider and wider, until I freely poured my essence into him. Malcolm's skin began to fill with color, and I could've sworn his lips seemed fuller. Even his dark irises seemed to dim to a more natural brown.

I turned my attention inward and focused on my essence. I channeled it from my heart and to my fingertips until white wisps of essence began flowing out of my palms. My essence crawled along the floor like fog.

The Aedes closest to us retreated several paces, and fear filled their eyes.

"Make her stop!" a woman cried.

I pulled the essence back to keep from scaring them and let it fill the space around Malcolm and me. We locked eyes and exchanged a smile.

Malcolm's grip relaxed, and he turned to the crowd of Aedes. "It appears there is some truth to the rumors. Davina who share themselves with us grow stronger with us."

And yet, I wasn't sure this was enough. I wasn't sure *I* was enough.

"Let my friends try," I requested.

Marek and Casey looked eager to give it a shot, but Allie and Kyle shrank away in uncertainty.

"We need as much power as we can get to close the portal, and I need my friends' help," I said.

Malcolm nodded in agreement.

"I'll go first," Marek offered.

Rob was beside him a moment later. "I want to try."

Marek and Rob faced each other. I didn't know how Rob channeled essence from one person into himself. There were no visual cues apart from the look on both of their faces. I witnessed Marek shiver and knew he must've felt the chill rise to his skin. Then I saw the wonder in his eyes and knew he must be feeling that channel open wider.

Without warning, a fireball shot from his hand. It was a real fireball this time, with red flames and everything. I felt the heat cross my face as it shot across the room and slammed into the corner. A pile of dry leaves instantly caught fire. Flames licked into the air for a second before fizzling out to embers.

I heard Allie's audible intake of breath and Kyle's curse of surprise. Casey exhaled slowly, like she wanted to say something but couldn't find the words. Marek's eyes widened. He looked more shocked than the rest of us.

"What. Was. That?" Casey asked.

Marek held out his palm, and red flames rose into the air.

"Does it hurt?" I asked.

Marek shook his head. It looked like the flames should be burning the flesh off his bones, but his skin remained unharmed.

"Let us try," Allie said, intrigued to give it a shot.

Malcolm gestured for another three Aedes to come forward. He paired each of them with one of my friends. Allie shivered when the first Aedes accessed her essence. She held out her palm and narrowed her eyes in concentration. I expected a fireball or fog to rise out of her hand, but nothing came.

"Maybe it only works for some Davina," I thought out loud.

Allie's face fell in disappointment. Just as she dropped her hand, a gust of wind passed through the room.

Her eyes lit up. "Was that me? Did *I* do that?"

I couldn't find the words to respond. Had Allie just controlled *air*?

She concentrated and swiped her hand through the air again. Another gust of wind passed by me. Allie was shaping the air to her will.

Allie jumped up and down in excitement. "Let's see what Kyle can do!"

Casey and Kyle tried at the same time. Casey paired up with a tall, muscular Aedes with long dark hair, and her power manifested almost immediately. She willed the rock Marek had used into her hand. Slowly, dirt across the floor rose around us, as if someone had flipped off the switch to gravity. Casey had the power to control earth.

Kyle took the longest to discover what his essence was capable of. After trying to control fire, air, and earth, he'd almost given up. Outside, the clouds began to darken with his mood. When Allie pointed out the poor weather, Kyle rushed to the window.

"And then there was rain," he said just as the first of the raindrops hit the ground.

Within seconds, the rain pounding against the roof filled the room with a deafening roar. A moment later, it stopped.

"I don't get it," I thought out loud. "Why do we all have these different powers?"

The old man cleared his throat again. "It's like the stories said. The Aedes can unlock the power of the gods."

"It makes so much sense," Marek said. "These are all earth-creating powers like the gods had."

"How can we have this power in our mortal bodies if Grace's power was too much for me?" I asked.

Marek pressed his lips together, stumped.

"Maybe Grace's power was different because it wasn't *yours*," Kyle thought aloud. "Maybe it was working against you somehow because it still belonged to Grace."

Allie nodded, like she thought Kyle had a good point.

"We must've inherited the gods' powers all along," Marek theorized. "We just forgot how to access them on our own. Our ancestors, the Sanctities and Divinities, coexisted. Maybe this was one of the reasons the two races of gods worked together. Because together, they were stronger. Only with the help of the Aedes do the Davina have the power to access their full essence and become who they truly are."

Excitement sizzled in my bones. "And only with the Davina can the Aedes survive. They can feed off Davina essence without hurting anyone. This was how it was always meant to be! We can work together. The Davina can finally give back to the Aedes!"

Malcolm frowned. "Only if we can shut down the portal."

Well, shit. There was still that.

"We can do it together," I said with conviction. "Together, we should be able to generate enough power to collapse the portal and keep the realms from touching."

I turned back to the large group of Aedes still staring at me. "It's time for the Davina and the Aedes to put our differences aside and come together. If we survive this and the other Davina see what we can do together, then we can live in true peace once all this is over. I'm sorry for how they've treated you and that they've never listened to you before. It's time for that to change. I can't make up for the past, but perhaps we can change the future. I'm a Davina, and I'm here listening."

Murmurs spread across the room, and the Aedes exchanged glances with one another.

"The least we can do is try," I said. "Either we survive by working together, or we perish together."

A chilling silence fell over the chapel. Would we all be able to set aside our pride and give this a shot?

They're going to say no, I thought. *They'd rather die than help us.*

Dread spread throughout my body. Turning to the Aedes was our last option, and now we *would* die—all of us.

Ayden stepped forward on shaky feet. "I will follow Malcolm, whatever he decides."

"I will, too," a woman behind him agreed.

A chorus of agreement broke out across the church, raising my hopes.

I turned to Malcolm for confirmation. "You'll help us?"

He nodded once. "What do we have to do?"

I let out a shaky breath. "Follow me."

26

*H*undreds of flapping wings followed behind me. I knew they were all Aedes, but the strange thing was that they sounded entirely Davina. Without looking back, I could imagine the group following behind me *were* Davina. We really weren't so different after all.

The clearing loomed up ahead. From this distance, the trees blocked my view of the ground, but I could see the rippling air of the portal rising above the tree line. Fear entered my chest. The portal had grown to massive proportions. I only hoped we weren't too late.

I passed above the outer edge of the clearing, and my fear quickly melted away. Instead, complete and utter hopelessness filled my body. The flapping of my wings faltered for a moment, and I dropped several feet before catching myself again.

Hundreds of Davina sat in the clearing facing the portal. I thought for sure we'd only have to fight off a few Davina Council members, but this was a whole freaking army.

Good thing I brought my own army, I thought.

I heard the collective gasp below us as the Aedes following behind me swooped down into the clearing. Davina hurried to their feet. Essence shot from several people's hands before I had a chance to truly process my surprise.

I landed hard in the grass and raced forward toward the angry crowd of Davina. "STOP!"

"They've come in peace!" Marek shouted from beside me.

Davina hesitated when they spotted me and my friends at the front of the crowd. Several didn't seem to care and aimed more essence at the Aedes behind us. Black essence flew back in their direction.

Allie whirled around toward the Aedes. "No, wait! You have to show them you're better than this! We didn't come here to fight."

I opened my mouth to shout toward the Davina, to try to explain, but before I could say anything, a figure landed in front of me. I recognized Grace's large wings before I noticed her dark curls and white dress.

She faced the Davina and held her hands up. The chaos within the clearing calmed, leaving only the sound of rushing wind whipping through my hair. The burning smell had intensified and was so strong it made me want to hurl.

Grace slowly turned toward me. A hard expression settled on her face. "What are you doing, Ryn? You're ruining these last few moments the Davina have together."

"What are *you* doing here?" I couldn't help but let the accusation slip from my tongue before answering her. Was she *guarding* the portal from me?

Grace held her head high. "I thought it'd be best to wait out the end together."

"But it doesn't *have* to end," I argued. "The Aedes have agreed to help us."

Grace's lips turned down, and she eyed Malcolm beside me. "They can't help us. When are you going to accept that this is the end? There's nothing more you can do."

"But we can," I insisted. "The Aedes make us stronger. With their help, we can access more essence than we ever have before. We can collapse the portal!"

Davina exchanged glances with one another. Whispers spread across the clearing.

"You said it yourself, Grace," I pointed out. "You're not strong enough to do it on your own, but you're *not* alone. We can do this together. The Aedes and Davina are *meant* to be together."

Grace's features hardened. "I have no idea what you're talking about." The way she said it told me she was being honest.

"We'll show you," I offered.

I glanced to my friends. Together, we took a collective breath, and then all at once, we exposed our new powers. Fog lifted from my hand. Beside me, flames burst into the air out of Marek's palm. Kyle directed his hands toward the sky, and the clouds began to darken above him. Dirt rose from the ground in front of Casey and gathered into her hand. Allie produced a small whirlwind, causing the grass below her to blow out in all directions.

The entire crowd of Davina gasped and took a step back.

Even Grace stepped away from us. "What—?"

"Join our fight!" I called out above the wind. "Share yourself with the Aedes, and together, we can save our world!"

"NO!" Grace shouted. "This is insane! Ryn and her friends don't believe in our new world!"

"Nobody here will survive in your new world!" I spat. "You want to end the fighting, Grace. That doesn't start with genocide or whatever fresh start you're hoping for. It starts right here, with the Davina and the Aedes on the same side!"

Grace lowered her voice so only I could hear. "Just let it be, Ryn. The realms will die eventually, no matter what we do."

"They don't have to die *now* if we can prevent it," I argued.

"Ryn's a traitor!" Grace roared.

She looked out into the crowd of Davina, as if expecting them all to rush forward with murder in their eyes. They only stared back, unsure of who to follow.

"It won't hurt to let us try—" I started, but I was cut off when a white ball of energy whizzed between Marek and me.

The essence slammed into the Aedes behind me, knocking him out. His limp body fell into the Aedes beside him, and they caught him on his way to the ground. It took only a split second for my gaze to travel to the assailant. The essence had come from a young Davina boy who looked about fifteen. He stood there in shock, like he couldn't believe what he'd just done.

A moment later, chaos erupted in the clearing. Screams flew through the air, and Aedes and Davina rushed forward all around me until the two groups merged.

I instinctively ducked as essence rushed by my head. A strong hand gripped mine, pulling me back to my feet.

"Come on!" Marek shouted. "We have to get closer to the portal!"

I reached out for Allie, and we raced along behind Marek as he barreled his way through the crowd. I caught sight of Davina fighting Davina. One Davina took ahold of an Aedes's hand and shouted something in his ear. It looked like they were forming an alliance, but I was past them before I could see the outcome. Above us, Davina and Aedes flew through the sky. In only a matter of seconds, the two groups were evenly dispersed across the clearing, some of them fighting and others teaming up. It was impossible to tell who was on whose side.

My friends and I broke through the edge of the crowd just a few yards from the portal. Marek skidded to a halt, stopping so fast that I nearly rammed into him. I momentarily forgot about the fighting happening all around me as my eyes took in the portal in front of us.

It'd gone from being the size of a doorway to the size of a large house. The air rippled so violently that I couldn't make out the shapes swirling through it. I wasn't sure if I was looking beyond the portal to the trees anymore or if I was seeing Malum's landscape.

"Holy—" I started as I stared up at the grand feature in front of me.

Grace dropped down in front of me, blocking my view of the portal.

"Quick!" I shouted to Marek, Allie, and Kyle. Casey was nowhere to be seen. "Get as many people as close as you can to the portal—now!"

Kyle and Allie rushed away immediately to follow my orders.

"But I—" Marek started.

"I've got this!" I yelled at him.

"You never give up, do you?" Grace snarled.

I ignored her question. "It doesn't have to end like this."

Grace's lips curled into an evil, sardonic smile I'd never seen cross a Davina's face before. In that moment, it was clear that Grace would do whatever it took to hold me off until the world she'd come to despise was destroyed. My chance to convince her otherwise had long since passed. Grace had the power to end me in a heartbeat—and I could see in her eyes that she wanted to. I'd never be able to fight her.

"I need your help with Allie and Kyle!" I rose my voice at Marek.

Marek hesitated.

"Go!" I screamed. I wasn't going to let him stick around and watch me die.

Marek looked like it physically pained him to turn away, but he did as I asked and rushed into the crowd to help round up people on our side.

Grace's hand twitched, and I knew instantly what was coming.

My death.

My life force would be severed right here at the foot of the portal.

No, I told myself. *I'm not going to die today.*

The thought passed through my mind in an instant. Grace's hand swung out. Just as purple electricity shot from her palm, I flinched away from her and threw my hands over my head like I was trying to protect myself from an avalanche.

Because that's totally going to help, Ryn, I told myself.

Shock hit me when I realized thoughts were still racing around in my head. I should've been knocked to my feet when Grace's essence hit me. It should've killed me. Grace was standing there ready to use her magic on me, and I had no time to get out of the way and no weapon to use against her.

Had she not attacked me?

I slowly peeled my eyes open and gasped. My foggy white essence had spread out from my hands and collided with Grace's crackling purple essence. It was like my essence acted as a shield against hers.

Well, Ryn. It looks like you were right. You're not going to die today.

I smiled at my inner voice.

My eyes met Grace's. A moment of confusion crossed her face, but it was instantly replaced by anger. The sounds of battle faded around me as I channeled essence into my palms.

"Not today, bitch," I muttered under my breath.

Essence exploded out of me, sending Grace's power back toward her. Grace flew off her feet and landed several yards away. I approached her with my newfound confidence. Essence snaked out of my hand and wrapped around her body. Grace dug her hands and feet into the ground and tried to distance herself from it, but it wrapped around her like a transparent rope, securing her arms to her sides. Her eyes widened.

I couldn't explain the strength that overcame me or how I knew what I was doing. All I knew was that I felt strong. *Damn* strong. And that I could use that strength to stop Grace. I guided my essence upward, pulling at Grace's body. Her feet dangled several inches above the ground.

"So this is what it's come to?" she choked out. "You're going to kill me?"

Her question hit me like a punch to the gut. I'd already killed too many times, but I couldn't let Grace get away with this. If I let her stop us, the end of the world was on my shoulders as well as hers.

"I'll do what I have to do," I stated in a strong voice. And I meant it.

Grace struggled to breathe. "You almost had me convinced."

My hold on her unexpectedly weakened, and I fought to squeeze tighter.

Grace shook her head, as if the whole thing amused her. "I was right all along. If teaming with the Aedes is the only way to stop this, it was never meant to be. Sooner or later, you will bring destruction down upon each other."

"You don't know that!" I shouted. The ground swayed beneath my feet, and I knew my energy was quickly draining.

"The gods lived in peace, and they destroyed each other," Grace pointed out.

"We're not the gods," I challenged. "We're different."

"You're right." Grace barely got the words out.

Without warning, purple electricity burst from the center of her chest. It spanned the air above me, crackling just inches above my head. My essence fizzled away, and Grace dropped to her feet. The drain of energy had disoriented me just long enough for Grace to gain her composure.

"You're nothing like the gods," Grace said a moment before her fist connected with my jaw.

Pain shot through my face, and I stumbled backward. The taste of copper filled my mouth.

What the hell? For a lady who'd spent thousands of years sleeping, you'd think her muscles would've atrophied, but Grace was *strong.*

I immediately shot a white fireball in Grace's direction, but my eyes were beginning to blur from the exertion. I missed completely.

Grace's hands were on me a moment later, gripping my shirt. "*I'm* the closest thing to a god now, and your weak essence can't defeat me."

Grace whipped me around and held my face just inches from the portal.

"NO!" I shrieked. I had no idea what would happen to me if she pushed me into the rippling air. I didn't want to find out.

Grace only laughed and yanked my body back. I landed hard on the ground several feet away. I gasped for the air that had been knocked from my chest and pushed myself onto my elbows.

My shoulders shook, but I forced my voice to remain strong. "Why do you care so much that you take everyone down with you?"

Grace didn't answer. Instead, she stared down at me with a smirk. Purple energy pulsed down her arm, and she readied herself to throw it at me—to end me.

I threw my hands in front of me again to block her attack. Tension built in my muscles as I fought to direct essence out of my body and toward her. Every inch of my body ached, as if I'd just run a marathon without any prior training. The essence I expected to shield me never came.

Grace raised her hands, and in that moment, I knew this was it. I didn't have the energy left to save myself.

Just as the thought crossed my mind, the earth began to shake beneath me. I thought for a moment that I might be having some sort of seizure, that all the fight had drained me to the point where my body gave up, too.

But then I noticed the mix of confusion and fear on Grace's face. She felt the violent shaking as well as I did, and just like me, she had no idea what was happening.

A sound like thunder filled the clearing, but unlike thunder, it wasn't met with a moment of silence following the initial *crack*. It

continued, filling my ears to the point of pain. I couldn't even hear the violent winds over the sound of canons coming from inside the earth.

Then, the sound didn't seem to matter anymore. One moment, I was watching the grass shake beneath us. The next, the earth split, forming a massive cavern just feet from me.

I scurried backward and tried to get to my feet, but every time my hands left the ground, the intense shaking of the earth knocked me down again. I dared to glance back. The cavern was expanding, growing wider and wider by the second. Grace had fallen to the ground on the other side, and she stared at it in horror.

The cavern stretched along the length of the clearing and stopped at the portal. I drew in a sharp breath when I looked up to see what the portal had become. The air was no longer rippling in the center. Instead, a massive image of a new landscape formed. It was as if someone had punched a hole straight through the air. Dry, cracked sand and dark skies stretched as far as the eye could see.

Sheer terror ripped through my body.

This was Malum. And it was going to destroy us.

27

Grace's eyes darted to the portal, then back to me. Fear melted from her face, and a calm expression took over. It was the look of someone who'd found their peace.

"Marek!" I screamed, but I could hardly hear my own voice over the sound of the earth shattering around me.

His eyes met mine through the crowd. He raced toward me, pushing past people to get to me as fast as he could.

"We have to finish this. Now!" I shouted.

Marek reached me and pulled me to my feet. We stumbled as the earth continued rumbling beneath us, but I managed to stay upright without his support.

"We have to throw everything we've got into the portal," I instructed.

Allie and Kyle stumbled forward, trying to stay on two feet as they made their way toward us. Casey dropped out of the sky and landed next to me.

"Now!" I shouted.

Red flames shot from Marek's hands and into the portal, while Casey concentrated on trying to steady the earth. Color drained from her face as she strained to help. Allie and Kyle reached us and immediately began using their powers on the portal. Kyle summoned the power of the weather, and lightning struck down in front of us. Allie pushed the wind coming from the portal backward, using its energy against itself.

Fletcher landed beside Allie and focused on the grass beneath us. It grew and shaped to his will, tangling into the portal.

I gritted my teeth and fought to direct my essence toward Malum. Wisps escaped my hands in bursts, but it was nothing compared to the essence I used before. I glanced behind me quickly. Hordes of Aedes and Davina flocked away from the portal, but others still fought like they had nothing left to lose.

"Malcolm!" I shrieked.

Essence shot out of his palm and hit a Davina in the chest. His eyes met mine.

"We need help!" I yelled.

Malcolm gestured to a group of Aedes nearby for them to follow him. Moments later, he was beside me.

"I'm running out of energy!" I shouted over the deafening noises around us. "We all are. We need to access more!"

All around me, Davina and Aedes paired up. I noticed Gabe and Mr. Harris among the willing Davina. Aedes shot dark essence at the portal, while Davina used their new powers.

"No! Stop!" Grace shouted.

Malcolm gestured to another group of Aedes, and they took flight and dove toward Grace. Her scream ripped through the air as two of them grabbed her arms and dragged her into the sky, away from the portal.

"Take my essence, Malcolm," I demanded. "There's only one way to do this, and that's together."

Malcolm held his chin up. He didn't look scared at all; he looked brave. He nodded once, and then his strong hands were on my shoulders, pointing me back in the direction of the portal.

A chill spread across my skin, and I knew he was channeling my essence into him. The more he drew it out, the wider I felt the channel open. My body stopped shaking despite the ground moving beneath my feet, and I sensed my strength slowly return.

Essence fell from my fingertips and drew toward the portal in a stream. All around me, powers grew. Marek's flaming fireballs turned to a stream of fire, as if there was some sort of fuel suspended in the air for him to burn through. Kyle's lightning bolts hit one after the other, sending thunder echoing throughout the clearing. Aedes essence continued to shoot into the portal.

But all our essence did was distort the image of the landscape on the other side. The ground continued to shake, and the portal continued to widen.

"It's not working!" Marek shouted.

I can see that! I wanted to yell back, but I couldn't break my concentration.

My essence hit the portal and expanded inside of it, swirling as if it'd hit a wall. Every muscle inside my body tensed as I willed it to do something… *anything.* I bit down on my lower lip until I tasted blood.

Why wasn't this working? We were collectively stronger than Grace, weren't we? Surely, together we had more power than the sixteen Originals had when they'd destroyed the portals the last time.

Maybe the portals weren't this strong.

Maybe they did something different.

Doubts raced through my mind. Any moment now, the earth would crack in half and destroy us all.

Aedes essence crossed my path, slamming into my stream of magic. My essence flickered from white to black and then back to white again. An electric tingle traveled along my skin.

A sharp breath passed my lips as a moment of clarity struck.

The only way to do this is together, I reminded myself.

Though we were working together as allies, we weren't working together as *one.* And that was the only way we'd survive.

I was the answer. I was the only one who could bring these people together. I had the power in me all along.

I pulled my essence from the portal and directed it into a large globe above us. My foggy essence spread out like a force field, and it only continued to grow.

"Stop aiming at the portal!" I instructed as loud as I could. "Fire at my essence instead!"

A confused expression crossed Marek's face, but he didn't waste a moment to comply. He shot his fire into the opening I'd left for him. It bounced around inside the giant orb, unable to escape.

Several people down the line took notice and followed suit.

Soon, everyone was sending essence into one concentrated area. Fire, wind, lightning, and more whirled together. My force field expanded to the size of the school as power grew and sizzled inside of it. It was hundreds of times stronger and more electric than I'd ever felt from Grace's power.

I sealed off the force field, locking the collective magic inside of it. And then I squeezed, pulling all that magic together. The massive, powerful globe hovering above us glowed every color of the rainbow as the various types of essence bounced around inside, struggling to escape, begging to explode.

And they would... together.

A piercing cry ripped out of my lungs as I aimed my essence at the portal. It took everything I had to manipulate it, so much that I thought the exertion might tear me apart. A moment later, I felt the tethers of my magic break away from me.

And then came the blinding light and the deafening *boom* of a crumbling realm.

My ears were ringing. Why were my ears ringing? I should be dead. Ears don't ring when you're dead.

"Ryn!"

That voice. That beautiful angel's voice...

Angels didn't exist in death. What was one doing here?

"Ryn! Oh, shit. Please don't be dead."

I hate to break it to you...

"Marek," another voice said softly.

Marek?

Suddenly, everything that had happened to me since moving to Eagle Valley came rushing back in a blur, everything right up to that last moment, when our realm collapsed.

I blinked my eyes open. Warm sunlight caressed my face, almost blinding me.

"She's okay!" a female voice shrieked.

A strong force wrapped around my body and squeezed me tight. I struggled to breathe. The faint scent of leather hit my nose. It was so familiar. It was...

"Marek!" I cried as my eyes finally focused.

He pulled me into him tighter, burying his face into my tangled hair. He drew away from me only to place kiss after kiss on my lips. "I thought I'd lost you, but you're okay! You're okay!"

I finally had a chance to look around. Allie, Kyle, Casey, Malcolm, and Fletcher stood in a circle, surrounding me. Beyond them spanned a stretch of thick grass, and then a forest of trees. We were still in the clearing, but the roar of the wind and the shaking of the earth were gone. The large cavern remained, like a scar carved into the earth, but the portal was nowhere to be seen.

"What happened?" I asked.

"It worked!" Allie cried in excitement. "Your plan worked, Ryn. We collapsed the portal!"

"So, we're safe?" I asked, barely able to believe it. "And the war?"

Fletcher and Malcolm exchanged a glance.

"I think it's time we declare this war officially over," Fletcher said.

"Yes," Malcolm agreed. "I think it's finally time peace is restored."

Those words meant everything to me.

Malcolm reached out and pulled me to my feet. I was still trying to wrap my head around what we'd accomplished together. All this time, the Aedes and Davina had the power to work together as one.

This, I realized, was our divine fate.

EPILOGUE

*H*appiness filled me on our first day back at school over a week later. Aedes and Davina alike roamed the halls after class. The school was almost crowded now that Aedes were allowed to attend with us, but it was crowded in a good way, like we were all attending an amazing party together. New class schedules had been issued, and we were now training alongside the Aedes and learning how to harness our powers together.

I turned down a secluded hallway and gently knocked on Mrs. Presley's old office door.

"Come in," a male voice called from behind it.

I pushed the door open. Mr. Harris sat behind the large desk near the window, and Malcolm sat in one of the chairs across from him.

Malcolm stood when I entered the room. Color filled his skin, and his black irises had faded to brown. It was as if only Davina essence could restore the Aedes' health. Malcolm wore navy blue pants and a white button-down shirt. It was strange to see him in regular clothes and looking so… human.

No one knew exactly what happened when we destroyed the portal, but ever since then, the Aedes have been able to interact with our world. Fletcher theorized that when we destroyed the portal, we also destroyed Malum. He believed that their second curse—the one that kept them from fully existing here and from the humans being able to see them—was somehow tied to their realm and that when we destroyed it, we broke their curse. Somehow, their first curse remained, the one that marked them with darkness and made their feathery wings black and their essence dark.

Luckily, there were already Davina in government positions, which made assimilating the Aedes into our society easier than I would've thought.

"You wanted to see me?" I asked.

Mr. Harris leaned forward in his chair. "Let me start by apologizing."

I took a seat beside Malcolm. "You don't have to do that."

"I do," Mr. Harris said. "On behalf of the entire Davina Council, I hope you will find it in your heart to forgive us. As you may know, Anthony Lucas has resigned as the head of the Davina Council, and I've been voted in to take his place. However, we have decided to dissolve the Davina Council altogether. A new alliance is forming, and we're inviting members of all races to be a part of it."

He smiled cheerfully. "We cannot reveal ourselves to the entire population until a treaty is established. Naturally, humans are a bit wary of us. Our new alliance will need somebody to bring us all together and facilitate peace among our three races. We would like to offer you a position serving as a spokesperson for the alliance."

I glanced between Mr. Harris and Malcolm speechlessly. Was this some sort of joke?

I was surprised to find them both smiling back at me. They meant it. They wanted me to be their leader.

"Isn't that your job?" I asked Mr. Harris.

He smiled. "Yes, but we believe that you would serve us better in that role. The Davina and the Aedes found peace through you, and the humans need someone to listen to."

I shook my head. "Peace didn't come from me. It came from inside all of you. It was there all along. I just helped you realize it was possible."

"See?" Malcolm said. "That's why we need you."

I should've been jumping for joy at the offer, but I couldn't see myself in the position they saw me in. I was just a teenage girl trying to survive high school.

"I'm sorry," I said, "but I think I'm going have to respectfully decline. Politics aren't my thing."

Mr. Harris looked disappointed, but he nodded in understanding. He stood and reached his hand out. "Please let us know if you change your mind."

I shook his hand. "I will."

Malcolm crossed the room with me and smiled wide when he swung the door open. I never realized how much I took the simple act of opening a door for granted. Malcolm's whole life, he'd watched other people open doors but could never do it himself. It was strange how destroying the Aedes' chance at a true home had created a home for them here.

Malcolm followed me out of the office. "Do you mind if I have a word with you, Ryn?"

"Sure." I stopped in the middle of the hall.

He waited for a freshman to pass by us before speaking again. "I just wanted to know..."

I held my breath. I could already tell I wasn't going to like his question.

"Did he suffer?"

I thought I might vomit in response to those three words, but I managed to swallow down the lump in my throat and keep my lunch where it belonged. "Malcolm... I—"

"I'm not trying to blame you again," he interrupted. "I understand that you were only protecting yourself. I know now that Trenton made a sacrifice to create a new and better world. I just want to know if his sacrifice was... I want to know if..."

I wasn't sure Malcolm knew what he wanted, but I knew I could help him find his own peace.

"Malcolm," I interrupted.

His eyes lit up hopefully.

"He didn't feel a thing."

Malcolm relaxed, and then he reached out his hand. "Thank you."

I took his hand in mine and shook it. "I hope our new world ends up being everything you hoped for."

~

"Where have you been?" Kyle asked once I reached the common room. He sat on one of the big cushy chairs in front of the fireplace.

Allie sat on his lap with her head rested against his shoulder. Marek had his legs draped over the armrest of the chair next to them.

"Hey," Casey's voice came casually before I could answer Kyle. "Long time, no see."

She sat on the couch beside an Aedes guy with dark eyes and long black hair. He had a muscular arm wrapped around her and a smug expression fixed on his face. I recognized him as the guy who first paired up with Casey in the church.

"Yeah," I said like we were old friends. "What have you been up to?"

"Oh, you know." She shrugged and glanced to Mr. Tall Dark and Handsome. "Making new friends."

Kyle scoffed and muttered under his breath, "Is that all?"

"Hey," Casey snapped the same time her boyfriend's jaw tightened. "I didn't ask your opinion."

"It's called free speech, Harris," Kyle said with an eye roll while Allie lightly elbowed him in the chest.

Some things never change, I thought.

"Anyway..." Casey turned back to me. "I never got to tell you that what you did was pretty awesome."

I couldn't help but smile. "Thanks. You were great, too."

"Of course I was," Casey teased. "I wouldn't have it any other way."

"No, you wouldn't," I replied with a laugh.

Casey beamed.

I turned to my friends. "Ready to go?"

Marek stood and laced his fingers in mine.

"Racing?" Allie asked in excitement.

Marek smirked. "What else?"

Allie hopped to her feet, and Kyle followed.

"Have fun," Casey called over her shoulder. I wasn't sure how much she meant it, but I appreciated the gesture.

We exited the back doors of the school. A figure in the distance caught my eye, and I paused.

"What?" Marek followed my gaze toward Grace, who sat in the grass across the lawn.

I dropped Marek's hand. "I need a minute."

He hesitated.

"I'll be fine," I promised. "Go have fun. I'll meet up with you soon."

Marek caught up with Allie and Kyle while I approached Grace. Her eyes were closed, and she inhaled deep breaths. I could tell she noticed my approach, because her eyelids flickered slightly, like I'd disrupted her concentration.

"Mind if I sit?" I asked.

Grace shook her head.

I lowered myself beside her. "How are you doing?"

She finally peeled her eyes open, but she ignored my question. "I'm sorry for all the trouble I caused."

I wasn't sure what to say, but Grace didn't give me a chance to respond before she spoke again.

"I don't just mean I'm sorry for not trying hard enough to save this world. I mean..." Her voice trailed off.

"What?" I asked curiously.

Grace met my gaze. "I'm sorry for letting the Council hurt your friend. You should know that I was the one who followed you to Malcolm's."

I inhaled an audible breath.

Grace's eyes dropped back to the grass. "I'm sorry I didn't believe you, Ryn. I didn't think that the Davina and the Aedes could truly come together. I didn't believe any of us deserved this world, but you have shown me that I was wrong."

I noticed her hands shaking, as if this was incredibly difficult for her to admit.

She swallowed hard. "You were right. Peace is possible."

I was amazed to hear the words come out of her mouth.

"There are more people out there who need convincing," I said. "Will you help us unify them?"

Grace shook her head. "My reputation has already been ruined. I think that job is best left to you."

I smiled shyly. "Mr. Harris already asked for my help, but I turned him down."

"Why?" Grace looked surprised.

I shrugged. "I'm not a leader. And let's face it, I don't know enough about the Davina to lead them. I have to stay here at Galen and graduate."

She nodded like she understood.

A silent beat passed between us, and I dared to break it. "So, if you're not going to help the Davina, what will you do now?"

Grace hesitated. "I'm leaving, Ryn."

My brow furrowed. "Where will you go?"

She took a long breath. "I'm going to join my family."

"But your family… Grace, you're talking about death."

"I've already made my decision," she said. "The Davina and the Aedes are strong enough together without me. There's no place for me in this world anymore."

"But, you're immortal," I pointed out.

"I will never die of old age," Grace explained, "but that doesn't mean my body can't be destroyed and my life force severed. I've already talked with Fletcher, and he is willing to help me find my peace."

"What?" I asked breathlessly. "How?"

"I will not bore you with the details," Grace answered. "My tomb will be moved from your house and placed inside Galen High. Tonight, I will enter an eternal slumber, and this time, I won't ever wake up."

Oh, wow. What was I supposed to say to that? Rest in peace?

"I'm sorry about how I treated you," I said instead. "I know you were only doing what you thought was best."

"Yes, but your way was better," Grace admitted. "I failed as a leader. You will be the Davina's new hope now."

I looked toward the line of trees that met up with the lawn, contemplating her words. "I don't know if I want people to look up to me."

Grace breathed a heavy sigh. "I made a lot of mistakes, but I think the one thing I did right was choosing you. You didn't need to wake me to make the difference."

"But I did," I argued. "You pushed me in the right direction. We wouldn't be here without you."

Grace smiled. Silence passed between us once again, but finally, she turned to me. "Before I leave, I'd like to do one thing right."

My curiosity piqued. "What's that?"

"I'd like to leave you with a piece of advice. You say you don't want people looking up to you, but they will. Be careful what you say and do, Ryn. Someone will always be watching, and they'll be searching for inspiration. So please, keep doing what you're doing, and *inspire* them."

My jaw went slack as I tried to come up with the right words. It was strange to think that so many people would look up to me, but I couldn't deny that this was my destiny, whether I wanted it or not.

I held my head high. "I'll do my best."

Grace nodded. "I know you will."

It seemed like several minutes passed before I spoke again. "Do you want me to stay with you until…?"

Grace shook her head. "No. I know my peace is coming. I don't need any more comfort than that."

I thought, for a moment, she was only saying that to spare me the trouble, but she looked like she meant it. Grace had finally found her peace.

Once Grace said goodbye, I headed down the trail toward the valley. The bright sunlight filtered in through the leaves above my head, casting dancing rays along the forest floor. It was so beautiful that I couldn't believe these woods had once scared me.

I broke out of the trees to see black and white wings all throughout the valley. The last time I saw something like this, we were trying to kill each other. Now the Aedes and Davina were becoming friends.

I jumped back in surprise as Allie streaked past me. She raced laps around the valley with her wings spread wide. Marek flew by behind her a second later, followed by Kyle.

A wide smile spread across my face. I flexed my shoulders and jumped into the air to follow behind them. For the first time since discovering what I was, I felt like a normal Davina.

～

The day grew long as more Aedes and Davina joined us in the valley. I lay on my back in the grass with my wings spread out beneath me, staring up at the pink sky.

"Hey."

My heart flipped at the sound of Marek's voice. I turned my head to see him approaching. He knelt to one knee beside me and held his hand out.

"Come on," he encouraged. "What do you say about one last flight?"

I let my head fall back to the comfortable grass. "No, that's okay. I'm exhausted anyway."

A smile crept across his face. "I'm not asking you to race me. I'm asking you to follow me."

I didn't ask any further questions. I took his hand, and Marek pulled me to my feet. The wind whipped through my hair a moment later as I followed along through the sky beside him.

We landed at the top of the rocky hill outside of town—*our hill.* Marek pulled his wings into him and sat on the ground over-looking town. I joined him and snuggled into his bare chest.

Marek placed a kiss on the top of my head. "I love you, Ryn."

My heart fluttered at the sound of those magical words. "I know, Marek. I love you, too."

He reached out to touch my chin and pull my gaze to his. "You saved me, you know."

I saved him?

"From what?" I asked.

"From myself," Marek replied. "I see the world differently now, and it's all because of you."

A smile crept across my face. "I hope that's a good thing."

Marek laughed lightly. "Of course it is."

I snuggled back into him and inhaled his soothing scent. We stared out at the sunset for several minutes before Marek spoke again.

"Ryn? How do you feel, now that things are over?"

How do I even begin to answer that question?

I took a deep breath before speaking. "I feel… at peace."

"Even after what happened with Trenton?" Marek asked.

I carefully considered the question. I still wished I could take back what I did, but I knew wishing for such a thing was futile.

"Yeah," I answered honestly. "The Aedes have finally found their home. I think that if Trenton were here, he'd be smiling for them."

Marek nodded. "I think so, too."

My gaze dropped to the feather around his neck. "Marek, what do you think will happen next? With us, I mean."

Marek shrugged, but he looked deep in thought. "We'll graduate…"

"And then what?"

He returned his gaze to the landscape in front of us. "I still want to protect, like always."

"But the war is over," I pointed out. "There's nothing to protect *from*."

Marek breathed a heavy sigh. "We won *this* war. But there are many other battles to be fought."

"Does that mean you're going into the armed forces?" I asked.

Marek paused, as if considering the idea. He rested his head on mine before answering. "I was thinking law enforcement, like becoming a police officer."

I was so relaxed in his arms that my voice fell to a soft whisper. "That sounds perfect."

Marek trailed his fingers across the back of my hand, sending shivers up and down my spine. "What about you? Where do you want to go after graduation?"

I thought about the question for several moments. What *did* I want?

I laced my fingers through his. "I think I'd still like to become a chef. I could open my own restaurant. I don't want to be a part of the fighting anymore. I just want to live a quiet, normal life raising kids and baking cookies."

"Mm… cookies," Marek responded with a smile.

I beamed back at him. "I'll make you cookies anytime you want. No matter what happens, I'll follow you anywhere."

Marek squeezed me tightly, like those were the exact words he'd hoped to hear. "Are you ready to face our future together?"

"Yes," I said without hesitation. "Because I know that no matter what, we'll be together."

I barely finished the sentence before Marek's lips were on mine, sending a surge of passion throughout my body.

For the first time in my life, everything was absolutely perfect.

END OF BOOK THREE

The Davina return in book one of the Divine Descendants Duology, *Concealing Magic*.

ABOUT THE AUTHOR

Alicia Rades is a USA Today bestselling author of young adult and new adult paranormal fiction. When she's not dreaming up magical stories, she's either binge-watching paranormal shows, meditating, or spending time with her family. She has an unhealthy obsession with psychic characters and writes with a deck of tarot cards next to her computer.

www.ingramcontent.com/pod-product-compliance
Lightning Source LLC
Chambersburg PA
CBHW061103310726
48974CB00002B/372